CALEDO(

Book One of the Vetera.

By: William Kelso

Visit the author's website **http://www.williamkelso.co.uk/**

William Kelso is the author of:
The Shield of Rome
The Fortune of Carthage
Devotio: The House of Mus
Hibernia – Book Two of the Veteran of Rome series
Britannia – Book Three of the Veteran of Rome series
Hyperborea – Book Four of the Veteran of Rome series
Germania – Book Five of the Veteran of Rome series
The Dacian War – Book Six of the Veteran of Rome series
Armenia Capta – Book Seven of the Veteran of Rome series

Published in 2013 by FeedARead.com Publishing – Arts Council funded

A CIP catalogue record for this title is available from the British Library.

To: Tamara

ABOUT ME

Hello, my name is William Kelso. I was born in the Netherlands to British parents. My interest in history and in particular military history started at a very young age when I was lucky enough to hear my grandfather describing his experiences of serving in the RAF in North Africa and Italy during World War 2. Recently my family has discovered that one of my Scottish and Northern Irish ancestors fought under Wellington at the Battle of Waterloo in 1815.

I love writing and bringing to life the ancient world of Rome, Carthage and the Germanic and Celtic tribes. It's my thing. After graduation, I worked for 22 years in financial publishing and event management in the city of London as a salesman for some big conference organizers, trying to weave my stories in the evenings after dinner and in weekends. Working in the heart of the original Roman city of Londinium I spent many years walking its streets and visiting the places, whose names still commemorate the 2,000-year-old ancient Roman capital of Britannia, London Wall, Watling Street, London Bridge and Walbrook. The city of London if you know where to look has many fascinating historical corners. So, since the 2nd March 2017 I have taken the plunge and become a full-time writer. Stories as a form of entertainment are as old as cave man and telling them is what I want to do.

My books are all about ancient Rome, especially the early to mid-republic as this was the age of true Roman greatness. My other books include, The Shield of Rome, The Fortune of Carthage, Caledonia (1), Hibernia (2), Britannia (3), Hyperborea (4), Germania (5), The Dacian War (6), Armenia Capta (7) and Devotio: The House of Mus. Go on, give them a go.

In my spare time, I help my brother run his battlefield tours company which takes people around the battlefields of Arnhem, Dunkirk, Agincourt, Normandy, the Rhine crossing and Monte

Cassino. I live in London with my wife and support the "Help for Heroes" charity and a tiger in India.

Please visit my website http://www.williamkelso.co.uk/ and have a look at my historical video blog!

Feel free to write to me with any feedback on my books. Email: william@kelsoevents.co.uk

Chapter One – Mons Graupius

September 83 AD

The massed ranks of Caledonians stood along the upper slopes of the hill. Their small round shields and beautifully forged iron swords glittered in the morning sun. The nobles mounted on their lightweight chariots with their small shaggy horses rode up and down before the battle line. They were proud men, adorned with bronze torcs and elaborately decorated helmets. Some wore chainmail armour but others were bare-chested, showing off their full body tattoos. The charioteers were calling out to the Romans down the gentle slope, boasting of their prowess and fighting skills, recalling the names of long-dead ancestors and challenging the enemy to step forward and engage them in single combat. Behind them the tens of thousands of Caledonian warriors looked on, shouting encouragement and heaping insults on the Romans. Then from further up the hill came the haunting and defiant blast of a carnyx, the boar-headed Celtic war trumpet. The noise rolled down the slope towards where the long lines of silent Roman auxiliaries stood waiting for the order to advance.

Gnaeus Julius Agricola, governor of the province of Britannia, sat on his horse, inspecting his enemy with tense excitement. He had waited for a very long time for this day to come but now at last it had. His lips moved silently as he muttered a prayer of thanks to immortal Jupiter. To the civilians on his staff the sight of the fierce barbarian army up on the hill would be terrifying. But he knew his enemy. He knew what these men of the north were like. For seven long years he had fought them. For seven years he had watched and studied them. But today he would end it. Today he would end their struggle, end their independence and humble their pride. He had the enemy where he wanted them. All summer he had waited. Two battle groups, one formed around the Ninth and the other around the Twentieth Legion, had sat patiently on either side of the Pennines, waiting for his signal to march north. That signal had finally come when Roman scouts had reported that Calgacus, the Caledonian confederate leader, and the tribes were mustering in great numbers in the land of the Taexali, far to the north. Agricola's eyes burned with feverish excitement. Calgacus had finally decided to make a stand and confront the Romans in a pitched battle. It was the mistake he had hoped and prayed for. A smile appeared on Agricola's face. Today would see the climax of his twenty-four-year-long military career. Today was his day. The day upon which he would enter history as the man who conquered all the island of Britannia. It would be a worthy memory, he thought. An achievement nearly as great as that of another Julius, one Gaius Julius Caesar.

Agricola stared up the hill towards his enemy. Some of the Caledonians were stark naked despite the cool September weather. It was, he knew, their way of showing their bravery and contempt for death. Others had painted their faces with blue woad in order to frighten his men. He grunted as he heard the boastful cries, insults and challenges to single combat. Had they learned nothing? For a moment he felt a pang of sad admiration for his enemy. Their naivety in thinking the Romans would fight in the old-fashioned, single combat, ritualistic manner was touching. Damn fools, he thought. Damn heroic fools. They would have done better to have kept on hiding in the hills and forests. He shifted his gaze further up the hill hoping to catch a glimpse of Calgacus but the Caledonian high command were out of view. Still, he thought, he needed to be careful; the enemy outnumbered him three to two and he was far from his southern supply bases.

"I estimate they have thirty thousand men, sir," a young tribune at his side said tensely. "They outnumber our auxiliaries nearly four to one. With such numbers they will be able to envelop our front line. Should we not bring up the legions?"

Agricola kept his eyes fixed on the Caledonians. "No," he replied sharply, "keep them out of view. The Caledonians will not attack our front line if they see our full strength. I want them to come down from that hill and attack the auxiliary cohorts. Pay attention, boy – I explained my plan to all of you this morning, did I not?"

The six military tribunes, all of them young, inexperienced youths from noble and wealthy families, clustered around him like pupils around a teacher. The one who had spoken out blushed at Agricola's rebuke. Agricola looked away and smiled as he remembered his own time as a military tribune assigned to the staff of Governor Paulinus. That had been twenty-four years ago. Leaving behind the soft luxurious life of a civilian and joining the army was indeed a big and hard step in a young man's life.

"Numbers do not decide battles," Agricola snapped.

"What does, sir?" a tribune asked.

"I do," Agricola replied. He was enjoying himself now. The officers were waiting for orders, he realised. Well let them wait. This was his day and he was damned if he was not going to enjoy it. From the corner of his eye he saw Atticus, his young auxiliary cavalry commander, riding towards him. Atticus had chosen to ride along the front ranks of the auxiliaries in between the two armies. Agricola suppressed a pang of irritation. Atticus was showing off. Agricola had forbidden any man in his army to accept a challenge to single combat from the enemy and Atticus, by riding out in front of the troops like he was doing, was getting dangerously close to breaking that order. The Roman auxiliaries however, their large oval shields resting against their legs, raised their spears in the air and cheered Atticus on as he rode down the line.

"Are your men in position?" Agricola growled as Atticus rode up to him.

"They are, sir," Atticus replied in his thick Germanic accent, unable to hide the excitement in his voice. The young man turned his horse and glanced up the hill at the Caledonians. "They are showing no sign of wanting to come down and attack our centre, sir."

Agricola turned to look at the enemy. "If they don't want to attack we will need to encourage them a little," he replied grimly. He turned to a tribune. "Sound the order for the artillery to open up. Let's see how long they will stand up to that." Agricola turned to Atticus. "Ride back to your men. When you hear my signal, you will execute the plan as discussed. Time your attack when the enemy is fully committed, not before then. Only when the enemy is fully committed. This is important. Is that clear?"

Atticus nodded and Agricola allowed himself a smile. "Atticus," he said slowly, "our victory will depend on the timing of your attack. Your ancestors will be watching you today – do not disappoint them."

Atticus seemed to stiffen in his saddle and a furious blush of pride appeared on the young man's face.

"My men and I will do as ordered," he replied hoarsely.

Agricola watched his young auxiliary cavalry commander ride away and suddenly his mood mellowed. It was time to send his boys into battle. He turned to his tribunes.

"Do your duty for Rome today and win yourself the respect of your peers. Today you will discover what kind of men you really are."

A Roman trumpet blast echoed off the distant hills and a moment later the first catapults opened fire, sending a hail of rocks and burning incendiaries up the hill and into the enemy ranks.

Chapter Two – Marcus

Marcus sat quietly on his horse, trying to master his nerves. He was tall with a handsome, boyish face and reddish hair that looked out of place amongst the dark and blond-haired men of his cavalry troop. The red hair was a gift from his mother, a reminder, she had once told him, of his Celtic heritage. To his decurion and commanding officer Bestia, however, his red hair had been nothing but a source of amusement and scorn. From the first day that Marcus had joined the Second Batavian Auxiliary Cohort, a mixed infantry and cavalry unit, Bestia had submitted him to a barrage of insults, verbal and physical humiliation, all because he was easy to pick on, all because he was the only Briton serving in the unit. The Second Batavians were nearly exclusively recruited from the Germanic tribes of the lower Rhine and when they spoke in their own language Marcus could not understand a word. But now as the men sat waiting, none of that mattered.

His cavalry troop had taken up positions on the right of the Roman line. To his left the long lines of Batavian and Gallic auxiliaries stretched away into the distance. The infantry had not moved for over an hour. It would not be long now. Marcus felt his mount shift nervously. The horse knew what was coming. He patted her on her neck.

"Alright, alright," he murmured.

His mouth had dried out and he swallowed with difficulty. He could see the same tension on all the men around him. They avoided looking at each other, each man struggling with his own fear. Marcus tightened his grip on his spear and checked his armour for the hundredth time. Apart from a brief cavalry skirmish this was going to be his first big fight. He was twenty years old. He glanced at his friend. Pigface, the men had nicknamed him, because he did indeed look like a pig. Pigface was sweating and his breath was coming in short, sharp gasps. It was going to be his first battle too. Marcus could see that his friend was in a bad way. He lowered his spear and nudged him and managed a smile but Pigface did not turn round. Close by a veteran muttered something in his guttural Germanic language. Across from Marcus another rider started to sing quietly to himself. Marcus stared up the gentle grassy slope towards the enemy and as he did so he raised his left hand and touched the sacred amulet that hung around his neck on a leather cord. The bronze phallus was a gift from his father intended to ward off the evil eye.

Was this how you felt, Father, when you served the eagle god? Marcus hated his father. The man had been a violent, drunken bastard who had beaten him up whenever he felt like it. His father had shown his family no love and he had eventually driven Marcus's mother to suicide. At the age of seventeen Marcus had told him that he never wanted to see him again. That same day Marcus had bought his way into the Second Batavian Auxiliary Cohort. That was three years ago now. He had not seen his father since and he had no idea what had happened to him or where he was. He didn't want anything more to do with that arsehole, but today, waiting for the battle to start, he suddenly felt himself thinking of his father again. Ruthlessly he forced the man's image from his mind. Whatever happened in the coming hours he was going to show these tall German marsh dwellers, these Batavians, that he was no coward. He was not going to let them down. His survival and that of his mates was all that really mattered. Suddenly he felt calmer. Yes, that was all that really mattered: he had to survive, if for no other reason than to go on hating his father.

Down the line to his left he caught sight of Atticus riding back to the main cavalry force who stood drawn up hidden from view in the woods. Atticus was not much older than him, a shade over twenty, but he was a nobleman and on that distinction alone he had been given command of 3,000 horsemen. Marcus liked Atticus, however; he was a good man and an excellent soldier. When Atticus was around, the decurions, the cavalry officers, would not dare use their whips on their men. The young equestrian had even once publicly humiliated that bully Bestia.

A sudden trumpet blast tore across the battlefield.

10

"Prepare!" he heard Bestia cry out in Latin. Marcus's heart began to thump wildly. His horse kicked her hooves. Suddenly the air was filled with missiles. The Roman artillery had opened fire. The huge stones and incendiaries curved gracefully up the slope and smashed into the Caledonian ranks. But the enemy stayed put and took the pounding with impressive discipline. The tide of verbal abuse did not slacken and above the din came the terrible deep-throated blaring of the carnyx. The Roman cavalry horses whinnied nervously.

"Shields!" Bestia screamed. Marcus brought up his shield just in time as a hail of Caledonian arrows plunged from the sky. Another trumpet blast. To his left the long line of Batavian and Gallic auxiliaries lifted their shields off the ground and started to advance up the slope towards the enemy. Then came the cry that he had been waiting for.

"Second Batavian Cohort will advance!"

Marcus dug his heels into his horse's side and the massed cavalry surged forwards. It took all his riding skill to keep his position as the riders began to pick up speed. Up upon the slopes of the hill the Caledonian charioteers had turned and were thundering towards the advancing cavalry. Chariots and cavalry sped towards each other, closing the gap in seconds. Marcus had no time to think. Ahead of him a chariot crashed into three horsemen and a Caledonian was catapulted over Marcus's head and on down the slope. A broken chariot wheel spun past him, swiping a rider from his saddle.

"Kill them all! Kill, kill!" he heard a Latin voice scream.

Marcus surged up the hill but the Caledonian chariot charge had already been broken. The remaining charioteers were fleeing towards the safety on their own infantry battle line. Had it been so easy? The dead and dying lay on the ground and riderless horses, eyes bulging in terror, ran in all directions, some dragging the remnants of chariots and men behind them. A Batavian horseman at Marcus's side suddenly tumbled to the ground, his throat pierced by a spear. A fine layer of blood splattered Marcus's face. To his left Marcus caught sight of a lone chariot which had broken away from the retreat and was making a solitary charge at the advancing Roman line. The charioteer had a spear in his hand. Marcus screamed, raised his own spear and charged.

His opponent was a big man flying a large black pennant from his chariot. His face was covered in blue tattoos. The Caledonian was the first to fling his spear. The projectile slammed into Marcus's shield with such force that it ripped the shield from his hand. Marcus flung his spear at the man. The Caledonian was a fraction too slow in his reaction and the weapon punched into his chest with such force that it knocked him clean over the side of his chariot. Without shield or spear Marcus wildly drew his cavalry sword from its scabbard.

To his left the Roman auxiliary infantry had made contact with the main Caledonian battle line and were locked in savage close-quarters fighting. From behind the cover of their large shields which they were using as battering rams, the auxiliaries were stabbing their opponents with their short swords. The Caledonians, however, were holding their ground, having the advantage of fighting downhill. Then the Batavian cavalry crashed into the Caledonian ranks. Marcus heard someone screaming and was dimly aware that it was his own voice. A Caledonian, stark naked, swung a long sword into an auxiliary infantryman and in one stroke decapitated him. A horse slipped over a body and crashed sideways, screaming into the desperate fighting men, crushing them beneath its weight. An auxiliary infantry man turned from the battle line and ran away in terror. An officer swore and yelled at him but there was no time to haul him back.

Marcus's horse reared up and nearly threw him to the ground but somehow he managed to hold on. There was no way through the solid struggling, fighting mass of men up ahead. He turned and galloped along the line to his right. The Caledonians vastly outnumbered the auxiliaries and already Marcus could see that they were starting to envelop the Roman flank. Gods, what was Agricola waiting for? If the Caledonians got behind the auxiliaries, the battle would become a massacre. A young Caledonian, no more than a boy, saw him coming, turned and ran. Marcus thundered after him but at the last moment the boy flung himself flat on the ground and Marcus's slashing attack missed. Marcus charged on towards the right flank, his earlier fear consumed by a mad bloodlust.

Chapter Three – Emogene

From her vantage point, close to the crest of the hill, Emogene stared down anxiously at the battlefield, trying to spot her husband. Her long, childish black hair fell to her waist and her face was covered with blue woad. Was it only a few months since Beltane, she thought? She could still picture the feast to mark the start of the summer and to bless the land and its people with fertility. The whole village had joined in and she had danced around the fire with her husband and celebrated her eighteenth summer. That night she had kissed him under the mistletoe and promised him three strong and healthy sons. Later that night the two of them had run up to the highest cliff overlooking the sea and had stared in awe at the glowing festival fires that stretched away to the horizon. The tribes were all celebrating. They had made love and she had fallen asleep in his arms listening to the sound of the waves breaking onto the rocky shore. Life had been good. She had been happy. That was all she really wanted: a home and a family of her own. Had it been so much to ask for? The happy time had been short, however, for a few weeks later the summons had reached her village and war had entered her life. That war, the reason for which she still did not fully understand, had brought her here.

With one hand she gripped the collar of Bones, her husband's war dog, and in the other she held the wooden staff her father had given her. Bones stood perfectly still, just like he did when he spotted prey in the forests back home. He was grey and huge, weighing over two hundred pounds, with a broad mouth and loose skin above his brows. Around his neck he wore a ring with metal spikes. His alert yellow eyes were fixed on the fighting down the hill. Then he barked.

"I see him too," she said, gently tugging at the dog's collar.

You shouldn't have come, her husband had told her. He had tried to stop her from joining him on the long ride south to this nameless hill but it had been in vain, just as he knew it would be. She had refused to leave him. She had not wanted him to go. It had been a selfish desire. Every man in Caledonia was heeding the call. Who was she to hold onto him when every woman in the land was letting theirs go?

But I am a daughter of the moon. Is that why the spirits chose me?

The dream had come to her on Samhain, nearly a year ago. The Samhain festival marked the start of winter. It was the time when the cattle were brought down from the summer pastures and livestock slaughtered. As a child she had always worried about Samhain, marking the day's approach with dread, but as she had grown older she had become increasingly curious about it too. The druids had said that on the night of Samhain the door to the otherworld would open and that the spirits of the dead would wander freely amongst the living. But the dead were not the only ones to stalk the land that night. The druids also spoke of demons and shapeless, nameless things that preyed on the living and the unwary.

Emogene had lain on her straw bed in her father's house on top of the hill. Her father was the clan druid and as usual on Samhain had brewed a potion which the villagers said caused one to forget everything. When her father had not been looking Emogene had stolen a couple of mouthfuls of the bitter liquid. That night her sleep had been disturbed and she had tossed and turned. The spirits that could show the future and the past had come to her. They had taken her to the other world, the world that existed beyond the material and there, for a brief moment, they had drawn back the veils that hid the future. She had been terrified by what she had witnessed. She had seen burning houses, men butchered and enslaved, women raped, children abandoned and dying of hunger and disease. They had been her people. She had cried out in her sleep, tormented by the vision. Something terrible was going to happen to her village and her people.

A great loss you shall suffer. But if you, Emogene, remain true to your people, then hope shall return and a new love will find you.

She had woken covered in sweat and screaming. The intensity of the dream was like nothing she had ever experienced before. What had it meant? Her father had sat watching her with his wise pale-blue eyes but he had said nothing as she had fled from his house in embarrassment.

Emogene glanced across the hill towards where Calgacus stood surrounded by his closest clansmen and the tribal chieftains. He was a tall, powerfully built man and looked like a leader of men should, she thought. For a moment she tried to hate him. His summons had put the promise of her happy life in danger. But she could not feel any anger. Her father trusted Calgacus and supported him and so would she. Calgacus had achieved a miracle when he had united the tribes for the first time since anyone could remember. But would it be enough? Would her brave countrymen be able to defeat these Roman demons? The stories she had heard about the power of the Romans had unsettled her. None could defeat them, it was said. Nor could any magic stop their relentless march north. They had the support of powerful gods, the strength of bulls and the cunning of the fox.

Amongst the prominent warriors that surrounded Calgacus, she suddenly caught sight of Baldurix and her heart sank. He seemed to be looking straight at her. She gasped. How could Calgacus tolerate that man in his retinue? It was Baldurix after all, a leading clan leader of the Decantae, who had been Calgacus's main rival for the position of war leader. With the support of the druids and her father the matter had been decided in Calgacus's favour. It had been no surprise that her father had supported Calgacus. Ever since she could remember there had been a clan blood feud between Baldurix's Decantae and her father's clan, the Vacomagi. Her father had told her that the feud had started with the murder of a young Vacomagi druid. It had happened before she was born but still today men risked their lives by entering the territory of their blood enemy. Only Calgacus's authority as supreme war leader and the Roman invasion had allowed the two clans to gather without blood being spilt.

A carnyx bellowed its defiance. Others further down the hill joined in when suddenly she saw the Roman missiles hurtling into the Caledonian ranks. She felt Bones tense under her grip. He was a war dog and wanted to join his master.

"No, Bones, stay," she whispered.

He looked up at her with that inquiring look of his.

"When we are victorious you may go to him," she replied, avoiding his stare.

Calgacus was pointing at the flanks of the Caledonian army and conferring with his chiefs. What was his plan? Did he have one? Then she heard a great thundering of hooves. The Roman horsemen on the flanks were charging and turning to face them were the Caledonian charioteers. Emogene stared as the two forces smashed headlong into each other. In a fraction of a second it became impossible to tell friend from foe. Her husband would be down there in his chariot fighting with his closest kinsmen. Then she caught sight of the black pennant flying from his chariot. The world seemed to slow. She opened her mouth to scream but no sound came out. The Roman rider's spear had knocked him clean over the side of his chariot. No man could survive such a blow. Her body felt numb, stunned by the suddenness of it all. Her husband had told her he would be alright. Now he was gone. She stared down the hill, unable to look away. Then as a tear trickled down her cheek she felt a terrible resolve take hold. No, she thought savagely, she would not mourn for her husband, she would not cry. He was not dead. She refused to accept that he was dead. She would see him again.

Chapter Four – Gods Let This Battle Finish Soon

The Caledonians were starting to outflank the auxiliaries. Groups of warriors were coming down the slopes of the hill and looping round to attack the Romans in the rear. What the fuck was Agricola doing? Couldn't he see what was happening, Marcus thought. The flank of the Roman line had splintered into small groups of men, some fighting back to back as they desperately tried to fend off the Caledonian attacks that were coming in from all sides. Marcus raced towards a small tight group of dismounted horsemen who were trying to hold back the growing Caledonian tide. The horsemen were nearly surrounded by a furious enemy. The Caledonians had started to sense victory and it seemed to give them extra strength and courage.

A bearded warrior came at Marcus wielding a huge axe. The weapon slid off Marcus's parrying sword and sliced into his horse's neck. Blood welled up from the wound in a great gushing fountain and the beast crashed sideways to the ground. Marcus was thrown clear and landed painfully. The wind was knocked out of him and for a moment he was disorientated. Then a terrible roar brought him back to reality. The bearded warrior was coming at him once more, swinging his axe. Marcus rose to his feet just in time as the axe slashed past his face. Then in a single movement he punched his sword into his attacker's face and heard the crunch of metal on bone as it cut straight into the man's head. There was no time to watch the Celt die. Wildly he scrabbled on the ground, groping for a discarded infantry shield. Then he was among friends. The small group of dismounted cavalrymen had formed a protective circle. A Caledonian, naked from the waist up, his torso covered in tattoos, flung himself too carelessly at his enemy and the auxiliary beside Marcus smashed his shield boss into the man's face before stabbing him.

"Nice of you to join us," a voice beside Marcus hissed.

It was Bestia. The decurion managed a crooked half-smile. The officer was nearly twice as old as Marcus but he was still one of the fittest and most dangerous fighters in the troop. The rumour at camp had been that during the Batavian rebellion, Bestia had tortured Roman legionary prisoners by cutting off their balls and making them eat them.

"If that fuck Agricola leaves us here to die I am personally going to ram my cock up his patrician arse!" Bestia screamed. No one answered him. Marcus felt a heavy blow land on his shield and the force of the attack travelled up his arm. Blindly he stabbed with his sword. Someone cried out in a foreign language. Then something hit his helmet. He cried out in pain and felt blood trickling down his ear. A Caledonian raised his arm to fling a spear but collapsed with a spear protruding from his back as another desperate auxiliary came staggering towards the small group. Marcus raised his sword hand and tried to wipe the blood from his eye. As he did so one of the auxiliaries in the group collapsed.

"Agricola, you fucking prick," Bestia hissed, blocking a slashing sword with his shield.

Suddenly a trumpet blast echoed off the hills. It was followed moments later by a second answering blast. Then the ground began to shake. Marcus had no time to see what was happening. The thunder of hooves was coming closer. Then a man screamed.

"Atticus is coming, Atticus...!"

The Caledonians had heard the sound too but they had no time to react. Within moments the small band of auxiliaries and the Caledonians who swarmed around them were engulfed. A long wave of horsemen swept through them and crashed headlong into the rear of the Caledonian line. Then another wave followed and then a third. Marcus screamed in savage delight. Atticus had arrived just in time. The main Roman cavalry force must have skirted around the edge of the battle and had fallen on the enemy's rear. The battle was as good as won.

"Kill the fuckers, kill them!" Bestia roared. They all felt it. The violent release of so much pent-up terror. It was time to finish the enemy. The Caledonians knew it too for suddenly their line began to waver. Attacked from the front and now the rear was too much for any man. It only took a second but then the rout spread like wild fire. The Caledonians turned and began fleeing back up the hill in great numbers. Marcus felt the brutal bloodlust. All around him Atticus's cavalry were cutting through the fleeing enemy, mowing them down like corn during harvest. This was the time when most men would die. This was the moment when the battle became a massacre. The slopes of the hill were becoming littered with bodies.

"Kill them, kill them all…!"

Up the slope he caught sight of Bestia's bloodstained face. The decurion was laughing as he finished off the enemy wounded. Marcus wanted to laugh too but in that instant something caught his attention. A short distance away a Roman cavalryman had fallen from his horse and lay pinned beneath the dead beast. The man was screaming something in Latin and with a shock Marcus realised that the man was calling out his name. It was Pigface. He stumbled towards the dead horse and knelt down beside his friend. Pigface was still yelling his name. His legs were trapped under the dead horse.

"Shut up!" Marcus shouted.

He got his hands under his friend's armpits and heaved.

"Marcus, watch out!" Pigface yelled.

A Caledonian with wild, terrified eyes came running towards him with a raised sword. Then the man tripped and stumbled. Marcus sprung forward but as he did so the Caledonian dropped his weapon and fell to his knees, raising his hands. He was weeping. In one hand the man held up a sprig of mistletoe.

"No more, no more; a truce, I beg you," he cried in his Celtic language. Marcus stared wildly at the Caledonian warrior and the sprig of mistletoe. He knew the meaning. His mother had taught him that in Celtic society, no warrior may fight on in the presence of mistletoe. The plant was sacred. It was also a desperate act. A dishonourable act. Celtic warriors fought to the death. The truce would last for a whole day. He kicked the man in the head. The bloodlust was fading.

"Stay where you are. If you move the truce is broken!" he shouted in his mother's language.

He retreated to where Pigface lay trapped. His friend's shouts had turned to deep groans and gasps of agony. Behind him the Caledonian with the mistletoe had risen to his feet. The man was about to say something when a spear embedded itself in his back and a gobbet of blood shot from his mouth. A Roman rider charged past as the Caledonian fell to the ground. Marcus crouched beside Pigface. His friend was crying now. After the third attempt he managed to drag Pigface free. The young rider's legs had been crushed. He would never walk again. Pigface's head lolled from side to side. Then he slipped into unconsciousness. Marcus pulled him into his lap, leaned back against the dead horse and cradled him in his arms. The sight of his wounded friend had a sobering effect. Suddenly he felt very tired. The bloodlust had gone and his hands began to tremble as he suddenly realised what he had just witnessed. Gods let this battle finish soon, he thought.

Chapter Five – Vellocatus

Vellocatus picked his way carefully across the corpse-strewn battlefield. The hill was littered with the debris of war as far as the eye could see. The cries of the wounded and the dying could still be heard. Vellocatus's nose twitched as he caught the scent of thousands of dead men. Neither the smell nor the corpses bothered him. He was used to seeing the dead and the dying. He paused to look up at the sky. It was growing dark. It would be too dark soon to continue. He would have to hurry. He was a tall man of thirty-two and was wearing an expensive coat made from pure white bearskin. With an expert eye he took in every detail of the battlefield. To the Romans and the Caledonians who had just fought in this great battle, this nameless hill was a place of death, of shame and of glory, but to Vellocatus the place was nothing more than a gigantic goldmine. Once he'd overheard a slave comparing him to a vulture. He'd had the slave buried alive. No one had tried to compare him with anything after that, not even those who pretended to be his friends. But the slave had been right, he thought. His profession made him act like a vulture.

The dead and dying lay in great heaps and scattered amongst them were discarded shields, bloodied swords and spears, helmets, dead horses and overturned chariots. The story of that day's battle could clearly be seen in where the dead lay. Vellocatus ignored the dead. They were of no use to him. There was a hungry, excited look on his face. The gods knew how long he had waited for this day. They knew how hard he had worked to be here. How much money he had poured into this venture. And now after all that effort, the time had finally come for him to harvest his investment.

"Water…" a wounded Caledonian cried out nearby. Vellocatus glanced across at the warrior. The man lay on the ground clutching his stomach. His fingers were stained black with blood and dirt.

"No good," the slave who was following him with a stylus and a wooden writing tablet muttered.

Vellocatus stared at the wounded man. The slave was right. The man would be dead by nightfall. There was no use in dragging him back to the slave pen. There were healthier prisoners still out there whom he could take as slaves. Again he glanced up at the sky. If only the light would hold a little longer. Ignoring the dying Celt he started up the hill. Oh what a day it had been. That morning as soon as the outcome of the battle had been decided he and the mercenaries he'd hired had clustered around Governor Agricola waiting tensely and anxiously for his permission to storm onto the battlefield and start collecting the enemy prisoners. He had bagged sixty-nine slaves so far. All of them had been dragged from the battlefield or found hiding in trees. He had clasped them all in neck irons. By nightfall he was hoping to make it eighty. Tomorrow he would have another look but from experience he knew that the best slaves would all have been snapped up by then or managed to flee.

Eighty new slaves was his target. The price he could fetch for each one would vary of course, depending on the state of the particular slave, but he had already calculated that with eighty slaves, sold at a fair price, he would be able to repay the debts he owed to the Jewish moneylenders and still have enough money left over to build himself that villa which he had always dreamed of owning. His newfound wealth would finally allow him to marry Clodia, the young patrician lady on whom he had set his sights. Lady Clodia was the sister of Governor Agricola's wife. It was only by his incessant lobbying of her that he had finally managed to get Agricola's permission to take the slaves. With such a marriage, he, Vellocatus, would be propelled into the elite circles of Roman society in Britannia. He smiled at the prospect. Oh yes, the battle that had just been fought was going to change his life alright. Legally the slaves taken on the battlefield all belonged to Agricola and the army but Agricola had already agreed to sell them to him for a pittance of what he, Vellocatus, would get when he sold them in the great markets of Londinium and Eburacum. Life was good. He was going to be a rich man. The last time that a slaver had been able to make such a fortune had been twenty-three years ago, well before his time, when Governor Paulinus had destroyed the druids on Mona Insulis and routed that bitch Boudica.

Vellocatus strode on up the blood-soaked hill. Here and there he came across a Roman soldier robbing the dead. The soldiers, however, would drift away as he and his men approached.

"Fucking slaver," a voice cried out suddenly from close by.

Vellocatus stopped in his tracks and turned to look at the badly wounded Roman auxiliary who lay half covered under a heap of corpses. The soldier was staring up at Vellocatus with dull, listless eyes.

"We do all the fighting," the soldier muttered, "and you take all the rewards. I curse you – may you rot forever in the belly of the gods of the underworld!"

Vellocatus didn't hesitate. He took two steps towards the wounded man, bent down and with a quick movement cut the Roman's throat. Then he stood up and without looking back started on up the hill.

"Master," the slave carrying the stylus and the writing tablet said, touching his arm. "Over there beside the dead horse. He looks unhurt."

Vellocatus stared in the direction in which his slave was pointing. The Caledonian lay beside the dead beast. He was young, little more than a boy with dark curly hair. He seemed to have witnessed the killing of the Roman soldier for the boy's eyes widened in alarm as Vellocatus approached. The slaver kicked the boy in the thigh.

"How old are you?" Vellocatus asked, speaking in his native Celtic language.

"Fourteen," the boy replied with a trembling lip. He looked up in terror at the slaver and his men as they crowded around him.

"Don't kill me," he pleaded.

"Show me your teeth," Vellocatus demanded.

The boy did as he was asked. Vellocatus grunted in approval.

"Bestia, we will take this one," he cried over his shoulder in Latin. From the gathering gloom the decurion appeared. His face was still splattered with blood and in his hand he clutched several torcs and finger rings which he had robbed from the dead. He grinned as he saw the latest prisoner to be turned into a slave. Whether it was the killing he had just witnessed or Bestia's blood-splattered face, the boy suddenly turned pale with terror.

"Please, I don't want to die," he cried out. "Spare me, let me go free and I will tell you about a secret. I will tell you what I know."

Vellocatus was already moving on when he stopped in mid stride. Slowly he turned round to look at the boy.

"Wait," he raised his hand. He stared at the boy cowering on the ground. "What secret do you know that could possibly interest me?"

There was a sudden movement beside the boy. A Caledonian warrior with a deep gash along his side stirred and opened his eyes. The man tried to lift his head but he lacked the strength.

"No, Conall..." he muttered, trying to reach out to the boy.

Bestia was at the man's side in a single bound and a fraction of a second later the warrior was dead. The boy's eyes opened wide. Then he rose and cried out a name. There was an unmistakable grief in his voice. The cry was cut short as Bestia slapped him hard across the face.

The boy sat down heavily on the ground. Tears started to stream down his red cheeks as he stared at the warrior Bestia had killed. "Promise to let me go," the young Caledonian cried as he recovered his voice. "Promise me that you will let me go."

Vellocatus smiled and shrugged and the mercenaries around him sniggered. "Why not," he said smoothly, "if that is what you want so badly."

The boy was still crying. Then as Vellocatus, Bestia and the others waited he managed to compose himself, wiped the tears from his face and quietly, with the dejection of someone who had lost all hope, he began to speak, his words little mumbles in the gathering darkness.

Chapter Six – Beware of the Latrines

They stood in a semicircle around the wounded man. Pigface lay on the back of a cart wrapped in an old woollen army blanket. He looked glum and pale. Marcus stood by his side.

"We managed to collect this for you," Marcus said. He handed over a small leather pouch. "Maybe you can use it to learn a new trade?"

"Like what?" Pigface muttered. "Who will take a man with no legs?"

The troopers were silent, each man struggling to find something to say. It could have happened to any one of them, they knew, but it had happened to Pigface. Marcus stared at the long line of wagons that were preparing to take the wounded south to the coast.

"Your most important piece of equipment is still working isn't it?" he said, turning to his friend with a faint smile.

"Girls on top from now on, Pigface," one of the troopers added.

"Just like Batavian riders," another quipped.

Pigface managed a smile and his face brightened. "I am going to miss you bastards," he replied. "I am going to miss how much you stink."

They smiled at that. "Where are they taking you?" a trooper said at last.

"Eburacum," Pigface replied. "Doctor says he will give me a final examination once we are there. After that they will discharge me and send me back to my village along the Rhine. I suppose I can help my sisters with the weaving and I can fish. Maybe they will let me ride a horse…?" his voice petered out.

"We will come looking for you whenever we can get the leave," a trooper said solemnly.

"I would like that," Pigface nodded his appreciation. Then he stared at where his legs used to be. The group fell silent. When Pigface looked up there were tears in his eyes. He raised his hand and clenched it into a fist.

"It meant something didn't it, this battle? I didn't lose my legs for nothing?"

Marcus clasped his hand around his friend's fist and after a brief moment, one by one, the troopers stepped forwards and joined in. Marcus leaned forwards.

"We are veterans of Mons Graupius, my friend," he said quietly, "and we shall carry that honour wherever we go. Nothing can take that away from us. They will build monuments to us, you will see."

There were grunts of approval from the troopers around him.

Marcus did not stay to watch the column of wounded move out. Instead he made his way out of the marching camp. It was the day after the battle and the army had not moved on. There was too much to do. The wounded had to be found and treated, prisoners interrogated and sold into slavery, the dead had to be buried and the loot from the battle had to be gathered and handed out in equal measures to all the soldiers. Besides, everyone was exhausted.

He made his way to the army latrines. It was an odd place to find some peace and privacy but that was just what he craved. He found them beside the large and deep V-shaped ditch and the wooden palisade that protected the marching camp. The latrines were nothing more than a single shallow trench covered by wooden planks with round holes cut into them at intervals. When Marcus arrived there was just one other occupant. The man sat with his head in his hands, deep in thought, his garments at his ankles.

Marcus sat down a couple of holes away and nodded to the other occupant before he dropped his underclothes to his ankles. A moment later he too had his head in his hands, his thoughts far away.

"The Batavian cohorts won the battle yesterday; they are fine soldiers. The legions are green with envy."

For a moment Marcus did not realise that his neighbour was talking to him. Casually he looked up at the man and his eyes widened in shock. The soldier on the toilet, a few holes away, had raised his head from his hands. It was Governor Agricola. For an insane moment Marcus fought the urge to stand to attention and salute.

"Yes, sir, sorry, sir, I didn't recognise you," he blurted out.

Agricola smiled at the commotion he had caused. "Don't embarrass yourself, soldier," he growled. "In my army every man has the right to a have a shit." Agricola grinned at Marcus. "You look like you are from one of the Batavian cohorts – did you fight yesterday?"

"I did, sir, on the right wing; Second Batavian Cohort."

Agricola nodded and turned to look towards the battlefield. "You Batavians are some of the finest soldiers that I have ever encountered," he said. "I remember what it took to subdue your rebellion fourteen years ago. That was such a waste of good men. That rebellion should never have happened."

Marcus cleared his throat. "My name is Marcus; I am named after my grandfather. I am with the Second, sir but I am not a Batavian. My father was a legionary with the Twentieth and my mother was a local girl from the tribe of Trinovantes. I was born at Camulodunum."

Agricola turned to look at Marcus in surprise. "Your father served in the legions, in the Twentieth. That is my old legion. What was your father's name?"

Marcus was annoyed with himself. He had said too much but now he had to answer the governor.

"Corbulo, sir, First Cohort. He rose to the rank of tesserarius; he was the watch commander of the Second Company, First Cohort. He was with the legion for twenty-five years."

Agricola seemed to be searching his memory. Then his eyes lit up and a huge grin appeared on his face. "So you are Corbulo's boy!" he exclaimed. "Yes I remember your father now. We shared a boat during the assault on Mona. He called me an unwashed prick. Then later on," Agricola paused and nodded, "he was loyal even when some in the Twentieth were not. How is he doing these days? He must have retired by now?"

"I don't know, sir, I have not seen or heard from him in nearly three years."

There was a tightness in Marcus's voice that made Agricola hesitate. The governor glanced at him thoughtfully. "So your mother was a British girl, so you must speak the local language of these Britons?" he said.

"I do, sir," Marcus replied solemnly. "She taught me much about her people."

Agricola nodded and looked away. He was silent for a while. "I lost a good man yesterday," he said at last. "Atticus is dead, did you know that?"

"No, I didn't know that. I thought he was leading the pursuit, sir."

"Well he isn't. He was too eager and careless," Agricola murmured. "They told me that his horse carried him too deep into the enemy ranks. Rome lost a good man yesterday, a man not easily replaced."

Marcus found himself thinking about Pigface and his amputated legs.

"He is not the only one, sir," he said quietly.

Agricola muttered something beneath his breath. Then he looked up. "You have British blood in you, soldier," he said. "Tell me then, will this battle, my victory, break the will of these Caledonians? Will they now give up the struggle and subject themselves to the Roman peace or do I have to keep chasing them from hill to hill and forest to forest?"

Marcus blinked in surprise. Was Agricola really asking him this? He took a moment to consider the question.

"We defeated them yesterday, sir," he replied carefully, "and no doubt some will come seeking peace but others will refuse and keep on fighting. Why should they make peace when our army is followed by a horde of tax collectors and slavers whose only interest is in the exploitation of the conquered? Would you, sir, make peace when that means accepting the enslavement of everything you value?" Marcus's voice petered out. He swallowed nervously. *Fool, do you want a flogging?* Once again he had said too much.

Agricola looked unimpressed. He muttered something under his breath and his eyes wandered back to the battlefield.

"A horde of tax collectors and slavers," he repeated, louder this time. His face darkened. Then with a curt nod to Marcus he reached for his garments, pulled them up and strode away without another word.

Chapter Seven – The Victor of Mons Graupius

Governor Agricola stood at the entrance to his tent looking out into the camp. It was getting dark and his men were busy preparing their evening meals. They huddled around their small fires laughing, joking and eating. They had done well, he thought. Tomorrow he would issue the orders to break camp and march north. A few cheerful souls were singing but most of his men just looked tired. Agricola sighed. He was going to miss the army and camp life. It wasn't official yet but once news of his great victory at Mons Graupius reached Rome, Emperor Domitian would almost certainly order his recall. The order to return to Rome was bound to come like spring following winter. The emperor could not afford to let him win more military glory than he already possessed. Agricola's popularity and fame could become a threat to the emperor if he did and the devious, cunning advisers that surrounded the emperor would never tolerate that. He understood the reasoning although he hated the men who imposed it. That was the way it went for a man who had achieved what he had achieved. There was no higher position than that which he had now reached. Only the position of emperor was more prestigious. Agricola smiled. In Rome the emperor would start by thanking him and hailing his great victory. There would be sacrifices in his honour, speeches full of flattery, maybe the senate would even vote him a triumph. Then when the people and the soldiers had seen enough and had returned home satisfied that their hero had been properly treated, he would be quietly retired. He would be given a country estate in the provinces and slowly his family would be marginalised and allowed to be forgotten. Maybe, if the emperor felt especially threatened, he would make use of a slow-working and untraceable poison to kill him off. The emperor cannot tolerate a man who is more successful than himself.

Agricola's smile broadened. How many of Rome's great generals had found themselves where he stood now? Some had chosen to take the final career step and make a bid for the purple. To raise the banner of revolt and march on Rome. Men like his kinsmen Gaius Julius Caesar. Men like his old friend and patron Vespasian. They had been unable to content themselves with obscurity; they had found it impossible to leave their troops and the power that an army gave to a leader. But a man's fate was not his alone, Agricola thought; the gods had a cruel way of playing their games on mortal men. He had seen what had happened to Galba, to Otho and to Vitellius and he had not envied their fate. What would the gods do if he chose to ignore the emperor and marched his army on Rome? Would they really allow him to seize ultimate power in the empire and start a dynasty like Vespasian had done? The thought of his old friend and patron brought about a sudden mellowness. No, he could not do that to his friend's memory. He could not dispose of the youngest son of his friend, however obnoxious and tyrannical Domitian was. However much some senators were urging him to. No, when the recall came he would obey and lay down his power just like the consuls of the Republic had once done. Rome would remember him as dutiful and successful. That way his family would have a chance to survive and prosper.

He closed the flap to his tent and returned to the chair at his desk. There was still important work to be done before the victory feast that he was hosting for his senior officers that night. He glanced at a copy of Pytheas's book, *On the Ocean*. He had purchased the copy in his home town of Forum Julii just before he had set out for his governorship of the province of Britannia. Some may deride the ancient Massalian-Greek explorer as a liar but he had found the man's four-hundred-year-old writings and maps of these northern lands fairly accurate. Pytheas's book was the only written record on the far north that existed within the empire and Agricola had used it extensively on his march north.

He turned his attention to the letter he had been writing. It was to the emperor. He stared at the wax tablet, suddenly conscious of the power at the tip of his stylus.

...and our fleet has established beyond doubt that we are occupying an island. In the last seven years of my governorship

of Britannia I have conquered and pacified all the southern tribes. Now the northern Caledonian confederation has been destroyed and I am confident that Rome and you, my father, to whom I offer this great victory, will, by persistent and dedicated occupation of these northern lands, bring these Caledonians into the fold of the empire and civilisation. The Caledonian spirit is strong and wild, for these men live close to the edge of the world with its nameless demons and so do not fear like others do, but I am confident they can be civilised over time...

Agricola paused, frowned and then wrote down an extra sentence in the margin.

...as long as we show a mind for fair, good and effective administration.
To complete the conquest of the island of Britannia, which your father Vespasian first instructed me to carry out, I have drawn up plans for a line of forts to be built at the valley entrances that lead up into the hills where the remainder of the enemy sulks. I have also designated a spot for a new legionary fort and my men shall spend the winter building new roads between our camps. If these measures are allowed to continue then in a few years we shall have peace on the northern border. It may even be possible then to withdraw some of our men for duties elsewhere. But if you feel that the time has now come for me to return to Rome then I implore you, my father, instruct my successor to follow these policies. I humbly beg you, do this in memory of the soldiers who died to win you this glorious victory...

Agricola laid down his stylus. He had been hoping that yesterday's battle would conclude the conquest of the island. How could he let such vain hopes go to his head? That soldier, Marcus, whom he had met down at the latrines. He had been spot on with his analysis. What man would want to make peace when confronted by the rapacity of Rome's tax collectors and slave merchants? What did these Caledonians have to lose by continuing to fight? Nothing. Nothing at all. Agricola shook his head. He had been hoping to enter history as the man who had conquered all of Britannia. That was a worthy achievement. That was how he wanted to be remembered. But the gods were playing their games once more. They were meddling with his fate, denying him his place in history. The cruel, heartless gods were laughing at his vanity. The Caledonians would continue to fight and he had run out of time. Another governor would now accomplish what he had wanted to achieve. Agricola pushed back his chair and suddenly roared with laughter.

"Sir, a visitor to see you," one of his bodyguards announced as he stepped into the tent.

"Who is it? I am busy," Agricola growled, annoyed at the intrusion.

"The slaver, Vellocatus," the bodyguard replied. "Shall I send him away, sir?"

Agricola's face darkened in disgust. He didn't like Vellocatus but his wife had nagged him to allow the man to have the first pick of any slaves that his army secured. She had been acting on behalf of her sister of course. Vellocatus had his eye on the girl and his charms must be working but Agricola had seen through the man. Vellocatus was the illegitimate son of queen Cartimandua, queen of the Brigantes, and her armour bearer. Vellocatus had been born to illustrious Celtic nobles but the son had inherited nothing of value apart from his name. The bastard son was nothing more than a self-serving, back-stabbing rat of a man whom Agricola did not trust an inch. His wife's sister was making a big mistake by flirting with him. He had told his wife his opinion but when it came to matters of the heart she had ignored him as usual.

But today, Agricola thought with sudden grim satisfaction, he would confront the bastard.

"No, show him in," he snapped.

A moment later the tent flap was thrown back and Vellocatus entered. There was an urgent, excited expression on his face that took Agricola by surprise. He strode right up to the desk and Agricola raised his eyebrows as he saw that the man's whole body was shaking with excitement.

"Congratulations on your great victory," Vellocatus bowed. "The Caledonians have suffered a crushing blow. Not since the great revolt have we had such a battle. I salute you, Governor."

"The victory belongs to my men, the living, the wounded and the dead," Agricola replied sharply as he rose to his feet. He was about to continue when Vellocatus interrupted him. There was a strange gleam in his eye.

"It's not about the slaves, Governor," he said quickly. "There is something else that I would like to talk to you about." Vellocatus paused. "I found a prisoner on the battlefield. The boy has a rather strange and interesting story to tell. I think you would like to hear what he has to say, Governor."

Chapter Eight – Flight

Emogene stood on top of a large boulder as all around her the Caledonians fled. Her cheeks burned but she would not cry for her husband. She was not going to accept that he was dead. The warriors swarmed past her, heedless of any pride or dignity, obeying only the primitive urge for self-preservation. Bones stood beside her on the boulder growling at the swarming masses. The Roman horsemen were surging after the running mob. They would reach her soon. She stared desperately at the spot where she had last seen her husband but down the hill all was chaos.

"Run, girl, all is lost!" a warrior yelled at her as he stormed past.

She ignored him. Her eyes were on the horsemen and the Roman infantry who were charging up the hill towards her. Everything in their path was being slaughtered. She turned to look at where Calgacus stood. The Caledonian supreme commander, surrounded by his kinsmen and the finest warriors of the land, had not moved from his position. Surely they would fight. Surely they would not run. She had heard the warriors boast a thousand times over that they would never run. If they ran now it would be all over. It would be the end. Calgacus, distinguishable by his great black beard and black cloak stood rooted to the ground as if in shock. He was staring down the hill at his fleeing army. Then she saw Baldurix tug at his arm. Emogene gasped in dismay as Calgacus and his kinsmen turned their chariots around and rode away, joining the fleeing masses.

"We must run," she whispered, turning to Bones.

Emogene tore across the crest of the hill. Bones was ahead of her, bounding through the colourful heather. For such a huge dog he moved incredibly fast. Men ran past her. Some in their haste and terror bashed into each other or tripped and went tumbling along across the ground. Emogene dashed through a clump of trees. Two men were climbing up the branches.

The thunder of hooves was drawing closer. She didn't look back. The only men still riding horses would be Romans. A warrior ahead of her tried to grab Bones by his collar but the big war dog snapped his jaws into the man's hand and flung the screaming warrior to the ground.

"He's my dog!" she yelled as she stormed past.

The warrior was howling in pain and staring at his hand from which Bones had ripped three fingers.

The horsemen were very close now. Behind her she heard the screams of men being cut down as they ran. She was starting to tire and her breath came in ragged gasps. No, she was not going to be caught. She was going to stay alive. She was going to see her husband again. These Roman demons were not going to stop her. They were not going to prevent her from seeing her husband. Her eyes were fixed on the thick forest just a hundred yards away. If she could get in there she would have a chance. The horsemen would not be able to follow so closely. *Come on, run*, she willed herself. *Come on, just a little further.*

Suddenly a dark shape loomed over her and too late she saw the sword flash. The blow caught her on the shoulder and sent her spinning to the ground. A man clad in armour cried out in a strange language. The sun reflected on his armour, blinding her for a split second. She tried to scramble to her feet. From behind her she heard a deep-throated growl. A grey object shot past her and with a mighty leap, Bones went for the horse's head. The force of his charge and jump was so great that the horse screamed in terror and rose up on two legs, throwing her rider to the ground. Then the horse was bolting away across the hill. Bones, his snout covered in blood, had attacked the fallen rider. The Roman was screaming in panic as the war dog went for any exposed flesh that he could find.

Emogene was on her feet and running again.

"Bones, Bones," she cried.

A moment later the big war dog was at her side, his flanks heaving. His snout was drenched in blood and a strip of meat, horse or human, had got stuck in his jaws. There was a wildness in his yellow eyes. Then they burst through the trees and into the cover of the forest.

Wearily she stumbled the last few yards to the stepping stones across the stream. It felt like she had been running and walking for hours. Her long black hair was tangled and filled with dirt, twigs and sweat. She had discarded the wooden staff that her father had given her and taken a knife from a corpse. Sometimes, as she had picked her way up the long wooded valley, she had heard the thunder of hooves and the cries of the enemy echoing off the barren highlands. She had run into a small band of fugitives who had told her to go west. They were off to the western islands to hide and regroup. She had asked about Calgacus but they had not known what had happened to him.

She paused as she reached the stream with its flat stepping stones. Bones barked and idled up to her side, panting lightly. Her husband and the men who lived in his house and that of her father had agreed that if things went badly they would try and meet back at this place before deciding what to do. Bones barked again and it was then that Emogene noticed the man across the stream. He was sheathing his sword and was about to set off up the valley. She recognised him at once.

"Bodvoc, it's me, Emogene! What of the others? Have you seen them?" she cried.

Bodvoc was a young man, a year older than herself. He was her husband's cousin. He turned and stared at her but he didn't move from his side of the stream. A bloodied rag had been tied around his left arm.

"I saw your man fall," he replied, lowering his eyes. "We will honour him when we get home, Emogene."

Emogene shook her head fiercely. "He is not dead," she shouted.

Bodvoc raised his gaze and looked at her. Then slowly he shook his head. "He is dead, Emogene, the spear went straight through him. I saw his body myself."

Emogene's voice was shrill and emotional. "He is not dead!" she screamed. Her scream echoed across the hills.

Bodvoc's face hardened. "He is not coming home, Emogene. You must accept that. The Romans are killing the wounded."

She ignored him with an irritated shrug of her shoulders. Bodvoc glanced up the path leading out of the valley.

"Arlen and the others came through an hour ago," he said. "We are going home. We all fought together but in the rout I got separated." He paused. "Devlin is dead and Jodoc was wounded but alive when I last saw him. His boy decided to stay with him. That's all I know."

Emogene's eyes widened.

"Conall? You left them on the hill?" The words shot out of her mouth before she could think. Bodvoc nodded.

"Come, Emogene," he said, stretching out his hand to her, "we must get back home. The battle is lost. The Romans will be looking for survivors."

Emogene felt a sudden chill as if something invisible had just touched her. She bit her lip.

"You know my father's law," she said sharply. "We are all sworn to obey his law. You know its importance. We die in battle or we come home. We do not leave one of us behind alive. My father warned us specifically about that. We must go back and find Jodoc and Conall."

"Yes I swore to obey his law," Bodvoc snapped, "but to go back now is suicidal. That hill will be crawling with Romans. They will catch us. No, we cannot risk being caught, Emogene. Jodoc and Conall will be dead by now. The Romans are killing our wounded. The dead cannot talk."

Emogene clenched her hands into fists.

"Bodvoc," she cried out, "we must go back to make sure. The Romans must never discover what we know. That is why my father made you swear to obey his law. Now obey him!"

Bodvoc shrugged. "Come with me, Emogene, I am going home. Don't stay here. You know what the Romans are doing to our women."

Once again he extended his hand and once again Emogene felt a chill pass through her body. This was wrong, she thought.

"Tell my father that I obeyed his law," she snapped.

Bodvoc stared at her for a moment. Then he turned and started up the path.

Chapter Nine – The War Dog

Emogene watched him disappear. When he had finally vanished from view she slumped to the ground beside the stream and bowed her head. What was going to happen now? Part of her ached to go after Bodvoc, to return to the comfort and security of her father's house, to shelter behind his protective power and to make herself as small as possible but it would be the wrong thing to do. If she did that she would know in her heart, forever, that she was a coward. She had to go back to that nameless hill. She wrenched herself back up onto her feet and turned to examine her shoulder. There was just a bruise from where the Roman had hit her and a little blood but nothing serious. The Roman must have struck her with the side of his sword. Her eyes widened. He had meant to capture her. The thought of captivity made her stomach turn. They had all heard the stories of what the Romans had done to women from the tribes to the south. She glanced down at the knife that she had taken from the dead man. Once more she bit her lip. She would end herself before she allowed these foreigners to catch her. Her father had made her swear to obey him for a reason. She would obey. The thought of her father suddenly seemed to give her new strength and hope.

She turned to look at Bones until she had eye contact with the dog. Bones lay stretched out on a boulder, panting slightly, his large red tongue hanging from his mouth. His yellow eyes looked back at her.

"Come here," she commanded.

The dog obeyed instantly. She grabbed him by his collar, crouched and dipped her other hand into the stream and began cleaning the blood from his snout. He whined and tried to back away but she silenced him with a sharp command.

"We are going back to the battlefield," she spoke quietly to him as she washed away the worst of the gore. "We are going to look for Jodoc and Conall. They must not be taken alive, you see. That is what Father says. You understand, don't you."

The war dog's yellow eyes stared back at her.

She stood up and turned to look in the direction from which she had come. She would return when it grew dark. The night would protect her. The Romans liked to live in towns and camps, she knew. They would not venture out at night. Her people still owned the night. She turned to look to the north-west in the direction of home. The sun was already low on the horizon. Soon it would be gone. For a moment she thought she could hear the dull boom of the waves breaking onto the rocky shore. She closed her eyes and pictured her father's face. Long ago before she was even born he had made every man, woman and child in his village swear an oath of silence. Out there in the ocean was something that had to be kept secret from everyone who did not live in her village. Not a word was to be uttered. The people of her village had understood the reason and none had argued against her father, for he was a clan druid and such men were always obeyed. Her father had devised a simple and effective law and all had sworn to obey him. Until now, she thought. Two of her kinsmen were missing. She had to find out what had happened to them.

Emogene crouched on the ridge of the hill watching to see if anything was moving in the darkness below her. It was night and the moon cast its pale light across the land. In the distance she could see the myriad of Roman campfires. The enemy were feasting their victory inside the huge fort they had built. The size of their camp had stunned her. With what magic had these foreigners built such a thing in such a short space of time? The battlefield below her had fallen silent. For a while she listened to the noises of the night. The soft call of an owl. The distant howling of a wolf in the mountains. *The Romans may be the masters of the day but we still own the night*, she thought. The night held no fears for her apart from on Samhain when no one went outside. She glanced up at the moon and muttered a silent prayer to the spirits of the rocks who lived on this nameless hill. Then she pulled her cloak closer around her body and turned to look down the hill to the spot where she thought she had last seen her husband. He would be alright, she thought. He would have managed to escape. He was probably hiding in the forests before he made his way back home. She would see him soon enough.

For a long time she crouched on the ridge letting her eyes and ears probe the darkness. At last she seemed satisfied.

"Bones, come," she whispered.

The war dog padded up to her side. She fumbled for his collar and then pressed a rag into his nose.

"Find them," she whispered.

Bones bounded off into the darkness. Her husband had trained him well, she thought. He was good at training dogs. She remembered the warrior who had tried to grab Bones's collar on their mad flight earlier that day. Yes, the war dog would be worth a lot. Bones had been trained to fight against two armed men at the same time. He had been trained to bring down horsemen and of course he was an excellent hunter and guard. Bones had been her husband's most prized possession, even more valuable than his chariot.

She crouched and waited, feeling the tension grow. Her shoulders started to ache and she could hear her heart beating inside her chest. She would need to find some food soon. She strained to catch any signs of movement but the night was silent. Time began to drag. Her eyes began to grow heavy with tiredness. She bit her finger and pulled at her ears in an effort to keep herself alert. She would need to find a hiding place before it grew light. That meant she may have to walk for miles to find a suitable place. Tiredness and despair began to conspire to lower her spirits. She was just about to whistle for Bones to return when suddenly he appeared from out of the darkness. He padded slowly towards her and sat down. She brought her face close to his so that she could just about see his eyes. Normally she could read the dog's reactions quite well but Bones seemed indifferent and uninterested by what he had found.

"Show me," she whispered, taking a firm grip of his collar. Bones smacked his lips together and emitted a deep-throated growl. Then he started off down the hill into the night. She followed at his side.

Corpses began to litter the grass and rocks and she had to tread carefully to avoid tripping over them. Bones led her onwards down the slope. She was heading straight for the Roman camps. With her right hand she drew the knife from her belt. Then at last Bones stopped and sat down on his hind legs. She crouched and looked around her. The dead lay everywhere. The fighting seemed to have been particularly fierce here. Amongst the dead lay horses, weapons of all kinds and – her eyes widened in shock – the bodies of Romans! She moved over to one of them. The corpse was nearly entirely clad in armour. She bent down so that her face was nearly touching the dead man and peered into his eyes. It had been the first time she had seen a Roman this close up. She straightened up. They were not giants or magicians, she thought with sudden contempt. They were not invincible. They were just men, like her husband. The sight of the enemy dead brought her some comfort. These Romans could be killed just like any other man.

Bones whined. The dog had not moved but she could sense his impatience. He was hungry. He wanted to hunt. She laid her hand on his neck and stared around at the mass of tangled corpses. Bones was never wrong. He had brought her here for a reason. Then she saw him. It was Jodoc. He was half sitting up and his open eyes were staring straight at her. There was a long dark gash down his side. Emogene yelped in shock. Jodoc was her brother-in-law. She squatted down beside the dead man and touched his forehead. Stone cold. Gently she closed his eyes and muttered a prayer to help his spirit find the path to the next world. She had never gotten on with Jodoc but as she crouched beside him for the last time she felt her lower lip quiver. Quickly she rose to her feet. Bodvoc had said that they had all fought together. Where was the boy, Conall?

In the pale moonlight she searched the dead men one by one, rolling corpses onto their backs to get a good view. Slowly she widened her search. When she finally gave up she was exhausted and weak from a lack of food. She sat down beside

Bones and closed her eyes. There was no sign of the boy. He was not amongst the dead.

The mystery unsettled her. She needed to get away from the battlefield before dawn came. The night was already well advanced. She needed to find food and shelter but somehow she couldn't leave. Some stubbornness was holding her back. What had happened to the boy? Think. What had happened to the boy? The question refused to go away. Had he managed to escape? If so why had he not made it to the stepping stones like they had agreed? Was he a corpse further up the hill? Was he even now making his way back home? She glanced up at the moon, willing the spirits to give her a clue.

The Roman campfires within their huge fort were still glowing. There were hundreds of them. She blinked and stared at the Roman camp and the answer was suddenly there. They had taken him. Conall was alive. The Romans killed the wounded but took the unhurt prisoners as slaves. Slaves were valuable. That's what the men in her village had told her. She stared in the direction of the Roman camp. She was right; she always knew when she was right.

"Bones, come," she whispered urgently.

Chapter Ten – Governor Agricola's Victory Feast

Agricola frowned. The tent had fallen silent after Vellocatus had finished recounting his tale. He had been expecting that the slaver had come to complete the purchase of the slaves. He had just been about to reprimand Vellocatus but the slaver had surprised him. Agricola did not like surprises, especially from a man like Vellocatus, and his irritation was clearly visible. Vellocatus, however, seemed not to have noticed. His face was glowing with excitement. Agricola grunted and clasped his hands behind his back.

"So you believe the boy's story?" he growled.

Vellocatus nodded. "He was speaking what he believes is the truth."

Agricola glanced down at the paperwork on his desk. "A man will say anything if he thinks it will save his life. Fear makes people talk," he snapped.

Vellocatus nodded again and a gleam appeared in his eye. He glanced around at the opening to the tent but the two men were alone.

"Governor," he said, lowering his voice, "what if the boy is speaking the truth. Think about what that could mean for men like you and me. Think what we could do. Think about how it could change our lives."

Agricola tensed. He stared at Vellocatus with a stony expression. Vellocatus smiled. His eyes gleamed. "The boy says that many men guard his village. I do not have the resources to go there myself but if we acted together, if we came to some sort of agreement on how to share the spoils, then it would be possible wouldn't it?"

"What would you need?" Agricola said sharply.

"A single ala of cavalry should be sufficient," Vellocatus replied instantly. He paused and examined Agricola from across the desk. "With such resources a man may even be able to buy the loyalty of the Rhine legions. Domitian is not very popular in Rome these days I hear…"

Agricola grunted. He had heard enough.

"A cohort of cavalry is out of the question," he said. "I cannot spare the men. I will need more proof that the boy is telling the truth before I can authorise an expedition."

"Then may I suggest that you question the boy yourself?" Vellocatus replied.

Agricola nodded. That seemed fair enough.

"Did the boy tell you where his village is?" he asked.

Vellocatus looked disappointed. "He described it in fair detail but as to its exact location he wasn't much use. The boy has never seen a map in his life. All he could tell me was that his village was on the coast to the north. But maybe I will be able to persuade him to act as our guide," Vellocatus grinned.

Agricola looked thoughtful. Then he nodded.

"Fine, bring the boy to my tent at dawn tomorrow. That will be all."

Vellocatus bowed, turned and stepped out of the tent.

"Prick," Agricola muttered to himself. He would deal with the other matter concerning Vellocatus later, he thought. Despite his dislike for the slaver, the man's tale had intrigued him. If the story was true he would need to give some careful thought on how to handle the information. Yes he would need to be careful. Once the news got out, many ambitious and dangerous men would be coming north. He would have to deal with all sorts of trouble.

That night Agricola's personal cook prepared the finest and most lavish dinner that he could afford from the provisions that he had taken on campaign. There was dormouse, freshly baked bread, olives, cabbage, hard Batavian cheese, duck and mutton all flushed down by the governor's finest wine. Agricola lay on a couch at the head of the table watching his fellow officers eating and talking. His officers were in a good mood and their laughter and boisterous voices filled his tent. A couple of slaves, clad in simple grey tunics, stood to one side, their faces expressionless. One place along the table, however, remained empty and the plate of food before it remained untouched.

"Where will you take us next, Governor?" one of the young tribunes cried.

Agricola smiled but said nothing.

"Maybe to Hibernia?" the Irish prince replied smoothly. "A single legion would make the high king shit himself. Once ashore I would be able to raise an army to fight at your side, sir."

"Would you really slay your own brother?" another tribune asked, turning to the Irish noble.

"That plan was discussed and rejected two years ago," the grey-haired camp commander of the Twentieth Legion and oldest soldier around the table snapped.

"But it was the reason why you built the great fortress at Deva!" the Irish noble exclaimed.

"I have already been to Hibernia," Agricola replied with a smile.

"Maybe we are to withdraw," Tacitus, Agricola's son-in-law and the only civilian in the party, said. The young man's words were met by a howl of protest but Tacitus persisted, raising his voice. "The word in Rome is that it is on the Danube frontier that we face our greatest and most dangerous enemy. The Dacians are causing trouble, a lot of trouble. Domitian will have to go to war against them soon. Many of you may find your next posting along that frontier."

"I thought you only liked the company of actors and whores?" the legate of the Ninth exclaimed.

The tent erupted in laughter and Tacitus smiled good-naturedly. "You must all be nice to me," he retorted, "for I am here to record your deeds. One slip of my pen could see your achievements erased from history."

The officers banged the table with their fists and roared with laughter. Tacitus grinned and spluttered as a hand slapped him hard on his back.

"What about Thule, Governor?" another Tribune cried. "Our fleet may have sighted the island but no Roman has ever set foot that far north. We could be the first. That would give Tacitus here something to write about."

Suddenly Agricola rose to his feet and as he did the tent fell silent.

"Gentlemen," he said, looking around the table at his officers, "if I may raise a toast to an absent friend."

All eyes turned to look at the empty seat and the untouched meal.

"Tonight he dines with us one final time," Agricola said, raising his cup in the direction of the empty place. The officers rose noisily to their feet and raised their cups.

"To Atticus," they murmured.

They lay down again on the couches with their joviality dampened. Agricola took his time to study their faces. He had known some of these men for nearly twenty years.

"I shall tell you what our next move is going to be," Agricola said at last. He was just about to speak when he was interrupted. The tent flap opened and the watch commander of his bodyguard entered. The man halted and saluted.

"There is a visitor here to see you, sir," the soldier said with a hint of excitement in his voice.

"What, who is it?" Agricola exclaimed, looking annoyed.

"Baldurix, a tribal leader of the Decantae, sir."

The tent fell silent as all turned to look towards the entrance in surprise. The silence lengthened. The watch commander cleared his throat.

"Shall I show him in, sir?"

Agricola looked thoughtful. Then he nodded. "Bring him," he ordered.

A moment later a tall, big and clean-shaven man stepped into the tent. He wore a black woollen cloak, underneath of which he had a finely made coat of chainmail armour. On his arms he sported two golden bracelets and tattoos. Around his neck Baldurix was a wearing a beautiful torc. The Roman officers rose noisily from their benches. Baldurix took a step forwards. He looked unconcerned as his eyes took in the plates of food and jugs of wine on the table. Then he turned to look at Agricola and nodded.

"I see that I have disturbed your dinner," Baldurix said in heavily accented Latin.

"You have," Agricola replied.

"My men have not eaten in two days. May they have some food?"

Agricola turned to his watch commander who had followed Baldurix into the tent. "Bring his men some food."

The soldier saluted and left. "Thank you," Baldurix murmured gratefully.

"I have heard of your name," Agricola said, clasping his hands behind his back. "Your tribe are known for their skill in ironwork, are they not? You trade with the southern tribes around Eburacum and Deva."

Baldurix nodded.

"What brings you here?" Agricola said sternly.

Baldurix lowered his eyes. "I have come to seek the friendship and peace of the Roman people," he replied.

Agricola nodded in approval and glanced at the large map of Britannia that stood on a tripod in the corner.

"I remember once offering the friendship and peace of Rome to all the Caledonian tribes," Agricola said, "and none would accept my offer. Why should I believe you now?"

Baldurix glanced towards the tent entrance. "I will give you my son as a hostage and the Decantae will pay an annual tribute to Rome. In return you shall leave us free to govern ourselves by our own laws."

"A conquered people have no rights," one of the young tribunes sneered. "You will do as Rome says."

"Silence," Agricola barked. The room fell silent. Agricola glared at the tribune who had spoken out. The young man's face burned with sudden embarrassment.

"Agreed," Agricola said at last as he turned to face Baldurix. "But when you die, in your will, you shall leave the territory of your tribe to Rome. I want your oath – kneel."

Baldurix stared at Agricola. He was a proud man and Agricola's order was causing him a lot of difficulty. The shame seemed to burn right through his face. Then slowly Baldurix got down on one knee and bowed his head. "I swear on the spirits of my forefathers that it will be so," he said.

"Good," Agricola said, looking pleased. "Now show me on this map where your people live."

Baldurix rose quickly to his feet. His face had gone red and he wore a resigned look as he followed Agricola to the map standing on its tripod. After a few moments Baldurix placed his finger on the map. "My people live here along the coast," he said.

"How many of you are there?" Agricola snapped.

"A thousand men will follow me," Baldurix said and there was a sudden hint of pride in his voice.

Behind them amongst the officers someone sniggered. Baldurix raised his chin. "My people are free born and follow me by choice," he replied as he tried to maintain his dignity. "My men are not paid to fight for me; they choose to follow me and they are fine warriors."

"No doubt," Agricola said smoothly, "and one day they will make a fine auxiliary cohort. But what of the others, the other tribes – will they make peace? What about Calgacus? Where has he gone?"

Baldurix shook his head. "We are scattered now," he said, staring at the map. "Calgacus's authority has been broken. The tribes will return to their homes but whether they will make peace I don't know. That is something each tribe will decide for themselves now."

Agricola looked thoughtful, then disappointed.

"There is something else," Baldurix said quietly. "I would like to have the support of your army. To the east of us live the Vacomagi. They are hostile to us. They are hostile to Rome and they are ruled by a druid. Their numbers are similar to ours but with the support of your army we will beat them."

Agricola glanced at Baldurix. "Why are they hostile to your people?" he inquired.

"There is a blood feud between us," Baldurix said, lowering his eyes.

Agricola grunted in understanding and turned to look at his map.

"Rome will not choose sides between two feuding tribes," he exclaimed, "but we will protect our allies if they are attacked." He jabbed his finger on the spot that Baldurix had pointed out earlier.

"Here," he exclaimed, "we will extend our line northwards to the coast. We will build a fort here at this place called," he peered closer at the map, "Cawdor. Yes, that fort should sit right in between you and your enemy."

Baldurix nodded his gratitude. "Your soldiers will be welcome to buy supplies from my people as long as they do not insult my warriors or chase their women."

Agricola glanced round at his officers. "You have my word that they will behave themselves," he said sternly. "We do not want a repeat of what happened with Boudica. My men will be under strict orders to leave your people alone."

Agricola stepped across to the table and lifted up two cups of wine. He offered Baldurix a cup and the tall barbarian took it. Agricola looked at him.

"To your newfound friendship and peace with the Roman people," he announced.

Baldurix raised his cup in salute and the two men drank the contents in one go. Agricola was wiping his chin with the back of his hand when the watch commander appeared once more.

"What is it now?" he growled.

"Another visitor, sir," the soldier replied. "It's that slaver, Vellocatus. He looks quite agitated. Insists he speaks with you at once, sir."

Chapter Eleven – The Boy

Emogene sat on the ground munching on the strips of dried meat that Bones had found on a corpse. She was waiting for the light to fade. Across the barren hillside, still littered with the dead, she could see the Roman camp. Vultures were circling in the sky and swooping down to inspect the dead bodies with high-pitched shrieks. Earlier that day she had glimpsed a pack of wolves too. The hunters had come down from the mountains to get their share of the bonanza of dead meat.

She had found shelter that night in the forest a mile away and had collapsed, exhausted and weak from hunger. She had been too tired to look for food and if Bones had not brought back the meat she would have had nothing. She had tugged, snarled and jostled with him for the meat he'd carried in his jaws. With one snap he could have broken her neck but she was not afraid of him. He was Bones, her dog; he would be loyal to her until death. Just like she would be to her husband, she thought. Maybe he had made it back to the village by now. She smiled as she pictured him sitting around the hearth telling the older folk about how he had managed to escape from the Romans. After she'd eaten she had lain back on the pine-covered ground and had glimpsed the moon through the trees. Bones had curled himself into a ball beside her. He would know if anyone or anything got too close. He would warn her. She wasn't afraid of sleeping out in the forest. The moon had reminded her of the druids. The druids were the guardians of all knowledge, her father had told her. They alone knew how to talk to the gods and the spirits of those who had passed on. *Do not fear death for the soul will never die*, her father had taught her. Only the body would perish; the soul would move on to rest in the other world until it would be born again into a new body. Only when you believed, truly believed, that the soul was indestructible would you know the highest form of courage. The druids knew, and they were fearless, truly fearless, and because they respected no fear, or threats, or authority other than their own, the Romans hated them and killed them wherever they found them. That was why her father had come north into the wild and free land of Caledonia all those years ago.

She had woken early and for a while had searched for forest fruits amongst the trees. Her hunger, however, had not gone away. It was Bones who had once again saved the day. He'd padded up to her with a dead duck in his mouth and the two of them had feasted on the raw fatty meat. Later that morning he had returned with more strips of dried meat which she had stuffed into her tunic for later. Her strength had returned and with it her purpose.

She crouched watching the Roman camp in the distance. The question had been bothering her for a while now. How was she going to get into the camp with its deep ditch and high wooden palisade? The Romans would see her coming. They would be guarding the place. It was impossible. She shrugged off her doubts. It would be best to try during the night when the darkness would give her some protection. But for every hour that she waited the higher would be the chance that Conall had talked. He was her nephew and she knew him well. The boy was weak and could be easily bullied. She knew because the girls in the village bullied him. They made him do stupid things. She bit her lip nervously. What if Conall had already told the Romans everything? What if they had already taken him south? She thought about Bodvoc's warning. Was she taking an unnecessary risk? Would it not be better to return to her village? But something drove her on. *No*, she thought, *they have him.* She knew it, she just knew it. The images that she had seen in her dream during Samhain came back to her. The welfare of her village depended on Conall keeping his mouth shut. She was going to find him.

The afternoon began to grow into evening. She was still watching the camp when she heard the thunder of hooves and the whinny of horses behind her. Startled, she scrambled behind some rocks and a few moments later horsemen rode into view below her. There were six of them. She gasped as she recognised Baldurix. What was he up to? What was he doing here with just six men? The riders halted on the slope of the hill and for a moment all six sat motionless, staring down towards the Roman camp. Then Baldurix urged his horse forwards. Emogene frowned, then her eyes widened as she realised what he had come to do. She resisted the temptation to stand up and yell obscenities at her blood enemy. The man was despicable. He was worse than worse. He was going to surrender to the enemy.

Her anger made her throw caution to the wind. "Stay," she snapped at Bones. This was something that she could only do on her own. Baldurix and his men were picking their way carefully across the battlefield and she had no trouble in catching up with them. A few Romans were out examining the corpses. They paused to stare at the horsemen as they rode by but took no action. Emogene hurried on fifty paces behind the last of the riders. If Baldurix turned he would see her but she was counting on his attention being on the Roman camp they were approaching. The Roman ditch and palisade got closer. She plodded straight for the gateway and the sentries that guarded it. From observing the camp she had seen other women enter the fort. She would pretend to be one of them. With a bit of luck the sentries' interest would be on Baldurix and not on her.

To her left outside the protective V-shaped ditch and wooden wall of the camp she suddenly noticed the tents belonging to the camp followers, the merchants, whores, soldiers' wives and shopkeepers who had followed the invaders and who made their living from the soldiers' pay. The sentries were advancing towards Baldurix demanding to know who he was, when she caught sight of a group of half-naked men sitting together on the ground beside a large tent. The men looked utterly dejected and miserable and each man's neck was shackled to a long iron chain that twisted through the group. The chain looked heavy and solid. A slaver's chain, she thought. She had seen one just like it in Tuesis once, but it had been smaller. She veered from her path and strode towards the group. Two armed men stood guard over them. There had to be seventy or eighty slaves. She felt her heart pounding in her chest. With every step she prepared herself to run but no one challenged her. She sat down beside a tree stump close to one of the tents and pretended to fiddle with something on the ground. The slaves were a dozen paces away. They looked exhausted and in a bad state. No one spoke; it was as if the very life force had been ripped from their souls. Emogene worked fast, her eyes searching one face after the other, but Conall was not amongst the slaves. She felt a spark of panic. Now what?

Just then a tall thin man wearing a beautiful white coat strode past followed by a couple of men.

"See that they are fed well and that their strength returns," the man in the white coat was saying. "I want them all fit for the journey south. I do not want to lose a single one of them, do you understand?"

The men following on behind nodded.

Emogene stared at the white-coated man as he disappeared into the large tent that stood alongside the group of chained slaves. The man had spoken in her own language. He was a Briton, a Celt. She lowered her eyes to the ground. Were her own countrymen helping the Romans? Were they profiting from her kinsmen's misfortune? She felt herself blush as she suddenly realised how little she knew about the world outside her village, how naive she was. Then she froze. One of the men guarding the slaves had noticed her. He approached holding a spear. She could see that he was a Briton. A long moustache covered his upper lip.

"Looking for your man," he said, slyly gesturing towards the slaves. "Take a good look, girl; this will be the last time that you see him."

Emogene crouched on the ground. Her knife was hidden in the folds of her clothes. She didn't know what to do. Without thinking she bared her teeth like Bones would sometimes do and hissed at the man. The Briton stared at her in surprise. Then as she hissed again he backed away with a guarded look.

"Stupid witch," he growled. "Get out of here. Go!"

Emogene rose to her feet and turned. It was then that she saw the boy. He was sitting in front of the large white tent, his neck and legs shackled to an iron chain that vanished into the tent. He was picking at his fingernails and staring at the ground. It was the same tent which the man with the white coat had entered. Emogene turned her back and quickly walked away. A fierce sense of triumph surged through her. She had found him and he was alive. She had been right to come back.

Chapter Twelve – Nothing Will Ever Be the Same Again

Emogene kept walking. Her spirit soared. She would wait until it was dark. Then she would return and get him out of that tent. A couple of prostitutes passed her going in the opposite direction and the girls stared at her curiously. Emogene bit her lip. More people were turning to look at her. Why were they looking at her? She was attracting too much attention. She fought the urge to run, to get away from this awful place. Something was wrong. Then she understood. Her face was still covered in blue woad. She had forgotten to wash it off. It looked out of place. No one amongst the camp followers was wearing any. That must have been why the guard had noticed her.

She quickened her pace and had just left the last tents and cooking fires behind when a hand caught her by the shoulder and forced her to halt. The fingers gripped her so tightly that she yelped in pain. She spun round and stared up at two men. One she recognised as the guard who had spoken to her at the tent. The other was older and a foreigner, a soldier, clad in armour. There was a cunning, knowing look on the older man's face.

"Yes, that's her," the Briton said with a nod. "She was watching the slaves. I think her man may be amongst them."

The older man was examining her carefully. It was his fingers that gripped her shoulder and forced her to stop.

"Why were you watching the slaves? What are they to you?" he said, speaking her language slowly and brokenly with a thick accent.

Emogene hissed at him, baring her teeth, but the soldier looked unimpressed. With his free hand he slapped her hard across the face. The blow caught her by surprise and the pain seared through her head.

"Answer me," the soldier shouted.

Emogene gasped and turned to stare up at the man. Then a wave of rage surged through her body. With a shriek she kicked out and her foot caught the soldier right in his groin.

Then she was free and racing away across the hill. When at last she dared look round she saw that there was no pursuit. From the corner of her eye she noticed Bones bounding towards her. The two men were where she had left them. The soldier she had kicked was on his knees, his hands pressed to his groin. Emogene cried out in savage delight and raised her hand in a crude gesture of defiance.

Carefully she wiped the sweat from her forehead. Night had finally come and the darkness hid her as she crouched just beyond the edge of the army followers' camp. The cooking fires filled the night with a reddish glow and she could clearly smell the delicious scent of roasting meat. She had eaten the last of her food and once more she was hungry but her hunger would have to wait. Her eyes peered into the darkness. Then slowly she rose and calmly, keeping to the shadows, she began to make her way towards the large tent. The slavers' tent was easy to spot for a huge fire burned before its entrance around which men had gathered. They were eating. She could hear their voices as she approached. Giving the fire a wide berth she circled round the back and crouched down beside a tree stump. So far so good, but this was the easy part. The back of the tent was a few yards away. The glow of the fire could be seen through the linen. A man laughed and the fire crackled and spat as someone threw another log onto it. Would there be others inside the tent? She had no way of knowing. Slowly she pulled her knife from her clothes and peered at the metal. A quick glance behind her. She was alone. Quickly she flitted up to the tent and raising the knife jabbed it into the linen. There was no sound of alarm. As quietly as she could she started to cut until she had made a hole large enough for her to crawl through. She stopped to listen. One of the men beside the fire had started to sing. Gingerly she lifted the flap of canvas and peered inside.

An oil lamp hung from the roof and in its glare she saw a bed and a table. In the corner was a large metal chest. Then she saw him. He was sitting on the ground, half hidden in the shadows, staring straight at her with wide, terrified eyes.

"Emogene," he whispered, "is that you?"

She slipped into the tent, glancing warily at the entrance and the fire beyond. The man outside was still singing. She turned to look at the boy, raising one finger to her mouth. He was blushing and there was an angry bruise around his eye that she had not noticed when she had first spotted him. Conall tried to rise and it was then that she saw that his legs and neck were chained together. Her heart sank. She had not thought about that. She stared at him, suddenly uncertain about what to do. The look of relief on the boy's face faded and he sat back down.

"What have you told them?" she whispered, advancing towards him.

Conall shook his head. "Nothing, I swear."

"Liar," she said, kneeling down beside him. "They would not keep you in here, separated from the others, without a good reason. What have you told them?"

For a moment he held his own, then his face crumbled.

"They promised to set me free," he whispered. "Vellocatus said it himself but they lied to me, they tricked me. You must believe me, Emogene."

She examined him closely. The boy was only a few years younger than her. She had known him since he had been a baby in his mother's arms.

"Your father is dead," she said.

He nodded and looked away, fighting back sudden tears.

"What have you told them?"

Conall closed his eyes and his head drooped in defeat.

"I told them about the secret out in the ocean," he whispered with a sob.

Emogene closed her eyes. So the Romans knew. She had failed. Her father's law had been broken in a most catastrophic manner. All her father's precautions had been in vain. The boy raised his head and pleaded with her.

"I thought they would set me free. They will never find our village."

Emogene looked at him with a sudden coldness.

"What else have you told them?"

61

"Nothing, I swear it," and this time she knew he was speaking the truth. She glanced at the tent entrance. The man had stopped singing. She closed her eyes once more and clenched her teeth. Her father's law was clear and all had sworn to obey it. Their village's secret had to be protected at all costs. Her village was in danger. The slavers would use the boy as a guide to find her village and then the dream she'd had on Samhain would become a reality.

When she opened her eyes her face was devoid of emotion. She leant forwards and took the boy's head in an embrace like an older sister comforting a younger brother. She felt his warm tears on her neck.

"Go to your father," she whispered as her left hand suddenly clamped over his mouth, "and be at peace, Conall, son of Jodoc," and with that she slid her knife across his throat in one swift sharp movement. She felt his body tense in shock, then go limp. Blood spurted onto her arm and clothes.

"Forgive me, Conall," she whispered, feeling a tear trickle down her cheek.

Gently she lowered his body to the floor. His blood was beginning to spread out across the ground.

She stared at the dead boy. She had killed her own nephew. She had done what her father had made her swear to do. The person who broke their oath of silence would be killed. They had all agreed to that. They had all agreed, for the sake of their village. The bonds of family and kinsmanship would be ignored. The secret that lay out there in the ocean had to be protected at all costs. At *all* costs.

Gently she brushed Conall's hair with her fingers. He looked so peaceful in death. Then her fingers started to tremble, her eyes widened and she opened her mouth and screamed. In that single moment it was as if everything she had been through in the past three days was released in one furious, high-pitched and heartfelt scream. Outside the tent men yelled in shock and alarm. Emogene rose to her feet just as the tent flap was thrown back and a man's face appeared. It was the soldier she had kicked earlier. He stared at her in alarm.

"You!" he shouted.

Then before he could do anything else, Emogene was out through the tear in the tent and had vanished into the night.

Chapter Thirteen – A Twist of Fate

It was still dark when a hand roughly shook Marcus awake. He was just about to curse the fool who had dared wake him when he saw that it was Bestia, his commanding officer. The man was holding a beeswax candle in his hand.

"Get up," Bestia snapped. He looked irritated. "The governor wants to see you in his tent immediately."

Marcus groaned as he felt his hangover. Then he swung his legs onto the ground. The eight-man tent in which he slept was quiet except for Bestia's breathing and the gentle flicker of the candle. The others seemed still to be sleeping or pretending to be asleep. Marcus rubbed his face with his hand. He was already fully clothed and it only took a few moments to fix his belt and strap on his sword. What on earth could Agricola want with him? Had he said something wrong whilst speaking to him in the latrines?

"Get moving," Bestia growled, "I haven't got all fucking day."

"Am I in trouble?" Marcus replied, sliding his feet into his boots.

"How the fuck should I know? Shut up and do as you are told."

Marcus finished tying up his boots. "I heard that a Caledonian girl kicked you in the balls yesterday," he said, turning away so that Bestia would not see his smile. There was a snigger of laughter from amongst the sleeping men in the tent. Bestia spun round and shone his candle at Marcus's comrades but they all seemed to be fast asleep.

"The bitch couldn't handle my size," Bestia muttered. He took a step forwards and slapped Marcus over the head. "Get moving, the governor is waiting."

Marcus had never been inside the governor's tent before. He ducked through the opening with a general feeling of apprehension. What did Agricola want? Bestia followed him in. The governor was sat behind his desk reading as Marcus stepped forward and rapped out a quick salute. Behind him

Bestia did likewise. Agricola looked up and gave Marcus a quick examination. In the corner of the tent stood another man who Marcus didn't recognise. The man was clad in a white bearskin coat. He was staring at Marcus with sharp, cold eyes.

Agricola rose and came round to have a closer look at Marcus. The flickering oil lamps in the tent hissed softly.

"When we last met," Agricola spoke quietly, "you mentioned that you had a British mother and that you speak the Briton language."

"Yes, sir, I do. My mother was from the tribe of Trinovantes."

Agricola nodded and glanced at his desk. "I have been reading your service record. Age twenty. No convictions, no deducted pay, no assault charges, no homosexual behaviour, no attempts to bribe his officers. You are an exemplary soldier, Marcus. I see a great career ahead for you."

Marcus stood to attention, staring straight ahead. His hangover had vanished. "Yes, sir," he said.

"And I knew your father, Corbulo," Agricola added. Agricola paused and for a moment it seemed as if he wanted to say something more but then he changed his mind.

"Where did you grow up?" Agricola said, turning his back.

Marcus stared into the distance. "At Deva, sir. My father was posted to the fortress. My mother and I lived in the town beside the fortress."

"So you grew up with the local tribes. You can blend in with the locals?"

Marcus nodded. The forests and marshes that surrounded Deva was the place he would escape to when his father's violent behaviour and his mother's misery got too much. As a boy he had loved going hunting. He had loved the wild freedom of the woods and marshes. His mother had taught him everything she knew about plants and herbs. She had taught him about the spirits that lived in every stream, rock and grove. She had taught him about her forefathers. She had taught him far more useful things than his father ever had. His father had only taught him the meaning of fear.

"I am at ease with my mother's people," Marcus replied.

Agricola looked pleased. He turned to the man clad in the white coat. "He is the perfect scout," he announced.

The man with the white coat stirred and stepped forwards, circling and examining Marcus as if Marcus were a slave being sold at auction. Finally the man turned to Agricola and grunted his approval.

Agricola turned to Marcus and his face mellowed. "I have a task for you, Marcus. It will be a dangerous mission but you are well equipped for it." He paused. "Bestia, you may leave us," he said.

Bestia snapped out a quick salute, turned and exited the tent.

"Soldier," Agricola said quietly, turning to Marcus, "what I am about to tell you stays strictly between us. You are to tell no one about your mission. Clear?"

"Clear, sir," Marcus frowned.

"Stand at ease," Agricola ordered and Marcus relaxed.

Agricola gestured towards the man with the white coat. "Vellocatus here made an interesting discovery on the battlefield. He came across a Caledonian boy who claims to come from a village where amber is found. The boy says there are huge quantities of it just lying around to be picked up. He says the people from his village collect the amber and store it in a cave, a sea cave. The boy says there is enough amber in that cave to build a small mountain. Problem is that the village is somewhere in the far north but we don't know where exactly. I require more evidence and proof that the boy's story is true before I can do anything about it. So I want you to find this village and find out whether this boy is telling the truth."

Marcus glanced at Vellocatus. The man was observing him closely. Amber, he thought in surprise, in Caledonia? It seemed unlikely. But it explained Agricola and this Vellocatus's interest. Amber was one of the most precious resources known to man. In Rome, even a small handful of the mineral would fetch its owner a huge price. Just a handful of this northern gold would be worth the same as an adult male slave in prime condition. The rich ladies used it as jewellery, in ornaments and also as incense. Such was the shortage of supply that when Nero had still been emperor a young knight had set off along the amber road to the shores of the Baltic and had returned with cartloads of amber that had made him into one of the richest men in Rome. Oh, yes, he could see why a lot of people would be interested in finding that cave.

"If you don't know where the village is why not ask this boy?" Marcus replied. "Why not get him to show you the way to the amber cave?"

Agricola smiled with sudden delight. Vellocatus, however, looked annoyed.

"It seems the boy was murdered a few hours ago," Agricola said. "He won't be guiding us anywhere."

"Murdered?" Marcus looked confused.

"A Caledonian woman," Vellocatus exclaimed sharply. "She managed to get into my tent and cut the boy's throat. It makes me believe that the amber story is true. I think the woman was there to make sure the boy did not show us the way. She killed him to protect the amber."

"So she managed to escape?" There was a hint of contempt in Marcus's voice as he turned to look at Vellocatus.

The slaver's face darkened. "I will find her," he muttered. "Don't worry, I will make her pay for what she did."

"You will go this morning," Agricola said. "Leave your Roman armour, shield and clothes behind but you may take your cavalry sword. I will have my slave bring you some Caledonian clothes. You may also want to give some thought to a cover story that will explain your presence in the territory of the tribes that you will come across. Remember, Marcus, I require proof that the amber exists. When you have that proof return to me at once. If you cannot find anything then return on the winter solstice. The winter up there is terrible. Clear?"

"Yes, sir," Marcus said, turning to Agricola. "Do we know anything more that can help me find this cave?"

"The boy said his village was beside the sea. The amber washes ashore from the sea," Vellocatus growled. "The village leader is a druid called Dougal. That's all the useful information that the boy could tell me."

"Maybe if you had kept the boy alive none of this would be necessary," Marcus suddenly snapped, turning on Vellocatus. The prospect of riding out alone into the trackless wastes of Caledonia had not filled him with much excitement. Now he had to risk his life because the Briton slaver here was incompetent.

"Watch your mouth, boy," Vellocatus hissed, speaking in the Celtic language. "Scouts are expendable, especially when they are all alone."

"Enough," Agricola barked. "Speak Latin when you are in my presence." The tent fell silent.

Marcus lowered his eyes. It was no use moaning about his fate. He had been given his orders. He raised his hand and pulled off the bronze phallic amulet from around his neck. For a moment he stared at the charm. Then he looked up at Agricola and stretched out his hand.

"If I find a soldier's death, then please, sir, give this to my father."

Chapter Fourteen – Fortune

Agricola watched the young man stride away into the night. A brave man, he thought, just like his father had been. He glanced down at the bronze phallic amulet that the soldier had given him. It was a cheap copy and mass produced down at Deva but someone had scratched three letters into the bronze. He allowed himself a wry smile. Then his features hardened and he stepped back into his tent. There was still some more business to attend to, unpleasant business. Vellocatus was watching him carefully. Agricola moved round his desk, closed Marcus's file and turned to look at the slaver. Really, what did his wife's sister see in this man, he wondered. The girl was an idiot.

"A toast to the start of our joint enterprise," Vellocatus said, glancing at the jug of wine that stood on the desk.

"No," Agricola retorted sharply. "There is one more thing that we need to discuss. It concerns the slaves that you are hoping to buy from the army. The deal is cancelled. The army will not be selling the slaves to you."

"What?" Vellocatus spluttered. He blushed, looking confused.

Agricola fixed his eyes on the slaver. "The deal is cancelled. I have changed my mind. I am going to sell the slaves to Paterculus instead. You may go."

"But why?" Vellocatus whined.

There was anger in Agricola's eyes now. Suddenly he slammed his fist into the wooden table, making everything jump. "You murdered one of my men," he roared. "You were seen cutting the throat of one of my wounded auxiliaries after the battle! Now get out of my sight before I have you charged with murder!"

Vellocatus's eyes widened in horror. He swallowed and stared at Agricola, his face burning with shame and humiliation.

"Get out!" Agricola roared.

"You will regret this," Vellocatus hissed. Then he stormed out of the tent and into the darkness beyond. "You will regret this," he shouted once outside. A bucket of water stood on the ground and with a mighty kick he sent it flying into the camp. He didn't feel the pain in his foot. He was ruined. Agricola had just ruined him.

"Fuck!" he screamed.

Chapter Fifteen – Corbulo

Rome, April 84 AD

The prostitute leaned over the table so that her tits were practically in Corbulo's face. Her long fake blond hair curled down to her shoulders and he caught a whiff of cheap perfume. The woman was old and ugly.

"Honey," she purred, "this is all you are going to get. If you have no money you don't get any action."

Corbulo was drunk. The bar, one of the many seedy drinking houses that littered the Subura neighbourhood of Rome, was packed. The Subura was Rome's slum neighbourhood where the poor, the sick, runaway slaves, actors, the unemployed, prostitutes and criminal gangs lived and worked. In the far corner an old man was playing soulfully on a harp. From the ceiling an oil lamp was burning incense but it could still not hide the smell of sweat and unwashed bodies.

"Well fuck off then," Corbulo snapped.

The prostitute raised her hand to her mouth and pretended to be insulted. Then quick as lightning she slapped Corbulo hard across his face.

"Your mother should have taught you some manners," she chided.

The whore was an experienced woman for she leaned back just in time as Corbulo's clumsy fist swung at her. He missed.

"See, you can't even fight like a proper man," she yelled. The tavern erupted in laughter, cat calls and jeering. Corbulo glared at the woman but did not rise from his chair. That was what the woman wanted him to do. He was not so drunk that he had completely lost his senses. The moment he stood up and had another go at her the bouncers on the door would have him. The whore was taunting him. She was trying to get him thrown out again.

"I served in the legions, woman," he growled. "Have some respect."

71

The whore spat on the floor. "Sure you did," she said, "and I am the goddess Aphrodite."

Corbulo shook his head in disgust and sank back into his chair. For a forty-six-year-old he was still in relatively good health. Long years of hard physical training and work had toughened his body but recently his grey hair had begun to turn white in places and just the other day he had lost another tooth. He sat on his own in his favourite corner close to the toilet with his back against the wall. The position allowed him to see who came in through the bar door.

He shouldn't be spending all his time in this shit hole, he thought. But what else was there to do? What did a retired soldier do? He should have used his army pension to buy a plot of land, build a farm and watch his family grow and prosper. Wasn't that was he was supposed to do? Wasn't that the model life that men strived for? But he had no family. His wife had killed herself and his son had left him, saying that he never wanted to see him again. His son's words and his departure had been worse than the many beatings and lashings he had endured during his twenty-five years of service with the Twentieth in Britannia. Now he had no family, no job and his army pension was nearly all gone too. He ran his fingers down his face. He had blown his army pension, fifteen years' full salary, in just eighteen months and he had nothing to show for it. He'd spent the money on wine, gambling and women. He started to laugh. Fifteen years' worth of salary gone in eighteen months! That surely must be a record. Now he was nearly broke; a few more weeks and he would be begging for bread beside the newly opened Coliseum or worse, he blushed, he would become a rent boy.

"Lucius, another pitcher," he bellowed at the barman.

The man behind the bar folded his arms across his chest.

"Don't you think that you have had enough," he replied.

Corbulo grinned and shook his head.

"Come on, just one more. For an old friend."

The barman sighed and reached for another jug of wine. "This is the last one that you are getting," he said, thumping the wine down on Corbulo's table.

"Thank you, old friend," Corbulo said, clasping Lucius's arm. The barman's nose wrinkled in disgust and he pulled his arm from Corbulo's grasp.

"You are no longer with the legions," he snapped. "You are not a soldier anymore and I am not your friend."

"What am I then?" Corbulo said.

The barman shook his head in disgust. "You have lost your way, Corbulo. One of these days you are going to end up in an alley with your throat cut."

Corbulo grinned and reached to pour himself another drink.

"They won't catch me," he cried as the barman returned to his bar. He took a long drink and then wiped his mouth with the back of his hand and burped.

He had been eighteen when he signed up with the Twentieth Legion, the Valeria Victrix. He had been sent to Britannia, first to the legionary base at Camulodunum where he had met his wife, a local girl. Then onwards to Deva where he had been based for most of his twenty-five years' service. He'd been involved in the river assault on the druids' stronghold of Mona Insulis. He had fought in the decisive battle that had ended the destructive career of the barbarian queen. He had helped conquer and pacify the Ordovices and the Brigantes. He had taken part in two retaliatory raids on the coast of Hibernia. He had remained loyal during the Year of the Four Emperors even when most of the men in the Twentieth had not. He had been wounded three times in battle. He had been both promoted and demoted by the legate Agricola within the same day. He had earned the respect of his comrades, his officers and his enemies but now it looked as if he was going to end his days begging for bread on the streets of Rome.

Corbulo shook his head. It was not right. His wife was dead and his son wanted nothing more to do with him. After his retirement he had intended to take his family back to his ancestral village of Falacrinae, close to the Roman colony of Narnia, some seventy-five miles north-east of Rome. But his wife had killed herself days before they were supposed to leave. She wasn't legally his wife of course because soldiers were not allowed to get married whilst in service and his son, his only child, had therefore been illegitimate and ineligible to join the legions. So alone, he had gone back to the village where he had been born, but the village had been full of new, unfamiliar faces and the few people who did still remember him had only been interested in getting their hands on his army pension. He had been gone for too long and the old roots were dead. He had drifted to Rome and had ended up living a riotous life in the Subura, drinking, gambling and whoring. Corbulo lowered his eyes and stared at the jug of wine. "What a fucking disgrace you have become," he muttered.

Corbulo sighed and slouched in his chair. "Lucius, any chance you have a job for me?" he cried, slurring his words.

The barman pretended not to have heard but when Corbulo repeated himself a little louder he turned. "Not a chance," Lucius snapped. "You will only drink everything that I have got."

"Well fuck off then," Corbulo grunted.

Through the open doorway he could see that it was still light outside. How long had he been sitting here? He couldn't remember. He burped again, louder this time. He could either stay here for a while or return to the crumbling rat-infested apartment block in which he lived. He weighed up the choice. Maybe the whore would forgive him? He looked round searching for her and saw her sitting on a man's lap a few tables away. The man was holding her by her wrist and his two companions around the table were mocking her. The prostitute was beginning to look uncomfortable. Corbulo took a long slurp of wine and rose to his feet. The earth swayed under his feet. The whore saw him coming and her face paled. She shook her head but Corbulo had already tapped the man who was holding her on the shoulder. The man turned to look up at Corbulo.

"Are you going to let her go or not?" Corbulo said with a crazy grin.

The man's face darkened. "Fuck off, granddad," he sneered. He was a big powerful man in his prime.

Corbulo's fist smashed into the man's face. With a hoarse cry he flung himself at his opponent. The whore screamed and went tumbling backwards into the table behind her as the two men wrestled on the ground, sending tables, chairs, jugs, cups and people flying in all directions. Corbulo had caught hold of the man's throat and was trying to throttle him. His opponent was squealing like a pig. The man was lashing out with his hands and feet but Corbulo's grip was solid. Someone hit Corbulo in his ribs but he didn't feel the pain. Then a chair came smashing down on his head and four strong hands yanked Corbulo upwards. His opponent was still on the floor, his face red and his mouth gasping for air. Corbulo's face was oozing blood from where the chair had struck him. There was a wild, crazy look in his eyes. Then the hands that gripped him were dragging him straight through the bar. He landed painfully on the stone cobbles as he was thrown out onto the street. Lucius, the barman, appeared in the doorway flanked by two of his bouncers.

"Don't come back!" he yelled.

Chapter Sixteen – Mercy

Corbulo stumbled through the alley. His head hurt and he was still bleeding from a cut to his eye. The alley stank of stale piss and rotting garbage. He passed a beggar with no legs. The man sat slumped against a wall holding out his hand. No one had left the man anything. On either side of him the tall four- and five-storey tenement buildings of the Subura crowded out the sky. The buildings had been erected without any planning permission or control and looked in a bad condition. Inside whole families would be living crammed into a single room with no running water and little chance of escape if a fire broke out, which was frequent in Rome. This was how the poor lived in Rome. For the ignorant, violent and needy mob of unemployed who made up most of Rome's population, life was generally hard, brutal and short. The poor lived in an utterly different world to the rich houses around the forum and on Palatine Hill. The poverty and violence that he had seen had even managed to shock a battle-hardened veteran like Corbulo. Here in the Subura you rarely saw your enemy. He would come up behind you and stick a knife in your back or he would poison your food or slip a venomous snake into your room whilst you were sleeping. In order to survive in this hellhole Corbulo had learned that it was vital to make friends in the right places.

He entered a wider street where little shops spilled out into the road. Traders cried out advertising their wares in loud voices, competing with each other to create a furious wall of noise. Groups of children, some barely five years old and nearly all of them without shoes, mixed with the throng of people, running errands or looking for easy takings from those unwary enough to keep their purses on display. Corbulo noticed a couple of big men with shaved heads lounging on a street corner. They would be members of the dozen or so gangs that controlled and ran the Subura and many of the streets in the surrounding neighbourhoods. No one touched those men unless they wanted to get involved in a vicious, bloody street war. Corbulo lowered his eyes and hurried on his way. As he thrust his way down the street he passed a well-to-do man wearing a toga and accompanied by a slave. The man was followed by a swarm of begging children whom the slave was unsuccessfully trying to drive away with a stick.

Alongside the traders' stalls were the small workshops of the craftsmen. Their owners sat in the front room working away at their products in plain view of passersby whilst in the back room their wives and families fed babies, did the washing and cooked the evening meal. The smell of garum, rotting fish soup, came wafting down the street and Corbulo suddenly felt hungry. There would be a free handout of bread at the gladiatorial games in the newly completed Coliseum if he could get in. But the games would only start tomorrow and the prostitute was busy making her living. Until then or until she returned he would have to remain hungry. The thought of another night being spent hungry did nothing to improve his mood. What a fucking awful day it had been.

He turned wearily into the alley along which he lived and stopped in his tracks.

"Oh fuck," he said with growing alarm.

Lounging outside the door to his apartment block were four young thugs. They were dressed in short grey tunics and each had a wooden club in his hand. One of them suddenly pointed a finger at Corbulo.

"There he is. Get him!" the young man cried.

"Oh fuck," Corbulo muttered again, louder this time. He had forgotten about the gambling debt that he had failed to settle. The young men had come to collect the debt on behalf of their boss. The thugs were running towards him. Corbulo turned and fled. Behind him he heard shouts and the pounding of sandals on the cobblestones. He shot back into the busy shopping street and struggled his way through the protesting crowd. Behind him he heard a scream and some foul-mouthed cursing. He dashed into a narrow alley and sprinted along it, hoping they had not seen him. The alley was barely wider than his body. He snatched a quick glimpse over his shoulder and saw that his pursuers had followed him. Damn, damn, damn. He rounded a corner and crashed straight into a woman, sending her bouncing into the wall. Then he was past her and her outraged squeal. The alley led him onwards, then it changed into another alley. He felt a stitch developing. Bloody wine, he cursed. If only he had been a few years younger he would be able to outrun these pricks but now he was not so sure. They were young men, strong and well fed. With those clubs they could easily batter him to death.

He heard their running footsteps behind him and knew that they were gaining. He skidded around another corner and stormed towards the wider street he could see up ahead. He may have owed a gambling debt but the man he had gambled with had cheated. He was not going to pay a cheat. He tore into the wider street and suddenly realised where he was. He was on the Argiletum, the booksellers' street. He felt the stitch in his side intensify. He was not going to last much longer. With his strength rapidly fading he burst into out onto the Sacred Way and the sunlight that bathed the forum. Behind him he heard laboured breathing. They were very close now. A few paces up the Sacred Way coming towards him was a closed litter being carried by four slaves, two at the front and two at the back. An imperious-looking man was clearing the crowd ahead of the litter with his staff. Corbulo staggered forwards, grasped one of the wooden beams with a hand and knelt down on one knee, lowering his head to the ground.

"Mercy, lady, mercy," he panted.

Behind him he sensed that his pursuers had halted a few paces away. The imperious official turned angrily towards Corbulo.

"Get your hands off that litter at once," he cried, raising his staff to strike at Corbulo's exposed back.

"Mercy, lady," Corbulo begged, keeping his eyes to the ground.

"Stop," a female voice suddenly commanded from within the closed litter. A thin curtain shielded the lady from public view but all knew who she was. The Vestal Virgins were well known in Rome. They were the priestesses of Vesta, sworn to celibacy and service to the goddess of the hearth and held in high esteem and respect by the whole population of Rome. It was through their purity of body and mind that the purity of Rome was guaranteed. Behind him Corbulo heard his pursuers muttering but none of them dared touch him, not now that he had claimed the protection of a Vestal.

"We will get you later," one of the thugs hissed. Then he heard them stomp off into the crowd. Corbulo kept his eyes on the ground as he struggled to recover his breath.

"What is your name?" the lady commanded from behind her veil.

Corbulo remained on his knee. "Corbulo, lady, former watch commander of the First Cohort of the Twentieth Legion," he replied.

"A soldier," there was surprise in the lady's voice. "Why were you running away from those men, Watch Commander?"

"A gambling debt, lady, I failed to pay but the man whom I owe the debt to cheated. He does not deserve the money."

"Ah." There was a long silence behind the veil. "Do you love your wife, do you treat her with the respect she deserves?" the Vestal said at last.

Corbulo felt the sweat trickling down his back. He swallowed nervously.

"I did, lady, but I did not treat her with the respect she deserved. She is dead because of me."

There was another long pause from within the litter. Then at last the Vestal spoke.

"Tomorrow go to Tiber Island and visit the temple of Aesculapius. You shall find solace with the god of healing. Your wounds are not those of the body but of the mind. Go and heal your mind, Watch Commander, and start acting like the soldier of Rome that you once were."

"Bless you, lady," Corbulo said as he let go of the litter and the slaves started off down the Sacred Way towards the Senate House.

Chapter Seventeen – The Games

Dawn had just broken when he woke in the doorway where he'd spent the night. He couldn't risk going back to his apartment – the thugs would surely be watching the place. He rubbed his eyes wearily. It didn't matter. He had not left anything of value behind. He glanced about him. A fishmonger was preparing his fish for the day's customers. Corbulo licked his lips hungrily. Further along, two women were studying an advert that had been written onto a wall. Today was a public holiday. Corbulo got to his feet. He would have to hurry if he wanted to get in. Everyone would be going to the games. He joined the throng of people moving in the direction of the Coliseum. There was an excited, expectant buzz about the spectators. The crowd provided a measure of safety. Corbulo, however, kept a watchful eye out in case the thugs were waiting for him. Yesterday's incident was still fresh in his mind. He could have got himself killed. For what? A stupid gambling debt. For hours that night he had not been able to sleep. Stupid, stupid; how foolish he had become. To still his empty stomach he drank his fill from a public fountain. The water refreshed him but he still felt weak. He needed to eat and soon.

The crowds were excited and the chatter was about what sort of games the young emperor had laid on for them today. Corbulo came round a corner and there, looming over the apartment buildings, rose the magnificent Coliseum. It was immense, dwarfing everything around it. The largest building in the empire. Corbulo craned his neck to get a better view even though he had seen the building many times before. He could not help but be impressed every time. It made one feel fucking proud to be a Roman. Eight years it had taken to build. When Emperor Titus had declared the Coliseum open there had been one hundred days of continuous games. Corbulo smiled sadly. Vespasian had been an excellent emperor, Titus, his eldest son, had been a good emperor but Domitian, the youngest son, was a tyrant. Domitian had none of his father's and older brother's qualities. He had never served as a soldier on campaign.

Vespasian had left him behind in Rome where the young man had been brought up at Nero's court with its intrigue, corruption and vice. The rumour on the street was that the young emperor stalked through the rooms of his palace afraid of his own shadow.

The crowds seemed to converge on the Coliseum from all directions and as they drew closer the noise increased. Thousands of people were already queuing to get into the building. Corbulo struggled through the crowd towards the entrance reserved for serving soldiers and veterans. Four men from the urban cohorts, clad in armour and holding spears, stood checking men into the entrance.

"Soldiers and veterans only," one of the men shouted.

Corbulo made it to the entrance. One of the urban policemen shook his head.

"I served with the Twentieth Legion!" Corbulo exclaimed. "I am a veteran. Let me through."

But the policeman blocked the way.

"You are not a soldier or a veteran," the policeman growled. "Read the fucking sign." He gestured to the sign above the gateway.

"I served twenty-five years with the Twentieth. I was a soldier before you were even born," Corbulo cried angrily but the policeman just laughed.

"Go on, get out of here," another policeman snapped. "You are holding up the queue, grandpa."

It was his clothes and appearance, Corbulo thought as he reluctantly moved off into the crowd. He looked like a homeless man. He blinked. He was in fact homeless. He gave the soldiers entrance a final wistful glance. The veterans would get better seats but it didn't matter. He would have to go to the entrance reserved for the poor and the unemployed.

He clambered up to the very top ring of seats in the arena. From here it was a very long way down to the middle of the arena where the gladiators would fight. But he didn't mind. It was still a magnificent view. Fifty-five thousand people could fit into the Coliseum. What a show. The noise when the gladiators came out would be deafening.

"Not afraid of heights are you?" the man sitting beside him said, grinning. The man's mouth was missing several teeth.

Corbulo shook his head and then rose to his feet as slaves started throwing loaves of bread into the crowd. The men around him scrabbled around wildly and when it was over Corbulo had managed to get hold of two loaves. Hungrily he devoured the first one, tucking the second away for later. As he finished off the bread he stared down at the imperial box. Domitian was standing before his throne taking the applause of the crowd. Beside him stood another figure wearing victory laurels on his head. The man was saluting the crowd. Corbulo frowned.

"Who is that man, standing next to the emperor?" he asked his neighbour, spitting some crumbs into the air in the process.

The man peered down into the arena.

"Have you not heard the news?" he replied, looking at Corbulo in surprise. "Agricola returned from Caledonia a few days ago. They say that he has won himself a grand victory. Domitian may give him a triumph."

"Agricola has returned from Britannia," Corbulo exclaimed. He stared down at the man who was saluting the crowd. When had this happened? He must have been too drunk to have noticed.

"I know him," Corbulo said.

"Who, Agricola?" His neighbour looked startled.

Corbulo nodded slowly, "The prick made me watch commander in the First Cohort. That was the highest rank I ever obtained."

The masses cried, shouted and hooted when the emperor signalled for the games to begin and they went wild with excitement when the first gladiators appeared. Corbulo, however, hardly noticed. He seemed sunk deep in thought. He hardly watched the gladiatorial contests and when the first batch of fighting was over he stood up and made his way out of the Coliseum.

He had been hiding in the doorway of the alley for nearly an hour before she emerged from the bar. Quickly he checked to see if no one was following her before he stepped out into the street. He knew where she was going. Her routine did not vary and nor did her job. As she approached the apartment where she lived he made his move. She squealed in alarm as he slipped his arm around her waist and pulled her into an alley.

"It's me," he said, pressing his finger to her mouth. "Look I am sorry about the other day. I shouldn't have tried to hit you. I was drunk."

The old whore with the fake blond hair stared up at him with a mixture of shock and anger. For a moment she was lost for words.

"Well don't ever come up behind me like that," she snapped. "Scared me nearly to death. I have a weak heart, you know."

He nodded.

"Well what do you want, Corbulo? I am not doing any more shagging today."

He shook his head, "I am not here for that."

"You don't find me attractive?" she replied, raising her eyebrows.

"You are a beautiful lady," he lied. "But I need my money. It's important. Can you get it?"

She leaned forwards and sniffed at his breath. "Well at least you are not drunk anymore. How much do you need this time? There isn't much left, you know."

"All of it," Corbulo replied. "I am going away for a while."

She studied him carefully but Corbulo looked deadly serious. When he had first come to live in the Subura and the whore had become his friend he had given her his army pension for safekeeping. It wasn't safe to leave the money in his apartment when he was away, nor was it wise to carry it on him, and the woman had some wonderful hiding places.

She sighed and for a moment he thought she looked sad.

"I will fetch it for you. Stay here," she said, avoiding his gaze. Then without another word she was gone. A few minutes later she was back carrying a small leather bag and a sword wrapped in leather. She handed them over and Corbulo peered inside the bag.

"Fuck," he muttered gloomily.

"I told you there was not much left."

She sighed again and looked around her. "So are you going to tell me where you are going?"

He unfolded the leather wrapping and gazed at his old legionary sword. He'd had this sword for nearly twenty-three years. The metal looked in good condition although the pommel was showing some signs of wear and tear. He took some coins from the bag, then closed it and slipped the purse into his tunic.

"It's better that you don't know," he said quietly. "There are some thugs after me. If they come asking tell them that I have gone back to Falacrinae." He pressed the coins into her hand and closed her fingers around them. "This is for you, old friend. Thank you for everything that you have done. Look after yourself."

The prostitute opened her hand and looked down at the coins. Her face had grown resigned. She looked up and managed a faint smile.

"Alright, Corbulo, I won't ask. But wherever you are going, make something of yourself. You are still young enough."

"Bless you, Aphrodite," he said as he pecked her on the cheek and slipped away into the street.

Chapter Eighteen – The Waters of the Tiber

The temple of Aesculapius, the Greek god of healing, stood on Tiber Island occupying the middle of the Tiber river. Corbulo paused on the Pons Fabricius and gazed across the green waters of the Tiber towards the temple. The Vestal had been right. He needed to heal his mind. He had been putting it off for far too long. There were few people about at this hour in the afternoon. The sun was high in the sky and he felt her heat on his face. The temple was nearly four hundred years old, built in the time of the Republic when Rome still only controlled parts of central Italy. It was one of the oldest buildings still standing in the city. Once when a plague had struck Rome the city fathers had asked the priests what they should do and the answer had been to build the temple of Aesculapius. When the ship carrying the sacred statue of the god arrived in Rome from the Greek city of Epidaurus, a snake was found onboard and promptly swam ashore on Tiber Island. The temple had been built where the snake had rested.

Corbulo stared at the temple. His mind seemed far away. Then he started out across the stone bridge. Inside the temple he halted before the statue of the god. The stone manlike figure seemed to be leaning on a staff that resembled a snake. A few priests were polishing the temple floor and a real snake lay coiled in a circle in one corner. He seemed to be the only visitor. Corbulo looked up at the statue and then slowly got down on his knees and lowered his head.

"Hear me, honoured Aesculapius," he murmured. "I know that I do not deserve your attention. I have not once visited your temple. I have not once made an offering to you so if you will not help I will understand." Corbulo paused. He was staring at the ground as he struggled with the words. "But please hear me now. I need your help. I have not been a good father nor have I been a good husband. I beat my son, I drank away my pay and pension, I was unfaithful to my wife." He took a deep breath. "She killed herself because of me. I am responsible for her death and I am responsible for driving away my son. I do love them and for what it is worth, I am sorry."

The stone statue of Aesculapius was silent. The priests were still busy scrubbing the floor. Corbulo suddenly gasped. He took another deep breath. Marcus would be twenty by now. He had not seen his son in three years, ever since Marcus had told him to his face that he never wanted to see him again. *I was more of a man to her than you ever were!* The boy's furious retort had struck deep and the wound had never properly closed. The drinking, the fighting, the whoring – it had all been to try and forget that pain, that searing, burning guilt. Corbulo's hand trembled as he ran his fingers across his face. He had been so wrapped up in his own affairs that he'd hardly had any time for the boy. He hardly knew his son.

He looked up at the statue with moist eyes. "Forgive me, Marcus, please forgive me for what I did to you and your mother. I beg you."

He rose to his feet. The priests paid him no attention as he left the temple and walked down to the riverbank. He looked up at the blue sky. Life had not much more to offer him. He was too old to serve in the army. His teeth were starting to fall out and he was nearly broke. Death was not too far away. He had maybe a couple of years left, maybe five if he looked after himself. He paused at the river's edge. Then slowly he began to undress. When he was stark naked he carefully piled his clothes together and stepped out into the water. The current was strong and he had to brace himself. On the Pons Fabricius a few people had stopped to watch. When he was neck deep in the river he halted. Then he pitched forwards. His head went under and everything turned murky. He was in a cool, dark world. He felt the tug of the current and the sharpness of the stones cutting into his feet. He opened his mouth and started to shout. The shout echoed off the temple walls as he erupted from the water, sending droplets flying in all directions. He spluttered, sucked more air into his lungs and roared and bellowed as he allowed the pain and guilt of many years to finally burst through into his mind. When it was over his eyes were large and scary and his hands and body were trembling.

"Forgive me, Marcus," he whispered.

Chapter Nineteen – A Roman Triumph

Corbulo stood on the steps of the Capitoline Hill staring down into the forum. It was mid morning. He looked like a new man. His untidy stubble had gone and he was clean-shaven and his hair was neatly trimmed. In a bath house he had given himself a proper wash, cut his fingernails and had rubbed ointments into his body until every muscle was aching and glowing. Now as he stood waiting he hardly felt the fabric of his new dark-grey tunic or his new leather shoes. He had burned his old clothes and shoes beside the Tiber. His old army sword that the whore had returned to him hung from his belt in a new sheath and he had tied his money pouch around his neck. He stood looking down into the crowds, searching the faces of the expectant populace. The forum was packed and they were all waiting for just one thing.

In a corner a man was standing on a barrel addressing the crowds in a loud voice. He was predicting the end of the world but the crowds were not listening. A group of bankers were trying to attract business by holding up bags of coins and rattling them in the air but no one was interested. The dozens of small market stalls were the only ones doing a brisk trade as the people bought refreshments as they stood waiting. All eyes were on the Senate House. The doors to the building had been closed for nearly an hour. The debate was still not finished.

Looming behind Corbulo was the great temple of Jupiter, the patron god of Rome. White marble pillars stood like sentries in a long row and on the highest point of the roof a chariot drawn by four horses glared down upon the eternal city. In the temple itself white bulls would be sacrificed after each triumph to beg Jupiter to sustain Rome's military victories. To Corbulo's right, the great imperial palace of the emperor sat high upon the crest of the hill flanking the forum below. Beyond the Palatine would be the Circus Maximus and to the south along the Sacred Way he could see the towering Coliseum.

As he stood waiting he remembered the last triumph through the city. It had taken place just under a year ago. He had stood beside the triumphal gate in the city's wall, the gate that was only ever opened for a triumph. First into the city had been the senators and the magistrates of Rome. They had walked into the city dressed in their fine togas followed by the prisoners of war. At the sight of the prisoners the crowds had started to laugh. Corbulo had not joined them for he could not bring himself to mock a Roman triumph. He had known too many men who had died to give Rome her glory and power. No, making a mockery of Rome was best left to the new emperor, Domitian, who had followed the prisoners, riding in a golden chariot drawn by four horses and surrounded by his lictors. Domitian had returned from campaign against the Chatti in Germania claiming great victories whilst he had achieved nothing of the sort. His triumph had been a publicity stunt, nothing more, and it had angered Corbulo for it insulted the honour and dignity of the city. The prisoners paraded through Rome that day had been German slaves purchased in the markets and actors dressed up to look like wild Germanic warriors. The show had been a farce. The crowds that had lined the streets had not been fooled and some bold spirits had even jeered the emperor as he had ridden past.

Suddenly his attention was drawn to the Senate House. The doors had been flung open and the senators in their purple striped togas were pouring out. An expectant hush descended on the crowd.

"No triumph, there will be no triumph," a senator cried. The crowds groaned in disappointment and here and there a few voices cried out in protest. The crowds always loved a Roman hero and Agricola was such a man. His splendid victory at Mons Graupius had been the talk of the city. Corbulo pushed his way through the crowds and down the steps leading to the forum. He had spent the morning asking anyone who looked like they knew something for details on the great battle that had been fought in Caledonia. But the details had been sketchy. His old legion, the Twentieth, had been there and so too had the Ninth, but most of the fighting had been conducted by the Batavian auxiliary cohorts. Casualties appeared to be light and the enemy army had been annihilated. Caledonia had been conquered and hostages had been taken. Agricola should have had his triumph, Corbulo thought as he struggled through the crowds. Domitian had no doubt vetoed the idea because he feared that the people of Rome may compare his own achievements unfavourably with those of Agricola, who had after all managed to win a proper, glorious victory. If the people of Rome sensed that Domitian was vulnerable and weak there would be riots. Up ahead the crowd suddenly began to part.

"Make way for the emperor," a lictor cried out. Corbulo stepped quickly aside as the first troop of praetorians marched by. The crash of their hobnailed sandals on the paving stones was enough to scatter the crowd. They were followed by a few senators and then finally by slaves from the imperial household carrying a closed litter. The litter was protected on all sides by stony-faced and fully armed and armoured praetorian guards. The procession did not pause but swept past quickly as if Domitian was eager to get back to his palace.

"He doesn't even dare show his face," a man beside Corbulo muttered, shaking his head.

Corbulo rejoined the throng of people in the forum. Suddenly the crowd cheered and raised their arms in the air. A man had appeared in the Senate House doorway. The man raised his arm in salute and the crowds cheered him again. It was Agricola. He was clad in a simple white toga and accompanied by a single slave. Agricola smiled and stepped out onto the Sacred Way, the road that led from the Capitoline Hill to the Coliseum. As Agricola made his way through the crowds the people closest to him reached out to touch his toga. An old man shouted a blessing and a woman held out her baby for the victorious general to kiss. Following on behind their patron was a large group of Agricola's clients.

Agricola had nearly left the forum when Corbulo stepped out in front of him and barred the way. Agricola halted in surprise. He stared at Corbulo and then his mouth opened and he grunted in astonishment.

"I know you!" Agricola exclaimed as he tried to recall a name.

"My name is Corbulo, watch commander of the First Cohort, Twentieth Legion, sir. We shared a boat at Mona during the battle with the druids. You were a young tribune then."

"That's right." Agricola's eyes gleamed as he remembered. "We were the first boat to land on the enemy beach if I remember correctly."

Corbulo nodded, his features neutral. "You threatened to have me and the others flogged if we weren't the first, sir. We all thought you were a right prick for making us do that."

Agricola grinned. The crowds around them had fallen silent as they watched the unexpected meeting, wondering what would happen next.

"That wasn't the only time we met was it," Agricola said.

Corbulo nodded. "Listen, sir, I am retired now. I have heard about your victory at Mons Graupius. My son is serving with the Second Batavian Cohort. They are a crack unit and I am sure that you will have used them in Caledonia. I want to know what has happened to my son. His name is Marcus; he's twenty years old. I hope very much that he is still alive. He served in your army, sir."

Agricola looked down at the ground and the smile on his face faded. The crowd seemed to be holding their breath. Then Agricola glanced up at Corbulo and his expression had changed and he was once again very much the stern disciplinarian that Corbulo remembered him to be.

"You are right. The Second Batavians were at Mons Graupius but I don't know what has happened to your son."

Agricola nodded to his slave and started to push past Corbulo but Corbulo pushed him back. The crowd gasped in surprise. Then the gasps turned to hissing and anger at his insolent treatment of their hero.

"That is not good enough, sir," Corbulo shouted. "He was your responsibility. You were his commanding officer. I want to know where my son is and I am not leaving until you tell me."

"Move aside, citizen," a voice cried from the crowd. It was followed by more hissing and booing. The people were getting restless.

Agricola, however, did not look angry. He fixed his eyes on Corbulo and Corbulo, ignoring the growing vitriol in the crowds around him, sensed something else in Agricola's expression. Sadness. The general was feeling sorry for him. He staggered backwards in alarm. It could mean only one thing. Marcus was dead. He would not have a chance to redeem himself after all. He would go to his grave and live with his son's hatred for all eternity. Agricola was watching him carefully.

"Tomorrow come to my house on the Caelian and we shall talk," Agricola said.

Chapter Twenty – The Old Days

The queue of people stretched out into the street. It was dawn. Corbulo stood waiting patiently to enter Agricola's house. He had spent the night sleeping in another doorway, his hand never far from his old gladius. The young thugs would not have given up looking for him. He had to be on his guard. It would only take one person to recognise him and pass his location on and his plan would be in tatters. Those thugs would never give up. That was why most people paid up even when they had been conned.

A freedman stood beside the iron gate ahead of him handing out small gifts to the people in the queue. It was part of the patron–client relationship. In exchange for gifts such as food and money a client was supposed to support his patron. That was the essential truth to how Rome was organised and run. Clients would scratch their patron's back and he would do the same for them. A similar structure had existed in the legions amongst some of the officers and the men. The men had bribed their officers to go on leave. The officers had bribed their men to keep quiet about matters that could affect their careers. Corbulo understood how the system worked. But he had never been very good at playing it.

When his turn came he stepped through the gate. The freedman noted down his name and handed him a silver coin before ushering him down an entrance hall whose floor was decorated with the mosaic of a dog. Corbulo turned the coin over in his fingers. It was newly minted and showed Domitian's sham victories over the Chatti.

"His name is Corbulo," he heard a slave announce him.

He had entered the atrium of the house. A rectangular basin full of rainwater had been sunk into the centre of the room. Fine paintings of mythical scenes adorned the walls and expensive-looking furniture stood casually arranged around the large room. Agricola was sitting in a comfortable chair behind a table on which lay rolls of parchment, clay tablets and papyrus. Behind him the house opened up into a small garden complete with a fountain from which a steady stream of water poured forth. The gushing water made a soothing and pleasing noise. Corbulo sniffed. Someone was burning incense.

Agricola looked up and gestured for Corbulo to take a seat. His face was unreadable. He snapped his fingers at the slave who had accompanied Corbulo into the room.

"That's it for today. I will see the rest of them tomorrow," Agricola said.

The slave bowed and turned away, closing the atrium doors as he left. Corbulo sat down and glanced around the room. They were alone. Agricola was studying him from behind his desk.

"Do you know if my son is alive? Can you find out where his unit is based? Are they at Deva?" Corbulo exclaimed, unable to contain himself any longer. Agricola hesitated. Then he picked up his stylus and tapped it thoughtfully on the table.

"I had a son once," he said. "He died when he was one year old. I never even saw him when he was alive but it hasn't stopped me thinking about what sort of man he could have become. The gods are cruel when they take our children and yet we still look to these gods for strength and guidance."

With a supreme effort Corbulo managed to contain himself. Agricola looked at him sternly. "As it happened, yes I did get to know Marcus briefly," he continued. "He told me that you were his father. He didn't seem to like you much if I recall." Agricola paused and stopped tapping his stylus on the table. "I had a requirement for a scout, a man who was familiar with Britannia and its peoples and who could speak their language. Your son was the perfect match. In September last year I sent him north and ordered him to return by the winter solstice but we never heard of him again. He vanished. When I left the island there were no sighting reports for him. I presume that he is dead but I cannot be sure. The army has listed him as missing. So I spoke the truth yesterday. I really don't know what has happened to your son."

"A scouting mission?" Corbulo said. "What was all that about?"

Agricola's face became guarded. He studied Corbulo carefully as if he was making up his mind about something.

"Do you remember the second occasion that we met?" Agricola said. There was a faint smile around the edges of his mouth now.

Corbulo was staring at the floor. His earlier panic had subsided. The news was not good but there was at least a chance that Marcus was alive.

"I do, sir," he replied without looking up.

Agricola nodded. "The Twentieth Legion, Valeria Victrix," he said, weighing up the name. "Not a very loyal legion during the Year of the Four Emperors was it?"

"No, sir," Corbulo shook his head.

The Year of the Four Emperors had been fifteen years ago now. It had started with Nero's suicide and within the space of a single year had seen four men make a bid to become the next emperor. The civil wars had devastated swathes of northern Italy, Gaul and Spain and had killed thousands. It had seen legions fighting against their fellow legions. It had facilitated the Batavian uprising and it had only come to an end when Vespasian had been hailed as emperor. Vespasian had succeeded in his bid for the purple because he had the support of the Eastern and Danube legions. The Twentieth Legion had, however, supported Vitellius and a vexillation of the legion had even embarked for Italy to fight for Vitellius.

"Vespasian made me legate of the Twentieth with orders to punish them for their disloyalty," Agricola said. "You remember that that rogue Coelius, the officer whom I replaced, had led his troops in open mutiny against the governor of the province. Vespasian wanted the men punished for their lack of discipline. So he sent me to teach them a lesson."

"I remember, sir," Corbulo replied.

"And on my first day in camp who is it that I find chained to a tree outside the camp walls and surviving on a reduced ration of barley?"

"That was me, sir."

Agricola grunted. "Yes you, Corbulo, and when I inquired into the circumstances of your punishment I learned that you were the only man in your cohort who had refused to join the mutiny against the governor. So your officers had you punished for being a loyal soldier."

"It didn't feel right somehow," Corbulo muttered.

Agricola raised his eyebrows. "Do you remember what happened next?"

"Yes," Corbulo nodded. "You had me freed and promoted to watch commander of the First Cohort. On getting my freedom back I went straight up to the centurion who had punished me and smacked him in the face. So that same day you had me demoted again. I remember it all, sir."

Agricola was studying him again. The room fell silent.

"Are you still a loyal man, Corbulo?" he asked at last.

"I am, sir."

"Good," Agricola nodded. "I appreciate loyal men. Despite your temper you were a fine soldier, Corbulo. You would have made an excellent centurion if you hadn't had such an atrocious disciplinary record."

Agricola seemed to make up his mind.

"What I am about to tell you must remain secret, do you understand?"

Corbulo nodded his agreement. Agricola glanced down at his table. Then he pushed all the other letters to one side and unrolled a large parchment map of Caledonia. He beckoned for Corbulo to come closer. When Agricola had at last finished telling his story he pointed to the map. "I made your son memorize this map. It would have been too dangerous for him to take a copy with him in case it was found. As this amber cave is supposed to be somewhere along the coast Marcus said that he would start scouting the shore from the north-east and go as far west as this wide river here. The local tribes call it the great river and it is said to slice Caledonia into two parts." Agricola looked up at Corbulo. "The land beyond the river to the west is unknown to us. But one thing is certain – most of the tribes are still hostile and have refused to make peace with us but you will find that we have allies amongst the Decantae." Agricola peered at the map. "They live around our most northern fort, here at Cawdor."

Corbulo was staring at the map. "So my son was sent to find proof that this amber really existed. That's a fine fucking mission indeed." Corbulo paused. "This Vellocatus that you mentioned, where can I find him?"

"He has a house at Eburacum," Agricola replied gruffly. "He was a slaver until I put him out of business. I don't know what he is doing now. My wife's sister no longer has any contact with him."

Agricola paused and leaned back in his chair. "So what are you going to do?"

Corbulo looked up and there was purpose on his face and in his voice: "There is something that I must do before I die," he said. "I wronged my son and now I must make it right. I am going to go and find my boy and bring him home. I need to see him." Corbulo stared at Agricola. "There is nothing more important than that, sir."

Agricola looked away. He was silent for a moment. Then he stood up, walked across the room to a cabinet and returned holding something in his hand. Corbulo blushed as he recognised the object in Agricola's hand.

"Your son gave me this just before he departed. He said that I should give it to you in case he didn't return."

Agricola stretched out his hand and Corbulo took the bronze phallic amulet and stared at it. It was the amulet he had given Marcus when the boy had been thirteen years old. So Marcus had kept it all this time. The three initials he'd scratched into the bronze stood for his own name, his wife's and Marcus. Corbulo suddenly turned to look away so that Agricola would not see his face. The room fell silent.

"Very well," Agricola murmured at last. "Take this map and go and find your son then."

Corbulo rose to his feet and saluted. The salute brought a wry smile to Agricola's face.

"And, Corbulo," Agricola said carefully, "if you do happen to find the source of this amber be sure to tell me about it first."

Corbulo paused as he caught sight of the Flumentana gate in Rome's walls. He was leaving Rome and it was likely that he would never see the eternal city again, he realised. He glanced back towards the forum and as he did so he muttered a silent prayer to Jupiter. Then he turned his back on the city and headed for the gate. Beyond the Flumentana lay the great northern road, the Via Aurelia, which would take him in stages to Pisae and across the Apennines. From there he planned to take the Via Postumia into Gallia Narbonensis. He had decided he would walk. He would walk the fifteen hundred miles to the Caledonian frontier. He didn't have the money to buy passage on a ship or even to buy a horse. The distance did not unsettle him though. He had marched all his life.

"You are alive, Marcus," he muttered as he shifted the carrying pole on which his army pack and all his worldly belongings hung. Around his neck was the bronze phallic amulet that Agricola had returned to him. It was time to go. As he approached the gate he suddenly heard a shout.

"There he is!" a voice cried excitedly.

Lounging close to the gate were the four young thugs. Corbulo's heart sank and he cursed his own stupidity. The thugs had finally caught up with him. He should have known that they would be watching the city gates. He kept on walking towards the gate. The four thugs spread out as they came towards him. He could see they were carrying their wooden clubs under their cloaks. Corbulo glanced beyond them at the policemen from the urban cohorts who were guarding the gate. They wouldn't help him. The urban cohorts only got involved if there was a danger to the public peace. He was on his own.

"Let's settle this matter outside the walls of Rome," he cried.

The thugs smiled. They knew that they had him and they were confident in their ability.

"Sure, whatever you say, grandpa, but we want our money," one of them shouted.

"There won't be any Vestals to help you this time, you cocksucker," another whined.

Corbulo passed through the gates and out of the city of Rome. The guards had noticed the confrontation and had gathered together to watch. After a few paces Corbulo halted and slowly lowered his army pack and his belongings to the ground. Then he turned to face the young thugs. They had gathered around him in a semicircle and now held their clubs in their hands.

"Go home," Corbulo said. "I haven't got the money that your boss wants."

"That's too bad," one of thugs said, "for he told us that if you didn't pay we were to hurt you, to hurt you badly."

"What are you, fifteen, sixteen years old? Can't you leave an old man alone? I haven't got the money so piss off," Corbulo growled.

"Fuck you, grandpa," one of the thugs hissed.

"And what are you going to do with those clubs?" Corbulo snarled.

"What do you think, arsehole?" From the corner of his eye Corbulo caught a sudden movement. One of the boys came at him wielding his club. In an instant Corbulo's gladius was in his hand. He ducked and the thug's club sliced into empty space. Corbulo's sword gleamed briefly in the sunlight before he rammed it straight into the boy's chest. There was a sickening crunch of bone on metal. The boy gurgled up blood. Then Corbulo ripped his sword from the boy's chest and the lifeless corpse flopped to the ground. Corbulo turned to face the three remaining thugs. Blood was oozing out into the sand. He crouched, panting.

"Well what are you waiting for!" he bellowed, feeling the adrenaline coursing through his veins.

The three boys were staring in horror at their dead friend. They looked stunned by the speed with which Corbulo had killed him. Then slowly they turned and stared at Corbulo.

"Fuck this," one of them muttered. Then the three of them were retreating towards the gate, their pace increasing rapidly. Corbulo watched them go. Then slowly, without giving the corpse another glance, he picked up his carrying pole and started up the road towards the Tiber river. Behind him one of the urban guards at the gate raised a ragged cheer.

Chapter Twenty-One – The War in the Highlands

July 84 AD

Emogene crouched behind the rock and watched the Roman foot patrol moving through the bleak valley below. There were eight of them led by two officers on horseback. She had learned to recognise the different Roman uniforms and armour. The soldiers had come from the Roman fort at Balnageith. They were Batavians. Contemptuously she spat onto the ground. Her small war band had been tracking their progress all morning. It looked like a routine patrol but the Romans had been known to make hit-and-run raids on the tiny settlements that lay dotted about in the highland glens. It was a form of terror. It was intimidation, but today her war band would have the upper hand. The Romans were riding straight into a trap.

"Let them get further up the trail," Bary the war band leader whispered. "When they see the trail is barred, that's when we attack. Wait for my signal."

He was a big man with black hair and a handsome face. His men crouched beside him in a line, hidden behind the rocks. On the other slope of the narrow valley the other half of the war band under Finlay would be doing the same. In her hand Emogene held a bow. A quiver full of arrows was slung over her back. She had taken the weapons from a Batavian she had killed last month. Carefully she pulled an arrow free and strung it to her bow. Her face was covered in blue woad. At her side Bones knelt on the ground like she had taught him to. His yellow eyes were watching the Batavians closely.

The men in Bary's war band were not all from her own tribe, the Vacomagi. Some like Finlay were from the lowlands, refugees from the Roman stranglehold over Caledonia's most productive agricultural land. All of them, however, were determined to fight against the invaders. The war band had formed within days following the defeat at Mons Graupius and Emogene was the only woman to have joined them.

"Wait," Emogene snapped, sensing Bones's impatience. Across her chest she wore rough leather torso armour. She glanced across at Bary. He was staring down into the valley, the tension clearly showing on his face.

"Attack!" the cry reverberated along the valley.

Emogene blinked in surprise. Bary had not cried out but someone had. Then she saw Finlay and his men charging down the slope towards the Roman patrol.

"Damn him!" Bary cried out in alarm. "He was supposed to wait for my signal. Attack." He and his men rose to their feet as one and went charging down the hill shrieking their battle cries. Emogene sprang up onto the rock, crouched and pointed her bow towards the Romans, seeking a target. Her first arrow slammed into the flank of a horse, sending the creature and its rider crashing to the ground. A grey object streaked across her vision. Bones was always the first to reach the enemy. The big war dog took a mighty leap and tore into the head of the second horse. A high-pitched scream followed. Emogene strung another arrow, squinted and aimed for a Batavian at the back of the patrol. Her aim was good and the arrow punched into the man's torso, sending him tumbling backwards onto the ground. Down in the valley all was chaos. Finlay and his men reached the Romans first and by the time Bary and his men came charging up the fight was over. Six Batavians lay dead on the ground; the one thrown clear by Bones's attack was wounded and crawling across the ground. Two riderless horses had bolted back down the trail and the remaining officer stood before them trembling, his face ashen with fear. The man had thrown his sword onto the ground in an act of surrender. One of the Caledonians grabbed him and forced him down onto his knees. Finlay, a smallish red-haired man with a nasty-looking scar across his face, held a knife up to the Batavian's throat. There was delight in his eyes as he looked up at Bary.

"Shall I cut his throat and send him on his way to his gods?" he cried.

Bary took two steps forward and struck Finlay with a mighty punch, sending the smaller man flying.

"I told you to wait for my signal," Bary roared. He took another step forward, his fist raised to strike again, but his own men rushed to hold him back. On the ground Finlay was wiping the blood from his chin. He looked bruised but defiant.

"Yeah well, we got them all, didn't we," he snapped, rising slowly to his feet and giving Bary a contemptuous glance.

"Please spare my life. They will exchange me for four of your own held at Cawdor. I promise," the captured Roman officer suddenly said, speaking in the Caledonian language. The prisoner's eyes were fixed on Emogene.

The war band turned on the captive in surprise and Emogene suddenly realised that she had been wrong. The man was not a Batavian, he was a Briton. Her eyes widened and she felt a strange unease as the prisoner continued to stare at her. The man's gaze was broken when Bary slapped him across the head.

"How come you speak our language?" he growled. "Where are you from?"

The prisoner remained on his knees and looked up at Bary. "The Brigantes were my tribe and I served Queen Cartimandua once. That was long ago. Now I serve Rome, the rulers of the world."

"Not in this valley they aren't," Bary growled. The war band fell silent. The prisoner turned his head and stared again at Emogene.

"Exchange me and I promise they will hand over four of yours in return," the man repeated.

"They took Kegan and three of his brothers to Cawdor a few days ago," Finlay said, glancing at the prisoner. "Maybe we should do as he suggests? They would be a welcome addition to our band. They are my kin."

"I don't know," Bary said, circling around the prisoner. "It could be a trap." He kicked the prisoner in his thigh and the man yelped in pain. "Why would Cawdor exchange you for four of ours? What's so special about you?"

The prisoner rubbed his thigh painfully. "I am important, I have friends. They will do what I tell them," he muttered.

"Kill him, kill him now," Emogene said suddenly. Her face was cold and harsh. A few of the men murmured in agreement but Finlay shook his head.

"Exchange him and get our boys back. Then when he comes out here again we will kill him. That is a better bargain."

Emogene felt Bones sidle up to her and lick her hand. Her eyes, however, were on the prisoner. Her sense of unease had not gone away.

"I say kill him." She raised her bow and took aim at the prisoner but Bary raised his arm and moved to block her.

"No," he snapped. "Finlay is an idiot but on this occasion he is right. We must look after our own. We will do the exchange."

Emogene lowered her bow and scowled.

"How?" Finlay said. "How are we going to do the exchange?"

For a moment Bary looked uncertain. Then his eye fell on the wounded Batavian groaning on the ground. He stepped up to the man, rolled him onto his back and gave him a quick examination.

"Tell him that we are prepared to exchange their officer for four of our own. Tell him that if his people accept we will do the exchange tomorrow at noon. Dump this demon close to their fort and make sure they see him. If they don't show up we will know that they have refused. Then we will kill him," Bary added, glancing at Emogene.

"I will arrange it," Finlay said, gesturing to two of his friends.

Chapter Twenty-Two

Why Does He Not Come Looking for Me?

The highlands were covered in mist when the war band returned to their camp. The camp was perched on the summit of a treeless hill. It was nothing more than a scattering of holes dug into the ground and covered over with blocks of peat, wood and grass. A cow stood tied to a pole and chickens pecked their way through the burnt-out cooking fires. Further out along the slopes of the hill numerous sheep were grazing. A boy of around fifteen and armed with a spear suddenly emerged from the mist and challenged them. Bary raised his hand in greeting. The boy had been left behind to guard the camp.

The men drifted off to their sleeping places and Emogene sat down in front of her own and started to wax her bow. After she had murdered poor Conall and had escaped from the Roman camp she had returned home hoping to see her husband. But he hadn't been there and in the weeks that followed he had not come. Her father had provided her with no comfort. He had just sat there watching her with his wise pale-blue eyes. She had told him about Conall but he had said nothing even though she knew he approved of what she had done. Her father rarely talked.

She had been naive to think that life would return to normal after the battle. The men in her village were restless and some had started drifting off into the hills to join the small war bands that were forming to fight the Romans. Her husband must have a reason why he had not returned, she thought. Maybe he too had joined one of the war bands? Life in her village had become unbearable so one day she had packed her things, called out to Bones and set off into the highlands to fight and Bary and his men had welcomed her. That had been six months ago.

The Romans had been busy that winter. The soldiers had started constructing a long chain of forts from Cawdor southwards. The forts had been built at the entrances to the glens that led into the highlands. It was as if a gigantic snake had coiled itself around the mountains and was slowly squeezing its people to death. That's how Bary had described the enemy plans. The Roman forts had done something else as well. They had started to separate lowlander from highlander, hunter and herdsman from farmer. Bary and his men had attacked the forts but the Romans had been expecting that and had easily beaten them off. Now the war had entered a new phase, one of ambush, hostage-taking and terror. Emogene had killed her first Roman a month ago.

Emogene looked up as Bones padded across to her and lay down at her feet.

Why had her husband not come looking for her? When she would try to understand her mind would become foggy and confused. Some of the warriors in the war band had tried to persuade her to become their woman. She had refused, telling them that she was waiting for her husband to return. The men had stared at her as if she were mad. Behind her back they had muttered and gestured. They all thought she was crazy. She knew what they thought but she didn't care. Her husband was dead, they had told her. He wasn't coming back. Well let them believe what they wanted. She spat onto the ground and placed her bow against a rock.

"Emogene, come walk with me." Bary was suddenly standing beside her. He looked serious. Bones raised his head but did not get up. Emogene rose to her feet and followed Bary as he strode out of the camp. The mist had thickened and the hills were silent. Bary glanced at her carefully. She had come to know him as an honest and fair leader.

"It is time, Emogene, that you chose a man," he said gruffly. "The longer you remain single the more restless the men are getting. We have already had one nasty fight over you. I don't want any trouble within the camp. Fighting the Romans is difficult enough."

Emogene shook her head. "I already have a husband, I have told you many times. I don't need another."

A pained expression appeared on Bary's face. He grabbed her by her shoulders and twisted her round to face him.

"This is what I need to talk to you about," he said. "Your husband died last year in battle. Your kin who were with him confirmed it. I spoke with them myself. He is dead. He is not coming back." Bary paused, looked away and sighed. "You have not mourned for him yet, have you? You refuse to let him go. But you must, Emogene, you must face that reality and move on. Loyalty must end with death. He is gone. Waiting for him will bring you no happiness."

Emogene shook her head. Then with surprising strength she ripped herself free from his grip and stormed away into the mist.

The Roman prisoner had been tied up to the same pole to which the cow was pegged. His arms were twisted behind his back and his uniform was covered in mud and dirt. His chin was resting on his chest and he seemed to be asleep when Emogene stormed back into the camp. Her face was flush with anger. She strode up to the prisoner, yanking her knife from her belt. The Roman had just enough time to look up and see the knife plunging towards him. He yelped but before she could strike Emogene was knocked to the ground.

"What do you think you are doing?" an angry voice cried. She screamed and struggled to get up but the men were too strong for her.

"What happened?" She recognised Bary's voice.

"Emogene just tried to kill the prisoner," one of the men replied.

For a moment all was silent apart from her own ragged breathing.

"Get up," Bary said at last in a weary voice. The pressure on her arms was relaxed and Emogene scrambled to her feet. The men of the war band were staring at her in some puzzlement. Emogene ignored them and turned to the prisoner. The Roman was looking at her in horror. She spat at him.

"Why did you try and kill him? We decided to have him exchanged," Bary snapped.

Emogene pointed a finger at the Roman.

"There is something not right about that man. I don't trust him. He is going to get us all killed. He surrendered too easily."

"What nonsense!" a man exclaimed. "How can you know this?"

Emogene shook her head but made no reply. The group fell silent.

"Bary," a voice suddenly cried out from the edge of the camp. It was the boy. "We have company."

All eyes turned in the direction from which the boy had called out. Then three figures emerged like ghosts from the mist and strode towards the camp. Finlay halted as he caught sight of them and nodded.

"It is arranged," he said. "The Romans have accepted the exchange. We do it at noon tomorrow at the ancient circle of stones."

Chapter Twenty-Three – The Prisoner Exchange

Emogene studied the stone circle carefully. She lay on the ground, hidden amongst the rocks on the windswept ridge peering down. The others were doing the same. There were twelve stones in all and they had been set up in a circle in a meadow. No one knew who had erected them but the druids claimed that it had been done a very long time ago when the earth mother was still young. Her father had told her once that the stones had magic inside them and that people had once come to the stone circle to be blessed and healed. Other than that the druids had been silent on the matter.

Emogene glanced up at the sky. The war band had taken up their positions early. There was still roughly another hour to go before noon. She turned back to the ancient standing stones. There was no sign of the Romans.

"Are you sure they got the message?" Bary said, glancing at Finlay. The two of them were crouched behind a rock.

Finlay nodded. "They will come; there is still time."

Emogene turned and stared along the ridge towards the Roman prisoner. The man sat with his back against a slab of rock. Two men were guarding him. He caught her looking at him and smiled. Emogene looked away. Suddenly she felt her heart beating in her chest. Why was he smiling at her? Why was that man always looking at her? Had he never seen a woman before?

She forced herself to look the hundred paces down the slope towards the standing stones. The meadow in which they stood was open and flat and from the ridge where she and the war band lay hidden they had a good view of all the country around them. That view was why Bary had chosen the circle of stones as the location for the exchange. There was little chance of them being surprised up here. From the corner of her eye she suddenly caught sight of the boy running towards her. He ran half bent over and there was urgency in his movement. He flopped to the ground on his stomach beside Bary, gasping for breath.

"Bary, we have visitors," he panted. "On the hill behind us. Another war band. I counted twenty men."

"Another war band," Bary frowned. "They are ours? Are you sure?"

The boy nodded vigorously. "They are not Romans for sure but I couldn't get close enough to see who they are."

Bary turned and looked over the boy's head towards the wooded hill behind them. "What were they doing?" he snapped.

"Nothing, just resting; they made no effort to conceal themselves but they are armed and I think I saw horses but I am not sure."

"Horses?" Bary's eyes gleamed in sudden alarm. "How did they manage to get hold of horses? The Romans are taking away every beast they can find."

The boy shrugged. Bary glanced at Finlay but the small southerner shrugged as well. "Could be just chance that they are here," Finlay said.

Bary grunted and then turned to the boy. "Alright, go back to your position and keep an eye on them. If they move or anything changes you are to warn us right away. Understood?"

The boy nodded, turned and slithered away.

"I don't like it," Bary muttered suddenly. He glanced at Emogene and then at Finlay and then along the ridge towards the prisoner.

"Too late for that now," Finlay hissed. "Look, they are here."

All eyes turned to look down at the circle of standing stones. A troop of Romans had appeared on the trail leading up to the meadow. Their armour glinted and reflected in the sunlight as they marched slowly up to the stone circle. They seemed to be in no hurry. Emogene counted twenty armed men. The Romans had come in force. At the rear of the column she suddenly noticed four men stumbling along. Their hands had been bound to a long thick rope that was being pulled along by a Roman on horseback. The men looked exhausted, dirty and emaciated. The Roman officer in charge halted beside the stone circle and looked up at the ridge. Then he barked an order and the four prisoners were pulled to the front and forced down onto their knees.

Emogene checked her bow and then glanced at Bary. The leader of the war band looked anxious. Then he nodded to Finlay.

"Alright, get on with it. Let's get this done quickly."

Finlay rose to his feet and still crouching made his way towards the prisoner. A moment later the four men rose calmly to their feet and started down the slope. Emogene crouched, lifted her bow and took aim. Beside her Bones growled in anticipation. She watched as Finlay drew closer to the stones. The Romans had formed a line behind the four prisoners but didn't move. Emogene saw Finlay call out to the Romans. He was calling on them to release his kinsmen. Then the Roman officer suddenly shouted. A moment later four of his men flung their spears into the kneeling prisoners. The men were impaled and toppled over to the ground.

"No – betrayed!" she heard Bary cry in alarm.

The next moments were blurred. Finlay, seeing what had happened to his kinsmen, tried to kill the Roman prisoner but the man had been anticipating this moment and he managed to dodge the axe blow. Then he was off racing down the slope towards the Roman line, his hands still bound together. Nine Romans stormed to his aid across the meadow. They were running straight towards Finlay and his two companions. Finlay was shouting, then he and his companions were running back up the slope with the Romans in pursuit. Emogene closed one eye. Her bow was at full stretch. She took a deep breath, held it and released. The arrow hurtled straight into the back of the running prisoner, sending him crashing and tumbling to the ground. There was no time to congratulate herself. Bary and the remaining men of the war band were on their feet and charging down the hill in support of Finlay. Emogene sprung up onto a rock to get a clearer view. She already had notched another arrow to her bow. Bones had leapt after Bary and his men. He had not waited for her command. Suddenly she felt a chill pass through her body. Something was not right.

She stared in shock as a Roman's spear brought Finlay down. Bary and the others were screaming their battle cries. They had almost reached the Roman line. Then she froze as from behind her she suddenly heard another yell. It was high-pitched and urgent. In dread she turned to look behind her. The boy was floundering across the rocky plateau towards her. His mouth was open and he was screaming.

"Bary! Bary, they are coming, they are coming up the hill behind us!"

Emogene's eyes widened in shock. It was the other war band. They were going to cut off the retreat. They were working together with the Romans.

"It's a trap," she gasped. "We have been lured into a trap."

She opened her mouth but before she could shout out she knew it was already too late. They were never going to escape from so many men.

Bary and his men had halted in confusion as they heard the boy behind them. Then Emogene saw them. Twenty men, some on horseback, had appeared no more than thirty paces from her. They were running and galloping with their weapons in their hands.

Emogene gasped, turned on her heel and sent an arrow straight into one of the men closing in on her. Then she cried out with all her might.

"Bones, run, run home. Go!"

She caught sight of him. His ears had pricked up as he heard her and his head had turned in her direction.

"Run, go!" she screamed.

For a moment the big war dog hesitated. Then with flattened ears he was off bounding away across the meadow. A moment later a fist came smashing into her face and everything went dark.

When Emogene finally regained consciousness it was late in the afternoon. She spat a bit of blood from her mouth and tried to move but her hands and feet had been bound tightly together.

Someone had dumped her against one of the standing stones. She blinked and felt the pain in her head. On the slope she suddenly caught sight of the bodies of the men from her war band. They were all dead. Bary, Finlay, the boy, all of them. A Roman soldier was trying to wrest a finger ring from one of the corpses. Emogene felt a tear appear in her eye. It trickled down her cheek slowly but she couldn't wipe it away. Why was she still alive?

Carefully she turned her head. The pain was a dull throb. The Roman officer and some of his men were talking with the men from the war band that had attacked them from the rear. It had all been a trap. The Roman patrol, the Briton who had surrendered so easily, the exchange. It had all been a carefully prepared trap and it had worked. She leaned back against the stone and closed her eyes. But they had not managed to catch Bones. She couldn't see him anywhere. He must have escaped. The thought brought some comfort.

"The girl is awake," a voice said from behind her. She couldn't see the man but there was something strangely familiar about his voice that she couldn't place. The man had spoken in her own language.

"Is it her?" another voice said.

"Oh yes, it's her," the familiar-sounding voice replied. "I am not going to forget that pretty face for a while."

Emogene opened her eyes. The Roman officer and another man, a Celt, were walking towards her. She blinked. The Celt looked familiar. Then as he drew closer her eyes widened. It was Baldurix, her father's blood enemy.

"The girl is mine," she heard Baldurix say as he approached. "That was our bargain. You get to kill the warriors and I get the girl."

The Roman officer and Baldurix halted before her. Both of them looked down at Emogene in sudden amusement.

"If you think your dog is going to come back and free you then you are a fool," Baldurix said. "My men will kill him with bow and arrow before he even gets close to our camp."

Emogene refused to look at them. Instead she stared sullenly at the ground.

"I heard this girl escaped from you twice before, Bestia," Baldurix said with a chuckle as he glanced over her head at the man behind her. "I trust that you won't allow it to happen a third time?"

"She won't get away," Bestia growled. "I will look after her. I am to cut her throat if you try to take her or if she dares to escape. My employer is keen to protect his investment, if you know what I mean."

For an instant Baldurix's face darkened but he said nothing. Emogene felt the blood rush to her cheeks as she remembered the incident with the Roman outside the army camp the previous autumn. What was Baldurix doing with these Romans?

"You know who she is, don't you, Baldurix?" another voice said behind her. "She is the daughter of Dougal, the Vacomagi druid. He is our blood enemy. Should we not kill her for the sake of the feud? It is our right."

Baldurix grunted and for a moment he seemed to consider the suggestion.

"No," he said at last. "Even if we publicly tortured her in front of her father, I know that old druid. He would be unmoved and nothing would change. He doesn't give a rat's arse what we do to his daughter. Only Dougal's death and the massacre of the Vacomagi will end the feud. No, we stick to the original plan. I have a friend who is very interested in meeting this girl. He will be very happy to see her. Very happy indeed."

"Just so that you remember, nine of my men died to get her," the Roman officer growled, speaking brokenly in Emogene's language.

"And you will be well rewarded as a result," Baldurix replied smoothly. He glanced across at Bestia and then up at the sky. "Come, we should not delay any longer. I need to be at Inchtuthil by the full moon. Get her up and onto a horse."

As one of Baldurix's men caught hold of her arm Emogene sank her teeth into his hand. The man cried out in pain and staggered backwards in shock.

"Feisty bitch, isn't she," another man laughed.

"Yes, I am quite looking forward to that," Baldurix said darkly.

Chapter Twenty-Four – Hearts of Darkness

Saturnalia, December 83 AD

The round house felt cold. The fire was dead. Vellocatus was hurriedly packing his belongings into a trunk. Outside the fields were covered in fresh snow. A black bird was croaking loudly in a nearby tree. Dark circles surrounded Vellocatus's eyes as he cast a furtive glance at the door. Had that been movement outside? He was alone in his house. The whole civilian settlement that had grown up around the legionary fort at Eburacum had gathered in the great hall to celebrate the festival of Saturnalia. But Vellocatus was not joining them. He was preparing to flee southwards to Londinium. In Londinium he would be relatively safe. From there it should be possible to catch a ship and make it to Gaul. He had relatives in Gaul.

He slammed the trunk shut and locked it. Then he cast his eye around his house. Had he forgotten anything? There was no time for a sentimental goodbye to the place he had called home for five years. He turned for the door with his trunk in his hand. He was just about to step outside when a figure loomed up in the doorway. Vellocatus staggered backwards in horror. The man ducked into the house. He was followed by another and then another. The men were armed and clad in warm woollen cloaks. One of them had a hood pulled over his head.

"Going somewhere, were you?" the hooded man said, glancing at the trunk.

Vellocatus didn't reply. His chest was heaving in nervous tension.

"You know why we are here, Vellocatus," the hooded man continued. "You borrowed money from us a year ago and now we want it back plus the interest. Well, do you have it?"

"I was going to get it just now," Vellocatus muttered.

The three men laughed. "Sure you were. Is that why your horse outside is saddled and loaded for a long journey? Come on, Vellocatus, do you take us for fools? We want our money back – now do you have it or not?"

"He doesn't have it," one of the men growled. "You can see his answer on his face."

Vellocatus was staring defiantly at his three visitors.

The hooded man sighed. "One more day, Vellocatus," he said, looking up at the slaver. "We will return tomorrow and if you don't have the money by then I am going to put an iron ring around your neck. You know the law. If you can't repay your body will become my property and you will become a slave."

Vellocatus's breath was coming in short sharp gasps but he said nothing. The three men turned for the door.

"And don't try to escape," the hooded man snapped. "My men will be watching your every move. If you so much as set a foot outside this settlement we will cut your throat. Is that understood?"

Vellocatus felt a helpless rage surge through his body as the three men left his house. Then he let go of the trunk and it thudded onto the ground. He strode across the single room and hammered his knife into a wooden wall post and opened his mouth in a silent scream. Then he slumped down into a chair and stared listlessly at the far wall. The Jewish moneylenders and their Atrebate allies would keep their promise, he knew. He had borrowed the money to finance his slaving expedition in the wake of Agricola's advance northwards. He had been hoping his investment would be handsomely rewarded by the slaves he could have picked up after the battle. He had arranged everything with Agricola. Then the governor had betrayed him. Agricola had reneged on their deal and he, Vellocatus, had returned home empty-handed, in debt and a ruined man. He stared at the far wall and his face blushed a dark red. He couldn't become a slave. He would not allow himself to become a slave to those moneylenders. He had been born a free man of the Brigantes. His mother had been none other than Queen Cartimandua herself. He was of noble blood. He could not become a slave – anything but that.

Vellocatus closed his eyes. But what could he do? He didn't have the money. His mother was dead and so was his father. The Brigantes were no longer an independent nation. He was an illegitimate bastard and none of the remaining Brigante nobles wanted anything to do with him. He had relatives in Gaul but they were simple farmers and poor. What was he going to do? He had a day to find a solution. Slowly he opened his eyes. Then he got to his feet and stomped out of the door. It was freezing outside and he pulled his cloak closer around his body as he made his way through the snow towards the great hall from where the faint sound of music and laughter was coming. As he plodded across the snow-covered field with its scattering of round houses and tradesmen's workshops he became aware of two dark shapes following him. He didn't look round for he knew who they were. The Jews were keeping an eye on their investment.

In the distance to the north across a small river he could make out the turf and wooden ramparts of the legionary camp. The Ninth had just returned from active service in Caledonia for the winter and the smoke from hundreds of cooking fires drifted away into the grey sky. The soldiers' return had been greeted by much enthusiasm from the people in the civilian settlement for the presence of the soldiers was the main reason why the growing town existed at all.

The great hall was a long, low rectangular building made of peat and wood and it had a thatched roof. Smoke was pouring out from two chimneys. As he approached Vellocatus could hear music and singing. A drunk staggered past him towards the river but was violently sick before he could make it to the bank. Vellocatus ducked into the doorway and entered the meeting hall. It was dark inside and the noise was tremendous. Flickering oil lamps along the walls and two coal fires provided the only illumination. Vellocatus paused to allow his eyes to adjust. People clad in gay costumes were sitting around tables, eating, drinking, talking, laughing and singing. Others were dancing or banging their hands on the tables. Vellocatus did not join in. Instead he searched the hall until he found the person he was looking for. Brusquely he made his way through the crowd. The woman was laughing as he approached but the laughter faded abruptly as she caught sight of him. Vellocatus pushed a sleeping man aside and sat down beside her. The girl had begun to look decidedly uncomfortable.

"I need to see her at once!" Vellocatus exclaimed loudly.

"She doesn't want to see you anymore," the woman replied.

Vellocatus grabbed the woman's arm and held it tightly. There was a desperate gleam in his eye.

"Where is she? Why won't she receive me? What have I done wrong?"

The woman wrenched her wrist free. She turned to face him and there was disgust on her face.

"She is in the Roman camp. The soldiers will not allow you in. She is leaving for Gaul soon. You will never see her again."

Vellocatus stared at the woman in dismay. For many months earlier that year he had been courting the sister of Agricola's wife. The girl had been rather plain-looking but her family connections and wealth made up for all of that. But ever since he had returned from Caledonia the girl had refused to see him and his presents had been returned.

"It's all Agricola's fault, isn't it," he hissed. "He has poisoned her mind against me."

The woman looked at him with growing disgust.

"No," she shook her head, "it is not that." The woman paused. "It's you and your particular tastes. There are rumours going around that you have an appetite for sexual deviancy." The woman rose to her feet and glared at Vellocatus. "You are sick. You are a beast. Don't come here again."

Vellocatus staggered out of the great hall. The two men who had followed him were watching him from beside the river. In the trees the blackbird was still croaking. It had always been a foolish hope to expect Agricola's wife's sister to settle his debts but he couldn't think of anything else he could do. Moodily he

119

kicked at a snowdrift and as he did so his eyes glided towards the last house in the settlement. The woman was right. He had urges, dark deviant desires that he knew he had to keep hidden, for society would hate him if they ever knew about them. They would cast him out and maybe even threaten his life if they knew about his cravings. He snorted. What difference did it make? He was doomed after all. A final visit to the merchant who provided satisfaction to his cravings would do no harm. He licked his lips in anticipation and started out towards the round house at the end of the settlement. Not many people knew what went on inside that house. The merchant who owned it had a very select group of clientele and he was very careful about whom he allowed inside. But Vellocatus needed no introduction – he was a regular. He approached the house and then paused. The two men shadowing him were still there. He smiled and banged on the door. A few moments later it opened and a man's face peered out. He nodded quickly as he recognised Vellocatus.

"The usual price," he said sternly and Vellocatus nodded in agreement. Then he stepped through the doorway and into the house. The merchant closed the door behind him. Vellocatus stood in a dimly lit room and looked around. Another man whom he didn't recognise was sitting on a chair.

"I have another customer," the merchant said, gesturing for Vellocatus to sit. Vellocatus stared at the stranger. He was a big man and from his polished torc around his neck and the rings on his fingers he looked wealthy too. The stranger glanced up at Vellocatus and suddenly he grinned. Vellocatus found himself grinning in return as if the two men were sharing a guilty secret.

"My name is Baldurix," the stranger said, rising to his feet. "I have come from the north on business."

"And for pleasure it seems," Vellocatus said with a knowing look as he shook the man's hand.

Chapter Twenty-Five – Axis of Evil

The fire crackled in its hearth as Vellocatus threw another log of wood onto it. It was evening and he was back in his own house. Sitting beside the fire sipping a cup of wine was Baldurix. The big warrior from the north glanced carefully at Vellocatus as the slaver sat back down in his seat. For a moment the two men said nothing. Then Vellocatus leaned forwards.

"I have a problem," he said cautiously. "I won't lie to you. I owe some men some money. They are threatening to come here tomorrow and throw an iron ring around my neck if I don't pay up. I don't have the money."

"Sounds awful," Baldurix replied, taking another sip of wine. "Is that why you asked me to come to your house?"

Vellocatus nodded and studied the fire.

"You said you were here on business. You have a boat and you have ten armed men who follow you," Vellocatus muttered thoughtfully.

Baldurix wiped his mouth with his hand. "I sympathise with your problems, Vellocatus, but I don't see how I can help you."

Vellocatus looked up at him and in the firelight it seemed as if his face was on fire.

"If you kill these men to whom I owe money I will show you where they have hidden their fortune. If you kill these men for me, you can take three quarters of the money that they have."

The house fell silent. Baldurix was staring into the flames. He raised his hand and slowly stroked his chin.

"I do not fight against Romans," Baldurix said at last. "I am allied to them now. But this fortune you talk about, how large is it?"

"How large do you need it to be?" Vellocatus answered.

Baldurix looked at him. "I would need a fortune that is large enough so that I can bribe two complete Roman forts and nearly one thousand Roman soldiers."

121

Vellocatus whistled and looked impressed. He paused for a few moments.

"These men are not Romans, they are Jews. There are only six of them. Your men can handle them easily enough."

"Who are the Jews?" Baldurix frowned.

"It doesn't matter, but the Romans don't give a damn about them. No one does."

"How much money do they possess? Is it enough to get me interested?" Baldurix insisted.

Vellocatus leaned forwards and touched Baldurix on his knee. "Do this for me and you will gain a loyal friend. I know things. I have many friends amongst the Romans. I have connections that will be useful to you. I can even introduce you to Agricola's wife's sister. I have influence with Agricola himself."

Baldurix took another sip of wine.

"Six men you say? But you still haven't told me how much gold these Jews have?"

Vellocatus nodded and there was a triumphant gleam in his eye. "Lots – enough to satisfy all your men. But that's just the start." He paused. "I know how you can get the wealth you need. A few months ago just after Agricola's victory I happened to come across a boy who had a rather interesting story to tell…"

Baldurix was silent as Vellocatus recounted the tale of the captured boy and the secret of the amber cave. When Vellocatus finally fell silent the leader of the Decantae looked intrigued. He raised his index finger in the air.

"So this girl with the blue face, she murdered the boy to keep the stones a secret. To prevent the boy from showing you where they are?"

"Yes, that's what we believe." Vellocatus stood up and poured some more wine into Baldurix's cup. "I believe that this cave does exist," he said quietly. "A Roman scout was sent north to look for the place but there has been no news from him. He is probably dead." Vellocatus paused and his eyes suddenly sparkled with excitement. "Baldurix, don't you see, if we can get hold of this amber and it's there in the quantities that the boy told us it was, then think what we could do. With such wealth a man could do much more than bribe two Roman forts – a man could buy the loyalty of an entire legion!"

"Yes but why do I need you to find this amber?" Baldurix retorted.

The house fell silent. Vellocatus nodded.

"A fair question," he murmured. "You have the manpower, you know the land, but I, my friend, am the only one who knows what this girl looks like. Without her we could spend years looking for this cave. The girl is the key. She will be able to guide us to this cave and I am the only one who can identify her. That's why you need me."

Baldurix grunted and swirled the wine in his cup. He looked moody.

"So we will need to find this woman first. How do we do that?"

Vellocatus smiled. "When she first appeared one of my men mentioned that she had a big war dog as a companion. You know, one of these dogs trained to fight in battle. These dogs are fairly rare and they are valuable. There won't be so many of them in Caledonia. Have your men scour the hills and villages when you return and if they hear anything about a girl and a war dog then send word to me. I in return will send you one of my men who can positively identify her."

"I thought you said that only you know what she looks like?"

Vellocatus's smile widened. "I do. My man works only for me. He got to know the girl. She kicked him in the balls when she escaped. He is keen to meet her again."

Baldurix grunted and fixed Vellocatus with a cautious look. "I want three quarters of this amber; you can have the rest."

"It is done," Vellocatus nodded.

"Fine," Baldurix growled. His eyes blazed with sudden fervour.

"Why do you want to bribe two Roman forts?" Vellocatus asked.

Baldurix looked excited. "The amber will allow me to buy the services of the soldiers of the Roman forts and garrisons in the territory of the Vacomagi. The amber will allow me to tip the balance of power between the Decantae and the Vacomagi. Then," his eyes gleamed in triumph, "we will wipe them all from the face of the earth and my blood feud with them will be at an end."

Vellocatus laughed and raised his cup.

"Then are we agreed?"

Baldurix looked across at him and nodded. Their two cups clinked together.

"Agreed," Baldurix replied.

Vellocatus took a long sip of wine. Then he turned to study Baldurix.

"You know they hate us for what we are." He paused. "They call us sexual deviants, but I say fuck what other people think."

Baldurix grunted and raised his cup in the air again.

Chapter Twenty-Six – The Visitor

July 84 AD

It was noon and Eburacum shimmered in the summer heat. The small settlement had grown since the winter and the new white round houses along the riverbank gleamed and baked in the heat. Further along towards the single wooden bridge that connected the civilian settlement with the legionary fortress, new houses and workshops were under construction. The market stalls beside the bridge were doing good business as soldiers mingled with the throng of shoppers and stall owners. Down by the riverbank a party of children were playing loudly and from the workshop beside the meeting hall came the dull ringing metallic beat of a blacksmith at work.

Vellocatus and Bestia sat outside on two stools across a table beside Vellocatus's home. They were bare-chested and sweating. A jug of wine stood in the middle of the table and now and then the men would reach for it and take a long slurp. The air was hot, stagnant and humid. The two men were playing a game of dice and a pile of copper coins gleamed on each man's side of the table. The dice rattled in their cup as Vellocatus made his throw.

"I win again," Vellocatus said triumphantly. He scooped up the copper coins with a grin and handed the dice over to Bestia.

Bestia farted.

"Tell me, Bestia," Vellocatus said, leaning forwards, "did you really force those Roman prisoners to eat their own balls during the Batavian rebellion?"

Bestia sniffed and rattled the dice in their cup.

"Perhaps," he murmured.

Vellocatus laughed. "That's what I like about you, Bestia. I never know whether you mean something or not. The uncertainty kills me."

"I mean what I say." Bestia threw the dice and smiled.

Vellocatus scooped up the dice. "So do I," he replied. "Seven months ago some moneylenders here in Eburacum threatened to put an iron ring around my neck. Do you know what happened to them? The next day six corpses were dumped into the marshes down by the river. Bye bye, moneylenders. No one will ever know what happened to them."

"They didn't leave a record of their loans?"

Vellocatus grinned. "I made sure that I took all the documents. I burned them here. All gone. But the ledger made interesting reading. Did you know that the legate of the Ninth had borrowed a large sum? Maybe someone should go and tell him that it was I who erased his debt for him," Vellocatus said boastfully.

Bestia glanced at Vellocatus.

"Who took all the money?" he inquired slyly.

"You know who," Vellocatus grunted. "The same man who killed them."

"Baldurix," Bestia said slowly. "And no one made inquiries into the disappearance of these men? They can't have had many friends."

Vellocatus threw the dice and looked disappointed. "Well actually someone did come inquiring about them," he said. "A man from the south. The moneylenders had some friends amongst the Atrebates on the south coast. But no one knows what happened so he left without learning anything new."

"Still you should be careful," Bestia said, taking another slurp of wine.

Vellocatus nodded. "I am," he murmured.

Bestia threw the dice once more. "So you never finished telling me what happened to your mother, the queen?"

Vellocatus rose from his stool and strode towards a barrel of water that stood beside the door to his house. He plunged his head into the water and raised it again, sending droplets flying in all directions. He strode back towards the table and sat down.

"My mother, Queen Cartimandua, ruler of the Brigantes," he said, wiping his hair from his eyes, "loved only two things. Sex and power. She could never keep her legs together for long but she would cut your throat if you displeased her. I saw her do that once when I was a boy."

"And her support for Rome, her betrayal of Caratacus and the civil war amongst the Brigantes, what was all that about?"

Vellocatus was staring into space. "She made many enemies with her behaviour," he muttered. "Her husband hated her. He hated my father too. Most of the nobles supported him. They didn't want to bow to Rome. So I suppose she needed the power of Rome to help maintain her position." He blinked. "I had seven brothers and sisters once and now all are dead. I am her last living descendent and if I have inherited anything from her, then it's her lust for sex and power."

Vellocatus looked at Bestia and laughed and after a moment's hesitation Bestia joined in.

Their laughter was interrupted by the approach of a horseman. Both Vellocatus and Bestia rose to their feet as the rider came ambling towards them. The man was covered in dust and sweat lathered his forehead. A long bow was strapped to his back and a quiver of arrows was slung over his shoulder. The horse too was covered in sweat.

"Are you Vellocatus?" the rider said. "They told me that I could find him here."

Vellocatus folded his arms across his chest.

"Maybe – who are you?"

The rider looked annoyed. Then he got down from his horse and patted the beast on its rump.

"Baldurix has sent me to find you," he said. "I am to deliver a message to you. Baldurix says that he has found the girl."

Vellocatus went very still. For a moment he stared at the visitor but the man looked genuine.

"Baldurix has found her," Vellocatus muttered to himself. He glanced across at Bestia and then back to the rider. "Where is she?"

"We spotted her in the highlands," the rider said with a confident voice. "The girl and her dog are with a war band. They are hiding in the hills. Baldurix says that he has a plan. He wants to meet you at the Roman fortress of Inchtuthil. He says that he will bring the girl but he wants your man to be there to identify her first."

Vellocatus suddenly looked excited. "Excellent. Ride back to Baldurix and tell him that I will be in Inchtuthil by the next full moon. My man will accompany you and positively identify the girl."

Bestia turned on Vellocatus.

"I managed to bribe my commanding officer for this leave," he exclaimed, "but my unit are still expecting me back. If I do not report for duty soon they will list me as a deserter."

Vellocatus shrugged. "Then be a deserter. I need you to go with this man. If we can find this amber, Bestia, you are going to be rich for the rest of your life. You will be able to go anywhere. Who cares about your army career?"

Bestia took a long deep breath of air. His eyes were filled with sudden indecision.

"Fuck your unit – desert; I need you. Are you really going to turn down an opportunity like this?" Vellocatus exclaimed, jabbing his finger into the Batavian's chest.

"Alright, I will do it," Bestia hissed. "But if you fuck me out of my share I will cut your balls off…"

"…and make me eat them," Vellocatus finished the sentence and grinned. "Don't worry, I look after my old friends."

"My horse and I can do with some water," the rider said.

"Over there," Vellocatus replied without looking at the man.

Then he stepped through the doorway into his house. The cool interior was a welcome relief from the baking heat outside. Baldurix had found the girl. He hadn't been sure whether the tall Caledonian would keep on looking. He had secretly doubted the man's persistence. But Baldurix was proving to be a man of his word. Vellocatus grinned as he found his money pouch and counted out a number of silver coins. If they had the right girl he would force her to take them to the amber cave. Things were slotting into place. Their plan was going to work and he was going to become a rich man at last. Then those patrician Roman women would start taking notice of him again. Oh yes, then he would be welcome again.

"Vellocatus," Bestia's voice sounded strangely tense. "There is another visitor here to see you. Come outside."

Vellocatus frowned. He slipped the coins into a small leather bag and turned for the door. Outside he saw a white-haired man with a deep suntan. The man was in his mid forties and was leaning on a wooden stick. His torso was covered by worn-looking leather body armour. He looked Vellocatus straight in the eye.

"My name is Corbulo," the man said, "and you must be Vellocatus."

Chapter Twenty-Seven – Londinium

Corbulo had had a long journey since leaving Rome. It had been a journey through his past. Firstly there was his arrival in Londinium on the galley. He would always remember the galley nosing its way carefully up the swollen river. The tide was in and the dark water lapped hungrily against its banks. A thick reed bed had formed around the spot where a tributary stream joined and on the south bank a group of men were busy fishing. Corbulo stood at the prow of the ship, craning to get a first glimpse of the Roman bridge that spanned the Thames. He felt strangely excited. It almost felt as if he was coming home. He grinned. It was good to see Britannia again. He had spent twenty-five years of his life in the province. The greenness of the land was soothing to the eye and there was a certain softness of character about the province and its people that he had found lacking on the Continent. It was not the idle softness of the Greeks or the unemployed in Rome but a generousness of character, a willingness to let people live as they chose. The Britons, Corbulo knew, were at their most dangerous when they perceived that an injustice had been done. If one treated them fairly without tricks and cheating, then they were easily managed.

He grunted as up ahead he caught sight of the magnificent Roman bridge. It was huge and made entirely from wood. On the north bank, stretching along the river for a mile, the stone houses, wharves and warehouses of Londinium, with their new red roof tiles, glinted in the sunlight. On the marshy south bank Londinium's first suburb, Southwark, clustered around the road that led to the bridge. The ship started to angle towards the solid wooden quayside on the northern bank. Corbulo's grin widened as a thousand memories were awakened.

He had first arrived in this port as a young eighteen-year-old recruit on his way to join the Twentieth Legion. A few years later and already a veteran of two major battles, he had been with the men who had accompanied Governor Paulinus as he had hastened southwards from Mona. Corbulo's grin faded as he remembered the desperation in the townsfolk's eyes and voices as they had pleaded with Paulinus to stay and defend their town from Boudica's approaching army. But Paulinus had refused, saying he did not have enough men and he had ordered the town to be evacuated. Boudica had burned Londinium to the ground. Corbulo had seen the smoking, blackened ruins. In time, however, the town had rebuilt itself for it occupied a far too important and advantageous spot for it to be abandoned. Now as he studied the approaching city, Corbulo saw that Londinium was prospering once more. The bridge over the Thames and the port were driving the growth of the town. Surely the town must have overtaken Camulodunum in size by now, he thought.

Corbulo stepped smartly off the ship as two slaves fastened the mooring ropes to the waterfront. Then with a farewell nod to the boat's captain he strode along the wooden quayside and into the town. After Boudica had destroyed the city, the streets and houses had been rebuilt on the Roman model with a standard Roman street grid and stone houses closely built up against each other. The street grid was useful, he thought, for he had never managed to get lost when he had visited, even when he was drunk. The town extended half a mile or so northwards from the river. Corbulo strode along until he reached Watling Street. Then he turned left and entered the heart of the city. After the peace and quiet that he had endured on his long and lonely walk from Rome, the noise in the city was tremendous. A multitude of people from all across the empire – shoppers, children, slaves, tradesmen, merchants, bankers, soldiers and sailors – jostled along the narrow streets, talking, haggling and advertising their wares in loud voices. People barged into him without looking up.

Corbulo struggled on until he came to the forum. The marketplace and city centre was even more crowded and noisy. The merchant stalls were doing a roaring trade. He had forgotten how vibrant the place was. The people seemed so brash and confident, as if they had collectively forgotten about the horror and destruction that the barbarian queen had unleashed. He craned his neck to see if the old tavern was still there. It was. The name on the sign above the door read CUM MULA PEPERIT, but everyone had just called it The Mule. He grinned and felt a streak of sudden excitement. The tavern was just off the forum. He had first come to drink in the place twenty years before. It was the tavern where he and his army buddies would meet when on leave or if official business took them to Londinium. Maybe some of them would still be in town? After his long solitary journey he could do with having someone to talk to.

Absentmindedly he touched the phallic amulet that hung around his neck. Then he pushed his way through the crowd. The tavern was a simple two-storey building with a large room downstairs and several tiny rooms upstairs for the whores. Corbulo stood in the doorway and clasped the wooden door post with one hand. His eyes quickly swept across the room, taking in the faces of the drinkers. He grunted in disappointment. He didn't recognise anyone. Some of the men in the tavern looked like off-duty soldiers but all of them were young. None of them were remotely near as old as himself. He grunted again. A new and younger crowd visited the tavern now. Well, what had he expected, a welcoming committee of all of his old comrades? He licked his lips. He may as well have a drink for old times' sake. He shuffled across to the bar. An old fat lady was serving wine and mead. She looked up at him, frowned and then opened her mouth in surprise.

"Is that you, Corbulo?" she exclaimed.

Corbulo blinked. He had not recognised her. The woman was the wife of the tavern owner. She was still here after all these years.

He nodded and grinned at her, too embarrassed to tell her that he'd forgotten her name. The woman had been serving in the tavern for as long as he had been drinking there.

"Take over for a while will you," the fat lady said to the younger girl who was helping her. "I am going to have a chat with an old acquaintance."

The two of them sat beside a table tucked away in the corner. The woman looked sad.

"So do you know why she did it?" she said.

Corbulo took a sip of wine. He hadn't had a cup of wine in seventy-two days. The wine tasted delicious but his face remained glum.

"She was a good woman," he muttered. "She was loyal, I know that now and she was devoted to me and to Marcus." Corbulo sighed deeply. "I screwed it up. She must have been very lonely and miserable. I didn't give her the love she needed. I was hardly there most of the time. I beat my son and I was unfaithful. I drank too much but I reckon what drove her to kill herself was that I wanted to retire to Italy. I don't think she wanted to go but I was going to force her to come. Maybe she dreaded being alone in a foreign land."

The fat woman was silent for a while.

"And Marcus has gone missing?" she said.

Corbulo nodded and took another sip of wine. "He went missing late last year up north. I have come to find him." Corbulo looked up at the woman. "I have to make things right between me and my son. It's what my wife would have wanted. I want her spirit to know that at least I tried to make things right. I have to try and find Marcus. I believe he is still alive."

The woman gave him a smile.

"So you decided to walk for seventy-two days all the way from Rome with only enough money to buy yourself a new pair of sandals and the fare to cross the sea," she said, raising her eyebrows. "You have got balls, Corbulo, but then again you always did. I can see what that wife of yours once saw in you. Cut out the drinking and the whoring and you would be a fine man. I bet that was what you were when you were young, a fine man, a fine soldier."

"Any news from the others – you know, the boys who used to drink with me?" Corbulo said, changing the subject.

The woman shook her head. "No, haven't seen any of them in years. They are probably dead or retired by now. There has not been much military activity so far this summer. The

Ninth are up at Eburacum and the Twentieth are building a new fortress at a place called Inchtuthil in Caledonia. The auxiliary cohorts are all busy up north too, building forts all over Caledonia. I haven't seen one of them soldiers around here for over a year. Poor bastards. A man's got to get leave some time doesn't he?" She paused to catch her breath. "Heard that Agricola has been recalled. We will soon know who the new governor is going to be. It's a shame as I rather liked that old Gallic warrior. He came in here once, did you know that? He said that I ran a fine establishment."

"I know you do," Corbulo grinned.

"Oh," the woman said as she suddenly remembered something, "I heard that Quintus is up at Inchtuthil with the Twentieth. He was promoted to centurion last year. He was your friend, wasn't he?"

Corbulo nodded. "You are always surprisingly well informed about troop movements, aren't you," he said. "Gods forbid that the enemy were ever to use you as a spy."

"Maybe they do," she said tartly. Then she laughed. Corbulo finished his wine and rose to his feet. She looked up in disappointment.

"Won't you stay at least the night?" she said.

But Corbulo shook his head. "I must start heading north. Marcus will need me. I can't afford to waste any more time. Thank you for the wine. When this is all over my son and I will come and visit you. That is a promise."

The woman rose and pecked him on his cheek.

"Her spirit is watching you," she said quietly. "Death is not the end. Be bold, Corbulo, and the gods will reward you. I will pray for you."

Chapter Twenty-Eight – Eburacum

Corbulo undid his sandals and lowered his feet into the river. The water was cold and instantly refreshing. It was a beautiful baking hot summer's day. Nearby, two frogs leapt from the peaceful water leaving little ripples in their wake. He lay back in the grass letting his feet dangle in the water. Half a mile away the round houses of the civilian settlement of Eburacum gleamed in the sunlight. He could hear a party of children splashing and laughing in the river and further along the dull metallic ring of a blacksmith at work. Across the stream to the north he could just make out the fortifications of the legionary base. He had indeed forgotten how beautiful this green province could be in summer. He peered in the direction of the fortress. After he had retired he had never expected to see the old fort again. The Ninth had built it and had occupied it for most of the time but Corbulo had often made the journey from Deva. His final visit had been during his last winter in the province when he had been a member of the party that had accompanied the champion boxer of the Twentieth to the final match against the champion of the Ninth. The two army boxers had been competing for the title of best and greatest boxer in Britannia.

He sat up and began a careful examination of his body, as he had done each day since he had set out from Rome eighty-four days ago. He had lost a lot of weight. His cheeks had shrunk and his face was deeply suntanned. His tunic was stained and torn and he knew that he smelt like a sewer rat but he'd had no more money to buy new clothes or visit a bath house. He'd taken the leather torso body armour from a corpse he'd found lying alongside the road near Pisae. All his remaining army pension had been spent on food and the fare to cross the sea. Now as he sat beside the river he was down to his last few copper coins. His leg muscles were still in good shape, thanks to the long days of continuous walking, but every now and then he felt a twinge of pain in his joints, a gentle reminder that his body would not stand this exercise forever. And in Gaul he had lost another tooth. He sighed. He would not be able to keep up this pace for much longer.

When had he become an old man? When had that happened? It seemed only a few years ago that he had been at the peak of his physical fitness and prowess. Now raising his arse from the ground was an effort. How lucky the youth were, he thought enviously, but then again the young took youth for granted. They believed that they would always be young. He had worried about getting injured or sick. An injury would be the end of him and most likely Marcus too. So he had avoided the towns of Italy and Gaul. He had avoided people, only approaching them for food or directions. He had avoided confrontations and country taverns. Sickness lived in the cities and towns, an army doctor had once told him. The doctor had been convinced that it was rats that carried the plague that now and then reared its deadly head across the empire. Corbulo rubbed his calf muscle gently with his fingers. If he were to get injured badly enough to prevent him from walking then he would die. He would die beside the road. No one would care. Why should they? He himself had seen the corpses of people lying beside the road. Hunger, injury, disease and accidents killed more people than hostile tribesmen did. That was why he had started examining his body every day.

From his pack he took a loaf of stale bread and broke off a piece before replacing the rest in his pack. For a moment he munched quietly before reaching down and pulling his short sword from its scabbard. He grunted in satisfaction. At least the weapon was in good condition. He replaced the sword and glanced again at the civilian settlement. A worried look had appeared in his eyes. What if the man had already moved on? He swallowed the last mouthful of bread, hauled his legs from the river, slid his feet back into his boots and rose stiffly, brushing the crumbs and dust from his tunic. It was time to go and see this Vellocatus, the slaver that Agricola had told him about. Hopefully the man would be able to give him some clues as to what had happened to Marcus. The slaver after all was one of the last people to have seen his son.

The round house was made of white daub and wicker and it had a thatched roof. Corbulo was crossing the field towards the house when he caught sight of the two men lounging about outside the entrance. They seemed to be waiting for someone. A wooden table with an earthen jug standing on it and two stools stood abandoned beside the doorway. The men turned as he approached. One of them looked like a soldier; probably from an auxiliary cohort, Corbulo thought. The other was a native, a Briton with a large bow strapped to his back. Corbulo didn't like the look of either of them. The Briton was holding the reins of a horse. Corbulo halted and glanced at the two men warily.

"I am looking for a man called Vellocatus. The people in the market said that I could find him here?"

The soldier frowned and without replying called out to someone inside the house. A moment later a tall bare-chested man appeared in the doorway.

"My name is Corbulo and you must be Vellocatus," Corbulo said.

"I am him – what do you want?" Vellocatus replied tersely, as if he had been interrupted in the middle of doing something.

"Governor Agricola has ordered me to find you," Corbulo said quietly. "He has sent me to discuss the matter of Caledonian amber with you."

Vellocatus went very still. For a long moment he stared at Corbulo without uttering a word. His eyes gleamed dangerously.

"How do you know about the amber?" he said at last.

Corbulo cleared his throat. He had taken an instant dislike to the slaver. He paused. It was time to see if the ploy he had prepared would work.

"I already told you," Corbulo replied calmly, "Agricola has sent me. My patron wants to know how you are progressing with your search for the amber. He wants to know if there has been any news or developments."

"Why?" Vellocatus looked confused.

"Has there been any news from the scout who was sent north to investigate?" Corbulo said, ignoring the slaver's question.

Vellocatus was staring at him as if he had been caught off guard. For a few moments the man failed to reply. Then he found his voice again.

"Uh, no," he replied. "There is no news from the scout. Nor have I learned anything else since I last saw Agricola. Tell your patron that I now believe that the scout is probably dead and that the amber doesn't exist."

Corbulo looked Vellocatus calmly in the eye. The man was lying to him.

"That is a shame. Agricola was hoping to receive some good news. He will not be best pleased to hear about your progress."

"Yes well, that arsehole," Vellocatus suddenly retorted in a burst of fury, "ruined me. He reneged on our agreement. Why should I care a damn about what he thinks? Your patron is a prick!"

Corbulo gently wiped Vellocatus's spittle from his face.

"Agricola is concerned about his share of the proceeds. That is why he wants to know about your progress. He told me that if you are not capable of finding this amber cave he will find someone who is." Corbulo paused. "Now do we understand each other?"

Vellocatus's breathing had accelerated. He stared at Corbulo defiantly. "Agricola has been recalled to Rome. He is far away. What do I care?"

"No," Corbulo shook his head, "Agricola is in Londinium as we speak. He wants an answer from you right now or else he is coming north in person."

The standoff between the two men lengthened. From the corner of his eye Corbulo noticed that the auxiliary soldier's hand had dropped to the pommel of his sword. Vellocatus's eye had begun to twitch. Then abruptly a broad fake smile appeared on the slaver's face.

"Your patron may be a prick," Vellocatus said, "but I have no intention of crossing him, of course." He paused. "Tell your patron this: tell him that I am close to discovering the location of the amber cave. It's just a matter of time. I have allies in Caledonia now, men who know the land and its people. There is this woman you see, a Caledonian woman. She knows where we can find the amber and my allies have managed to track her down in the highlands. They are going to catch her and bring her to Inchtuthil. I am heading up there now. I will make this woman talk. She will guide us to the amber."

"What about the scout?" Corbulo asked. "Has there been any news at all? Do your Caledonian allies know anything?"

Vellocatus looked puzzled. "Who cares about the scout?" he muttered. "We will have the woman to guide us to the amber."

For a moment Corbulo allowed his mask to drop and his disappointment to show. Vellocatus was studying him with sudden curiosity.

"The scout was a friend of Agricola's," Corbulo said with growing desperation. "He was keen to find out what had happened to the man."

"Then why ask me?" Vellocatus retorted. "Why not send a messenger to the frontier forts to see if the scout has reported back?"

"Agricola has done so but there is no news," Corbulo replied defensively.

Vellocatus's face darkened. He stared at Corbulo with growing suspicion. The two men fell silent. Vellocatus was examining Corbulo's clothing.

"You are not acting on behalf of Agricola at all, are you?" Vellocatus said, suddenly taking a step towards Corbulo. "Who are you really?"

Corbulo made no reply. To his right the auxiliary soldier was gripping the pommel of his sword. The Briton, however, had not moved.

"I say again," Vellocatus hissed, "who are you?"

Corbulo cleared his throat. "The scout that you and Agricola tasked with finding this amber is my son. I have come looking for him."

"So you lied to me." Vellocatus's eyes bulged in their sockets.

"So did you," Corbulo replied calmly. "I can see now why Agricola ruined you. You are nothing more than an overgrown weed of a man. Your lust for wealth may have cost me my boy's life."

Vellocatus was panting.

"Get out of my sight you dumb fuck," he roared.

From the doorway of his house Vellocatus watched the stranger walk away. The man had fooled him. The stranger had tricked him into revealing what he knew about the girl and worst of all, what he was going to do. The man had known about the amber. Agricola must have told him or he must have heard it from somewhere else. It didn't matter. Vellocatus felt the violent rage building up inside him. His hand was trembling. And mixed with his anger was something else. Something he had not experienced for over seven months: fear. The stranger had managed to scare him. The man was a threat to his plans. He glanced across at Bestia and saw that the soldier was thinking about the same thing as he was.

"Did you get a good look at him?" Vellocatus growled.

Bestia nodded. His hand was still resting on the pommel of his sword.

"Good," Vellocatus nodded. He turned to Baldurix's man, who was still holding onto the reins of his horse. "Carry out the plan as we discussed. Tell Baldurix that I will meet him at Inchtuthil on the full moon. Tell him to bring the girl." Vellocatus paused and turned to look at the diminishing figure in the distance. "But before you do, kill that man. He knows too much. I don't want any rivals looking for the amber. I don't want him getting anywhere near Caledonia."

"He looks like he served in the legions," Bestia grunted. "I can always recognise old soldiers. There is something about the way they walk."

"He will be dangerous," Vellocatus snapped. "You had better be careful. But make sure that he dies."

"I think that I will do it now," Bestia said abruptly.

But Vellocatus shook his head.

"No, there are too many witnesses already. Do it outside the settlement, out on the road. Make it a painful death. I want that man to feel pain before he dies."

Chapter Twenty-Nine – The Hunter and the Hunted

Corbulo took the road north. He didn't want to stay in Eburacum. The meeting with Vellocatus had left a bad taste in his mouth. He was disappointed that the slaver had not been able to provide any further information on Marcus but it didn't matter. He was going to head north to where the Twentieth were building their new base. The place everyone called Inchtuthil. Maybe he would be able to glean some news from the soldiers. If they didn't know anything then he would head up further north along the chain of forts that the auxiliary cohorts were building until he came to the end of the world. Someone, somewhere had to know something about Marcus. He glanced back as he left the civilian settlement behind him. Some instinct was warning him about this Vellocatus. The man was profoundly immoral. Corbulo had sensed it during their conversation. He would have to be careful, he thought. The slaver looked like a man who was quite capable of murder.

A sudden restless urgency drove him onwards. If Marcus was in trouble then every hour was precious. He fought the urge to run. Discipline and a cool head was what he needed right now. He had to conserve his energy and he had to avoid injury. The steady pace that he had set himself day in day out would get him to his objective. Now was not the time to lose his head. Suddenly he felt hungry but he resisted the temptation to reach for his pack. *Come on, keep going*. He started to sing a tune that the soldiers in his company used to sing. It was the one which poked fun at their legate. They had intended to sing it whilst marching into Rome as part of their commander's triumph but that had never happened.

Soon he had left Eburacum behind. The road north was brand new and hadn't existed when he had still been on active service. So much had changed. So many new faces who didn't know him. Beyond Eburacum the gently rolling hills, forests and meadows stretched to the horizon. It was a hot day and soon Corbulo felt the sweat stinging on his back and trickling down his cheeks. In a dip between two slopes he suddenly glanced over his shoulder. To his left a thick and dense forest of bushes and fir trees came right up to the edge of the road. There was no one behind him. He paused. Then quickly he swerved and vanished into the forest. The wood was cool and dark and quiet. Some way in he crouched beside a tree and turned to look at the road. The branches and bushes obscured part of his view but despite that he could still see the rise over which he had just come. He crouched and waited. On the road nothing moved. Had he been wrong after all?

Suddenly a man appeared on the rise. The man was on horseback. He was quickly joined by another man, also mounted on a horse. The two men had halted and were staring up the road to the north. Corbulo grunted. His instinct had been right. He had been right to be cautious. It was the auxiliary soldier and his companion with the bow. So Vellocatus had sent his men after him. Question was, were they any good? He peered at the two men from his hiding place. If they were any good they would know where he would be hiding. He held his breath and willed the men to ride on up the road. His two pursuers were still staring up the road. Then the soldier swung himself onto the ground and unsheathed his sword. The metal glinted in the sunlight. The soldier had turned to look at the forest and to Corbulo it seemed as if the man was looking straight at him.

"Fuck," he muttered. They knew where he was. Quickly he glanced up at the sky. It would be another few hours before dark. He would have to hide.

He slipped away from the tree and began to run. His path took him deeper and deeper into the forest. As he ran he struggled to contain a growing panic. This was what prey must feel like, he thought. He glanced over his shoulder and thought he saw shadows moving amongst the trees. The men chasing him were younger and they would be fitter. He wouldn't be able to outrun them and the man with the bow looked like he was a hunter. He would have no problem picking up his trail. No, his only chance lay in finding a good hiding place.

He stumbled over a tree root and crashed onto the forest floor. For a moment he was winded. *Come on, get up, get moving*, an inner voice shouted at him. He stumbled on. He tried to remember what weapons he had seen the men carrying. The swords didn't frighten him but the bow, the bow was a terrifying weapon. An arrow could kill him before he even saw it coming. Oh how he hated bowmen. Those cowards who killed good men from a distance and then ran away when you closed with them. It was a pathetic way in which to fight. How could you fight back against a bowman without having a bow yourself?

He risked another glance over his shoulder but saw nothing. His breath was coming in ragged gasps and he knew he would need to pause soon. Then he saw it. A dark hole in the ground that was just wide enough for a thin man to crawl into. He fell to his knees and peered inside. The hole seemed to have no bottom. Behind him he suddenly heard an excited shout.

"Fuck," he muttered. They were closer than he'd thought. Without hesitation he thrust himself feet first into the earth and began to wriggle downwards. The hole turned out to be a tunnel and it was narrow. Thankfully he had lost a lot of weight during his long journey. He wriggled deeper until his head disappeared under the ground. Suddenly he felt the tunnel widen and he found himself in a tight little cavern. It was pitch black apart from the circle of sky at the end of the tunnel through which he had just come. Then his eyes widened in alarm as he heard a growl. His hand brushed against fur and then sharp teeth sank into his arm. He cried out more in shock than in pain. The animal that had bitten him, however, was not an adult beast. Its teeth were more like those of a kitten.

The animal growled again. Corbulo, ignoring the pain in his arm, fumbled for the beast, was bitten again and then clamped his hands around the animal's snout.

"Silence," he hissed.

From outside the hole he heard a sudden shout.

"See him?" a man shouted.

"He was here a minute ago," another voice replied.

Corbulo heard the crunch of footsteps drawing closer. The two men were close to the tunnel entrance now, practically standing on top of him. Would they be able to see him in the darkness?

"Wolf's den," one of the voices said. "Do you reckon that he crawled in there?" Corbulo felt his heart thumping in his chest. He had crawled into a wolf's den! The animal was trying to break free from his grip but the cub lacked the strength. Suddenly a sword was scraping away at the entrance to the tunnel. Then the sword vanished and a moment later an arrow embedded itself into the earth close to his head. Corbulo reacted without thinking and hurled the wolf cub out of the tunnel. The cub tumbled head over heels, hit the tunnel wall, landed on his feet and shot out of the den. Corbulo pressed his face into the cool earth and waited for the next arrow. Then he heard a man laughing.

"Look at the little fellow go. He can't be down there. Perhaps in the stomach of a wolf but not alive. No, I think he went that way. Let's search that ridge up there. He's an old man, he won't go far."

Corbulo raised his head. His eyes had finally adjusted themselves to the darkness. Where was the pup's mother? Off hunting? She wouldn't be gone for long. Outside he could hear nothing.

"It will be growing dark soon," one of the men said suddenly.

"Doesn't matter," the other said from further away. "He has got to die. You heard what Vellocatus said. Come on, let's find him and finish it."

Chapter Thirty – The Broken Hypocaust

It was dark when Corbulo crawled out onto the forest floor. The wolf had not returned. Maybe the pup's mother had caught his scent in her den and thought it wise to find another home. If she had returned, Corbulo thought grimly, she would have got his sword straight between the eyes. For a moment he crouched under a large pine listening to the noises in the night. It was a cloudless sky and a multitude of stars twinkled in the blackness. Satisfied, he slipped quietly through the trees in the direction in which he thought the road was. His pursuers would expect him to take the road but he had little choice. Following the road would be the fastest way to Inchtuthil. He couldn't waste any more time. But he would travel at night from now on and rest up during the day. The road was easy enough to follow in the darkness. But the whole episode with Vellocatus had left him annoyed and irritated. The amber and Vellocatus had complicated his search for Marcus just when he didn't need it. Suddenly he wished he had never approached the slaver, that he had not listened to Agricola's advice, but it was too late for that now.

He crouched in the bushes beside the road and paused to listen but all seemed as it should be. Keep going north along the military road and you will eventually reach Inchtuthil, the merchant in Eburacum had told him. Inchtuthil is the gateway into Caledonia. It should take you ten days on foot, the merchant had added. Fat chance of that, Corbulo thought. He took a piece of stale bread from his pack and ate it in a slow and measured way. On the journey from Rome he had learned to eat something every twelve hours. The quantity didn't matter. If he ate his food slowly the hunger in his stomach would recede for a while. Another trick was to fill his belly with water but he hadn't seen any streams since he had left Eburacum. He tried to remember what the two assassins looked like. He had only given them a cursory examination when he'd seen them standing outside Vellocatus's door. They seemed an odd couple. The Briton was no soldier. He had looked more like a tribesman, a hunter. What were an auxiliary soldier, a slaver and a Briton tribesman doing together? He frowned and shook his head. He'd been right about Vellocatus though. The man wanted him dead. It was probably because of the amber. He, Corbulo, knew too much. Vellocatus would see him as a threat. He understood that. There would be many desperate men stupid enough to have a go at finding the amber if they knew about it. But to murder a man solely based on what he knew from hearsay, without any evidence, that was not right.

It was dawn when he woke. He was lying in a drainage ditch beside the road. The ditch was bone dry. Cursing he scrambled to his feet and looked around him. He had intended to walk by night and rest up during the day but somehow his exhaustion had got the better of him. "Damn fool," he cursed himself. He relaxed slightly as he saw that no one was about. Then he noticed the wheat field a hundred paces away up the road. Wild blackberry bushes grew alongside the border of the field. He licked his lips: food. As he started towards the blackberry bushes he thought he heard a noise but when he looked round he saw nothing. He had just stuffed his mouth with the juicy forest fruits and had bent to pick up the one he had dropped when an arrow shot through the space where his head had been a moment before. He turned and his heart nearly stopped. Running towards him from the road were two men. One of them was fitting an arrow to his bow as he ran. Corbulo grabbed his pack and crashed through the bushes and into the wheat field beyond. Behind him he heard a shout and then another arrow zipped past him. Corbulo ran. How could he have not noticed them approaching? How could he have been so stupid? He had to be more exhausted than he realised. He tore on through the field. There would be no hiding place here. Another arrow whistled past him and instinctively he ducked. He snatched a glance over his shoulder. The auxiliary soldier was ahead of his companion. The man was gaining on him. There would be no point in turning and fighting it out. They would not give him a fair fight. The bowman would kill him from a distance. *Run.*

Suddenly as the field ended he saw sunlight reflecting on water. Beyond the field was a river. The water looked slow-moving and not very wide but its banks were steep and covered in nettles and tall reeds. He sprinted towards the river. His breath was coming in ragged gasps. How far behind him were they – thirty, forty paces? He leapt from the bank and crashed into the water. The coldness was shocking but he hardly felt it. He gasped and struggled his way into the dense tangle of reeds. The current was surprisingly strong and tugged at his body. He pushed himself deep into the water as his feet scrabbled on the riverbed to find a firm footing. Then when only his nose and eyes were above the water level he stopped moving. A moment later, through the reeds, he saw the auxiliary appear on the riverbank above him. The assassin stared at the ripples in the river. The man had a sword in his hand. Then he began to search amongst the reeds. Corbulo stared at him, willing him to pass on.

"He's hiding in the reeds," the man cried out.

The bowman appeared alongside his companion on the riverbank.

"Go fifty paces downriver and we'll work our way towards each other," the auxiliary barked. He turned towards the reeds. "You are not going to escape this time," he shouted at the riverbank.

The bowman moved out of view.

Suddenly a duck sprang quacking into the air from where Corbulo had disturbed it. Corbulo's eyes widened. The assassin was only a few paces away.

"I see him," the auxiliary yelled, pointing a finger.

Without hesitating Corbulo rose, took a deep breath and flung himself into the middle of the river. Frantically he kicked his feet to give himself some propulsion. He lost his grip on his pack. Behind him something large plunged into the water. Corbulo lashed out with his arms as the current seized him and bore him downstream. The auxiliary was in the river behind him, swimming after him, his sword held in his teeth. Where was the bowman? Wildly Corbulo stared up at the riverbank. Then he saw him. The Briton had notched an arrow to his bow and was taking careful aim. Corbulo sucked air into his lungs and disappeared underwater. The arrow hit the river a split second later and scraped along the skin of his left arm. Corbulo burst from the water, his lungs heaving. Lashing out he grabbed hold of a branch from an old willow tree beside the riverbank and pulled himself up and out of the water. He had no time to see what the bowman on the opposite bank was doing. As he flung himself up the riverbank an arrow buried itself into his left shoulder. Corbulo screamed and fell forwards onto the muddy embankment. Adrenaline was pumping into his veins. He was not going to die like this. He was going to find Marcus. With a savage roar Corbulo clawed himself up the riverbank. Ignoring the searing pain in his shoulder he reached the top and collapsed into cover behind the willow. In the river the auxiliary was yelling out instructions to the bowman who was crying out in protest and seemed reluctant to join him.

His chest was heaving with exhaustion, his wet clothes were weighing him down but the pain in his shoulder was far worse. This was the fourth time he had been wounded in his life. Grimacing, he risked a peek around the tree. The archer had his bow aimed straight at him. Corbulo pulled his head back just in time as an arrow zipped past his head. Then he was up on his feet and ignoring the screaming protests of his body, scrambling away through the bushes. *Run, run, you old bastard*, an inner voice screamed.

From somewhere he found the strength. He ripped and tore his body and tunic on the thorns and brambles but he didn't feel the cuts. It was as if his mind was blocking out the pain. Then he was through the bushes. Ahead was an open field and beyond that a ruined building.

He staggered across the field expecting another arrow but nothing came and when he snatched a glance behind him he saw only the auxiliary in pursuit. The man too seemed to be tiring. With a savage movement he reached across to his left shoulder with his right hand and snapped the arrow shaft in two. He bellowed in pain as a gush of blood welled up from his wound. His leather torso armour must have slowed the arrow down but the iron head remained embedded in his shoulder and his left arm dangled uselessly at his side. He bit his lip and bellowed again. The pain could not be denied any longer. Up ahead the ruin looked deserted. Corbulo staggered towards it. He would make his stand in the ruin. He still had his sword and his right arm.

He struggled into the courtyard. The ruin must once have been a farmhouse for it had a barn and a crumbling enclosure where cattle would once have been kept. In the middle of the courtyard was a well. The barn had burnt down. Corbulo stared at the jumble of charred and broken beams and stones. Weeds were growing up amongst the rubble. No one had lived here for years. The roof of the farmhouse had collapsed inwards but the stone walls were still standing. He came to a halt in the middle of the courtyard, pulled his sword from its scabbard and turned to face his pursuer.

Just then he heard something that made him turn. In the meadow just beyond the ruin, a black horse was staring across at him. Corbulo stared back at the beast as a sudden spark of hope came to him. He sheathed his sword and staggered into the ruined farmhouse just as the auxiliary burst into the courtyard. Corbulo stared at him through a crack in the wall as he tried to calm his heaving chest and catch his breath. The man had stopped in his tracks and was staring around at the ruined buildings. He was still alone. Maybe his companion could not swim or was afraid of crossing the river? But the bowman would surely not be far behind. Corbulo edged away from the doorway through which he had come and looked around at the debris and rubble that littered the house. Part of the floor was still visible and a few floor tiles had been ripped away, exposing the dark cavity of the under-floor heating system, the hypocaust. Corbulo crouched, lowered his feet through the hole and then dropped down through the floor into the space below. It was cramped but just high enough for him to crawl through on his stomach. Dozens of small pillars made of brick held up the floor above. As silently as possible he began to crawl away into the darkness. The arrow head in his shoulder was a dull ache now and his left arm was useless. He bit his lip until it bled. To his right he suddenly caught a glimpse of daylight. He turned and started to crawl towards the light. Then he froze as above him, he heard footsteps crunching on broken tiles.

"Come on out and fight me like a proper man. I am tired of all this running," a voice snarled in Latin.

Corbulo closed his eyes as he struggled to keep quiet.

"What's the matter with you," the voice above him called out. "Are you afraid, old man? Afraid you will piss yourself when you die?"

The man fell silent. Corbulo edged forwards and with his right hand reached out to touch the crack in the wall through which the daylight was streaming in. Whoever had built the wall had done a shoddy job. He pushed against the stones. Nothing. He pushed harder, gritting his teeth and this time one of them moved. He pushed again and one of the stones clattered away and the crack had turned into a small hole. Beyond the hole he could make out a green meadow and trees. Above him there came a triumphant cry.

"I knew you were hiding down there."

Corbulo raised his head and saw that the auxiliary had jumped down into the hole in the floor. Frantically he pushed at the stones with all his strength. Another came loose and then another tumbled away. From the hole in the floor he heard a shuffling noise. The man was under the floor and crawling towards him. Corbulo tore at the masonry in desperation. The hole was widening. Fuck, it would have to do. He heaved himself forwards and pushed his head through the hole. The stones scraped sharply against his skin and shoulders and he screamed in sudden agony. From close by he heard laughter. Then the man was coming for him, skittering like a running crab. With a savage thrust Corbulo wrenched his body through the hole and rolled out into the meadow and the sunlight. The shuffling noise under the floor had stopped. Corbulo grimaced and touched his shoulder. Then he edged up to the hole he had made. He paused as he brought his breathing under control.

"Now why don't you stick your ugly head out here," he cried.

There was no reply from his pursuer. Corbulo glanced at his shoulder wound. His leather torso armour was soaked black with blood. Gods he was tired. He'd lost his pack in the river. His pack had contained all his food. He glanced down at the hole and drew his sword. The auxiliary was the one trapped now but his companion, the bowman, was still out there. Wearily Corbulo leaned his head against the wall and closed his eyes.

"You are an idiot; you auxiliaries always were."

"Fuck off," came the muffled reply.

Corbulo opened his eyes and glanced at the black horse in the meadow. The beast had turned and was looking straight at him.

"Tell Vellocatus that I have no interest in the amber," Corbulo said. "I am not here for that. I just want to find my son. Tell him that his business is his own and that I don't want anything to do with him."

"It's too late for that," came the reply from inside the house.

Corbulo closed his eyes in disappointment. Then he forced himself up onto his feet and stumbled towards the horse. The beast tossed its head and stepped backwards as Corbulo gently stroked its nose.

"Blessed Epona must have sent you herself," Corbulo muttered. Then he swung himself on to the horse's back. The beast made no attempt to throw him.

"North, we go north," he whispered into the horse's ear as he held onto her long dark neck. "Now ride."

Chapter Thirty-One – Inchtuthil

It was early evening. The legionary fortress of Inchtuthil, with two labour camps close by, nestled on a small plateau on the northern bank of the Tay river. The turf ramparts that protected the rectangular fortress had been completed but the stone cladding was still not finished in parts. A V-shaped ditch ran alongside the wall to the gap in the rampart where one of the gatehouses was being built. The two guards on duty beside the unfinished gate stood in their wooden watchtower looking bored. After a hard day's construction work most of the legionaries of the Twentieth Legion had retired to their tents and cooking fires inside the labour camps. To the south across the shallow sand-banked river a simple wooden bridge connected the fortress to the path that led away into the forest. The light was fading fast when a figure on a horse appeared on the path. The beast crossed the bridge and swung left towards the two guards on their high platform.

One of the guards called down to his comrades below and a moment later four fully armed legionaries stepped out to bar the stranger's way. The rider was half hanging off his horse and he looked to be in a bad state.

"Quintus," the man muttered as one of the soldiers caught hold of the horse's mane. "Centurion Quintus of the First Company, Eighth Cohort, is that you?"

Then the rider slid from his horse and tumbled onto the ground.

Corbulo opened his eyes. He was lying on a camp bed in a large hall. Someone had placed an army blanket over him. The hot throbbing pain in his shoulder had gone and so had the fever. He raised his hand and wiped his forehead. He was still sweating but it wasn't as bad as it had been. He twisted his neck and drew back the blanket. A clean white bandage had been wrapped around his left shoulder. He lay back and closed his eyes in relief. His memories were blurred and confused. He remembered the horse and the jarring, cutting pain in his shoulder. The pain had got worse until he had hardly dared to move. Then the fever had come, bathing him in sweat and sucking the strength from his body.

A man wearing a leather apron was coming towards him. Corbulo raised his head and stared at him. The man was a Roman. Nearby he suddenly heard someone cough. He turned his head and noticed that he was not the only wounded man in the hall. The soldiers on either side of him looked pale and ill. Corbulo lay back and stared up at the wooden-beamed ceiling. He was in an army hospital. How had he got here? Where was he? What had happened to the horse?

"You are awake," he heard a man say in Latin.

A moment later the man with the leather apron was standing over him. He looked like an army doctor and there was something strangely familiar about him. The man touched Corbulo's forehead, grunted and gave his patient a stern look.

"Good to see you pulled through, Corbulo. If you had arrived here a day later I don't think you would have made it. That fever was eating you alive. You don't recognise me, do you?" the doctor said with a faint smile.

Corbulo stared up at the man, his mind racing. Then his eyes bulged as he remembered why the man looked familiar.

"You are the doctor who patched me up after I got that stab wound on Mona. That was what, seven years ago?"

The doctor nodded. "Welcome back to the Twentieth, Corbulo. You are at Inchtuthil, our new base. Give it another year and they will have finally finished building the place. I am a bit surprised to see you though. I thought you had retired and packed yourself off to Italy?"

Corbulo sighed. "I have – I am here on a personal matter." He paused and his face suddenly grew alarmed. "How long have I been here?"

"You have been more or less unconscious for eight days. I managed to remove that arrowhead from your shoulder," the doctor replied. "You should really have had that looked at earlier. The wound had got infected. That's why you got the fever. You were also exhausted. We had to force-feed you with porridge. It's the only thing you wouldn't throw up." The doctor shook his head. "I suppose you don't remember a thing about that, do you?"

Corbulo shook his head. Eight days! He had wasted eight days. He closed his eyes.

"But I am going to be alright now, am I not, Doc?"

"Yes, you are healing well but you need to rest. If you were still with the legion I would order you to stay here for at least another week. You need to regain your strength. You are not a young man anymore, Corbulo."

Corbulo was staring up at the ceiling.

"I remember now, I remember asking to see Quintus; he's the centurion of the First Company, Eighth Cohort. Is he here?"

The doctor nodded. "The guard brought you to him and he brought you here. I will go and tell him that you are awake."

The doctor turned to leave but Corbulo caught his arm. He managed a grin.

"Thank you, Doc; it feels good to be back with the legion," he said.

"Well fuck the sacred chickens, he's awake at last," Quintus bellowed as he caught sight of Corbulo lying on his camp bed. The centurion was clad in full armour and was wearing his centurion's helmet with its broad cheek guards, circular brass bosses and red horse-hair plume. Oblivious to the other wounded and ill men in the hall he strode straight towards Corbulo. Quintus was a big powerful man with a broken nose. He stopped beside Corbulo's bed and the two men shook hands in the legionary way.

"It's good to see you, Quintus," Corbulo grinned. "After my retirement I didn't think I would ever see you again but here you are and here I am."

"You look like shit," Quintus grinned. "I couldn't believe it when the watch commander carried you into my tent. You were half dead. What happened? What are you doing here? I thought you had gone back to Italy?"

Corbulo nodded. "You heard about my woman, didn't you. She killed herself."

Quintus's face grew solemn. "Yes I heard about that," he muttered.

"You remember Marcus, my son," Corbulo continued. "He signed up with the Second Batavians. A few months ago I heard that he had gone missing here in Caledonia. So I have come to find him." Corbulo looked up at his friend. "Have you heard anything from Marcus? Anything at all – rumours, gossip, any news? Doesn't matter if it's completely stupid."

Quintus shook his head. "No, I haven't heard anything. The Second Batavians are garrisoning some of the forts to the south of here. I didn't know that he had been listed as missing. Ah, that's bad news. I am sorry."

Corbulo looked disappointed. "Well I am going to find him, even if I have to go to the end of the world," he said.

Quintus nodded and folded his arms across his chest.

"These Caledonians," he said wearily, "they don't want peace. They don't want us here. They are too afraid of us to stand and fight in a proper battle. Instead they sulk in their forests and amongst their mountains and attack us when we least expect it. They don't do much damage but every ambush manages to kill one or two of our men. Then they flee back into the hills." Quintus sighed. "My men's morale is low. They want to fight but how do you fight against an enemy who acts like a ghost? It's the same with the auxiliary cohorts. Everyone is fed up with this kind of warfare. I wish Agricola was back in charge. He would put an end to this shit."

"Is it as bad as that?" Corbulo said, looking up from his bed.

Quintus nodded. "I was there at Mons Graupius. We all thought that would be the end of it, but it seems it was only the start."

"I can't believe they made you a centurion," Corbulo said with a wry smile. "How long is it before you retire from the legion?"

Quintus grinned. "I retire at the end of this year!" he exclaimed. "Makes you think that the legate was doing an old comrade a favour doesn't it. Shit, I served this legion for nearly twenty-five years and they only make me a centurion in my final year. I should have been an officer years ago."

Corbulo swung his legs onto the ground and stood up. For a moment he felt the earth sway beneath him. He steadied himself and turned towards Quintus. "Thank you, old friend, for what you have done for me. You saved my life. I cannot repay you for that now but I promise that I will remember and Marcus and I will look you up when this is all over. Now I must be on my way. I have wasted enough time already."

Quintus caught his arm.

"But not today, Corbulo," the big centurion said with a gentle shake of his head. "You can stay here for today. Tonight come to my tent and let's talk about old times. I would like that."

For a moment Corbulo looked undecided. Then he nodded.

"Let's talk about old times," he muttered.

Chapter Thirty-Two – The Twentieth Valeria Victrix

Corbulo rose from his sick bed at noon unable to contain his curiosity any longer. He was back with his old legion. He just had to have a look around and see if he recognised some old faces. The fever had broken but he still felt weak. Dressing himself in the new plain white tunic that Quintus had given him, he strapped on his gladius and leather torso armour and slipped his cloak over his shoulders. It was a beautiful day and the sun hung in a clear blue sky.

A work party of soldiers were labouring away on top of the turf ramparts and Corbulo climbed up to join them and to get a better view of the camp. The men ignored him. Corbulo grunted in satisfaction. Inchtuthil was a well chosen site, he thought as he surveyed the construction. He had expected nothing less. The Twentieth were after all the finest legion in the Roman army. The closeness of the Tay gave the fortress added protection whilst also providing the troops with fresh drinking water and access to seaborne supplies. Yes, it was a good location. He nodded in approval. Placing the camp just north of the river was yet another subtle message to the hostile tribes that Rome meant to conquer all the island of Britannia and not just defend the richest parts. As he stood staring down at the construction works Corbulo felt an upwelling of pride and for a brief moment he longed to be part of the legion again, the place he had called home for twenty-five years.

In the forest he could hear work parties chopping down trees and as he watched a large pine slowly toppled over and crashed into the woods. It was followed by the shouts of the wood cutters. Further to the north on the horizon he could just make out a line of heavily forested hills disappearing away to the north-east. How much more land was there beyond those hills? Did Britannia really stretch all the way to Hyperborea? He turned to look into the camp. The legionaries had only just started building the legion's huge granaries and workshops that would hold their winter food supplies and repair the legion's baggage train and the men's equipment. The barracks buildings, all sixty-four of them, were in an advanced state of completion but in the very centre of the fortress, on a clearly marked-out area. The soldiers still had to make a start on the legion's HQ where the legate and senior officers would be billeted and where the legionary standards, war diary and pay chest would be kept. The area had been levelled and prepared, but for now it was still covered in grass. The camp was crawling with soldiers and work parties. The shouts of officers and men mingled with the sound of sawing, hammering, the whinnying of horses, the rumble of carts and the bellowing of oxen. Beyond the main camp Corbulo saw the neat white tents standing in endless rows within the labour camps. Eight men would be assigned to a single tent. He grinned as the site brought back memories good and bad. Damn, he had missed the legion.

As he stared absentmindedly into the camp, a long supply convoy of carts pulled by oxen came rolling down the track from the south. The foremost carts were filled with thousands and thousands of long, shiny, brand-new iron nails. Corbulo started walking along the top of the turf ramparts. A wooden palisade was being built along the top and he had to be careful not to get in the way of the soldiers' work. Here and there he ran into an old comrade and the two of them would shake hands and have a brief chat before the men were called back to work. Corbulo had a broad grin on his face when a sentry high up in one of the tall wooden watchtowers suddenly cried out a warning.

"He's back, down by the river, look!"

The work party on the southern ramparts stopped what they were doing and every man turned to look in the direction in which the sentry was pointing. At the edge of the river on the southern bank, a hundred paces or so away, a big dog had appeared from out of the forest. The dog sat down and stared towards the fort.

"What is he doing?" Corbulo asked a soldier nearby.

The legionary gave Corbulo a quick examining glance. "He appeared yesterday," the soldier replied. "Just sits there by the river until our men try and catch him. Then he runs away.

Look, he's a big fellow, probably one of these Briton war dogs. He will be valuable."

Corbulo stared at the dog sitting across the river. The beast sat perfectly still. A spiked iron collar hung around his neck.

"Seems like he's waiting for someone or something," Corbulo muttered.

Corbulo was making his way back through the labour camp towards Quintus's tent when he suddenly froze. Ten paces away three men and a young woman had just emerged from a tent. The woman had a black eye and around her neck an iron ring shackled her to a slaver's chain. Corbulo didn't recognise her. She looked miserable and her eyes were cast down towards the ground. But it was not the woman that made Corbulo gasp. The three men were talking to each other. One of them gripped the end of the chain to which the woman was fastened as if she were a dog on a leash. Corbulo's hand dropped to the pommel of his sword. It was Vellocatus and his two assassins, the auxiliary soldier and the bowman. What were they doing here? For a fleeting moment Corbulo wanted to run but his legs refused to move. Vellocatus had not yet seen him. Then another man emerged from the tent. He was big and tall and looked like a Caledonian warrior. Corbulo did not recognise him but the four men seemed to know each other.

"Heh, fuck face, yes, you," Corbulo suddenly called out. "I want to talk to you."

Corbulo boldly took a step forwards. Vellocatus turned and his face went pale with shock. At his side the auxiliary suddenly looked embarrassed. Corbulo took another step forwards and pointed his finger at Vellocatus.

"Welcome to the Twentieth Legion, arsehole. I served in this legion for twenty-five years and I still have many friends here. Now I told your boy there that I have no interest in your business. I am here to look for my son. But he didn't seem to understand that. So I am going to tell you what is going to happen. You are going to leave me alone or else I am going to tell the whole legion about your little secret up north." Corbulo took another step forwards. "Now do we understand each other?"

Vellocatus was staring at Corbulo as if he was lost for words. He made no reply. Around them the legionaries had turned to see what was going on. Corbulo glanced at the girl but she didn't look up. Then he looked at the auxiliary soldier who was smirking at him.

"And if I see you again," Corbulo pointed his finger at the man, "I will kill you."

Then without another word Corbulo turned and walked away. His hand, however, did not leave the pommel of his sword until he had vanished amongst the rows and rows of white tents.

It was evening and Corbulo sat in Quintus's tent. The centurion of the First Company, Eighth Cohort, had a double-sized tent which also acted as the company's official area and where the unit's standard and trumpets were kept until the permanent quarters could be completed. The two men were alone. Quintus was cleaning his helmet and Corbulo was trying to mend the hole in his leather torso armour that the arrow had created. A fire ringed by stones spat and crackled close by.

"So you say that these men attacked you on the road from Eburacum?" Quintus said, looking serious.

Corbulo nodded as he passed the bone needle and thread through the leather. "They did. I am sure it's to do with this amber cave they talked about. I tried to warn them off but they don't seem to listen. I don't know what else I can do."

"The fourth man you described, the Caledonian," Quintus looked thoughtful, "I have heard of him. His name is Baldurix; he is a chief of the Decantae. They are our only allies amongst the native tribes. Baldurix is an important man. He speaks regularly with the legate when he comes here. If this Vellocatus is his friend then he will enjoy Baldurix's protection. You won't be able to touch them."

"I know," Corbulo said wearily, "but I could really do without their interference. I am here to find Marcus."

Quintus was silent as he finished polishing his helmet and started on his body armour.

"They had a girl with them. She had a slave chain around her neck," Corbulo said at last. He paused. "When I first met Vellocatus he mentioned that a girl was going to lead him to the amber cave. There was some sort of arrangement with his northern allies by which I presume he means Baldurix. I wonder if that was the girl which he mentioned? If so it looks like Vellocatus will be heading north too." Corbulo looked up at his friend. "I am going to leave at dawn tomorrow. I know you can't hold these arseholes but perhaps you could delay them for a while? I just need a few hours to get clear."

Quintus stopped polishing and glanced at Corbulo.

"I will see what I can do," he said.

Corbulo nodded his appreciation. The two men were silent for a while as they both worked on their chores.

"So have you given any thought to where you will retire?" Corbulo asked.

Quintus nodded, "I have. I am going to stay here in Britannia. It seems a fair decision after all the time that I have spent here. There is a hill, some six miles due south of Londinium. It's heavily forested but from there you have fine views for miles around including the city. I will buy my land there and build myself a farm and marry a fat local girl who doesn't mind an old soldier who farts in bed."

Corbulo grinned as he remembered the first time that he had met Quintus. His friend had been a few years younger than him. The Twentieth had been ordered to march west into the land of the Ordovices. There had been a lot of trouble that year. It had been the year that Governor Paulinus had destroyed the druids and Londinium had been burnt to the ground. It had been the year when Roman control over Britannia had nearly been lost for good. The Twentieth had known nothing about this when they had marched off into the bleak, lawless western hills to confront the druids across the straits that separated Mona

Insulis from the main land. Corbulo would never forget the sight of the fierce Celtic warriors lining the opposite shore or the Celtic women flitting in between them screaming for blood, or the white-robed priests holding hands in circles and calling down the wrath of the gods upon the heads of the Romans. The crazy and outlandish appearance of their enemy and the invocation of divine aid had struck terror into the hearts of the Roman assault companies. The druids had not feared death, they had been looking forward to it, and for a moment it had seemed as if the Roman attack was going to stall before it had even begun. But Governor Paulinus had been an experienced soldier; tough, cruel and unforgiving. He had ridden out amongst his men, shaming them for their cowardice and superstition, and the troops had finally grown ashamed and humiliated and had responded with a frenzy of blood. Corbulo and Quintus had been in the same assault boat as they had crossed the straits. They had been the first boat to come ashore. During the amphibious assault Quintus had been knocked out of the boat and had nearly drowned. It was Corbulo who had pulled him out of the water. The two men had been friends ever since.

"Do you remember that Agricola wanted to be on the first boat to hit the enemy shore at Mona," Corbulo said with a short shake of his head.

"Agricola was a prick," Quintus muttered with a faint smile. "He really did believe that that would get him noticed by the governor."

"Well he must have done something right. He managed to make it all the way to the top, didn't he," Corbulo replied. "Unlike us," he added with a grin.

"He did," Quintus conceded, "and I wish he was with us now."

The two of them were silent for a while as each seemed lost in his own memories. Finally Quintus laid his armour aside and rubbed his face with both hands.

"So what are you going to do now, Corbulo?"

Corbulo was staring at his leather armour. "I will go north," he said, "follow the supply routes that lead from fort to fort until I come to the end of the world. Someone in those forts must know something."

"And if they don't and you cannot find Marcus, what then? Do not be caught out by the winter. It's hell," Quintus replied.

Corbulo looked up at his friend and smiled. "I will find him. Marcus is alive."

Quintus looked away.

"You don't think I am doing the right thing?" Corbulo asked.

"I think you are desperate," Quintus replied with a sigh. "Desperate men die. Have you not considered that Marcus may be dead? Is throwing away your own life going to change that? Maybe you should stay here. Come back south with me at the end of the year when I retire. I could use a good man around the farm."

But Corbulo shook his head. "Maybe I am desperate like you say," he muttered, "but I have to try. I have promised my wife that I will try. I won't turn back now." Corbulo paused. "Would you be able to get a horse for me?"

Quintus shook his head. "No, they are in short supply as it is. The tribunes will never allow it, especially if the man is a civilian." He paused. "I can get you some provisions for the journey though. You looked all bone and no meat when you first arrived here; you still do."

Corbulo nodded his thanks.

"The hills and forests north of here are crawling with hostile tribesmen," Quintus said, staring sharply at his friend. "Our supply convoys have to have a strong escort just to get through. Stay off the main pathways and if they do catch you then you had better have a good story prepared. The Caledonians have a habit of nailing Roman prisoners to trees. I have seen their work myself."

"Same odds as against Boudica." Corbulo tried to smile.

"No," Quintus said, looking serious, "you are going to get yourself killed, Corbulo."

Chapter Thirty-Three – A Grey Friend

It was still dark when Corbulo slipped out of the labour camp. There was no moon and the sentries strolling along the ramparts did not see him go. Corbulo crouched in the field beyond the fortress and turned to listen. Nothing. The night was silent yet he felt uneasy, as if some instinct, born from a lifetime's soldiering, was trying to tell him something. He rose and set off eastwards, skirting the second labour camp until he came to the river. The water gurgled and splashed against unseen rocks and somewhere close by he heard an owl. Quietly he waded into the river. The water came up to his waist and he gasped at the cold. He was clad in his tough leather torso armour over which he wore an old palla, an army overcoat, with a hood. From his belt hung his gladius. He used the pilum, the spear that Quintus had given him, as a support as he struggled across the river. His old friend had been as good as his word. The centurion had managed to get him two weeks' grain rations, which he carried in a bag slung over his back.

"I shall ask the patrols to keep an eye open for you," Quintus had said, putting a hand on Corbulo's shoulder. There had been a touching concern in his old friend's voice. "Try and return before winter. Without shelter you won't survive up in those hills. You have no idea how cold, wet and dark it can get."

Corbulo struggled onto the southern bank and leaned against a tree, catching his breath. He was not yet fully recovered from his fever but he didn't dare waste any more time. Marcus needed him. He glanced towards the silent Roman fortress and suddenly he felt very alone. He was leaving his friends and the Twentieth behind. He could expect no help from them. He had deliberately crossed the river in order to confuse anyone who was maybe watching or waiting for him. With a bit of luck Vellocatus and his men would think he'd gone south. He would indeed go south for a while before turning and doubling back north again. From then onwards his path would take him north from Roman outpost to outpost into a war zone. Quintus had made him memorise the Roman forts from a map he'd shown him and he'd worked out the distance and time it would take to move from one to the next. His mastery of the Briton language was good for he had spent twenty-five years learning it but his accent would give him away. There was no way he could pass himself off as a local. He had planned for this moment ever since he'd left Rome. He'd been intending to pass himself off as a wandering merchant selling the wood carvings he'd made during the long lonely nights on the road but all the carvings had been in his pack and he'd lost his pack in the river when the auxiliary soldier had tried to kill him. There had been no time to devise an alternative cover. If the locals did catch him he would have to tell them the truth and hope for the best.

Dawn brought rain. The grey rain came streaming in from the west. Corbulo pulled his hood over his head and plodded on. The forest path he was following was narrow and twisting and he could hardly see what was around the next bend. The forest itself was in full bloom for it was high summer. Small animals scuttled away into the undergrowth as he approached and here and there, despite the rain, a butterfly danced on the breeze. The forest air was cool. Quintus had talked about highlands to the north which were devoid of trees, desolate places of stone where only sheep and fugitives lived. He had talked too about long winding river valleys, covered in perpetual mist and treacherous marshes that sucked men to their deaths. He had spoken of thousands of tiny flies that ate a man alive in the summer. *Maybe Rome was not meant to conquer Caledonia, maybe we should leave this cursed land to its inhabitants*, Quintus had muttered.

A sudden movement in the undergrowth caught his eye. Instantly Corbulo froze and lowered his spear in the direction from which the movement had come. Something was moving towards him. He steadied himself. A moment later a huge grey dog with a collar of metal spikes appeared, blocking the path up ahead. The beast's yellow eyes were staring straight at him. The dog opened its mouth in a silent yawn and gave Corbulo a glimpse of a row of large razor-sharp teeth. Corbulo slowly blew the air from his mouth. It was the same dog that he had seen sitting beside the river outside Inchtuthil only yesterday. What was the beast doing here? Then he saw what was wrong. The dog was limping. There was something wrong with one of its paws.

Leave the animal, go around it, he thought, but his legs refused to move. He stared at the dog with mounting indecision.

"Alright, let's see what's the matter with you," he said at last. If the war dog had wanted to attack him it would have done so already and if it didn't want his help then it would run away. Corbulo started towards the animal. The dog did not move. As Corbulo approached the animal emitted a low growl but it made no effort to run away.

"Alright, dog," Corbulo muttered as he stooped and gingerly lifted up the animal's paw. It was as he had expected. Several large thorns had torn their way into the flesh. Gently he removed them one by one. Then he let go of the leg and stepped back. The war dog was panting gently. Its yellow eyes were looking up at him.

"I don't have any food that I can share with you," Corbulo muttered. "Now go on, get out of here."

The dog did not move and its tail was swishing to and fro as if it was waiting for orders.

Corbulo frowned. It was a crazy thought but worth a try. "Go on, get out of here," he repeated speaking in the Briton language this time. The dog barked, turned and padded away into the undergrowth.

Corbulo watched it go. Then he smiled. Of course, the dog didn't understand Latin. It only understood the local language.

Up ahead the forest had begun to thin out and soon he was plodding across open fields and rolling hills. The land looked rich and fertile and now and then he noticed a field of crops and sheep. There were signs too that large animals had passed along the path. But he saw no people or settlements. It was as if the Caledonians had hidden themselves away from the outside world. For a while he followed a stream, checking his progress by the position of the sun in the sky. At one point

167

he saw smoke curling upwards from a small wood. *The people are sullen and resentful and easily angered*, Quintus had told him. *It is best to avoid them. They seem to reject the delights of Roman civilisation and stubbornly cling to their own traditions and customs. They are not interested in our civilisation. They honour their gods by throwing valuable objects into sacred lakes. They feud over the smallest insult. They paint their faces. They follow their druids. They are true barbarians.*

It was late in the afternoon when the pounding of hooves made Corbulo glance over his shoulder.

"No," he whispered in dismay.

Two men on horseback had emerged from the forest behind him and were galloping towards him. One of them was carrying a large bow strapped to his back. How had they managed to find him? Corbulo wanted to scream in despair but instead he started to run even though he knew it was pointless. He could not outrun men on horseback, men armed with bow and arrow. He made it to a small copse of trees and tangled undergrowth. His chest was heaving. It was not much of a defensive position but he couldn't go on. He turned to face his pursuers and lifted his spear into a throwing position. How suddenly he had come to the end of the road. He wasn't fated to find Marcus after all. He was going to die right here amongst these trees. He would meet his son in the afterlife.

He glared at the two riders as they came towards him. They were coming on without hurry now. They too knew that he was caught. The men halted fifteen paces away and carefully got down from their horses.

"Go back – I shall take at least one of you with me," Corbulo growled.

The auxiliary soldier sneered at him. The man had a large angry bruise around his eye that hadn't been there yesterday when Corbulo had confronted him.

"Hello, grandpa," the auxiliary snarled. "Thought you could leave without saying goodbye. We're not very happy about that."

"I told you that if I saw you again I would kill you," Corbulo snapped. "Now let's get on with it. I am not going to run from you any longer. It ends here." Corbulo aimed his spear at the auxiliary and pretended to throw it.

The auxiliary sneered again. "Brave words are not going to save you."

The two assassins moved away from each other so that Corbulo had to keep turning his head to watch them both. Slowly they circled around him like wolves waiting for the right moment to attack. His assailants seemed to be enjoying themselves.

"Shall I kill him with my bow?" the bowman said, speaking in the Briton language.

"You could do," the auxiliary replied in the same language, "but there wouldn't be much sport in that. No, let's see how long he lasts. Vellocatus wants him to suffer; we will make him bleed first."

"I could shoot him in the leg and then you could cut his head off. That's what Vellocatus said he wants, didn't he – his head?"

"There is to be no damage to the head," the auxiliary grinned. "I want him to be recognisable."

Corbulo said nothing. His eyes darted from one attacker to the other. The auxiliary soldier betrayed his attack with a slight movement of his head. Still he came in so fast that Corbulo barely had time to avoid the sword thrust. He jumped aside and flung his spear at the man but missed. The auxiliary laughed. Corbulo drew his sword.

"You legionaries are always so full of yourselves," the auxiliary sneered, "but we Batavians are the better soldiers. You will see soon enough."

Corbulo glanced quickly at the bowman. He had an arrow notched to his bow but he had not moved. The man was waiting for the outcome of the duel. If both of them attacked at the same time it would be over quickly.

"Let's kill him and take his head back with us. I am growing bored of this," the bowman announced suddenly.

The auxiliary grunted and crouched. Corbulo caught the malice in the man's eyes. How had his attacker received the bruise to his face?

From the corner of his eye Corbulo suddenly caught sight of something grey leaping through the air with incredible speed. Someone screamed in a horrible high-pitched voice that ended in a rattle. Corbulo stumbled backwards in alarm. The bowman was on the ground being ripped to shreds by a huge dog. The dog that was attacking him had ripped out the man's throat. Blood was gushing out of him in a small fountain. The beast's jaws opened and closed as he tore pieces of flesh from the fallen assassin. The bowman's screams faltered and ceased. The bowman's body did not move but still the huge dog would not let go. It was as if some violent demon had taken possession of the animal. Corbulo stumbled backwards again, his face pale with shock. He saw the auxiliary turn and run for his horse. With one swift movement the man was in the saddle and galloping away.

Corbulo watched him depart. Then he turned to look at the dog and the corpse. The animal was standing over the man it had just killed. For an insane moment Corbulo thought he detected pride in the dog's stance. Then slowly the dog turned its yellow eyes towards him. Its nose, snout, ears and jaws were covered in blood but Corbulo recognised the beast as the same animal that he had helped that morning. The dog must have been following him. For a long moment neither man nor beast moved. Then from the back of its throat the dog growled. The noise sent a shudder of fear right down Corbulo's spine but he stood his ground.

What was this? Had the gods sent a demon to protect him? Had immortal Jupiter heard his prayers and given his quest his favour? Slowly Corbulo walked over to where his spear lay and picked it up. The dog was still standing over the corpse like a lion standing over its kill. Corbulo stared at the beast with wide open eyes. Then he muttered a quick prayer of thanks.

He paused and examined the war dog closely. Then he turned.

"Come," he commanded using the Briton language.

He started walking. Behind him the dog stirred and started after him. Corbulo glanced back and shook his head in disbelief.

Chapter Thirty-Four – Desperate Men

Vellocatus strode along the lines of white tents that housed the soldiers who were constructing the fortress of Inchtuthil. He looked worried and agitated. Just that morning the man he'd left behind to look after his house at Eburacum had unexpectedly shown up in Inchtuthil. The man had brought bad news. A large band of men had arrived in Eburacum a few days after Vellocatus had left. They were Atrebates from the south and they had come looking for him. They knew his name and they knew what had happened to their allies, the Jewish moneylenders. The men had come seeking revenge. They had burned his house down and their leader had publicly vowed to place Vellocatus's head on a spear. There was no going back now, he thought grimly. He needed to find that amber or he was finished.

A Caledonian warrior was standing guard outside the tent. Vellocatus muttered the password that he had arranged with Baldurix, pulled back the canvas flap and ducked into the tent. He grinned in relief as he saw Bestia, Baldurix and the girl. The Caledonian girl was sitting crosslegged on the ground, her head resting on her chest. Her neck was fastened to a slaver's iron chain. A fourth man, the bowman, sat on the ground in the far corner eating an apple. Vellocatus shot Bestia a quick questioning glance and the auxiliary soldier nodded in confirmation. Vellocatus's grin widened as he stared at the girl. They had the right woman. He had found her at last; the amber was within reach.

Baldurix raised himself up from his chair and folded his arms across his chest.

"Good to see you again, Vellocatus," he said. He gestured to the miserable-looking girl. "As you can see I have kept my side of the bargain. Bestia says that she is the one who killed the boy in your tent last year. Now it is time for you to do your part of our agreement."

Vellocatus nodded. "Don't worry, Baldurix, give me a day and a night and we shall know the location of the amber cave."

"What are you going to do?" Baldurix inquired.

Vellocatus smiled. "It's best that you don't know. It will put you off your breakfast."

Baldurix grunted and glanced at the girl. "I don't want it done here in the camp. The Romans may get suspicious if the girl starts screaming. Take her out into the forest. My man here will show you the way to a sacred grove. You can do what you like with her there. I will meet you at the grove tomorrow at dawn. You had better have the answer by then."

Vellocatus nodded his agreement and gestured for Bestia to follow him. Vellocatus stepped out of the tent. He was followed a moment later by the others. Bestia had a firm grip on the slave chain.

"Mind if I have her after we are done?" he said, glancing at Vellocatus. "The bitch owes me something."

Vellocatus was just about to reply when a voice cried out.

"Heh, fuck face, yes you. I want to talk to you."

Vellocatus's face was pale and he was lost for words. For a long moment after Corbulo had disappeared amongst the tents, he just stood rooted to the ground unable to believe what had just happened.

"Is there a problem with that man?" Baldurix growled.

Vellocatus slowly turned to look at Bestia and there was growing fury on his face. Bestia blushed with sudden guilt. Then ignoring Baldurix, Vellocatus took a step forwards and smacked Bestia in his face with his fist. The auxiliary staggered backwards with a howl.

"You told me that he was dead," Vellocatus hissed. "You lied to me. You cheap sack of piss, you lied to me."

"I am sorry, I shouldn't have," Bestia mumbled.

Vellocatus's breath was coming in short sharp gasps. He turned to Baldurix. "He may be a problem. The man knows about the amber. He says he is looking for his son but I suspect that he too is after the amber."

"So we have competition," Baldurix muttered. He glanced over at Bestia and grinned at the deserter's discomfort. "Don't worry, my man here can track anything across any terrain. When that Roman leaves we will get him and kill him."

The sacred grove was a small pond. The thick forest crowded around as if the trees had fought long and hard to be the closest to the water. Vellocatus sniffed the air and stared suspiciously at the still black water. The druids believed that these groves were doorways between worlds. Insects buzzed and danced across the surface of the pond but apart from that they were alone. Vellocatus stepped up to the edge of the water, muttered a short prayer and undid a ring from his finger before casting it into the lake. The ring vanished with a small plop and ripples spread away in a perfect circle. The gods needed their share too, he thought. Now they too had a stake in his success.

He turned sharply and gestured for Bestia to force the girl to her knees. From the edge of the forest the bowman leaned back against a tree to watch. Vellocatus crouched before her and grabbed her chin with his hand, forcing the woman to look at him. He smiled.

"You know what we want," he said quietly. "Question is, will you tell us or must we inflict a great deal of pain on you before you then tell us?"

The girl opened her mouth and spat in his face.

Vellocatus rose and wiped the spittle from his face. He nodded at Bestia.

"Get started," he snapped.

The girl screamed and it was a scream of pure agony. It was evening. Bestia sat beside the fire he'd built and held up the white-hot poker. The woman was naked and tied hands and feet to a tree. Three burn marks already scarred her body.

"Again," Vellocatus ordered. Bestia pressed the white-hot metal into the girl's exposed flesh. There was a sizzle and hiss of burning meat and then an ear-shattering shriek of pain.

Vellocatus grabbed the woman's chin.

"Tell me where we can find the amber. Tell me where the amber cave is and the pain will stop."

The girl kept on screaming. Vellocatus slapped her hard across her face.

"Tell me," he roared, bringing his face close to hers.

Tears were streaming down the girl's face as she at last nodded her consent. Vellocatus stepped back with a triumphant look.

"Give her some wine," he snapped. He folded his arms across his chest as the bowman raised a skin of wine and forced some of the contents down the girl's throat. The remaining wine spilt down her chin and over her naked breasts.

"I have a ship waiting for us at the mouth of the Tay," Vellocatus snapped. "We will sail north along the coast. Where can we find the amber?"

The girl choked and her tears mingled with the wine and snot that was coming out of her nose. She rolled her head.

"My father's village," she gasped between sobs. "Look for a headland that pokes out into the sea. My people have built a fort on the headland. There is a sandy beach to the west. The cave is at the end of the headland. There is a cliff and rocks. You can only get to the cave from the sea."

Vellocatus's eyes sparkled with sudden hunger. "Good, good," he muttered. "I am glad that you have finally decided to cooperate." He studied the girl for a long moment. "I can see you are telling the truth but nevertheless I am going to take you with me just in case. You can guide us to the cave. Once we have the amber I will set you free."

The girl was still sobbing. "I will not be free," she cried. "I am going to die."

Vellocatus shrugged and turned to look at the bowman. "Go tell Baldurix that we have what we need."

The bowman turned and slipped away into the forest. Vellocatus glanced at Bestia.

"I was going to give her to you afterwards," he snarled, "but you lied to me so the girl will belong to me."

Bestia muttered darkly and flung the poker into the fire and looked away. "I deserted from the army because of you," he growled angrily. "They will have listed me as a deserter by now.

I have nowhere to go. Do you know the punishment for desertion? It's to be put into a sack with venomous snakes and thrown into a lake. That's what will happen to me if the army catches up with me. You promised that you would make me a wealthy man."

"And I will," Vellocatus retorted, "just as soon as we find the amber. Now stop whining and prepare us a meal. Baldurix will be here at dawn. Once we're done with him I want to be on my way as soon as I can."

Bestia blew the air from his cheeks and stared into the flames. "Are you really going to share the amber with that man?" he said suddenly with a cunning gleam in his eye.

Chapter Thirty-Five – The Plan

Vellocatus was staring at the girl when Baldurix stepped out from amongst the trees. It was dawn. Accompanying Baldurix was the bowman and a few others that Vellocatus had not seen before. He rose to his feet and kicked Bestia awake. The fire had died out and only a blackened circle of stones and ashes remained. The black waters of the pond were still and even the forest birds, so noisy most of the time, were silent.

Baldurix looked pleased. He glanced at the girl. She was still naked and huddled into a foetal position and shivering with cold. The burn marks on her body had turned black.

"The Roman who accosted you yesterday," Baldurix said. "He slipped out of the Roman camp this morning and crossed the river heading south. Some of my men tracked him. He turned north a short while later. They lost him when he re-crossed the river but my man here," Baldurix said, gesturing at the bowman, "will be able to pick up his trail. I suggest that this time we make no more mistakes. I don't like competition."

Vellocatus nodded and turned to Bestia.

"Go with him," he snapped, "and finish what you should have done a long time ago. Don't show your face to me if you fail again. I want that man's head in a sack, do you understand?"

Bestia snarled something in his Batavian language and then without another word he and the bowman stalked off into the forest. When they had gone Baldurix turned to Vellocatus.

"I hear that you got what we need from her," Baldurix said.

"I did," Vellocatus replied. "We can proceed with our plan." Vellocatus walked up to the edge of the pond and stared into the water. "I have a ship waiting for me at the mouth of the Tay," he said with his back turned. "I have managed to hire eleven mercenaries and a score of slaves. It's cost me every last coin that I had. I will take my boat and sail northwards. The amber cave is on a headland that sticks out into the sea. It can only be approached from the sea. I will take the girl with me.

She will help guide us to the place. After we have found the cave I will load up my ship and sail along the coast to your village where you can take delivery of your share of the amber."

Baldurix grunted. "When we have the amber I want the girl too," he said. "The woman is the daughter of my blood enemy. She will be useful to me."

Vellocatus turned round. "What, you didn't rape her on your journey to Inchtuthil? You do surprise me, Baldurix."

Baldurix was studying Vellocatus carefully. "And I want some of my men to go with you onboard your ship. Half the crew will be yours, the other half will be my men," the tall Caledonian chief said.

Vellocatus paused and stared at Baldurix for a long moment. Then he shrugged. "If you wish," he muttered. "Are your men ready to go? I am leaving the moment our business here is concluded."

"They are ready to go," Baldurix said firmly.

Vellocatus turned to look once more at the black pond. His reflection stared back at him.

"So what is your plan, Baldurix?" he asked curiously. "When we last spoke back in my home in Eburacum, you mentioned war and a blood feud."

Baldurix cleared his throat and glanced at the girl. "I will head north back to my home and my people," he said proudly. "Amongst my clan, a thousand warriors will follow me but there are some within my tribe who don't like it that I am a friend and ally of Rome. These men want to fight against Rome. So the time has come for me to settle the blood feud that has existed between the Decantae and the Vacomagi. Our feud unites all men of the Decantae. We hate the Vacomagi more than we hate Rome and we will slaughter them to the last child. When my people see how I, with the aid of Rome, have destroyed our blood enemy there will be no more resistance to my authority and leadership."

Vellocatus was silent for a moment. "What about the Vacomagi, won't they resist? You told me that in numbers they equal your own and they are led by a druid. All men fear the druids."

Baldurix snorted his disgust. "The druids are just men, like you and me. They bleed and die in the same way. I do not fear them. Rome is the future. The druids belong to the past; their time has come and gone."

Baldurix paused. "I have spoken with the commanders of the Roman forts at Cawdor and also Balnageith. They have promised me that they will do nothing to prevent the passage of my men into Vacomagi territory." Baldurix lowered his voice and glanced at the trees as if fearful that someone may be listening.

"The Romans have also promised me artillery support from their catapults and bolt throwers but they first want proof that the amber exists before they will act. I must show them some of these precious stones before I can attack. The Roman commanders are otherwise afraid that they will get into trouble with their superiors." Baldurix paused. "I am a rich man but I need that amber if I am to bribe nearly one thousand Roman soldiers into joining forces with me."

"I will be there, my friend," Vellocatus said cheerfully.

Vellocatus turned and glanced down at the naked Caledonian girl. "So do you want to fuck her first, or shall I?"

Chapter Thirty-Six – A New Love

Emogene shuffled along behind the slaver. The iron neck ring chafed her skin and every now and then her captor would give it a tug that would pull her forwards. The man was holding the other end of the chain and leading her on as if she were a dog. She didn't have the strength to fight him anymore. Her body was weak and exhausted and the burns that the torture had inflicted upon her stung and ached. They had been walking for hours with only a few pauses for rest. Baldurix's eleven warriors came on behind her. The men were silent and sombre and their hands were never far from their weapons. Emogene looked up at her surroundings with dull eyes. The pretty river was still to her right. A couple of ducks were bobbing up and down on the current. The slaver seemed to be following the river eastwards for the sun was now behind her. She stared at the green trees. Why did her husband not come and save her from these demons? The forest came up to the water's edge. She sniffed the air. They were close to the sea. She could smell the saltiness on the breeze. Where was the slaver taking her now? She didn't care; part of her had given up. Part of her did not want to live any longer. Everything had got worse and worse since she had seen Bary, Finlay and the rest of her war band killed and herself taken prisoner. She had recognised the Roman who together with Baldurix had taken her south. He had been the soldier who had confronted her in the slaver's tent, the night that she had killed Conall. And Baldurix? Baldurix had revealed his true self. The man was a traitor to his own people. During those days that it had taken her captors to ride south to the Roman fortress she had figured out what they were after and had resolved not to give them anything. If the Roman demons and these Caledonian traitors expected her to tell them about the stones that washed ashore from the sea then they were mistaken. She would tell them nothing.

Despite herself she started to laugh. It was not a happy laugh but laughter born out of despair, humiliation and the loss of hope. The pain from the white-hot poker had been unimaginable. It had broken her resistance. Now the very thought of that white-hot metal made her break out in a sweat.

The slaver glanced round. "Shut up, stupid bitch," he snapped.

Emogene fell silent. The slaver had raped her, then Baldurix had raped her and finally his men had had a go as well. A tear appeared in her eye as she turned to look into the forest. Why did her husband allow this to happen? Why did he not come and take her away from these men? She closed her eyes and wiped the tear from her cheek.

"Where are we going?" she mumbled.

"You will see soon enough – now no more talking," the slaver replied.

The old Roman naval supply galley sat at anchor along the north bank of the Tay river. Its sail was furled and its oars drawn inwards. A few men were lounging about near the prow. The slaver raised his hand and shouted at them and a few moments later two men clad in simple tunics and cloaks were coming towards her. The slaver muttered something in a language she didn't understand and one of the men took the chain and started to drag her towards the ship. The man strode across a plank that connected the ship with the shore and pulled her towards the mast in the centre of the galley. There he forced her to sit on the deck before he secured the chain to the mast.

"Water, something to drink," she pleaded.

"Shut up," the man retorted as he stomped off towards the prow.

Emogene leaned her head back against the mast and closed her eyes. Her mouth was dry and she found it difficult to swallow. The eastern breeze had picked up and the wind tugged at her long black hair. For a while she allowed it to play with her hair. Then she opened her eyes and looked up at the sky as if she had just awakened from a dream. Maybe her husband was dead. Maybe she had been wrong and everyone else had been right. She glanced down at the rowing benches. The rowers sat together resting and talking in quiet voices. Was that all they did every day? Row their master's boat in any direction he wanted? Was that their purpose in life? She stared back upstream along the pretty river and the beautiful forest with its multitude of different shades of green. This was her land, her beautiful green land. Her husband had died fighting to defend it. Her father fought to protect it and now it was her turn. Her moment to show if she cared or not. She felt herself blush. Her husband, her father, all the men in the village, they had been fighting for their land and their freedom. She hadn't really understood what that meant until now. Without freedom a person had no dignity. She stared at the distant hills smudging the horizon. Without dignity a person was little better than an animal. She had always known it, she just hadn't recognised it for what it was. There was something good and beautiful about this land that was worth fighting for. It was her home. It could never die. It was immortal. It would never leave her and it would never disappoint her. She would love the land and her people. If she was to be denied her husband then by the gods she would fill this land with all the love she possessed until it could take no more. She was done with men. She didn't want anything more to do with them, not after what they had done to her. She would never love a man again. Her eyes widened as she was suddenly reminded of a dream she'd had a long time ago now.

A great loss you shall suffer. But if you, Emogene, remain true to your people, then hope shall return and a new love will find you.

She glanced at the riverbank. Baldurix's warriors had come onboard the ship and the slaver was arguing with another man who looked like he was the captain of the galley. The slaver was pointing to the north and the captain in turn was pointing at the sky. She was too far away to hear their conversation.

"We sail north," the slaver cried in a loud voice as he came aboard. The captain followed him, shaking his head.

The rowers scrambled back onto their benches and pulled out their oars from where they had been stored. Emogene counted forty-three men onboard; twenty-two of them were rowers and crew and the remainder seemed to be evenly divided between Baldurix's men and those following the slaver. She looked down at the wooden deck and her face darkened with sudden shame. She had revealed the location of the amber cave. That was where they were heading now. The ship was taking her home.

A man was pulling the gangplank back into the ship when a lone horseman suddenly appeared on the river path. Seeing them the man frantically raced towards the ship.

"Wait for me, wait for me!" the man cried.

The galley was starting to drift out into the river as the man leapt from his horse and plunged into the water. He grabbed hold of a mooring rope as some of the slaver's men grabbed him and hauled him aboard. Emogene watched as the late arrival struggled to catch his breath. It was the auxiliary soldier, the man Baldurix had called Bestia. The slaver strode towards him with an inquiring look.

"Well, what happened?" he growled.

Bestia wiped the water from his face and got to his feet.

"Baldurix's man is dead. He was killed in the fight," he panted. "But the Roman is dead too. He leapt from a cliff. That's why I don't have his head."

Chapter Thirty-Seven – The Grey Sea

The grey sea was choppy and unsettled and the rowers had a hard time getting their oars into the water. The ship's crew had unfurled their sail and the canvas bulged and creaked as the galley's captain took full advantage of the south-eastern breeze. Emogene sat chained to the mast staring out over the wide expanse of water. The wind played with her long hair, blowing it up and letting it fall. To the west she could make out the dark smudge of land. The ship had been following the coastline all day but now it was late in the afternoon and the captain was bellowing orders to the helmsman to change course and head for the land. It looked like they would spend the night ashore. The greyness of the sea was matched by that of the sky. A storm was brewing. That was what the captain must have been trying to tell the slaver when they'd set out that morning. Emogene stared at the sea. She had lived all her life beside the sea and she knew its moods and the power of its rage when the sea spirits were angry. Silently her lips moved, muttering prayer after prayer, calling on the sea spirits to release their power and violence upon the flimsy wooden vessel in which she sailed.

Now and then she noticed that the rowers were glancing at her. There was apprehension on the faces of the crew and once that afternoon she had heard them muttering amongst themselves saying that she was going to bring them bad luck. That she had put a curse on the ship.

The slaver and Bestia had left her alone. The two men had spent most of the day in the prow of the boat staring towards the north. Her wounds still hurt and burned but the crew had given her water and a bowl of porridge, which she had wolfed down, and the captain had tended to her burns by rubbing a cool ointment into the skin. It had brought a little relief. The captain was a Roman and had little knowledge of her language so she had not understood his muttered words. Emogene closed her eyes and ended her silent prayers. She was going home. But the slaver was lying when he'd said that he would set her free. The man was never going to allow her to be free. Once he had no more use for her, he would kill her. Her only chance was to try and escape and for that she needed a storm.

Emogene opened her eyes. The slaver had turned and was making his way towards her. The man crouched down beside her and made a show of checking the chains that fastened her to the mast. He grinned.

"I have been curious about something," the slaver said. "When you entered my tent and killed that boy…" He paused. "You must have known him. Did you kill him to protect the secret of the amber?"

Emogene turned to look away but the slaver's hand caught her chin and forced her to look at him. She could smell his breath on her face.

"Well?"

"He was my kin," she muttered.

The slaver leaned back and his eyes sparkled. "Well, well," he muttered, "that must have been a hard thing to do, to kill one of your own." The man grinned. "But it was all for nothing wasn't it, for we got the secret out of you in the end. Doesn't that mean that you should kill yourself now?"

Emogene closed her eyes and refused to answer. She heard the slaver's soft mocking laughter.

"Who ordered you to kill the boy?" the man said suddenly.

"My father made us swear an oath of silence," she snapped angrily.

"The druid?" The man paused. "Of course, his name is Dougal. Baldurix has spoken to me about him. Will he prevent me from taking the amber?"

Emogene opened her eyes. "He will have you burned alive," she said with a sudden smile, "together with that friend of yours. Tomorrow will be your last day in this world."

For a moment the slaver looked alarmed. Then he got up to his feet and smirked. "Maybe, maybe," he muttered, "but at least I didn't break my oath like you."

He walked away as Emogene felt a surge of hatred choke in her throat. The man's words were just as potent as the white-hot poker. She wrenched her eyes away from him and glared out to sea. The slaver had been right. She had broken her oath, the oath for which she had killed Conall. She was a hypocrite. A tear appeared in her eye. She had failed her father and her people. She had been weak. Conall had died for nothing. Despair started to seep into her mind. High above her she suddenly heard the shriek and cry of a seagull. The white bird circled the ship, gliding gracefully on the wind. Then it swooped down and perched high up on the mast.

"Storm's coming," she heard one of the rowers cry.

She bit her lip and forced back the tears. No, she thought with sudden savage determination, Conall was not going to die for nothing. Her husband was not going to die for nothing. She was not going to let that happen.

The storm struck just as the ship made it into a small protected cove. The captain's will seemed to have prevailed this time for the slaver had not objected. That night, as torrential rain had come hurtling down and the wind had lashed out and roared across the land, the ship's crew had huddled together on the rocky beach, sheltering under any cover they could find whilst everyone waited for the storm to pass. Not a man had slept that night; the noise of the gigantic waves battering the shore and the howl of the wind had been too much. Now as weary faces peered eastwards hoping to catch a glimpse of dawn the storm's force was unabated. If anything the fury of the wind and rain seemed to be getting worse.

Emogene tugged at her iron chains. Her face and body were soaked as she sat chained to the slaver a little further up the beach. Vellocatus snarled at her not to move. The slaver too was soaked. He sat staring at the boiling sea with his arms folded across his chest and his legs drawn up together. From under the hood of his cloak he looked annoyed and irritated. Seeing the look on his face gave Emogene some grim satisfaction. She pulled again on her chains and the slaver's head whipped round towards her.

"When we get to the headland," she cried out, "I forgot to tell you. There are rocks in the sea. You must pass them to get to the cave. If you hit those rocks the ship will sink. I have seen it happen. I can show you where they are."

Vellocatus stared at her through the driving rain.

"Stop playing games with me!" he yelled.

Emogene tugged once more at her chains. "I am telling you the truth. I will show you the way to get to the amber cave but first you must take these chains off. If I were to fall overboard, I would drown and you would have no one to guide you past those rocks."

She held her breath as the slaver stared out into the rain.

"Where am I going to go in this weather?" she cried. "Where am I going to go with all your men onboard the ship? Take these chains off me."

Around them the wind howled and the rain came streaking in, plastering their faces. Vellocatus was silent. Then he turned.

"If you are lying to me, bitch," he snarled, "I will burn you with that poker."

The galley rose and pitched into the waves and a blast of salty seawater crashed over the prow, soaking the rowers. It was noon but in the grey sky there was no sign of the sun. The ship groaned and creaked. Emogene held onto the mast with both hands as the deck lurched up and down and then from side to side. Vellocatus had removed the chains from around her neck and the relief from their heavy weight was immense. The storm, however, was still raging. She glanced at the captain. The sailor looked furious. Vellocatus had forced him back to sea against his will. His rowers had nearly mutinied but the threat of physical violence and death had persuaded them to go back to their seats. Now they huddled on their benches in sullen silence trying to shield themselves from the waves as best they could. Their oars had been stowed but the main sail was still up.

Emogene turned her face into the wind. The sea spirits had heard her prayers. She felt the smooth cold power of the wind as it rushed across her face and tossed her hair up into the air. Her heart was pounding away in her chest. Would the men see the tension in her body? Over to the port bow the dark grey rocky coastline could be seen half a mile away. She saw the captain glance apprehensively up at the mast and sail. Vellocatus was in a hurry, she thought. He was taking a big risk by setting out into the storm. She peered through the rain searching for the slaver and saw him standing by the prow, one hand holding onto the ship, staring at the grey sea and the cloud-filled sky. This was the day upon which she had said he would die. A sudden movement caught her attention. A seagull was hovering over the ship, its wings spread with majestic ease as it glided effortlessly on the wind. To the north the sky had turned even darker. As she watched she saw a forked shaft of lightning stab into the sea followed moments later by the dull rolling clap of thunder. Emogene wiped the rain from her eyes. The ship was sailing straight into the eye of the storm. The captain turned and yelled something in a furious voice at the slaver but Vellocatus pretended not to have heard him. Emogene looked down at her hands. Her breath came in short sharp bursts. She was nervous. She glanced around. Bestia sat a few paces away holding onto the deck with both hands, his hood drawn closely around his head. He looked seasick. He had been throwing up all morning. Beyond him amongst the waves she suddenly caught sight of some flotsam, a wooden log that the storm must have ripped from the land. Without hesitation Emogene tensed, took three steps forwards and leapt from the ship into the boiling sea.

Chapter Thirty-Eight – Hope and Fear

Emogene plunged into the sea. A wave towered over her and then she was underwater in a dark green tumbling world. Panic-stricken she burst to the surface, spluttering, and received a wet salty slap in the face. She sucked air into her lungs. The water was cold, so cold, but she had been expecting that. The next wave came towards her but this time she managed to go with the swell and ride it out. She twisted her neck as she heard a shout behind her. The ship was already some distance away. A lone figure was standing at the rear pointing at her. He was shouting but she couldn't see who it was or hear what he was saying. The sea was tossing her about with contemptuous ease. She cried out with growing panic. What had she done? She was going to drown. *The sea spirits will help me. The sea spirits will save me.* The thoughts rushed through her mind like men running to put out a fire. She rose up with the next wave. Her fingers felt numb with cold. To the west she caught a sudden glimpse of the land as another long white foaming wave rolled in towards her. Down, down she went, then up and up and once more she caught sight of the land. She was a good strong swimmer but she had never been out in the sea in a storm like this. Another wave rolled in and her desperate staring eyes suddenly caught sight of the wooden log she had seen earlier. Despite herself she screamed in delight. The sea spirits were with her. Frantically she dug her legs and arms into the water but her pathetic attempts to swim seemed to have no effect. Suddenly she relaxed. It was no use trying to swim. Her fate was now in the hands of the sea gods. She was completely in their power. Soon she would know what they had decided. She gasped as another blast of icy water struck her face. The wind was howling and swooping over the unsettled sea. Another wave was sucking her down, down, then she was going up again and a moment later her body was slammed into the drifting piece of flotsam. Wildly she scrabbled to grab hold of the wood. The log was thick and long enough for her to half crawl onto it. Her legs and waist, however, were still in the water. A wave tried to tear her off the flotsam but she held on with desperate strength.

It was evening and out at sea the storm continued to buffet and lash at the waves. Emogene lay on the rocky beach where the current had washed her ashore. She could hear the crash of the waves on the rocks and the howling of the wind but the noise seemed distant and inconsequential. She was soaked to the bone but she couldn't feel the coldness. It was as if her mind had become separated from the rest of her body. Nearby the log that had saved her had become wedged between the rocks. As the waves crashed ashore a fine spray of water landed on her head and body. She moved in and out consciousness. Then at last she opened her eyes. The sea gods had protected her. They had not wanted her to die. She remembered the biting cold, the panic and the single savage thought that had dominated her mind. She had to hold on. She had to endure. She blinked and wearily raised her head and turned to look at the sea. She had endured. She had escaped. There was a sudden maturity about her that was beyond her nineteen years. Let any man try and do what she had done. She was their equal now. She looked up at the sky. Seagulls were circling over the cliffs to the north. She closed her eyes and ran her hand over her face. Then she got to her feet. She had to warn her father about the impending attack on her people. She had to warn him about Vellocatus and his plan to plunder the amber cave. She turned to look around. She hadn't got a clue where she was but if she followed the coast northwards the shoreline would lead her home. Home, she thought as she started to walk; her home was in danger. She quickened her pace. Her father was in danger.

Dougal stood alone at the edge of the high cliff looking out to sea. The sun was sinking into the mountains to the west, and above him, gliding gracefully on the sea air currents, the seagulls swooped and dived. Dougal was an old man, stooping and leaning on his gnarled oak staff for support. He was already well past fifty and now as he stared at the ocean his fingers carefully stroked his long grey beard. He was clad in a long flowing white robe embroidered with gold. The villagers had named him Dougal or 'dark stranger' when he had first arrived in their settlement as a young refugee from the south. But Dougal wasn't his real name. His true name was Greer and his true home had been Ynys Mon, the sacred island of the druids. Ynys Mon was gone now, destroyed and desecrated by the Romans. Now the place only lived in his memories. He would never be able to return to the holy island where his father and grandfather had learnt and practised the secrets of the druids. Greer lifted his head to look at the swirling sea birds. To halt the remorseless Roman advance he had seen the elders sacrifice a warrior of noble birth in an attempt to force the gods to intervene against Rome but the sacrifice had been in vain. The warrior had died for nothing. The gods had not intervened and the Roman war machine had not been stopped.

Some of his friends, young druids fleeing from the destruction, had urged him to come with them westwards, across the sea. Not to the island of Hibernia but across the great vast ocean to the continent that lay beyond. His friends had said they would be safe there. They had said that the druids would survive if they emigrated but he had refused to join them. Instead he and his son had fled north. The druids may know the secrets of nature and man. They may be able to read the will of the gods but he had become obsessed by a single question which he couldn't answer. Was it the will of the gods that Rome should rule all? The question remained and he had been unable to abandon his people. He had to find the answer for only then could he stand before the tribes and put the heart back into his people and make them believe in themselves and their cause. But the gods had been silent and for years now his divination had produced nothing.

The small peninsula on which he stood jutted out into the ocean towards the north-west with the sea surrounding it on three sides. On the western side a rocky beach curled slowly away and to the east the flat fields, covered with long grass and heather-encrusted sand dunes, vanished into the gathering gloom. In front of him, just a foot away, the steep cliff face dropped sharply down to the sea below. Behind him smoke was rising from the thatched round houses inside the promontory fort that was built on top of the headland. The low-slung thatched roofs were nearly touching the ground.

Greer gave the sea a final sullen look, then he turned and started to make his way back home. The fort was large and well populated but he didn't pause to talk to the people who came and went. The villagers were busy with their chores but they nodded to him in respect as he passed by. On the landward side the peninsula was defended by three impressive layered earthen and wooden ramparts with walkways behind them and an outer ditch. Greer approached the inner entrance and glanced in the direction of the chambered well. A young man stood guard outside the steps leading down to the well door. The warrior nodded at Greer but the druid ignored him. Trouble was coming. He could feel it in his bones.

He passed on through the two outer ramparts and crossed the muddy ditch. His house and that of Emogene's husband stood together on a small hill about a mile away from the fort. He had never told Emogene about her brother. She had never known him. He had refused to talk about his son. He ambled along at his slow but steady pace, his head sunk deep in thought. Trouble was coming. Could he really wait until Samhain? The proposal, although unexpected, did make sense. During Samhain the door between the world of the living and the dead would open. It was the perfect time to make the sacrifice and read the will of the gods but something was making him uneasy. Trouble was coming. Would he have enough time? Was it not better to end the matter now before events could distract him?

He was muttering to himself as he stepped through the doorway into his house. He lived alone now that his wife and son were dead and the others had gone to live in Emogene's dead husband's house. He closed the door behind him. One of the women who lived in the neighbouring house had lit a fire for him. He shuffled towards it and then stopped in surprise. A woman was standing beside the fire warming her hands. She turned. It was Emogene, his daughter. She looked exhausted.

Emogene turned and looked up into her father's wise pale-blue eyes. In the past she would have wanted to fling herself into his warm embrace but now something held her back. Instead she managed a smile of relief.

"Father," she said, "I am so glad to see you."

Greer didn't move, nor did he speak. He just stared at her. Then he dipped his head in silent recognition and greeting.

Emogene blew the air from her cheeks and wiped her forehead. She looked bedraggled, exhausted and hungry.

"There is much to say and I am afraid we have little time," she blurted out. "It has taken me four days to get here. I came as fast as I could but I may already have arrived too late."

She paused and stared at her father and there was urgency in her voice as she spoke. "I have news, important news which we need to share with all our kin. The Decantae led by Baldurix are planning an all-out attack. The Romans are going to support them. Baldurix thinks that with the support of the Romans he can defeat us. He intends to slaughter us all. You must warn our men. And there is something else," she swallowed nervously, "Baldurix and his friends know about the amber. They know where to find the precious stones. They are coming here to raid the cave. They may have done so already. We must post a watch on the cliffs."

Greer's face darkened. His body tensed and his pale-blue eyes stared at her with growing anger and suddenly Emogene felt a tingle of fear slither down her spine.

"How did Baldurix find out about the stones?" Greer's voice rasped. "I thought you told me that you killed Conall?"

Emogene looked down at the earth.

"They tortured me," she muttered. "They burned me with metal rods. I told them where they could find the cave. It is my fault that they know."

The round room fell silent. Greer stared at his daughter and as he did so Emogene felt her fear grow.

"You were weak," Greer's voice cut through the air like a knife. "Did you not once swear an oath of silence to me? Do you not understand why the stones had to be kept hidden? Why their very existence had to be kept secret? If the Romans find out about the amber it will just fuel their greed and they will be all over our land like rabbits in summer. They will never leave. They will never leave when they know about the amber." Greer paused for breath. "Is that what you want? Do you want these invaders to rule us for eternity?" the druid thundered.

"Of course not." Emogene shook her head. She looked at her father with a startled expression. "None of us want that but what is done is done. I have come here to warn you and our men. We must prepare ourselves."

Greer tightened his grip on his oak staff. "What is done is done," he repeated her words. Then he fixed his pale-blue eyes on her and there was something cold and heartless in the way he looked at her.

"Do you remember the punishment for breaking your oath?" he rasped.

Emogene felt her body grow cold. She stared at her father in sudden horror.

"Death," the old druid rasped.

"No, Father, please!" Emogene cried out.

"Bodvoc, come here at once," Greer shouted.

Emogene felt tears trickling down her face. She fell to her knees and tried to clasp her father's waist but he smote her angrily with his staff and she fell backwards.

"There will be no exceptions," he rasped.

"I am your daughter," Emogene sobbed as she lay on the ground. "You are my father. Please do not do this."

Her desperate pleas were interrupted as the door opened. Bodvoc stepped inside. He gasped in surprise as he saw Emogene on the floor.

"Take her to the well and lock her up inside," Greer snapped. "I have no more use for my daughter. She has betrayed us all."

Emogene remained silent as Bodvoc grasped her by the arm and pushed her down the stone steps that led to the chambered well. He had not said a word as he had marched her the mile from her father's house into the fort on the headland but she could sense that he was confused and unhappy about what he was doing. It was no use arguing with him or the young warrior who stood guarding the well. In this village and amongst her kin, her father's word was law. They would never disobey a druid. Her tears had dried but she still couldn't believe what had happened. She had not for a moment considered escape. How could she? He was her father. These were her people. Her family and friends. This was her home.

"I will come back later with some food," Bodvoc muttered as he unbolted the well door. He sounded apologetic and refused to look her in the eye. The door opened and he pushed her inside without another word. She heard the bolts slide shut behind her. With her fingers she touched the cool stone wall. It was damp. She turned to look around. She was in a dark chamber around four yards high and a few yards wide. The only light came from the small cracks between the door and the wall. To her right she could hear the gentle drip of water. The chamber was too dark for her to see the basin of water from which the fort drew its water supply. The basin was fed by a tiny underground stream. She leaned back against the stone walls of the well and slid slowly to the ground. She was exhausted. A sudden movement in the darkness startled her and she jumped back to her feet. Something had moved in the darkness.

"Who's there?" she cried in alarm.

A face appeared from out of the gloom. It was the face of a young man but the dirty beard, hollow cheeks and dull eyes were those of a sick old man.

"Marcus, my name is Marcus," the voice whispered. "Cavalryman, Second Batavian Auxiliary Cohort."

Chapter Thirty-Nine – The Amber Cave

Vellocatus stood at the prow of the galley as the waves tossed the vessel about. With one hand he steadied himself against the boat. His face and clothes were sodden but he didn't care. He was staring ahead across the grey sea at the dark storm clouds that were building up. The ship pitched and rolled and every now and then a huge wave would break across the deck, swamping everyone with stinging, icy cold seawater. The galley groaned and creaked in protest. Vellocatus's gaze was fixed on the northern horizon. Earlier that morning the captain of the ship he'd hired had had the temerity to protest to him about their journey. The captain had complained about the dangers of sailing out into a storm like this. His men had nearly mutinied. The captain had advised him to seek shelter ashore and let the storm blow itself out but Vellocatus was having none of it. He was in a hurry and storm or no storm, nothing was going to stop him from finding the amber cave as soon as possible. He glanced back and saw the captain staring apprehensively up at the mast and sail. It was such a shame that he needed the sailor and his crew, he thought. Otherwise they would have been feeding the fish by now. He squinted through the seawater spray. The girl was holding onto the mast with both hands. Good, he thought, she was coping better than poor Bestia. The auxiliary soldier had been seasick for most of the morning. He turned back to face the sea up ahead.

Baldurix was a fine friend and ally, he thought, but it would be such a waste to allow him to take three quarters of the amber. The Caledonian had no concept of the value the stuff could fetch when it was sold back in Italy or in Rome. No, the plan had changed, he thought. He would find the amber cave, load up his ship with as much of the stones as he could, kill Baldurix's men and sail away. Once he was clear he would order the captain to sail south. He glanced at the rocky shore, half a mile away. He was going to leave Britannia. There was nothing left for him to go back to. He would take his ship and his amber south until he reached Hispania. From there he would follow the coast and enter the middle sea through the pillars of Hercules. He would make for the great Egyptian city of Alexandria. He had heard that it was warm there, that the sun always shone and that the locals didn't ask questions. Yes, he would spend the rest of his days as a rich man in the sun. He grinned at the prospect.

Suddenly he heard a shout behind him. Someone was crying out his name. He turned and saw Bestia gesturing frantically at him. What did the man want? Then his face grew pale in shock. The girl. The girl was no longer holding on to the mast. Where had she gone? He staggered back towards the mast and as he got closer he could hear Bestia's words over the howl and shriek of the wind.

"The girl, the girl, she's jumped into the sea. The mad bitch is overboard."

Vellocatus's eyes bulged. He twisted his head and stared back across the side of the ship but he could see nothing apart from the grey rolling waves. The girl was indeed gone. Vellocatus turned and grabbed hold of Bestia's neck.

"You were supposed to be watching her!" he screamed. "How can she just jump overboard! Where the fuck were you?"

Bestia forced Vellocatus's hands from his throat. He looked pale and unwell.

"She will never make it to the shore," he shrieked. "Not in this weather. She is going to drown. We won't see her again."

Vellocatus turned away and roared his frustration into the howling wind. Then he closed his mouth and swallowed.

It didn't matter, he thought. The girl had told him enough for him to find his way to the amber. From the rear of the galley the captain was staring at him as if he were a lunatic.

"Not another word from you!" Vellocatus screamed.

It was night and the sea was flat and calm. The galley lay anchored off a flat rocky beach. As the stars twinkled in the sky Vellocatus crouched on the shore and peered into the darkness. He could hear the steady gentle crash of the waves on the rocks and the sucking noise as the tide retreated. It had been a difficult two days but the ship had come through it and the storm had finally blown itself out. They had spotted the headland after just a day of sailing to the west. It looked exactly as the girl had described it. Vellocatus turned to look at the two men who crouched behind him. He could just about make out their faces. They were Baldurix's men and they had insisted on accompanying him on his reconnaissance. He'd left Bestia in charge of his mercenaries onboard the ship. The auxiliary soldier may have been afraid of the sea but he would know how to keep the crew and Baldurix's men in check.

Vellocatus turned and peered again at the peninsula half a mile away. On the top of the high cliffs he could make out a number of glowing fires. Would the villagers in the fort have posted a guard? On spotting the headland he'd ordered the captain of the ship to sail past it and continue on to the west. That had given him a good opportunity to study the place. Then when the galley had sailed on and was out of sight of any watchers on the cliff he had given the order to double back and anchor half a mile away. He had been pleased with himself. He had timed the ship's arrival to happen during darkness and so they had.

"Come," he whispered.

He rose to his feet and set off along the shore towards the headland. Baldurix's men followed without a word. The waves breaking onto the shore masked the noise of their passing and they made easy and swift progress. The shoreline was open and flat. After a while Vellocatus raised his hand in warning and crouched. Looming up before them was a high timber-faced rampart and in front of it a muddy ditch. Vellocatus peered up at the top of the wooden wall but he could see no guards. It was a good sign. He started to edge towards the sea. The rampart and ditch, however, came right up to the water's edge. He grunted in disappointment. Whoever had built this place was not going to make it easy for him. Baldurix's two men crouched beside him.

"The girl said that the amber cave can only be approached from the sea," Vellocatus whispered. "We will have to wade into the water and swim around the headland. I think the cave is below those high cliffs."

Without waiting for an answer he rose and strode out into the swell. The water was cold but he was already soaked from having to swim ashore from the boat and his heart was thumping with excitement. He was close now. He could nearly smell the stones. They were within reach. Behind him he heard his two companions wading into the water. Vellocatus struggled on. The sea came up to his waist. Then it was up to his neck and he started swimming. Up ahead he could see the flickering red light coming from the villagers' fires. He had seen no guards on the cliffs as the galley had sailed past earlier that day but if he was right and the amber cave was located beneath the cliffs it would be very difficult, without being seen, to get his ship close enough to load the amber in the quantities that he wanted. He spluttered as he took in a mouthful of seawater. Then his feet were touching the ground. He struggled forwards. The sea tide was pushing him up against the rocks. He spat some water from his mouth in disappointment. He had been right. He would never be able to bring his galley in close without the danger of the ship being dashed onto the rocks and sunk.

Then he saw it. A dark cavernous opening in the cliff face. The sea cave. Behind him he heard his two companions fumbling their way along the rocks. They were still with him. Vellocatus felt his heart pounding away. He pushed himself off a rock and allowed the tide to carry him along. Then he grasped hold of another rock. He was there. He peered into the darkness. The cave was open to the sea. It was maybe a yard high and across, not much more than a hole but wide enough for a single man to enter. He wiped the water from his eyes and stared at the dark entrance. He could see nothing beyond. Then carefully he started moving along the rocks until he was directly opposite the hole. He glanced back. Baldurix's men had seen the cave opening too.

Without further hesitation Vellocatus waded through the hole in the cliffs and into the darkness beyond. He was in a tunnel. He steadied himself with both hands against the rock walls as he propelled himself forwards. The tunnel floor seemed to be rising and he had to stoop so that he would not bang his head on the rocks. Then abruptly the tunnel veered to the right. Vellocatus froze. There was light up ahead. Someone had lit an oil lamp. Carefully he edged along the side of the slippery rock walls and peered around the corner. Three oil lamps, standing in their metal holders, flickered and in their light he saw a large cavern. It was high enough for him to stand in. Stalagmites and stalactites littered the cave like the teeth of a long-dead prehistoric animal and heaped up in between them was a mountain of gleaming and sparkling amber. Vellocatus's eyes bulged in their sockets. He scrambled into the cave, banged his knee painfully on a rock but he wasn't aware of the pain. He fell to his knees and dug his hands into the mountain of precious stones. Then with both hands he held the stones up to the light. They were perfect, beautiful: green, red, blue, yellow, all the colours of the rainbow. He wanted to cry out in joy. He had found the amber. Behind him he heard Baldurix's men scrambling into the cave and their collective sigh of wonder. He turned and in the flickering light all three men grinned at each other.

Vellocatus lay back on the mountain of coloured stones and started to heap the amber over his body as if it were sand on a beach. He was laughing. He was going to be a very wealthy man.

"Baldurix needs a few of the stones to show the Romans," one of Baldurix's men interrupted. "We will take some of them with us and return for the rest when we have slaughtered these Vacomagi."

Vellocatus stopped laughing and sat up. He had told no one, not even Bestia about his real intentions for himself and the amber. He stared at the man who had spoken, his mind torn with sudden indecision. But the man was right. He couldn't bring his ship in close without it either being seen or sunk and the narrowness of the sea cave passage and the lack of a beach meant that loading up the galley would take time. It would indeed be better to wait until Baldurix's blood feud had distracted or killed the villagers. He made up his mind. He would go along with Baldurix's plan for now and then when the Caledonian had marched off to confront his enemies he would take his boat, return to the cave, take the amber and sail away. He would just have to be patient for a little longer.

He nodded at the two men. "Fine, take what you need and let's get back to the ship," he growled.

Chapter Forty – Corbulo and the War Dog

Corbulo stopped as he caught sight of the Caledonian settlement nestling at the base of the hill upon which he stood. It was mid morning and the sun shimmered in a beautiful blue sky. The village was large and he could see no wall or ramparts protecting the place. Beyond the cluster of round houses he could make out a river and farms with enclosures for cattle and sheep. Smoke was rising from an iron smelter's workshop. The settlement looked prosperous. He glanced round at the big war dog that was padding towards him. The dog had been with him ever since the beast had killed the bowman and saved Corbulo's life. Corbulo rather liked the dog's company. The animal responded to his commands with impressive understanding and obedience and it had confirmed his suspicion that the beast was indeed a war dog, for someone had trained him well.

Corbulo had headed north after the incident with the auxiliary soldier, following the rough patrol and supply tracks from Roman fort to fort. The chain of Roman defences stretched northwards following the line where the low rolling fields and hills gave way to the bleak treeless mountains of the highlands. Agricola's engineers had done well, Corbulo thought, for the Roman forts formed a barrier between the populous lowlands and the sparsely inhabited highlands. Agricola's strategy had become clearer the further north Corbulo had gone. The Roman forts had been placed along the valley entrances leading up into the highlands. Thus they prevented the small scattered war bands in the highlands from joining forces with the bulk of the population who lived in the more fertile and productive lowlands. Numerous smaller watch and signal towers and fortlets connected the larger forts with each other. These smaller Roman outposts had often been manned by just eight men.

Corbulo had moved from fort to fort but everywhere he had received the same reply. No one had heard of or seen the missing Roman cavalry scout. The soldiers in the forts had all been auxiliaries, mainly Batavians, and they had been tense and moody. The constant hit-and-run attacks from the Caledonian war bands were having an impact on Roman morale. *If they have captured him then don't waste your time, he will be dead*, the soldiers had told him. They had told him to go back south, to forget about his son. The Caledonians did not take prisoners and if they did it was only so that they could be sacrificed to the Celtic gods.

Corbulo had spent each night within the relative security of the Roman ramparts but the war dog had refused to enter the Roman camps. It had been the same with every fort and watchtower that they came across, but in the morning when Corbulo would set out again, the dog would reappear and follow him once more. Only once had he come across some local men. They had been out hunting by the look of the deer that they had slain, but the Caledonians had not approached him. They had been wary and soon vanished back into the forest.

He stared down at the peaceful Caledonian settlement. The soldiers had told him it was called Tuesis and that it was the Vacomagi capital. He had tried to avoid the Caledonians, hoping that the Roman auxiliaries would be better informed of what was going on in the area, but the lack of news was dispiriting. The Batavians had advised him not to enter the local villages on his own. The newly conquered population was sullen and resentful of the Roman presence and a Roman's safety could only be guaranteed if he came in a group. On his own he was likely to have his throat cut. But now as he looked down at the settlement Corbulo knew that he was growing increasingly desperate for news. Maybe it was time that he broadened his search and went into the local villages to see what the locals knew? He heard the gentle panting of the war dog and looked down at the grey beast. Besides he was not alone. The war dog would be his bodyguard. He made his decision and started off down the slope towards the settlement.

The inhabitants of Tuesis were indeed sullen and resentful. As Corbulo made his way through the place the people stopped what they were doing and turned to stare at him. They didn't want him here. He could see it in their hostile, unfriendly postures. But no one stepped out to block his path. The war dog padded along at his side. Corbulo's fingers played with the pommel of his sword. Idly he glanced at a large round house. The house had been constructed from turf and timber and had a low-slung thatched roof that nearly touched the ground. An old man sat in the doorway staring up at him from beneath a dirty beard. Further away he could hear the hammering of blacksmiths. Beside the large round house a woman was grinding flour using a stone and earthenware pottery. She looked up at him and her face darkened. Then she grabbed her pottery, turned her back and walked away. Corbulo moved on. He could hear a baby crying in a nearby house. The village was indeed a prosperous place, he thought. The houses were larger than the ones in other villages he had seen further south and as he strode on he noticed the black jewellery worn by women and men alike. He stopped as a man standing on a small chariot came riding towards him. The warrior slowed as he approached and Corbulo stepped out of the way as man, horse and chariot trundled past.

"Go!" the warrior shouted at him. Then the man disappeared amongst the cluster of houses.

Corbulo looked around him. He seemed to have come to the centre of the village. The circular open space before him was surrounded by round houses. He sniffed as he caught the scent of horse manure. To his left a woman was sitting out in the sun on a large stone. She was mending a cloak. He turned towards her and she looked up and scrambled to her feet in alarm.

"I mean no harm," Corbulo said, raising the palm of his hand and speaking in the native Celtic language. "I am looking for my son. He may have come through here towards the end of last year." Corbulo paused. "He is a Roman, on horseback and alone. He has red hair. His mother was from the south. Did you see this man? Do you know if such a man passed through here?"

The woman was staring at the war dog in surprise. Then she looked at Corbulo.

"A red-haired Roman?" She shook her head. "All the Romans around here are at their fort at Cawdor," she replied sullenly. "If you want to know about your son then go and ask your own people."

Corbulo looked disappointed. The woman turned to look again at the war dog and this time her face was filled with growing curiosity.

"Where did you find him?" the woman said, pointing at the dog.

"He found me. He came out of the forest a few days' walk south of here and has been following me ever since," Corbulo muttered.

The woman was studying the dog intently as if she knew the animal. Then she called out a name in a sharp commanding voice. The dog's ears pricked up and he barked but he didn't move from Corbulo's side. The woman muttered in surprise. Then she looked up at Corbulo and her expression became guarded.

"Do you know what happened to the dog's previous owner?"

Corbulo shook his head. "I have no idea," he replied. "Do you recognise the animal?" he said, glancing down at the dog.

"I do," the woman said. "He belongs to a girl. Her name is Emogene. She and her father come here now and then to visit their kin." The woman paused as a worried look appeared in her eyes. "I suppose something must have happened to her if her dog is here on his own…"

She looked up at Corbulo with sudden suspicion. Then before Corbulo could reply the woman was crying out to someone in a loud voice. A few moments later a man and two sturdily built boys appeared from the doorway to a blacksmith's workshop. The man and the boys were wearing leather aprons and their faces were covered with charcoal soot. They approached Corbulo and the woman. Corbulo took a step backwards and his fingers came to rest on the pommel of his sword. The man and the boys looked at him with a hostile inquiring expression. More people had appeared in the doorways to the houses. All were staring in his direction.

"Look," the woman snapped, "he's got Bones. That's Emogene's dog. What is he doing with her dog?"

Corbulo blushed as the hard, hostile faces glared at him, waiting for him to answer. He should have known. The dog was going home. He had only been tagging along with him because they were going in the same direction. For a split second Corbulo thought about making a run for it but he knew he wouldn't get far. Fool. The Batavian auxiliaries had been right. He was going to get his throat cut. He looked down at the dog.

"Like I said," he muttered, "the animal came to me in the forest. I never met this girl and I certainly did not steal the dog. He just followed me." Corbulo stopped as he had a sudden idea. "I shall trade with you," he said, turning to the woman. "Let me walk out of this village and if the dog follows me he is mine. If he decides to stay then he is yours. Agreed?"

The woman picked nervously at her fingernails. She looked undecided.

"That seems fair," the blacksmith growled.

Corbulo nodded and his earlier panic started to subside. He turned to the blacksmith. "I see that you are a skilled man. Do you have a bow and some arrows? I will exchange them for some Roman copper coins."

Corbulo undid a small leather pouch from his belt and shook the copper coins into his hand. Then he held them up for all to see.

The blacksmith peered closely at the coins and then at Corbulo. After a long pause he nodded. "I will trade with you."

Corbulo wiped the sweat from his face as he followed the blacksmith into his workshop. Quintus had given him the copper coins as a final parting gift. There was not much he could spend the money on up here. He had been saving them up in case he needed to bribe the Roman soldiers but investing in a bow and arrows seemed a better option. The bow would allow him to hunt and provide food for himself.

The workshop was boiling hot. A large kiln fired by charcoal formed the back of the turf-and-thatch building with the smoke escaping through a chimney. In the middle of the workshop was a large heavy wooden table. An array of metal objects in various states of completion lay upon it. The blacksmith shuffled across the space and stopped beside a metal rack from which hung an arsenal of finished weapons. He plucked a bow from the rack and handed it to Corbulo. Then he folded his arms across his chest. Corbulo had never used a bow in his life. He hated and despised bowmen but now he needed the weapon. He squeezed the wood and tried the bow string. It seemed sturdy enough. He looked up and nodded. Then he handed over the pouch of copper coins. The trade was complete.

He was just about to turn for the exit when his eye caught sight of a sword leaning against the rack. He froze. It was a spatha, a Roman auxiliary cavalryman's sword. There was no doubt about it. He stared at the long shiny steel blade with its rounded tip. It was definitely a Roman cavalry man's sword. What was it doing here? He raised his hand and pointed at the weapon.

"Where did you get that sword?" he exclaimed.

The blacksmith followed his gaze and grunted.

"That sword? I traded it from a man who lives in Bannatia, Dougal's village by the sea."

Corbulo stared at the spatha.

"How do I get to Bannatia?" he muttered, trying to hide his growing excitement.

The blacksmith gestured with his head.

"You cannot miss it if you keep going north from here. Bannatia is on a headland sticking out into the sea."

Corbulo wrenched his eyes from the sword and stepped out of the workshop. The villagers were still watching him. He nodded a farewell to the blacksmith and then turned to look at the big war dog. Would the dog come with him this time? The beast had not moved.

"Come," he called as he started walking. Behind him the animal hopped up and started to follow. Corbulo heard a gasp from amongst the villagers. The war dog was well trained and he was valuable. Corbulo kept on walking and as he did so he heard the villagers following on behind. At the edge of the settlement he glanced round. The dog was still with him. A crowd had gathered by now. Some of the people were calling out to the dog, trying to make it come to them. Corbulo kept on walking. He was out of the village now. The green rolling fields beckoned. He turned and looked back. The dog had sat down on the path. The beast was staring at him as behind him the villagers were calling out, enticing the animal to return to them. Corbulo made eye contact with the dog and sighed. The animal had been a good companion but he could see now that the dog was not going any further with him. The war dog had come home.

"Thank you," Corbulo said. The war dog had saved his life. For a moment Corbulo looked sad. Then he dipped his head respectfully at the dog and without another glance he turned and strode away across the fields. When at last he looked back the dog and the villagers had gone.

Chapter Forty-One – Cawdor

A thick mist covered the woodlands and fields. It was early morning. Corbulo trudged along the path. He could feel the warmth of the rising sun on his back. It had been two days since he had said goodbye to the dog and he was missing the animal's company. The road had been a lonely place. He had headed west in the direction of Cawdor. Quintus had told him that Cawdor was the last of the permanent Roman forts, and the most northerly, in the long chain of fortifications that stretched away southwards along the highland line. Slung over his shoulder he carried his newly acquired bow and quiver. The blacksmith had included seven arrows and Corbulo had made his first kill yesterday when he had brought down a fat duck. He had cooked the meat that night and it had tasted delicious. With the bow and his arrows he would be able to hunt for food. It would allow him to maintain himself a little longer as he searched for Marcus.

The Roman fort loomed up out of the early morning mist. The rectangular fort had been placed on the south side of the Nairn river with its northern ramparts protected by the river. As Corbulo trudged along the track towards it, he could see the thick turf-filled wooden ramparts and the tall watchtower with its thatched roof, beside the south-west gate. Two sentries were on guard. He raised his hand and cried out in Latin in a loud voice. He had done the same with each Roman fort he'd approached. It paid to be careful and to show that he had no hostile intent. The soldiers he'd met had been tense and quite happy to shoot first and ask questions later. The Batavian auxiliaries turned to look at him but did not answer. A scorpion, a tension-sprung bolt thrower that could fire a spear over a hundred yards, mounted on a tripod, stood beside the guards on the platform of the watchtower. As he drew closer to the southern gate Corbulo passed a blackened shrunken head that had been stuck onto a spear and planted into the earth.

He came to a halt before the deep V-shaped ditch that protected the fort's ramparts. The wooden gate ahead was closed.

"Who are you?" one of the guards called out in Latin.

"A friend," Corbulo replied, raising the palms of his hands. "I wish to speak with your commanding officer."

"About what?"

Corbulo stared up at the guards. "I have been told that you boys belong to the Ninth Batavians. If that is so, tell Prefect Chariovalda that an old acquaintance is outside waiting for him."

The guards glanced at each other. Then one of them turned and shouted at someone in the camp and a moment later the gate creaked open. Corbulo stepped into the fort and the auxiliaries hastily closed the gate behind him. He looked around. The fort seemed like any other he had seen. In the centre of the open rectangular space was a single-storey barracks building made of turf, timber and thatch. A few worn-looking soldiers' tents had been raised along the northern ramparts and inside Corbulo could make out the shapes of several carroballistae, bolt throwers mounted on wagons. He grunted in surprise. He had not expected that kind of weaponry in a fort of this size. Closer by, along the western wall, a horse and a cow stood tethered to a stake and beside them a couple of engineers were repairing a cart. They gave him a sour glance. He turned towards the barracks. Smoke was rising from a hole in the roof. Then he noticed an auxiliary soldier striding towards him. Corbulo nodded politely as he faintly recognised him. The prefect and commander of the Ninth Batavians was nearly the same age as himself. It had been a long time since he had last seen him. He didn't really know the officer but at Inchtuthil Quintus had made him memorise the names of the Roman forts, units and commanders that he was likely to encounter and he remembered the name of the commander of the Ninth Batavians. He had met him once before.

"Do I know you?" the prefect said in good-natured disappointment. "The guard said that you were an old acquaintance; I was expecting…"

"I am sorry," Corbulo interrupted. "I was afraid your men would not let me in. We met once at Deva. You and your auxiliaries came with my cohort when we raided Hibernia. It was about ten years ago."

The prefect stared at Corbulo as if he was searching his memory. Then a grin appeared on his face.

"Ah, the great raid on Hibernia, I remember. Yes, I recognise you now. Hibernia." He allowed the name to linger for a moment. "If I recall it rained every single day that we were there."

Corbulo nodded and grinned.

"We don't get many visitors up here," the prefect said wearily, "but I do know who you are. You are that watch commander from the Twentieth who refused to support Vitellius when all your comrades did. They chained you to a tree outside the camp and made you eat nothing but barley for a month."

Corbulo looked surprised. "You heard about that?"

"Everyone did," the prefect said with a bemused look.

Corbulo chuckled.

"So what brings you to our comfortable outpost on the edge of the world?"

Corbulo scratched his chin. "I am retired now," he said. "I have a son who served with the Second Batavians. He has been posted as missing. On his last mission he was sent north. He was on his own. I am looking for him." Corbulo paused. "Have you or your men heard anything? Maybe the tribes are holding him as a hostage or as a slave. His name is Marcus. He may have come through here late last year."

The prefect looked thoughtful. Then he shook his head. "Afraid I haven't heard anything about a missing Roman soldier," he replied. He raised his hand and pointed to the east. "Over there live the Vacomagi. Their capital is called Tuesis. You will have passed through their land to get here. They are hostile to us." The prefect turned and pointed to the west. "Over in that direction we have the Decantae. They have made a formal alliance with us. We patrol as far as the great river. My advice is that if you are looking for your missing son, go and ask the Decantae. They are friendly enough as long as you don't insult them or try and sleep with their women."

Corbulo turned to look towards the west. There was a resigned look on his face.

"The Decantae," he murmured. "How far is it to their principal settlement?"

"About fifteen miles," the prefect replied. "It's near the coast between the river and the sea."

"A day's walk," Corbulo said. He nodded his thanks and turned to leave. Then he hesitated. "Prefect," Corbulo said thoughtfully, "I seem to remember that the Ninth Batavians are an all infantry unit. Is that still the case?"

"Yes that's right," the prefect replied. "My command is spread across the whole district. In addition to my twelve watch and signal towers, half my men are here and the other half are manning the fort at Balnageith further to the east."

"So there are no cavalry units in the area?" Corbulo asked.

The prefect shook his head. "We sometimes use local horses to get around but we are all infantry. If you are looking for a cavalry unit, you will have to go south to find them. None around here."

Corbulo looked pleased. He turned for the gate.

"Stay and have some breakfast with us," the prefect said suddenly. "Like I said, we don't get many visitors. I could do with the company." He looked around and Corbulo realised that the prefect was bored. "This fort is the arse end of the world and I have to share it with a bunch of mindless recruits," the officer complained. "Come and have some porridge and tell me the news from the south."

Corbulo followed the man into the barracks. A line of auxiliaries were sitting along a table having breakfast. They looked up at him but no one said a word. The prefect was right, the men looked young. They sat down at a separate table to the men and a cook slapped two bowls of porridge onto the table.

"I have got two more years to go before I retire and earn my citizenship," the prefect said as he ladled the porridge into his mouth. "Two more years to go. I should have had a nice easy posting. Somewhere in the south, close to the sea. A place where the local market sells mussels. Gods, I miss eating mussels. The food we receive up here is shit."

The officer gave his cook a dark look but the cook pretended not to notice.

"Last winter was terrible," the prefect said. "Half this fort was built in the dark. But at least we don't have any trouble from the Decantae. All the attacks on my men come from the highlands to the south. That's where the Caledonians like to hide. We caught one war band only a few weeks ago. They had a woman fighting with them." The prefect finished his porridge and wiped his mouth with his hand. "The last time any of us here had a woman was nearly a year ago," he said wearily. "My men are getting a little frustrated. It's going to lead to trouble."

"It looks like you are in the middle of two feuding tribes," Corbulo said as he finished off his porridge.

The prefect laughed. "The Decantae and the Vacomagi hate each other more than they hate us and I am glad they do. Having to cope with these hit-and-run attacks from one tribe is just about all we can handle."

Corbulo was studying the prefect with a thoughtful gaze.

"I hear rumours," Corbulo said, "that amber can be found here, somewhere along the coast?"

The expression on the prefect's face changed abruptly. He looked away.

"No, I didn't hear about that. I don't know anything about any amber," the officer murmured.

Chapter Forty-Two – The Decantae

Corbulo looked troubled as he strode away from the fort. The prefect had been lying to him when he'd said he knew nothing about the amber. He had seen it in the man's eyes. The officer was hiding something. He passed the impaled head on its spear and turned westwards. Fifteen miles was not too far, he thought, but his legs felt heavy and clumsy with disappointment. Cawdor had been the last fort in the chain of Roman fortifications and now this village of the Decantae may well be the final place where he could ask for information about Marcus. His search was coming to an end. Apprehensively he glanced up at the sky. How long did he have before the dreaded Caledonian winter came? He didn't know. If the Decantae had no news then he wasn't sure what he was going to do next. He could, he supposed, ask around in the Caledonian settlements that he'd seen but he was wary of that after his last encounter with the locals, especially now that the big war dog was no longer at his side. His mood soured. Maybe that was what he would end up doing? Maybe he was destined to have his throat cut and be buried in an unmarked grave. He kicked at a stone and sent it flying through the air.

    The Decantae village nestled on a flat terrace overlooking the great wooded river valley that cut through the land towards the south-west. It was late in the day and the sun had vanished behind the grey mountains to the west. Corbulo paused amongst the trees of the forest and stared down at the place. The round houses had been built in a large circle, grouped around an open space with all their doorways facing north-east as if intended to keep out the wind. Like the previous settlement he had entered a few days ago this one too did not have a wall or any external defences. The Decantae, it seemed, feared nothing and nobody. The village was large and full of activity. Smoke was curling upwards from at least six kilns and Corbulo could hear the dull rhythmic banging of blacksmiths at work. The settlement seemed to be another centre for iron production and if the village produced iron goods then it would be wealthy. He studied the men and women at work in the nearby fields. The villagers had planted grain in the fertile fields that surrounded their houses and on the higher ground, enclosed by a stone wall, were herds of cattle, horses and flocks of sheep. The animals were being supervised by a group of boys who were shouting to each other in loud excited voices. A couple of dogs were barking out of sight. Large, well organised and prosperous, that meant men with power would reside in this place. Corbulo scratched his ear. He would have to be careful even though these people were the nominal friends and allies of Rome.

Corbulo stepped out from the trees and started towards the nearest house. To the north he caught a sudden glimpse of the sea. Two ships were anchored close to the shore. The people working in the fields stopped what they were doing and turned to look at him. As he approached the circle of round houses three armed men strode out to meet him. They halted and spread out, blocking his path. One of the warriors had a nasty-looking wound across his cheek that looked barely healed. All three of them stared at him suspiciously.

"I am a friend," Corbulo said, raising the palms of his hands. "I have come from the Roman fort at Cawdor. I want to speak with your leader."

"He is not here, he will be back tomorrow," one of the men replied.

"You speak our language very well for a Roman," another muttered. "Who are you and what do you want?"

"I am a friend," Corbulo repeated himself. "The commander of the Roman fort said that the Decantae are friends and allies of Rome. I am here to look for my son. He is a Roman, like the men at Cawdor, but he is missing."

The warriors glanced at each other.

"Very well, Roman," one of them said at last. "You are welcome to stay in our village tonight. We are going to have a feast – you may join us."

Corbulo nodded gratefully. "I would like that very much," he murmured.

It was night. Corbulo sat on the straw-covered floor inside the largest and most impressive round house in the settlement. The front of the house had been built from stone and turf and the entrance floor was laid out with large, smooth white stones. Inside the main circular room a ring of massive wooden poles and beams held up the roof. The building was large enough to have a second floor. As he looked around Corbulo noticed a ladder disappearing into a dark hole in the wooden ceiling. He sat close to the large crackling fire sipping mead from a leather flask that was being passed round the packed circle of warriors. Another smaller fire, set within a circle of stones, was burning in the centre of the room. The flickering and leaping firelight was the only source of light in the crowded and noisy house. The warriors were pissed. Their laughter, shouts and boasting filled the room as a whole glistening pig roasted slowly over the fire. Gobbets of fat exploded into the flames. The smell was delicious and Corbulo felt his stomach growling with hunger. The feast, someone had tried to explain to him, was in honour of the forthcoming victory over the Vacomagi. Corbulo had listened politely and had only been able to understand half of what the warrior had been trying to tell him. A woman appeared with another flask of mead. By the doorway, two men with red noses and cheeks from too much drinking had started to sing a song. Soon the others joined in until the whole house was heaving. Corbulo looked around him and tried to smile. If only Quintus could see him now, sitting in the midst of their former foes, getting slowly pissed on mead. His friend would never believe him.

The singing petered out. The first of the roast meat was cut from the pig and a woman brought up another flask of mead. As she bent down a man grabbed her by the arm and fondled her arse. With a swift slap in the warrior's face she freed herself and escaped to raucous laughter. Corbulo nudged the man sitting next to him. The warrior was one of the men who had confronted him at the edge of the village. He looked pissed. Mead had dribbled into his beard.

"I am here to find my son. He is a Roman soldier," Corbulo shouted into the man's ear. "He may have come through here late last year. Do you know anything about a Roman? He was a cavalryman. His name is Marcus. He has red hair. He can speak your language just like I can. Maybe someone enslaved him?"

The man swayed slightly and for a moment Corbulo thought he was going to be sick.

"Not around here," the man replied hoarsely. "But there is a rumour that Dougal the druid is keeping someone locked up in that well of his." The man opened his mouth and burped.

Corbulo stared at him. "What did you just say?" he cried.

Just then someone grabbed Corbulo by his neck and tried to heave him up onto his feet. A drunken warrior stood before him grinning foolishly. The man was huge but too much drink had caused him to lose his coordination. His hand lost its grip around Corbulo's neck and he staggered backwards, narrowly missing the fire. Corbulo ignored the drunken fool. His eyes were fixed on his neighbour.

"Where can I find this well? Is this the same Dougal who lives in Bannatia?" he cried.

His neighbour was laughing but not at Corbulo. He was looking at the drunken brute beside the fire. The warrior was coming towards Corbulo again.

"Roman, on your feet. I want to speak to you," the man shouted, slurring his words. He leaned forwards and made another grab for Corbulo's throat. A blast of bad breath struck him in the face. Corbulo leapt to his feet and smashed his fist into the man's jaw. Then he stepped forwards and slammed his foot into the man's crotch.

"Leave me alone, you fucking arsehole," Corbulo roared.

The warrior made a whimpering noise. Then he collapsed onto his back. There was a moment of complete silence in the house. Then the warriors bellowed with laughter and excited shouts. The warrior whom Corbulo had struck lay on the straw floor, whimpering and gasping for breath as he pressed his hands to his crotch. Corbulo gave him an angry look before sitting down. He turned to his neighbour. The man was laughing too.

"Where is this well? Is it in Bannatia?"

The man opened his mouth, "You know nothing, do you. Dougal is our blood enemy. Soon we are going to kill him and his people."

"Where is this well?" Corbulo said with growing irritation.

"Yes the well is in Bannatia. It's on a peninsula to the east," the warrior cried above the noise in the house. "It's fortified by three ditches and a strong wall. The sea surrounds the place on three sides. The well is inside the village. No one has ever managed to capture Bannatia. We are going to be the first."

Corbulo sat back. His eyes widened. He could feel his heart pounding away. He wiped the sudden sweat from his forehead and fumbled for the flask of mead. He took a long drink. Bannatia, the Caledonian fort on the headland sticking out into the sea. The cavalry sword, the spatha, had been purchased from a man from the same place. Could the blade have once belonged to Marcus? The prefect had confirmed that there were no cavalry units in the area. Corbulo turned to stare at his neighbour. The man was still laughing and paying him no notice. No one saw the flush of sudden excitement that had appeared on Corbulo's face. In the morning he would set off to find this Caledonian fort on its headland.

Corbulo was woken by a painful kick to his shoulder. It was morning and he lay curled up on the floor of the house. He glared and was about to cry out in protest when he saw six men standing over him. They looked sober and serious.

"Get up!" one of them snarled.

Corbulo rose to his feet and rubbed his shoulder. He stiffened as he caught sight of the big man he had kicked in the balls. The Caledonian was sober and his face was sullen and vengeful. A reddish bruise on his right cheek marked the spot where Corbulo had hit him.

"What's this about?" Corbulo muttered. "I said I was a friend."

The men moved to surround him. They looked unfriendly and Corbulo suddenly noticed that all of them were armed.

"This man here claims you insulted him last night," one of the warriors said, gesturing at the big man with the bruise. "He has called you out to single combat. What is your answer?"

"Single combat? You are joking!" Corbulo exclaimed.

Agricola had forbidden single combat in his army when he'd become governor. Corbulo's laughter ceased abruptly as he saw that the men around him were serious.

"You snivelling piece of goat's liver," the big man sneered. "Are you too afraid to accept my challenge? Well, what can a man expect from a Roman coward. You are not a man, you are a weed under my foot. I am going to crush you."

Corbulo took a step back in alarm. He glanced around at the men.

"What if I say no?" he said quietly.

"You don't say no. You have insulted this man. He has the right to try and take vengeance for that insult," one of the men growled.

Corbulo looked around at the sleeping men on the floor and at the pig carcass and the dead fires. They were not going to let him go.

"Then I accept your challenge," Corbulo replied quietly. He raised himself to his full height but even so his head only came up to the man's jaw. He turned on his challenger. "Well you are a right piece of maggot shit, aren't you," Corbulo said angrily. "So how are we going to settle this?"

The man with the bruise grinned.

"Each of us may choose just one weapon. The fight is to the death," he said.

Corbulo looked away. How had he managed to get himself into this mess? The prefect had warned him about insulting the Caledonians. These barbarians took any insult, real or perceived, extremely seriously. Now he was locked into a fight that he didn't want or need. But he had to stay calm. Any show of weakness would just make his opponent more dangerous.

It seemed as if half the village had followed them to the meadow above the cliffs beside the sea. Corbulo had been forced to hand over his bow and arrows. That just left him with his gladius. He strode up to the edge of the cliffs and peered down. The sea boiled and smashed into the rocks far below. There would be no escape that way. He turned and strode back into the centre of the grassy field. Corbulo looked angry and tense. His opponent was preparing himself. The warrior was holding an axe. The villagers had gathered around them in a semicircle. Some were calling out encouragement to his opponent. No one was shouting in Corbulo's defence. Was this where his long journey was going to come to an end? Just when he had a solid lead regarding Marcus? Corbulo kicked at a turf of grass and glanced at the warrior's axe. It was the weapon he dreaded. He had seen the damage they could inflict and it was horrible. In a skilled hand the blade was terrifying. He glanced again at his opponent. The man was younger than him. He would be stronger too and no doubt, judging from the scars on his arms, he had been in battle before. He would have to try and end the fight quickly before his opponent exhausted him.

"Go on, start!" a man's voice suddenly cried out. The villagers fell silent. Corbulo pulled his gladius from its sheath and steadied himself. *Dance, keep moving, wait for the opening, strike.* His opponent raised his axe in his brawny arm and bellowed something that Corbulo did not understand. Then confidently the man came towards him. His eyes were fixed on Corbulo. He was swinging his axe through the air as if the weapon weighed nothing.

"I didn't insult you," Corbulo cried out. "You were drunk. You grabbed my throat."

The warrior's dark eyes sparkled but he did not reply. Then he lunged and the axe came sweeping down towards Corbulo. He sprang aside and stumbled backwards. His opponent allowed him no time to recover. The axe came slicing through the air aimed at his neck. Corbulo ducked and charged forwards but the warrior spun away, avoiding the thrusting gladius. Corbulo was panting as he stared at his opponent. The man was coming towards him again. There was going to be no let-up in the attacks. This man was not going to give up until he was dead. The villagers had started to yell encouragement at their man. Corbulo felt a spark of rage. This ridiculous duel was preventing him from finding his son. But he was going to find Marcus. With a cry the warrior came at him, aiming his axe at Corbulo's torso. At the last moment Corbulo stepped backwards and the wild swinging blow sliced through empty air. Corbulo charged and smashed headlong into the warrior. It was as if he had hit a stone wall but Corbulo's rage had taken over. The force of his charge sent both men tumbling to the ground in a confused tangle of arms and legs. Corbulo heard himself screaming. The warrior was underneath him trying to hit him with his axe. Corbulo raised his head and smashed it into the man's skull. Pain exploded in Corbulo's head but he hardly felt it. A madness seemed to have taken hold of him. Blood welled up from his opponent's face. Corbulo just had time to catch the man's arm and force the axe blow to a halt. Both of them strained and groaned as they grappled with each other's arms and legs. Then Corbulo managed to raise his head and once more he smashed his forehead into his opponent's head. Then he did it again. He felt the warrior's grip slacken. In a frenzy he hit the man again. Blood was pouring from the man's face. His opponent coughed and spluttered. The blood was running into his mouth. Corbulo freed his right hand and tore the axe from the man's hand and flung it away. Then he brought up his fist and started pummelling the Caledonian's face with blow after blow until the man was no longer moving.

"What is going on here?" a voice suddenly shouted. The villagers, who had fallen silent as they witnessed the fall of their man, turned and stepped aside respectfully as three men strode boldly into the field. Corbulo looked up. His face was splattered with blood and his hands and arms too were covered in it. He stared at the newcomers and then rose to his feet in sudden alarm.

"You!" Vellocatus cried in surprise. The slaver's eyes bulged.

"You are supposed to be dead!"

Beside Vellocatus, Corbulo recognised the tall barbarian chief he had met in Inchtuthil and bringing up the rear was the auxiliary soldier who had tried to kill him. At the sight of Corbulo, the auxiliary froze and broke out in a deep blush.

"You!" Vellocatus pointed a finger at Corbulo, but the slaver was unable to add anything else. The man seemed speechless.

Behind the two men Corbulo suddenly saw the auxiliary turn and run. In an instant the man had disappeared into the crowd.

Vellocatus half turned and stared at the crowd of villagers.

"Bestia, you lying piece of shit, I am going to cut your balls off!" he roared.

"I said what is going on here?" Baldurix bellowed again. The shout from the Decantae chief silenced everyone.

"Kill him – he knows about the amber," Vellocatus snarled, pointing at Corbulo. "He is the man we met at Inchtuthil."

"Yes I recognise him," Baldurix nodded. He gestured at the warriors in the crowd. "Bring him to me," he ordered.

Corbulo wiped the blood from his eyes. Then as the warriors came towards him he turned, stooped, picked up his gladius and started to run. The edge of the cliffs drew closer. He heard a shout behind him. Then he was leaping into empty space, his arms and legs flailing in the air before he tumbled down towards the sea far below.

Chapter Forty-Three – The Chambered Well

Corbulo plunged into the water and went down in a stream of bubbles. Down, down he went into a green murky world. The cold water pressed around him. His lungs ached for air. For a moment he could not tell up from down. Wildly he scrabbled around with his arms. His fingers still gripped his gladius. A huge underground rock loomed up and vanished. Then he was going up again. He burst to the surface gasping for air. His leap had landed him six or seven yards from the boulder-strewn cliff face. He looked up. The cliff top was lined with people peering down at him. Then an arrow smacked into the water close to his head. Corbulo took a great mouthful of air and vanished underwater. He surfaced once more and as he did so another arrow smacked into the water close by. Instinctively he ducked his head. The cliffs were high and stretched away as far as he could see. There was no beach, just a tumble of rocks and boulders at the base of the cliffs. The villagers would have to jump into the sea if they wanted to catch him. He twisted his head and stared at the two galleys anchored further out. He could see no one aboard but the ships would be manned. He ducked underwater and swam towards the shore. Hopefully the angle of the cliffs would give him some protection from the arrows. He cut his foot on a sharp rock and cried out in pain as the saltwater stung the wound. With his hand he grasped hold of a rock and looked up. He had been right. The cliffs had a slight overhang. The villagers could not see him. He gasped and spat some seawater from his mouth.

The sun was rising to the east. Bannatia, the Caledonian fort was on a headland to the east. He pushed himself off the rock and started to make his way along the shore in the direction of the rising sun.

Corbulo sat on the rock as the sea surged and retreated around him. The spray from the waves struck his face but he didn't seem to notice. His heart was pounding with excitement and trepidation as he went over his plan one final time. It was night and in the heavens the stars twinkled and out at sea the moon cast its dim light across the rolling waves. Beside him the dark hole marked the entrance to the sea cave. He was exhausted and weak from lack of food and rest but he had made it. It had taken him two days to find the headland. Now he sat below the cliffs at the tip of the peninsula where the land gave way to the sea. There was no beach, just a jumble of fallen rocks and boulders. Somewhere above him was the Caledonian fort. He had glimpsed it as he had swum out to the peninsula tip earlier that evening. The landward defences looked formidable and he had quickly given up on the idea of trying to get into the fort from that direction but he had seen no walls along the seaward side of the headland. Maybe the defenders judged the sea and the cliffs to provide adequate protection.

At last he stirred and turned to peer up at the cliff face. The cliffs were high but they weren't smooth. Erosion and the power of wind and water had taken their toll and the jagged face was lined with natural cracks and ledges. He started to climb. It was slow going but not too difficult and he made steady progress. The sea dropped away and soon only the wind kept him company. He froze, spread-eagled against the rocks as he dislodged a stone and saw it clatter down and bounce into the sea. His ears strained to listen but all he could hear was the dull crash of the waves and the wind as it tugged at his sodden tunic. Gingerly he peered upwards. Would the Caledonians have posted a guard on the cliff top? He had not seen or heard anyone. He fumbled for the next handhold and heaved himself up. The climb was not too difficult but in the darkness he had to be careful he didn't lose his grip. He climbed on, fumbling blindly for handholds and ledges, testing them with his fingers and feet. Then at last he felt his fingers touch soft grass. He heaved himself up and rolled onto the cliff, panting for breath. The stars twinkled as he stared up at them. He got to his feet and crouched, peering into the darkness.

As his eyes adjusted he could make out a rampart to his right. The turf wall curved away towards the cliff edge. To his left he caught sight of another wall that he had not seen from the sea. The rampart stretched away in a straight line down the edge of the cliffs and off into the darkness. In front of him, between the two walls, was an open space. He rose and started forwards, slipping into the gap between the two defensive walls. After a short while a round house loomed up out of the darkness. Corbulo crouched beside the wall to listen. Nothing. Then he heard it, the gentle snoring of someone on the other side of the wall. He rose and moved on. Another house appeared and then another. The gap between the two defensive walls was widening. He was in the midst of the settlement. He paused to listen again but could hear nothing unusual. The fort was large and as he looked around he could make out the shapes of more and more houses, their thatched roofs nearly touching the ground. Where was the chambered well? He moved on silently, flitting past the houses. Then he flung himself flat onto the grass. Nearby a dog had suddenly started to bark. It was coming from somewhere to his left. He tensed, expecting to be attacked, but the dog did not come. The barking, however, continued. Corbulo rose and moved towards the noise. In the moonlight he suddenly caught sight of the animal. The dog was a sheepdog and it stood chained to a post. The animal growled and bared its teeth menacingly as he approached. Corbulo slid his gladius from its sheath, grabbed hold of the dog and slit its throat in one swift movement. The barking stopped. The dog's hot blood spurted onto his hand as he laid the body on the ground. He turned to listen. Nothing. Then suddenly he saw movement in the darkness. Someone was coming towards him.

"Girl, where are you?" a voice called urgently. Corbulo stooped and quickly cut the dog's lead with his sword and scooped it up before moving backwards. In the pale moonlight he saw a figure. The man was holding something: a spear. He stopped beside the wooden post and gasped as he caught sight of the dead dog. As he bent down to touch the animal Corbulo stepped up behind him, raised his sword and with a swift sharp movement cut the man's throat. There was a gurgle and hot blood spurted across Corbulo's hand and sword. He clamped his hand over the dying man's mouth and slowly lowered him to the ground beside the dead animal. Then he picked up the spear that the man had dropped. The watchman had been guarding something. He took a few steps in the direction from which the man had come and peered into the darkness. Nothing. He strode forwards and nearly fell down the flight of stone steps. He steadied himself just in time. In the darkness his breathing came in silent sharp bursts. His muscles ached with tension. He laid the spear on the ground and stared at the steps. They were leading down into the earth. He had found the well. This had to be the place. This was what the watchman had been guarding. Carefully he started down the steps. The ground towered over him, threatening to bury him as he descended deeper into the earth. His descent came to an abrupt halt as he nearly hit his face on a door. He reeled in surprise. Then he took a deep breath and felt his way across the door until he found the handle. He tried it but the door did not move. Damn. In the darkness his fingers explored the door. Of course, there would be a bolt. His fingers touched something cold and metallic. Then he had it. He took another deep breath and forced the bolt upwards. The door swung open of its own accord with a slight creaking noise.

"Marcus," Corbulo whispered hoarsely in Latin, "are you there, son, are you in here?"

He opened the door wider and peered into the dark chamber beyond. From somewhere he could hear the drip of water on water. A woman's face suddenly appeared from out of the darkness like a ghost. She looked startled. Corbulo yelped in pure shock and fright and without thinking smashed his fist into the girl's face, sending her spinning against the wall. He heard her head hit the stone and her body crumple to the floor. He leapt forwards and crouched beside her. She was out like a light but she was still alive. Corbulo's breath was coming in short sharp gasps as a crushing wave of disappointment swept over him. The rumours had been right. Someone had been kept prisoner within this chambered well but it had not been his son. It had been a woman.

Then the hairs on his neck stood up as he heard another voice. It was a man's voice and it was coming from deeper within the chamber.

"Marcus," the voice groaned weakly, "I am Marcus. I am a cavalryman. Second Batavian Auxiliary Cohort."

Chapter Forty-Four – Blood Feud

Baldurix opened his mouth in disbelief as he saw the Roman leap over the cliff. Then he, like the rest of the villagers, was running towards the edge. He halted at the edge of the cliff and peered at the sea below. By his side the slaver was doing the same.

"There he is," the man shouted. "Shoot the bastard."

One of Baldurix's men notched an arrow, took aim and fired. He missed. Far below them in the sea the Roman vanished beneath the waves. Baldurix watched as another arrow missed. Then the Roman was beneath them and they lost sight of him.

"I want two groups," Baldurix shouted. "One is to go west and search for that man along the coast, the other is to go east. If you find him you are to kill him. I will reward any man who brings me back that Roman's head."

Baldurix glared at Vellocatus as the villagers started to disperse.

"I thought you said he was dead," he snapped.

Vellocatus looked annoyed. "That's what Bestia told me," he said, casting about for the auxiliary soldier, but there was no sign of him.

Baldurix shook his head in disgust. Then he was off stomping back towards his village with the slaver following close behind. His plan had been going well until this unexpected surprise. Vellocatus had kept his word, had found the amber cave and had brought him some of the stones to show to the Romans. It was from Cawdor that he, Vellocatus and Bestia had just come that morning. The Roman prefect, on seeing the amber, had greedily asked them where they had found it but Vellocatus had told the officer to mind his own business. Vellocatus had kept the exact location a closely guarded secret. The prefect had eventually agreed to the terms they had discussed before and they had sealed their new alliance with a cup of mead. Now that the Romans were going to help him he was free to attack the Vacomagi and end the blood feud in his favour. It was time to gather his men and brief them on the plan of attack that he had devised. As he strode along he glanced at Vellocatus. The slaver had been remarkably loyal since they had struck their deal all those months ago in Eburacum. He had not really expected Vellocatus to honour his promises but he had. Baldurix smiled. The man was indeed full of surprises but he was also a blundering idiot. First he had allowed the girl to escape and now this Roman adventurer had reappeared.

Baldurix sat on the straw-covered floor of his house. The circle of warriors were watching him, waiting for him to speak. In the hearth the fire crackled and hissed. Baldurix remained silent as his woman finished passing around the drinking flasks. Then as she left the room he glanced up at Vellocatus who was standing leaning against one of the wooden posts that was holding up the roof.

"The time has come," he said, clearing his throat, "to end the existence of the Vacomagi and end this blood feud that has existed for so long."

There was a murmur of agreement from the assembled warriors.

"The Romans have pledged to support us. With their help we will crush our enemies and forever rid the land of this stain," he growled. "This morning I have sent word to all the men who are sworn to follow me. I have summoned them here. It will take some time before all our warriors arrive from the outlying settlements. We go to war at dawn in two days' time."

"How many will come?" one of the warriors asked.

"About a thousand men," Baldurix replied with a confident nod. "Now this is what we are going to do. Our first blow will be delivered by stealth. A small group of men whom I handpicked myself have already set off this morning into Vacomagi territory. They will go to Dougal's house. The Vacomagi look to him for leadership. For those of you who don't know, Dougal has a house just outside Bannatia. My men will attack the druid at night. They will kill the old fool. With their leader slain the Vacomagi will be disorganised and become dispirited."

The warriors glanced at each other in surprise.

"You know something about that, don't you," a voice muttered darkly. "Even a boy can sneak into another's house and murder his enemy when he is asleep. That is how this feud began. But where is the honour and the glory in doing that?"

"Silence," Baldurix bellowed. He glared at the man who had spoken out. "If I didn't know you any better, I would think that you were challenging me," Baldurix said in a dangerous voice. "Well, are you challenging me?"

The men in the room suddenly looked tense. There was silence. Then the man who had spoken shook his head.

"I spoke hastily, Baldurix, apologies," he murmured.

Baldurix looked at the others. Then he continued, "The Romans have promised to besiege Bannatia. The prefect has told me that his men will bombard the fort with artillery. The aim will be to prevent the men inside from joining forces with their friends and kin at Tuesis. This will give us the advantage of numbers."

"When will all of this take place?" a man asked.

"At dawn in precisely four days' time," Baldurix replied. He was about to continue when a voice interrupted him.

"So we are to fight as allies of the Romans?" the man said with a distinct lack of enthusiasm. "I don't know about you but the last time I saw a Roman I was with Calgacus and they were very much my enemy."

A few voices around the room murmured in agreement.

"The Romans are our friends. They are going to help us destroy the Vacomagi." Baldurix raised his voice, "Have you all forgotten the blood feud that exists between us? Have you forgotten our many dead and maimed? Have you forgotten about the houses that they burned and the cattle they stole from us? Have you forgotten the young Vacomagi druid who raped and murdered my sister?" He glared at the warriors in the circle. "The time for vengeance has come. The Romans will give us the advantage that we need. They will be our friends until I say they are not. If anyone disagrees with that then leave now and do not come back."

The men sitting in the circle held their breath. They glanced at each other but no one spoke. Then a single man rose to his feet and headed for the door. Baldurix watched him go.

"Anyone else?" He glared.

His question was answered with silence.

Baldurix nodded, satisfied. "Now the timing of our attacks is important. Our main force led by me will be assembled and ready to go at dawn in two days' time. We will move east down the Nairn valley, past the Roman fort at Cawdor and strike the Vacomagi in Tuesis, their capital. We will burn the place to the ground. Our assault must take place in exactly four days' time, at the same moment as the Romans begin their siege of Bannatia. We will take the Vacomagi by surprise. They will be leaderless, a quarter of their men will be bottled up in Bannatia and we will outnumber our enemy. We will slaughter their men and take the women and children as slaves." Baldurix looked round. "This feud will be over in five days."

"In five days," Vellocatus piped up, "all of you are going to be wealthy men. The Romans like wealthy men. They have invented many objects and pleasures for a man to spend his wealth on. You have no idea, but you will get to know them soon."

A grizzled white-bearded warrior who looked older than the rest raised his hand.

"I have lived all my life beside the Vacomagi," he said hoarsely. "In bravery and in numbers they match us." The old veteran paused and glanced at Baldurix. "The plan that you propose is risky. What if the Vacomagi catch wind of what we are up to? What happens if the Romans don't fulfil their promises? The druids have a habit of knowing what is going to happen. They speak with the gods. Have the gods given us a sign that we are going to be victorious?"

Baldurix's face darkened and he struggled to find an answer. It was Vellocatus who came to his aid. The slaver laughed.

"The gods sent me to you," he said boastfully. "My presence here is a sign from the gods that they will grant you victory. It was I who discovered the amber. It is I who convinced the Romans to join us. It is I who has turned the wind in your favour. What more do you need?"

The room fell silent. The old warrior looked unimpressed. Ignoring Vellocatus he looked directly at Baldurix.

"Maybe single combat would be a better way to settle this blood feud," he croaked. "Maybe you," he raised his hand and pointed a bony, gnarled finger at Baldurix, "should challenge the bravest and best of the Vacomagi to single combat. It is better to spill the blood of just one man than that of a whole clan."

"Nonsense," Vellocatus interrupted hastily. "It is too late for that now. We have promised the Romans a share of the amber. If we don't deliver there is going to be trouble. Besides, we gang raped Dougal's daughter. The druid is never going to let that go. He and his clan have to die. We have no other choice."

"He is right," Baldurix raised his voice, "It is too late for single combat. The Vacomagi must be destroyed. We leave at dawn in two days' time. Now get your men ready. There will be no delays."

Baldurix got to his feet and the circle broke up as the others rose and headed for the doorway.

As the warriors trooped out Baldurix gestured for Vellocatus to remain behind. Then when they were the only two left in the house he spoke.

"At dawn, the day after we have left, you will sail to Bannatia and start taking the amber from that cave," he said. "Try and time your arrival to coincide with the appearance of the Roman soldiers. The Romans should provide enough of a distraction and protection for you and your men to get in close."

Vellocatus grinned. "Don't worry, I won't let you down."

"I know you won't," Baldurix nodded with a serious expression, "because some of my men will be coming with you on your ship. When you have the amber you are to return here and we shall share the spoils. After that we can go our separate ways."

The grin faded slowly from Vellocatus's face. "Won't you need every warrior that you can muster to be with you?" he said. "Honestly, there is no need to have your men accompany me. I can handle it."

Baldurix shook his head. "I trust you, but my men will go with you nevertheless. The amber is what is making all of this happen. I want to make sure all goes well."

Vellocatus looked away. For a moment he looked unhappy. Then abruptly he smiled and stuck out his hand.

"It is not a problem. I shall see you in five days' time then," he smiled.

Baldurix gripped the slaver's hand. His eyes twinkled mysteriously. Then he smiled in return.

"Goodbye, Vellocatus. Till we meet in five days," he said.

Chapter Forty-Five – The Battle of the Clava Stones

It was noon two days later and Baldurix stood staring at the cairn. A circle of standing stones surrounded the ancient stone burial chamber and there were two other cairns to his left. The three stone burial chambers formed a line, angled along the winter solstice, from north-east to south-west. The chambers were sealed with coloured stones and covered with a domed mound of earth and grass around four yards high. No one knew who had built these monuments. The druids had no collective memory of their construction and there were no songs or tales told about them around the fireplace. The burial chambers were old, really old. They belonged to his ancestors. But Baldurix knew who lay buried inside. These were the graves of long-dead heroes, of great men, of powerful warriors from a time long ago. One day he too would be carried into such a tomb and laid to rest, together with his armour, jewellery and weapons. When they sealed him into that chamber he would become immortal and generation after generation would wander past his tomb and know that a great man resided within.

Behind him hundreds of his warriors poured past in a large disorganised mass as they headed east along the Nairn. Baldurix shifted his gaze and stared at the river that flowed beyond the cairns. The water level was low for it was high summer. The cairns had been constructed on a flat gravel terrace above the river and a few trees lined the bank. Beyond the river the land rose to the crest of a grassy ridge. He glanced again at the cairns as old memories stirred themselves. The young druid who had raped his sister had been Dougal's son. Baldurix had only been a boy when it had happened. He'd lain in the darkness on the straw on the second floor of his father's house and had heard his father's enraged voice bellowing below. He had heard his sister crying. Dougal's boy had raped his sister. So that night Baldurix, still only thirteen, had taken his father's sword and slipped out of the house and alone and unaided he'd gone to the druid's home and had murdered Dougal's son as he lay sleeping. He had avenged the insult to his family's honour. It was a few days later when news of the murder had spread that he'd found his sister's body floating face down in the lake. Murder had been answered with murder and from that day onwards a blood feud had existed. Over the following years the feud had grown rapidly to include nearly all the men of the rival tribes as raid and counter-raid had deepened the mutual loathing and bitterness.

A horseman suddenly appeared on the ridge across the river. Baldurix frowned as the rider, seeing the column of warriors, wheeled his horse round and came galloping towards him. The horseman splashed through the river. As he drew closer Baldurix caught sight of a human head hanging around the horse's neck. The man was shouting something. Baldurix's face grew pale as at last he recognised the rider. It was one of the warriors he'd sent to assassinate the druid. What was the man doing here? The rider veered towards him.

"They are right behind me," the man cried out as he pulled up beside Baldurix. "We failed. They were waiting for us. The others are dead."

Baldurix stared at the rider's exhausted face in stunned silence.

"Who is behind you?" he said.

"Dougal and his men," the rider gasped. "The Vacomagi are right behind me. They are coming with their full force."

Baldurix turned to stare at the ridge beyond the river in sudden alarm. It wasn't possible. How could Dougal have reacted so quickly? Then he closed his eyes in silent, bitter resignation. Someone had warned the druid. Of course, it was the girl. She had heard him and Vellocatus discussing what they were going to do. Vellocatus, stupid idiotic Vellocatus had allowed her to escape. He should have realised that the girl would survive the sea and warn her father but it was too late for all of that now.

The mournful bellowing of a carnyx shattered the stale noon air. The noise had come from behind the ridge across the river. Then a few moments later a lone chariot appeared on the crest with two men standing on its platform.

"Dougal," Baldurix hissed as he caught sight of the druid's white robes and long beard.

Baldurix turned to his warriors behind him. The men had heard the carnyx and had turned to see what was going on.

"The Vacomagi are here in full force," Baldurix roared. "Prepare to fight. Form a line. I want a shield wall along the cairns. Move, move, move!"

For a moment the mass of warriors did not move. Then the warriors broke out into a great mass of disorganised activity as war bands, fathers, sons, brothers and friends rushed around looking for each other.

Baldurix turned to stare at the ridge to the north. Very well, he thought. If he could not surprise his enemy then he would fight him here amongst the burial chambers of the ancients. Around him chaos reigned as his warriors rushed to take their place beside their friends and kin in the growing shield wall. Baldurix grabbed hold of the cairn and clambered up the domed roof that he'd been admiring only a few moments ago. As he reached the top the deep tones of another carnyx could be heard and then another. He turned to look at his men. The shield wall was several men thick and stretched away in a gentle C formation with the wall facing the river and the three cairns breaking up the line. There was no cavalry or charioteers. This was going to be an infantry battle. Then he heard cries coming from across the river. On the ridge a long line of men had appeared. The druid had spotted him for Baldurix saw Dougal raise his oak staff high in the air and point it in his direction. The warriors on the ridge began to swarm down towards the river. The hillside turned black with moving men. Baldurix felt a bead of unease worm its way into his mind.

"Men of the Decantae," he cried, turning to the shield wall, "you will stand your ground. You will win this fight. You will do so under the gaze of the ancients. They will be watching you. Do not disappoint them."

The warriors in the wall shouted their battle cries and raised their weapons in the air. Then they turned to grimly await the enemy. The Vacomagi were surging down the hillside. Their foremost men splashed through the river and slowed to a walk as they got to a hundred paces from the shield wall. Then they halted and began to form their own line. In dress and weapons there was no difference between the two feuding tribes. But war band and friends would fight together and know each other by face and name. There would be no confusion about who was on whose side during the battle. Baldurix peered at the enemy ranks as they formed up but he couldn't see the druid anywhere. He unbuckled his heavy two-handed war hammer and slid down the roof of the cairn and onto the ground in front of his shield wall. The weapon was heavy but it could kill a man with a single blow. His men cheered as they caught sight of their leader. Baldurix raised his hammer in the air to show all his men where he had chosen to take his position.

The Vacomagi wall looked ready and for a few moments the thousand or so men on each side stared at their enemy in grim silence. Baldurix lowered his hammer and turned to face his enemy. Most of the Vacomagi were not wearing armour but here and there he noticed a man with leather body armour or a bronze breast plate strapped across his torso. The enemy shield wall was lined with long oval shields made of hide-covered wood with metal ridges and spines and engraved with a multitude of different designs and patterns. Then he noticed a figure pushing his way towards the front. The white-robed druid stepped out beyond his men and raised his oak staff without saying a word. The warriors around Baldurix tensed. Then the druid's staff came swooping down and a great shrieking yell rose from the Vacomagi ranks as their warriors leapt forwards and came running towards him in a mad chaotic charge.

The enemy warriors came on like the tide rushing across the beach. The men were screaming their battle cries. A volley of spears and javelins tore into the charging men, impaling and tumbling men to the ground, but the momentum of the charge was not lost and a moment later it smashed into Baldurix's shield wall and kept on going. In an instant the cohesion of the shield wall was broken by the force of the charge and the battle descended into chaos. Baldurix roared and swung his two-handed hammer into a man's head. He caught him clean on the neck and the blow sent the warrior flying back into the ranks of his charging comrades. Baldurix turned and swung his hammer in a wide circle around himself, catching a man on the back of his knee and sending him somersaulting into the air. A head flew over the battle field and landed on top of the domed roof of the burial chamber. Around Baldurix men were hacking and stabbing at each other, screaming, yelling and pushing. A warrior swung his long sword at Baldurix, missing him by inches. Baldurix nearly tripped over a corpse. He roared his battle cry and swung his heavy hammer in an arc before him, hitting someone full on in his chest. The man collapsed without making a sound.

Wildly he glanced over his shoulder. He had no idea how the battle was going. Was he winning, was he losing? The fight seemed to have descended into a gigantic brawl. A man came at him with an axe but Baldurix thrust his hammer head into the man's face, sending him crashing backwards against the wall of the cairn. One of his men finished the enemy off by stabbing him in the chest. Where was the druid? A madness seemed to have taken hold of him. He was going to kill that old maniac just like he had killed his son all those years ago.

"Dougal, where are you!" he roared. "I am coming for you."

Baldurix swung his hammer with great force and skill but by now his enemy had become wary of him and the weapon and as he stepped forwards they gave him a wide berth.

"Fight me!" he screamed. "Fight me, you cowards!"

But no one did.

Then behind him he heard a shout that made his blood grow cold.

"The Decantae are fleeing, they are fleeing. After them!"

A great roar rose up all around him and Baldurix suddenly knew that he was surrounded. Warily he took a step back so that his back was protected by the cairn. "To me, to me," he roared.

A few of his men stumbled towards him. Baldurix twisted his neck to look around the cairn and gasped. A great horde of men were running away back the way he'd come that morning. They were his men. The cowards were running away. They had left him here to die. In frustration he took a step forwards and swung his hammer at the enemy who were now pressing closer from all sides. The Vacomagi were laughing now and jeering. They had him trapped against the cairn. Baldurix roared his battle cry and caught a man on his shoulder and sent him spinning into his own ranks.

"Come on then!" he screamed. "Who of you thinks he is going to kill me?"

But no one took up the challenge. Around him the small band of brave men who had tried to protect their leader dwindled as one after the other was cut down and killed. Baldurix lunged time and time again but he could not turn the tide. The battle was lost. As the last of his companions collapsed to the ground he flung himself onto the cairn and with desperate strength clambered up the earthen mound. On top of the dome he crouched, panting for breath. The Vacomagi surrounded him on all sides. They were insulting him now. Baldurix stood up and raised his hammer in the air.

"I am Baldurix of the Decantae and you shall not take me alive!" he yelled in defiance.

Then something hard hit him in the back of his head and he toppled over and tumbled from the cairn and onto the ground.

When he came to he was lying on his back. Baldurix tried to move but his feet and hands had been bound tightly together. His head ached and the hair on the back of his head was soaked with blood. He stared up at the sky and blinked. Then his vision was filled by a face. An old man with a grey beard and pale blue eyes was staring down at him. There was no emotion at all on the druid's face. Then quick as lightning a bony hand grabbed his throat, with surprising strength for such an old man, and started to squeeze it. Baldurix coughed and spluttered and his eyes bulged in their sockets. He stared at the druid's pale blue eyes, unable to look away.

"You killed my son," a voice whispered. "You killed your sister. Did you not realise? I am going to tell you the truth of what happened. The truth, which in your heart you have known about from the start. Your sister was not raped. She wanted to be my son's woman. I was going to marry them. They loved each other but your father forbade the match. But they decided to go ahead with it anyway. Then you killed my boy and in her grief your sister killed herself. So you see, it was you who murdered your sister, not us."

The druid's pale blue eyes seemed to be on fire. Baldurix felt the air slowly being driven from his lungs. He spluttered and gasped.

"Admit it," the voice whispered. "In your heart you have known all along that this is the truth. You know they wanted to be together."

"Give me a warrior's death and bury me next to my ancestors," Baldurix gasped as the bony fingers squeezed and squeezed. "Then I will admit," he wheezed, "that that is the truth of the matter."

The pale blue eyes stared down at him for a long moment.

"No, your head will be placed on a spear for all to see and when it is rotten and disfigured I shall throw it into the sea," the voice whispered cruelly. "Then your soul will be doomed to wander for all eternity. You will never find a final resting place nor shall you see your forefathers again. So this feud will come to an end and my son's murder will be avenged."

"No," Baldurix gasped in terror.

Chapter Forty-Six – The Dream

Vellocatus strode up and down the shoreline staring at his ship that lay anchored a hundred paces away. He looked impatient and tense. It was noon. Baldurix and his warriors had marched away that morning and Vellocatus had been left with nothing to do but wait. He wasn't very good at waiting. The galley captain had told him that the wind was likely to remain unfavourable if they were to sail east. They would have to rely on the oars and their progress was likely to be slow. He picked up a stone and flung it into the sea. And there was something else that was making him nervous. What if this Corbulo, this Roman adventurer who was pretending to look for his son, found the amber cave before he could make it back to Bannatia? Baldurix's search parties had found no trace of the man. He had vanished. The shock of seeing that man still alive had unnerved him. Who was he working for? Had Agricola set up his own expedition to find the amber? That would fit, he thought bitterly. He had seen enough about the Romans to know their avarice was boundless.

He picked up another stone and flung it into the waves. But Baldurix had given him strict instructions to leave at dawn tomorrow and only arrive at the amber cave at dawn in two days' time. Vellocatus glanced furtively across at the four men lounging about on the rocks. They were Baldurix's men and they had started to follow him everywhere. Even when he'd gone to have a shit he'd noticed one of them lurking nearby. They were not letting him out of their sights, not for a single moment. The presence of the men unsettled him. It felt like he was a prisoner. It felt as if his every move and thought was being studied. Did Baldurix no longer trust him? The tall Caledonian warrior may share his sexual vices but outwardly he appeared to be a man who kept his word. Vellocatus could recognise untrustworthiness in people but he had seen none of it in Baldurix. He grunted to himself. It was more likely that Baldurix was taking precautions to protect his investment. Vellocatus looked away and smiled grimly. Well two could play that game.

His own mercenaries, all ten of them, sat a little distance away; two of them were gambling with dice and the rest lay stretched out in the sun, dozing or looking bored. Vellocatus stopped walking. He had spent everything he had on this venture. The mercenaries, the ship, the captain and his crew. The expense had cleaned him out. He was not going back south without the amber. He would do anything to get his hands on the coloured stones. His life depended on them. He raised his hand and beckoned for one of his mercenaries to come over. The man rose to his feet lazily and Vellocatus pressed his lips together in silent irritation. Bestia was good at handling the insolence of these mercenaries but there had been no sign of Bestia since the auxiliary soldier had run away. Bestia was probably halfway to Rome by now, Vellocatus thought darkly. The man could have collected his pension and become a Roman citizen if he'd only remained in the army for a few more years. Now he had deserted. He'd become a fugitive, with no pension, no amber and with nowhere to go. Damn that man and his lies. He'd asked the soldier to do a simple straightforward job and he had failed twice and what was worse he had lied to him twice. A man who lied to him was useless. A man who lied to him was showing disrespect. But Bestia's disappearance didn't change anything. He would never see Bestia again and if he did he would kill him. The auxiliary would forever be a piece of worm beneath his boot.

The mercenary came up to him and raised his chin in an inquiring gesture.

"Get the men ready. The plan has changed – we are going to go now," Vellocatus growled. Then abruptly he turned and strode away. As he splashed through the surf towards the small log boat that would take him across to the galley he noticed Baldurix's men rise to their feet. They came towards him.

"Where are you going? Baldurix told you to leave at dawn tomorrow," one of them said.

"Well Baldurix is not here and I am going now," Vellocatus retorted.

The four men exchanged glances. They were armed.

"My captain says the wind is not favourable," Vellocatus said. "I just want to make sure that we arrive on time as planned."

"Then we are coming with you," another replied.

"Is that really necessary?" Vellocatus said wearily. "Baldurix and I are friends. Do you not trust me?"

"Not in the slightest," another man murmured, fixing him with a challenging eye.

The rowers heaved and strained as their oars plunged into the sea, propelling the galley along the coast. Vellocatus stood at his usual place in the prow. He looked annoyed. Behind him Baldurix's warriors crowded the deck. There were more of them than on the first leg of their journey and they outnumbered his own mercenaries by two to one. He had protested of course but short of starting a fight there was not much he could do about it apart from gnash his teeth in frustration. The men had said that they were acting on Baldurix's instructions. They had refused to listen to him and one of them had even insulted him. No matter, he thought. He had managed to speak to his mercenaries. Once they reached the amber cave he would take half of Baldurix's men with him to help collect the amber and whilst they were ashore his mercenaries would pounce on the remainder of the warriors, kill them and dump their bodies overboard. Then when he and the others returned with the sacks of amber his mercenaries would ambush Baldurix's men as they came onboard. With his rivals dead and disposed of he would be free to sail away with the amber.

"The rowers are exhausted," a voice said suddenly. "It's getting late. We should make for the shore and put up for the night."

Vellocatus recognised the captain's voice. He looked up at the sky. For once the captain was right. It would be dark in an hour or so.

"You were right about the wind," Vellocatus said, making a huge effort to be polite. "Take her into the shore and find us a spot where we can spend the night, unobserved if possible."

The captain nodded and walked away. Vellocatus closed his eyes. He had to be polite to the captain and the rowers. When the time came to murder Baldurix's men he needed the crew to remain neutral.

Vellocatus woke with a start. It was still dark. Around him the ship's company were asleep. Someone was snoring and he could hear the gentle lap of the waves on the shore. The dream had been so vivid that he'd thought it had been real. He had been lying on his back in a grassy field. He had been hot; the heat had been all around him, drenching him in sweat, but he could not escape. He had looked around for the heat source but there had been nothing, just a blank world. In his dream he had gotten hotter and hotter. Then he'd woken. He stared up at the star-filled sky. His forehead was drenched in sweat. Dreams like this did not just happen. This was a sign. The gods were talking to him. What had they been trying to tell him? He rubbed his eyes. Then it came to him. The heat! He had heard that it was always hot in Alexandria. He smiled. The gods were telling him that he would succeed.

He raised himself up on his elbows and looked around the camp. Bodies lay asleep everywhere. As they had anchored off the cove the previous evening he had toyed with the idea of murdering Baldurix's men in their sleep. The plan, however, had been thwarted by the insistence of Baldurix's men that they sleep onboard the galley whilst the crew and his own mercenaries slept ashore. They had refused to accept anything else and he had been forced to go along with it. Vellocatus turned to glance out to sea and as his eyes adjusted to the darkness he caught the outline of the galley riding the gentle waves. No doubt a sentry would be keeping a close eye on him from the ship. It was nearly, he thought with a frown, as if Baldurix's men were expecting him to attack them at some point. But how could they know what he was planning? The tension onboard the ship had been very high when he and the rest had waded ashore.

He lay back down again. There was not much he could do about that now. His thoughts returned to the strange dream. The heat, the heat, he smiled. He had been born into a noble family; his mother Queen Cartimandua of the Brigantes had been wealthy and powerful. He may be her bastard son, driven from his land and position after his mother's downfall, but wealth and power were still his birthright. Agricola and Baldurix had inherited their wealth and status, this Corbulo was just a common opportunist, but he, Vellocatus, he really deserved the amber, he deserved to live like his mother had once lived. Yes he was entitled to be rich. The amber belonged to him. He had a right to be richer than the common man.

Chapter Forty-Seven – Amber

Vellocatus counted the leather sacks one more time. Then he nodded, satisfied. It was still dark outside. He stood in the captain's tiny cabin onboard the galley holding an oil lamp as one of the mercenaries knelt and tied a rope around the leather bags.

"How long before dawn?" Vellocatus murmured to the captain who stood behind him.

"Another hour or so," the captain replied.

Vellocatus handed him the lamp and stepped outside onto the deck. A cool fresh breeze was skipping across the waves. The galley pitched and rolled in the gentle swell. The rowers lay hunched over their oars. They looked exhausted. It had taken them a whole day and most of the evening before Vellocatus had at last sighted the unmistakable headland jutting out into the sea. That had been last night. The ship had spent the night at sea and with each hour of darkness the tension onboard had grown. He glanced at Baldurix's warriors. They sat in a group clustered around the prow having taking over the whole front half of the ship. Vellocatus turned and spat into the sea. They had taken over his favourite spot. One of his mercenaries brushed past him. The man's hand was gripping his sword pommel.

"Is everything ready?" Vellocatus muttered softly.

The man nodded and disappeared into the gloom.

Vellocatus touched his own sword and felt the reassuring cold steel. He turned to look at the dark headland that was just visible in the moonlight. He wondered how Baldurix was faring. Baldurix had said that the Romans would start to besiege the Caledonian fort at dawn. As soon as he caught sight of the Romans he would launch the small boats that the Decantae had loaned him and set off for the cave. They would load the amber into leather sacks and transport them back to the galley. If the Caledonians had posted a watch on the cliffs above the cave they would surely spot him very quickly but with the Romans attacking them from the landward side there would be little they could do to intervene.

He felt his way forwards along the deck until he saw the large group of warriors sitting ahead of him. They all looked wide awake. There was a sullen, forbidding atmosphere about the group.

"Dawn's in an hour," Vellocatus called softly. "When we launch the boats I want half of you to come with me to the cave and help me load the sacks." He paused. "There are so many stones, you won't believe it."

"Is that so?" a voice replied from the darkness.

There was no reply from the rest of the warriors. Vellocatus was conscious that the men were staring at him in a strange way.

"Just be ready when I give the order," he snapped. He turned and nearly tripped over a heavy iron chain that someone had carelessly left about on deck. He was just about to swear when he recognised the chain. It belonged to him. It was the neck irons in which he had held the girl captive. He frowned. Had he really just left it lying here?

In the gloom one of Baldurix's men laughed. Vellocatus stumbled back towards the spot where his mercenaries were sitting, feeling his heart thumping in his chest. Oh it would be such a relief to see those men's corpses floating in the sea. He bit his lip. In a few hours time he would be rid of Baldurix's men for good. In a few hours he was going to have wealth equal to that which that prick Agricola possessed. He undid the small leather pouch from around his belt and touched the piece of amber he'd taken for himself on his first visit to the sea cave. The stone felt smooth and hard. For a moment he allowed himself to enjoy the touch. Then he slipped the stone back into its pouch. He could not celebrate yet.

As the first glimpse of the sun appeared to the east Vellocatus jumped to his feet and looked up at the watchman who was standing high up in the ship's mast.

"What can you see?" he shouted. "Have the Romans arrived?"

The man took his time in answering.

"No, can't see anything," he shouted.

Vellocatus shook his head impatiently and clenched his hand into a fist. If he waited for too long the Caledonians would surely notice the galley half a mile out to sea. If the Romans had been delayed or the plan had changed it would give the men in the fort time to intervene. In frustration he looked up again at the watchman.

"Nothing? What is happening now? Can you see anything?"

"There is no sign of anyone," the lookout cried.

"Damn it," Vellocatus hissed. What had happened to the Romans? They were supposed to be in position outside the fort at dawn. He turned to look at his mercenaries. Everyone was looking at him, waiting for him to make a decision. At the front of the boat Baldurix's men had stood up.

"We go," Vellocatus shouted. "We can't wait for the Roman attack. Get the small boats into the water. You," he pointed at Baldurix's men, "half of you come with me. The rest will stay here. Bring the empty sacks and the rope."

The ship broke out into a hive of activity. The rafts and log canoes were dropped overboard and men swung their legs over the side of the ship and jumped into the sea. Vellocatus turned to his mercenaries. Some of them were smiling at him with knowing looks. Vellocatus nodded.

"Stay here, you know what to do," he said quietly.

Vellocatus moved to the side of the ship and swung his legs over the edge. He was just about to drop overboard when the captain appeared. The man folded his arms across his chest.

"I want double what we agreed upon," the sailor demanded.

Vellocatus's face darkened. "What is this?" he hissed. "I don't have time to negotiate with you. We made a deal, we are going to stick to it. Now fuck off."

But the captain didn't move. He looked at Vellocatus with a stubborn expression.

"I want my share doubled," he repeated.

Vellocatus shook his head in disbelief. He had no time for this.

"Alright, agreed," he growled as he made a mental note to add the captain to the corpses that would be floating in the sea. Then he jumped down into the sea and grabbed hold of a log canoe.

The sea was calm and Vellocatus had no difficulty in getting into the hollow tree trunk boat. He pulled the oar from the bottom of the small narrow vessel and dug it into the waves. When he looked round he noticed that only six of Baldurix's men were following him. The rest had remained on the galley. He twisted his neck and yelled at the warriors but the men onboard ignored him. Damn it, what were they up to? Had he not told half of them to follow him? Angrily he turned to face the cliffs of the headland. The sun was rising steadily and it was growing light. He looked up at the tops of the cliff but could see no lookouts. What the fuck had happened to the Romans? They were supposed to be besieging the Caledonian fort by now. Well he would have to hurry. Maybe he would just fill one cargo of sacks instead of the two runs that he had planned. He dug his paddle into the water and began to force his way towards the rocks beneath the cliffs.

The shore looked just as rugged as he had imagined it to be when he had slipped in at night a few days ago. The waves crashed against the rocks, sending white spray flying up into the air. A seagull drifted on the breeze and then swooped down towards the sea. Vellocatus pushed on, glancing now and then up at the cliffs but he saw no one. With a bit of luck the villagers would not know what was going on until it was too late. He snatched a glance over his shoulder. Baldurix's men were still with him, strung out in a line behind him.

Then after what seemed an eternity he was under the cliffs and close to the shore. He swung himself into the water and grabbed hold of a boulder and with his other hand pushed the canoe up onto the rocks. The narrow, dark sea cave opening was a few yards to his left. He turned and pointed at it, guiding the men behind him to the right spot. Then he hauled himself up onto the rock. All around him the sea broke onto the boulders with its gentle rhythmic routine.

"Pass me the sacks," he cried impatiently as the last of Baldurix's men dragged themselves up onto the boulders.

One of the men handed them to him and Vellocatus snatched the tied bundle of empty sacks and turned for the cave entrance.

"Two of you follow me and help me load up the amber," he snarled.

Without waiting for an answer he slid down the boulder into the sea and started edging his way towards the cave entrance. Then he was through the dark entrance and inside the tunnel. He felt his way forwards until he came to the bend to the right. Then he paused to listen. He could hear nothing apart from the noise of the sea. He glanced back. A shape was following behind him, blocking out the early morning light. Vellocatus felt the cold steel of his sword touch his leg as a sudden idea came to him. In the darkness his face hardened.

He started forwards and scrambled into the cave. The torches were still burning. Someone must have replaced them. Why would they do this? He frowned but everything was forgotten as he saw the great mountain of coloured stones just as he had left them. He sniggered in delight and threw the bags onto the cave floor. Then he stepped aside to allow the man behind him to get into the cave.

"Beautiful aren't they," he said as the second man scrambled out of the tunnel and grunted in surprise at the sight of the multicoloured mountain of amber. "There is enough here to fill an entire galley," he said, stepping up behind the two men. Then swiftly he drew his sword and stabbed one of the men in the back. The man cried out and collapsed to the ground with blood pouring from the wound. His companion just had enough time to shout and half turn towards Vellocatus when he was stabbed in the chest. The force of Vellocatus's blow sent the man tumbling into the mountain of stones. There was an animal-like fury about Vellocatus as he stabbed the man again and again. Then at last he stopped and scrambled to his feet. The man he'd killed lay half buried under the amber. The other lay on the cave floor in a large pool of blood. Vellocatus was breathing heavily. He wiped the sweat from his face and covered the corpse completely under the stones. Then he stooped and dragged the other body to the far end of the cave. From the entrance passage he scooped some seawater in one of the bags and cleaned away the blood. When he was done he paused to catch his breath and stare at the amber. The cold stones were indeed beautiful; they were so beautiful they were worth killing for. He turned and with a last glance at the amber entered the tunnel. When he could see the daylight up ahead he called out.

"We need two more of you to help us in here."

From outside there was no answer. Vellocatus took a step forwards and repeated himself. Again there was no answer. Carefully he sheathed his sword and clambered towards the cave mouth. The four men were sitting on the rocks watching him as he emerged.

"What, are you deaf?" Vellocatus cried. "I said that we need two more men to help us in there."

Then he choked as if someone had just placed a hand around his throat. Lying on a rock before the cave entrance was the heavy metal slaver's chain he had last seen onboard the galley. Baldurix's men must have deliberately placed it there. As he stared at the neck iron the four men unsheathed their swords. Their faces looked hard and brutal.

"What is this?" Vellocatus stammered.

As he spoke he heard a terrified high-pitched scream coming from the galley. The boat was closer to the shore than when he'd left her. He stared at the ship and his eyes bulged in horror. There were bodies floating in the sea but they were not Baldurix's men. They were his mercenaries.

"What is going on?" he croaked. "What is the meaning of this?"

"You know what is going on," one of the men replied as they slithered towards him. "Do you really think that we didn't know that you intended to kill us all and take the amber for yourself? A pity for you that your plan hasn't worked."

Vellocatus stared at the boat in absolute horror. As he did so he saw two men hold up one of his mercenaries whilst a third cut his throat and kicked his body overboard.

"Look I can make a deal with you," Vellocatus cried as he retreated into the cave entrance. "Did Baldurix make you do this?"

The men closed in on the entrance with drawn swords and knives.

"Baldurix thinks you are a blithering idiot," one of the men grinned. "Of course he planned this. He wasn't going to just let you get away with all the amber."

"We can share the amber – you can have as much as you like. Baldurix can have as many of the stones as he wants," Vellocatus cried out, holding up his sword in a futile effort to force the men back.

"In exchange for what?" one of the men asked.

Vellocatus leaned against the wall of the cave entrance.

"Let me go free with a single sack of stones. I will go right away. You will never see or hear from me again."

The men exchanged looks.

"Agreed. Lay down your sword and come out of the cave," one of them growled.

Vellocatus turned to look at each man in turn. Then he waded forwards and placed his sword on a rock. One of the men kicked it into the sea. Then two others grabbed his arms and dragged him roughly up onto a boulder. They pinned his arms down as the fourth man picked up the slaver's chain and raised it in the air with a smile.

"But we agreed!" Vellocatus cried out in alarm. "You would let me go! What is this? Treachery!"

"Yes," the man holding the chain nodded. "I told you what I needed to tell you in order to get you to come out of that cave. You could have held up an army in that confined space but now I am going to place these on you." He held up the slaver's chain for Vellocatus to see.

"No! You promised," Vellocatus roared with sudden fury.

One of the men struck him in the face and Vellocatus cried out in pain as his head bounced into the rock beneath him.

"I may have been inclined to honour our agreement," a voice whispered close to his ear, "if you hadn't killed my two friends inside the cave."

Then Vellocatus felt the cold wet iron clamp shut around his neck.

The two men pinning down his arms turned him over onto his back and his hands were bound tightly behind him. Then they dragged him higher up the boulder until he was leaned against the rugged, jagged cliff. Out to sea he could see bodies floating up and down on the waves. One of the men disappeared into the cave and reappeared dragging one of the corpses by the arm. Vellocatus looked on horrified as the second neck ring in the slaver's chain was placed around the dead man's neck. They were chaining him to a corpse.

"What are you going to do with me?" he muttered.

"Baldurix will decide what to do with you," one of the men answered.

Suddenly a great roar rose up from the galley a hundred yards away. Vellocatus blinked in surprise as he saw men tumbling overboard into the sea. The four men around him rose to their feet in alarm.

"What is going on over there?" one of them shouted.

As Vellocatus stared at the galley he saw another man being knocked over the side by a blow from an oar. Someone screamed. Then there was another high-pitched shriek and two more men tumbled into the water.

"The crew," one of his captives said in shock, "the crew have taken control of the ship. Look, those are our men in the sea."

Vellocatus strained to see what was going on. He heard another scream. Some of the men in the sea were still alive. They were shouting and raising their arms towards the shore. Then as he stared at the spectacle the galley sail came rolling down and a few moments later oars poked out of the ship's side and began to dig into the waves. One of the oars bounced off the waves and sliced into a man's head as he bobbed in the sea.

"She is leaving us," one of his captors snarled. And sure enough the galley was heading out to sea. Despite his condition Vellocatus started to laugh. It seemed as if the ship's crew had had enough. The sailors were going to have the last laugh. As the ship began to pick up speed Vellocatus caught a glimpse of the captain standing beside the helm, staring in his direction.

"Double my share," he cursed, "you fucking weasel."

High above him on the cliff top a carnyx suddenly rang out in an angry blast. The trumpet blast was followed by another and then another. His captors peered up in sudden fright.

"What's that?" one of them said nervously.

"Let's get out of here," the man who had placed the neck iron on Vellocatus murmured. "It sounds like the Vacomagi know that we are here."

"What about him? Baldurix said to bring him," another exclaimed, pointing at Vellocatus.

"Fuck him, leave him here. He won't get far chained to that body. Let the Vacomagi have him. I am going," one of the men said as he slithered down into the sea.

"No, don't leave me here," Vellocatus cried. "Give me a chance, give me a chance."

"Fuck you," one of the men said, giving him a kick. The three remaining men lowered themselves into the sea, pulled their log boats free from the rocks and set off after their comrade as he paddled away along the cliffs. Then they were gone.

Chapter Forty-Eight – The Smell of Roasting Pork

Vellocatus was left alone on the rock but he could hardly move. His hands were tied firmly behind his back and the heavy chain weighed on his neck. He forced himself up onto his feet and stared at the sea. His captors were right. If he went into the water the weight of the heavy chain and the attached corpse would in all likelihood drown him. He looked around for his sword but it had gone. His captors had released the remaining boats when they'd left and as he stood up he saw his drifting away on the waves. He turned and shuffled towards the cave entrance and felt the weight of the corpse pull him backwards. The men he'd killed inside the cave had had weapons. Maybe he could use them to at least free his hands. He sat down on the boulder beside the cave entrance and glanced down at the water. He blinked in surprise. The seawater was very clear and suddenly on the sea bed, a yard or so down, he saw a multitude of coloured stones glinting back at him. He gasped as he realised what they were. The amber was everywhere. The sea was washing the stones onto the shore. He turned to stare at the cave entrance. That must be why the villagers above him stored all the stones in this cave. They must sweep the shoreline and pick up any stones that they found and bring them to the cave. That was why there was such a mountain of the stuff in one place. The villagers didn't want anyone to know about or find the amber. That was why the girl had murdered her kin. She had done so to protect a secret. His mouth opened in astonishment. What sort of man could have been behind such a careful plan? Whoever had devised the idea of the amber cave would have known about the value of the stones. They would have understood what would happen if the amber source was ever revealed. So they had thought up a plan that would keep the source of the amber secret. Vellocatus's eyes widened as at last he understood. And whoever had come up with the whole idea had been prepared to spill blood in order to maintain the secret.

As he stared at the cave entrance a log dugout canoe nosed its way carefully around the rocks. It was followed by three more. Vellocatus stumbled backwards against the cliff as he caught sight of a pair of pale blue eyes coldly staring up at him.

He lay on the grass inside the headland fort to which they had brought him. The druid with the pale blue eyes had not said a word to him. Vellocatus looked up at the sky with listless eyes. What had happened to Baldurix? What had happened to the Roman attack? The Romans had never shown up. Something had gone wrong, terribly wrong. But at least the men had removed the iron chain from around his neck. He turned as he saw smoke rising up. Nearby someone had started a fire. A woman was feeding the flames with wood and coal. The wood crackled as it caught fire. His captors sat in a small circle a few yards from where he lay on the ground. They seemed to be waiting for a feast. He watched as two men appeared carrying two metal tripods and a spit used for roasting meat over to the fire. The men were silent as they placed the spit over the rapidly growing fire. They looked solemn. No one looked at him.

From the corner of his eye he saw the white-robed druid coming towards him. His long flowing robes fluttered in the breeze. The druid stopped before him and Vellocatus got up on his knees.

"I am just a slave," he whined. "Please, you must believe me. I am a friend. I was an oarsman on the galley. The men onboard my ship forced me to come with them. They put the chains on me when I said I wanted to go back. Honestly, I don't know what they were doing here. Please, that is the truth."

The druid said nothing. Then the man stooped and before Vellocatus could react he ripped the leather pouch from Vellocatus's belt. The man turned the pouch upside down and out rolled a single piece of red amber.

"That's not mine," Vellocatus stammered with a sudden furious blush.

The druid examined the stone in his hand and then crouched beside Vellocatus.

"My daughter said that one day men would come to try and take the stones," he said quietly, "but I thought you would be better prepared than the bungling that I witnessed from up here." The pale blue eyes seemed to bore into Vellocatus. "Tell me your name?"

Vellocatus gave the druid his name.

The white-robed man stroked his grey beard for a long moment.

"Was it worth it? Your quest for the stones?" he said at last. "Will there be others coming after you? If you tell me the truth this time I will give you a clean, quick death."

Vellocatus stared at the druid in sudden terror.

"I have friends," he protested with a panicked splutter.

"Baldurix is dead, I killed him," the druid said quietly. "Your friends will not be coming to rescue you. Now tell me what I want to know."

"I want to live," Vellocatus suddenly cried out in growing terror.

The druid's bony fingers shot forwards and clasped Vellocatus by the throat. Vellocatus choked and spluttered.

"Tell me," a voice whispered.

"There is no one else. I told no one else about the stones," Vellocatus gasped.

The druid stared at him and for a brief moment it seemed as if the old man could see straight into Vellocatus's soul.

Then the man released his grip and rose.

"You lie," he hissed. Then the druid was gesturing to the men sitting in the circle in the grass.

"Do it," he nodded.

The men rose to their feet. They looked serious and solemn. They grabbed Vellocatus and flipped him onto his stomach. His ankles were bound tightly together so that he could no longer move his legs. Then his arms were pulled over his head and his hands bound tightly. Finally two metal chains were wrapped around his torso and fastened into place. When they were done the men stepped back. Vellocatus turned and twisted his head to try and see what was going on. Then he felt a cold metal rod being inserted through the ropes and chains that bound him. His eyes suddenly bulged and his mouth opened and he screamed in pure terror as he finally realised what was happening. The druid was planning to roast him alive over the fire, as if he were a pig. He opened his mouth, sucked air into his lungs and screamed and screamed. Still screaming the men hoisted him up into the air and carried him over to the fire. The smoke blew into his face. Then with a metallic clang the spit was set in place. The fire crackled and burned beneath him. He could feel the heat from the fire. It was burning. The heat, the terrible heat was scorching his skin and flesh. He screamed again as someone started to rotate him like a roasting animal. Round and round he went as the fire burned and blistered him. As the agony steadily grew he suddenly remembered the dream he'd had two nights before. The heat, the growing heat. The gods had not wanted him to succeed. They had been warning him. Just before he slipped into unconsciousness Vellocatus's final glimpse of life was of a girl and a big dog striding purposefully towards the druid.

Chapter Forty-Nine – Father and Daughter

Emogene could hear the man screaming from outside the fort. The warriors guarding the entrance gate through the first wall looked nervous and uncomfortable as she and Bones approached Bannatia. Emogene said nothing as the men recognised her and called out to her but when one of them tried to block her path she angrily shoved him aside. The warriors let her go.

"Where is my father?" she cried to a woman hurrying along in the opposite direction. In reply the woman turned and nodded her head in the direction from which the screaming was coming.

Emogene strode on through the second wall without another word. After the surprise nocturnal visitor had knocked her unconscious she had come to whilst it was still dark. The Roman who had been imprisoned with her had gone and so had her assailant but the man had left the door open for her. Outside she had found the body of a guard and a dead dog. She had known about the young Roman prisoner for a while. Her father had lured him to Bannatia and had locked him up in the chambered well after the man had been heard asking questions about amber in Tuesis. That had been just after Samhain a year ago. Her father had decided not to kill the man right away. He was intending to sacrifice him on Samhain as an offering to the gods. But now the prisoner had escaped and that was a problem. The young man knew about the amber, and he had guessed where the amber cave was. He had told her so during the long bored hours they'd spent together in the dark.

That night she fled to Tuesis and there, still reeling from what her father had done and intended to do, she had been reunited with an old friend. Her kin in Tuesis had welcomed her and told her that the war dog had arrived one day in the company of a stranger. A Roman, they had muttered uneasily. They also knew about the attack that Baldurix was planning. Her father had warned them. He was, they told her, going to launch a pre-emptive strike. He'd also gotten some of the war bands in the highlands to come down from the hills and keep the Romans busy in their forts. So her father had listened to her after all. The realisation had given her courage. But their relationship had changed. Bodvoc had told her he thought her father was not serious about executing her. He was only showing that the law applied to all, even a druid's daughter. But Emogene had not believed that. She had seen the glint in her father's eye as he had condemned her. The old man had meant every word. So she had spent many hours thinking about what to do until at last a solution had presented itself. She would go to Bannatia and confront him.

She passed the third wall and strode up the slope towards the edge of the cliffs. Bones padded along beside her. As she passed the steps leading down to the well she refused to look at the place. She would never drink water from there again. Something was about to change. The man was still screaming but his cries were getting weaker and weaker. Emogene did not pause as she caught sight of the sickening scene. She couldn't see the man's face nor did she care. The warriors feeding the fire with wood looked pale, uneasy and subdued. Her father stood to one side, watching the man slowly roast to death. He turned as he heard her approach. She halted a few paces from him.

"I have come back," she said, staring him squarely in the face.

For just a tiny fraction of a moment she caught a glimpse of surprise on her father's face. The pale blue eyes examined her coolly but he said nothing.

"I have come back," Emogene repeated, "to tell you how I managed to escape. A man, I believe a Roman, came in the midst of the night, killed the guard and knocked me unconscious. He came for the prisoner but the young man, whom you refused to kill, knows about the amber. He has guessed that the cave is right here beneath our feet. He has guessed that the amber comes from the sea. He told me all of this. I don't know where he has gone but if he and the man who freed him make it back to one of their forts then the location of our secret will be revealed."

Emogene raised her chin. Her eyes blazed.

"You," her finger suddenly shot out and pointed at her father, "broke our law. You should have killed the prisoner when you had the chance. Now your decision has placed us all in danger."

"Enough," Dougal's sharp voice interrupted. "I have heard enough. My decision has been made, Emogene. It is you who nearly ruined us. You told this man here where to find the amber."

Her father gestured for the warriors around the fire to seize her. The men, however, hesitated.

"No," Emogene snapped. "One word from me and by the gods I swear I will order Bones to rip out your throat."

Her father's pale blue eyes shifted to look at the dog.

"Bones, come here," he bellowed but the dog did not move.

"I am your daughter," Emogene said, "I have your blood. You failed us, you failed to protect us. It is I who warned you about Baldurix and it is I who killed Conall to protect the stones. You no longer have the authority to lead us. Go home, old man, go home and brood on your failure."

Dougal angrily took a step towards her but a sharp command from her brought Bones up onto his feet.

"I know what you have been seeking all these years," Emogene cried out, "I know the question that frustrates you. You wonder why the gods don't answer. You despair at being unable to stop the Roman conquest. That is why you were planning to sacrifice the prisoner on Samhain. That's why you kept him alive. You needed a sign, a great sign, from the gods to show us that they will support us in our struggle for our freedom."

Emogene placed her hands on her hips.

"Well I am that sign!" she yelled. "I survived. I survived war, I survived rape, I survived torture, I survived the sea and now I will survive you. This is my land and it will be here long after we are gone. These are my people and it is my freedom that you claim to protect but if you cannot do so then what use do we have for you?"

"You cannot speak to the gods, only the druids can," her father retorted, raising his oak staff threateningly in the air.

"You can no more speak to the gods than I can," Emogene sneered. "But I know this. We do not need the gods to give us hope. We are strong. The strength to win this war is already within us. We just have to believe in it. As long as we continue to believe in ourselves then one day we will regain our freedom and the Romans will leave. That is what you should be telling people."

Her father hurled his oak staff at her and it struck her shoulder. Emogene stooped and picked it up. Then in a swift action she snapped the staff over her leg and threw the broken pieces onto the ground.

"Go home," she cried at her father.

The druid was staring at the broken staff in disbelief. Then he looked up at her and it was as if something within him had changed.

"I will go after the Roman prisoner and kill him," Dougal said, turning away. "He is weak and feverish. He will be moving slowly. After the escape I sent men to watch the Roman forts. If he tries to escape by that way, they will catch him."

"No," Emogene shook her head, "I will go. Those two men must not be allowed to escape. You will stay here and mend our relations with the Decantae. Then after I return, I never want to see you again."

Chapter Fifty – What Reconciliation?

The hair on Corbulo's neck rose as he heard Marcus's weak voice in the dark. He had found him, he had found his son. He'd been right. Marcus was alive. Shaking he stepped over the girl and into the well. It was too dark for him to see anything. Then he heard a moan close by.

"Marcus, it's me, are you hurt?" he whispered.

His question was answered by another groan. Then Corbulo's foot touched something and a moment later his fingers felt a head and a shoulder.

"Go away," a voice mumbled in Latin.

Corbulo took a deep breath, stooped, found Marcus's armpits and heaved the young man up onto his feet. Marcus's head lolled from side to side and Corbulo had to hold him up to prevent him from falling over. His son was in a bad state. He couldn't see his face but the stench of bad breath, sweat, shit and piss was overpowering. Without another word Corbulo stooped to one knee and threw the young man head first over his shoulder. Then slowly he forced himself up. Marcus weighed less than he had expected. Corbulo blushed; no wonder, he must have been inside this well for a very long time. The boy was a sack of bones. Carefully Corbulo picked his way past the unconscious girl. On his back Marcus groaned and muttered something he didn't catch. Then they were outside in the cool night air. Corbulo moved up the steps, pausing now and then to listen but all was quiet.

"Can you walk, Marcus? Can you walk, I need to know," he whispered urgently.

There was another unintelligible groan from over his back.

"Where are you taking me?" Marcus muttered.

"It's me, Marcus, your father," Corbulo whispered. "I have come to rescue you. We're going home but you must be quiet. We are in danger."

The body on his back was silent. Corbulo blew the air from his cheeks and began to move up the gentle slope between the houses, towards the cliff edge. If his son could not walk they were both in trouble. He couldn't carry him on his back forever. If Marcus could hardly stand how was he going to get him down the cliff face and into the sea? He snatched a glance at the sky. He still had some time before it grew light. Like a ghost he flitted in between the silent round houses moving as fast as he could. Then after what seemed an age he saw the sea in the pale moonlight. It looked impossibly far away. He crouched by the edge of the cliff, panting slightly, and lowered Marcus onto the grass. In the faint light he caught sight of a unkempt beard and a shrunken face. The boy had his eyes open and was staring up at him. Corbulo tried to smile. He had found him! He had found his son.

"We're going over the cliff face and down towards the sea," he whispered fiercely as he tied the piece of rope he'd taken from the dead dog around Marcus's waist. "You are going to have to climb down. It's not too hard but its dark and you will need to concentrate. I will be holding the rope but it's too short to lower you all the way. Can you do it?"

Corbulo heard his heart beating in his chest as Marcus blinked and stared up at him with dull eyes.

"Damn it, soldier," Corbulo whispered fiercely with sudden authority in his voice. "Get your arse down that cliff and don't you dare fall off. That is an order – now move it and stop pussyfooting around, you spineless whelp!"

Then before Marcus could reply Corbulo was dragging him to the edge.

Marcus yelped. Then he was over the edge and Corbulo felt the rope tighten. He turned, gave the sleeping fort a final glance and swung his legs over the side and began to climb down after his son.

The sound of the waves crashing onto the rocks got louder and to Corbulo it was the best noise he'd heard in a very long time. When at last he felt the rope slacken he looked down and caught a glimpse of a dark shape sitting on a boulder with his legs drawn up close together. Corbulo slithered down the last few feet. Then he crouched beside Marcus.

"You came back for me – why?" Marcus said quietly.

"Ah, you know," Corbulo was suddenly glad that the dark hid his face, "I heard you were missing. I couldn't just leave you here to die. I am your father. Isn't that what fathers are supposed to do?"

In the darkness he heard his son laughing softly.

"Come, we can't stay here," Corbulo whispered, suddenly glad to have something to do. "We must get as far away from this place as we can before they discover you are gone. We are going into the sea. Hold on to the rocks and follow me."

He slipped from the boulder and into the sea and a moment later he heard Marcus follow him in. The seawater was cold and now and then a wave swamped him so that after a while he was utterly soaked and bedraggled. When at last he waded through the surf onto the flat beach Corbulo was exhausted. Marcus staggered after him and collapsed onto the beach, his breath coming in unhealthy-sounding gasps.

For a while the two of them lay on the sand too exhausted to continue. Then at last Corbulo rose and dragged Marcus to his feet.

"I can walk," the young man muttered, "but my leg hurts. I am wounded. Do you have any food? I haven't eaten in two days."

Corbulo sighed. He had nothing to give his son. "Come on," he said, slipping his hand around the young man's waist and pushing him forwards, "let's go. I will cook you a lovely rabbit stew tonight."

"Where are we going?" Marcus muttered as he undid the rope and dropped it into the sand.

Corbulo let go of his son and glanced up at the stars. Then he looked back at the fort on the headland. For a moment he didn't answer.

"They will expect us to head for the nearest Roman fort," he said. "Cawdor is at least a day and a half away if you were fit and healthy, which you are not. We would never make it and Balnageith is even further away. No," Corbulo said with a firm nod, "we will go west. They won't expect that."

265

"West, west," Marcus slowly shook his head, "what is there in the west?"

"Agricola told me once," Corbulo said, scratching his chin, "that the land west of the great river valley is unknown to us. Well, we are going to be the first Romans to go there. Once beyond the river we will turn south and try and find our way to one of our outposts."

"But that means crossing the highlands," Marcus muttered as the two of them started off along the flat shoreline. "Those hills are crawling with hostile war bands."

"Yes, I know, so let's get moving," Corbulo grunted.

For a while the two of them trudged on in silence. Marcus kept up as best as he could but he was limping heavily. The shore was easy to follow and as long as they kept close to it Corbulo knew they were heading in the right direction.

Marcus suddenly took a deep breath and staggered as if someone had landed a punch. Corbulo grabbed his arm and steadied him.

"I haven't spoken with anyone in a very long time," he gasped. "They brought me a little food each day but no one talked to me. Then a few days ago they imprisoned a girl with me. You have no idea how good it was to talk to another person. What happened to her? Did you kill her?"

"I hit her," Corbulo replied, "but she was alive when I left her."

Marcus was quiet for a while. Then at last he spoke.

"Some things don't ever change."

"Sometimes they do," Corbulo shot back.

"You are an arsehole."

"I know," Corbulo muttered, "I know."

Chapter Fifty-One – Survival

"Come on, eat these," Corbulo said as he lifted up his son's head and forced a handful of black berries into Marcus's mouth. Marcus groaned but managed to swallow the food. The boy was in a bad state. He'd lost a huge amount of weight and his clothes were rags and his hair and beard were crawling with lice. His face looked like it had shrunk and his cheekbones were clearly visible. He'd stunk like a sewer when Corbulo had first carried him out of the well but the swim in the sea had washed away the worst of the sweat, piss and shit so that the smell was odious but tolerable. For two days now they had been heading west, following the coastline but that morning Marcus had been too weak to continue. He needed rest and food but Corbulo could offer neither. It was evening and they had spent the whole day hiding amongst the undergrowth in the copse of trees. Corbulo had gone off in search of food but the only thing he'd been able to find were the blackberries. He fed them into Marcus's mouth until he had none left.

"I saw a farm about a mile away," Corbulo said as he wearily leaned back against the tree. "When it's dark I will go back and try to steal a chicken or some eggs."

"That would be nice," Marcus muttered in a faint voice. His eyes were closed as he lay on the ground.

Corbulo nodded and closed his eyes too. Over two days Marcus had told him the story of what had happened to him. The druid who had imprisoned him had wanted to kill him at first. It was because he knew about the amber. The druid had spent many days interrogating Marcus, trying to find out who else knew about the coloured stones, but Marcus could only repeat what he knew: that Agricola had sent him north on a mission to establish whether the amber really existed. The druid had not been satisfied but after a while he seemed to have realised that Marcus did indeed know nothing more than that. Corbulo opened his eyes and glanced down at his son. The boy had a sharp mind. He had bought himself some time by offering to be a human sacrifice on Samhain. The druid had agreed.

"How did you know about Samhain, the druids and human sacrifice?" he asked, poking his son gently in the side.

"My mother," Marcus stirred. "She taught me," he coughed, "about the druids and the Celtic festivals. She told me, the door between the worlds is opened on Samhain. It is an important day for the druids. It was all I could think of to stop him from killing me."

"Oh." Corbulo looked embarrassed. "I didn't know she taught you those things."

"There was much about her that you didn't know," Marcus murmured.

"Like what?"

But Marcus looked like he had fallen asleep.

It was dark when Corbulo stumbled into their hiding place. Marcus managed a weak warning cry before Corbulo called out that it was only him. He crouched beside his son and there was a triumphant note in his voice.

"Look, look what I managed to find," he whispered, holding something up. Marcus muttered something and raised his hand to touch the object.

"A whole chicken," Corbulo grinned. "I wrung its neck. I also found six eggs. We got food. We are going to make it, son, just let anyone try and stop us."

In the darkness Corbulo did not see the smile appear on Marcus's face.

"You were always good at stealing," Marcus whispered. "Not good for much else but you were good at stealing. I remember the time we had to hide the centurion's money bag when he came looking for it."

Corbulo was digging a hole in the ground with his hands.

"I didn't steal his money," he murmured, "I won that in a fair contest."

"That's not what the centurion told us."

Corbulo shook his head but did not reply. Instead he scooped more earth from the hole. Then he rose and started hunting around for stones. When he had enough he placed them at the bottom of the hole and piled in dry wood and a few pieces of charcoal. Then he took out the flint he'd taken from the farmhouse. Starting a fire, even if it was partially concealed in a hole, was a risk, but they were going to die if they didn't eat. He pulled out his sword and sliced the chicken's head off. As the dry twigs caught fire he carefully fanned the flames with his hands. Then taking his sword he rammed it through the length of the chicken and balanced it over the hole. Next he carefully laid out the eggs on the ground. He moved over to Marcus, raised his son's head, broke open one of the eggs and forced it down Marcus's throat. Then he took another and did the same.

"Tomorrow we must move on, we can't stay here," he murmured. "I need you to be strong. Now eat and rest. Everything will come right in the end."

Marcus nodded but did not open his eyes. Hunger had made him listless and inactive. The boy was close to giving up. Corbulo looked concerned. He had seen the same expression on the faces of starving villagers when the crops had failed but this was worse, this was his son. Whatever happened, he thought savagely, nothing and nobody was going to take his son from him.

Corbulo woke with a start. It was morning. Something had moved in the undergrowth. He snatched his sword from the ground and leapt up into a crouch. Then he saw a squirrel racing away up a tree and he relaxed. Marcus was still asleep but his breathing was stronger and more regular than before. The food that Corbulo had been stuffing into him was having an effect. He glanced at the hole. The fire had died. He laid down his sword and filled the hole with earth. The chicken had tasted delicious. He'd been careful to feed Marcus only small pieces in case he vomited the food back up. But the meat had been effective. The meat had made him feel stronger. He glanced around him but the small wood seemed peaceful. Corbulo moved across and nudged Marcus awake. His son blinked, sat up and scratched his beard.

"We must go," Corbulo said, "but first of all I am going to cut some of that hair from your face. You look like you haven't shaved in a year."

"I haven't," Marcus muttered, "but you don't have a knife."

"I have my sword and it's sharp," Corbulo said. "Now keep still. It won't be pretty but I will get the worst of it."

As he cut the bushy hair from his son's face he was conscious that Marcus was watching him. The boy looked stronger now that he'd eaten something and had rested for a day and a night.

"Why did you come back for me?" Marcus asked suddenly. "You never used to give a damn about us. I was gone for a whole week once when we lived at Deva. You didn't even notice that I was not there."

"Keep still," Corbulo growled. They were silent as the hair fell to the ground in thick wisps. "I know I was not a good father," Corbulo said at last. "For what it is worth I am sorry. I am not that man anymore. In Rome I went to the temple of Aesculapius on Tiber Island. I made a promise to the immortal gods that I would find you and bring you home. That's what my wife would have wanted."

"The temple of Aesculapius," Marcus raised his eyebrows. "Well that settles everything then. From now on everything will be fine. I will just forget all the beatings and humiliation you put me through. I will just forget that my mother killed herself because you were a complete arsehole."

"Give me a chance," Corbulo said.

"I will think about it," Marcus retorted angrily.

Corbulo laid down his sword and examined his handiwork. "We need to get some new clothes for you," he said. "That tunic of yours is crawling with lice. I will try and steal some from the next farm that we come across. You could do with a weapon as well. Any preference?"

Marcus nodded. "I am a cavalryman – anything will do but a horse would be preferable." He sniffed. "While you are at it, there is something else," he said. He turned onto his stomach and pointed down at his calf muscle.

"I think it has become infected. It hurts like hell."

Corbulo peered at the ugly gash in the flesh. The wound was jagged, long and deep and yellow pus oozed from underneath the black scab. Carefully Corbulo touched the wound and felt Marcus tense up. He sat back.

"It looks bad," he said. "How long has it been like that?"

"I cut myself in the well." Marcus shook his head wearily. "I honestly can't remember. Everything that happened in that place is blurred, days didn't mean much."

Corbulo looked concerned. "The faster we find some horses the better. Until then you will just have to endure the pain. Come on, let's go, we have wasted enough time already."

Chapter Fifty-Two – "I am a poor swimmer"

Corbulo paused and glanced around him. It was dusk and they were still following the coastline. Marcus nearly bumped into him.

"What's the matter, why have you stopped?" he said wearily.

"I think," Corbulo said, turning to look at the cliff top meadow, "that this is the spot where I jumped into the sea."

"You did what?"

"Never mind, I will tell you the whole story one day," Corbulo grinned. "But it also means we are not far from the great river valley."

"We need to rest and look for some food," Marcus said.

"I know." Corbulo looked thoughtful. "There is a large settlement not far from here. The people are allies of Rome but I don't think we will find a warm welcome with them. I had to fight in single combat because some prick believed that I had insulted him."

Corbulo turned his back on the sea and gazed inland.

"I think we will turn inland, skirt around the Caledonian settlement and cross this great river further to the south."

"We need to find a place to hide, it's nearly dark," Marcus said.

"No," Corbulo shook his head. "We push on, I don't want to spend the night around here. We can rest when we are across the river."

With a final glance at the sea Corbulo turned inland. The night drew on and for a long time he was haunted by the idea that he was blundering straight towards the Decantae village. It was difficult to find a path in the dark forest and they scraped past branches and tripped over tree roots. The only noise was the occasional swear word, the crack of twigs under their feet and their own laboured breathing. The two of them did not speak. Then at last in the moonlight Corbulo swore in relief as they emerged onto a barren hillside. The night was cold but it didn't rain. Their pace increased as they trudged across the barren hills, navigating with the help of the stars. Corbulo set the pace and he was heartened to see that Marcus did not complain, not once, despite the pain he must be enduring in his leg with his limp.

As the night sky started to turn a dark blue he cast around for a place where they could hide and rest. But there were no obvious places. The barren hills, covered in purple heather, treeless, stretched away to the horizon in every direction. As dawn approached Corbulo felt a growing sense of panic. Where was the damned river? They should have come across it by now. When the dawn came they would be visible for miles. He was just about to veer towards a clump of rocks when he heard a dog barking somewhere to his right.

He held up his hand in warning to Marcus and crouched down on the ground. Marcus limped up to him.

"We're lost, aren't we," he whispered.

"Maybe," Corbulo replied. He glanced across at the boulders he'd spotted earlier. "Get yourself into cover and get some rest. I am going down there. That dog must be guarding something. If I don't come back, keep heading south, then cross the river. You know the plan."

Marcus limped away without a word and Corbulo rose and flitted across the heather until he had a good view of the deep and narrow valley below him. Nestled on the shore of a small lake was a farm. Corbulo stroked his chin as he stared at the building. He hadn't spoken with anyone apart from Marcus since they had escaped from the headland but now he had little choice. Marcus was right, they were lost. He had to know in which direction to go. They also needed food. Another risk, another compromise. How many would it take before they were caught? He glanced up the slope in the direction of the boulders. Marcus may be stoic about his pain but sooner or later his body would refuse to move if it didn't get some food and proper treatment. He had no choice. The wind had picked up and was sweeping across the hills, flattening the heather.

The farm looked run-down. The main building was a small round house. In the growing light Corbulo could see that the thatch roof was in poor condition. Someone had tried to mend it for a ladder leaned against one side. At the back of the house, bordering the lake, there was an animal enclosure but he couldn't see any pigs or chickens and in places the stone wall had collapsed. Corbulo waded across a shallow stream and approached the farmhouse. He could hear the dog barking from around the back. The animal must be tied up for it would surely have come to investigate him by now. He paused to listen beside the doorway. Nothing.

He glanced up at the steep valley slopes but the bleak hillside looked deserted. Then he smelt it. Food. Someone was cooking. The food smelt delicious and his stomach suddenly felt empty and hollow. Carefully he lifted the leather hide that covered the doorway and peered inside. The room was empty; straw lay on the ground and a ladder poked up into a hole in the ceiling. There must be another floor up there. Where were the people who lived here? Then he caught sight of the large pot hanging over a fire. Boldly he stepped into the house. A small bronze knife lay on the table and he snatched it. Then he moved across to the fire and bent down to sniff the contents in the pot. It was a stew. He reached out and lifted the pot gently from the iron spit.

Suddenly there was a slight movement behind him and he whirled round and slid his sword from its scabbard. In the gloom he suddenly saw two small children staring at him with large frightened eyes. They couldn't be older than four or five. Corbulo froze in sudden embarrassment. Then after a long awkward silence he raised his finger to his mouth, gesturing for the children to be quiet. Above him he suddenly heard a woman moan. Keeping his eyes on the children he edged towards the ladder. Then he looked up at the dark hole in the ceiling and holding his sword in one hand he began to climb. The woman's moans and groans were getting louder and more urgent. Then as Corbulo poked his head through the hole he heard her cry out. He blushed as he caught sight of a woman lying on her back with her legs spread wide. She lay on a bed of straw. A naked youth of no more than sixteen or seventeen was on top, thrusting himself into her with an increasing rhythm. He was grunting as Corbulo scrambled up through the hole.

The woman was the first to see him and she screamed in fright. The youth turned in mid motion and stared at him in horror. Then with a speed that took Corbulo by surprise the naked boy bolted for the open damaged section of the roof and without hesitation leapt towards the ground. Corbulo swore and rushed towards the gap in the thatch. He was just in time to see the naked youth tumble onto the ground, roll head over heels and spring back onto his feet. The boy snatched a glance at Corbulo to see if he was following. He looked panic-stricken. Then he was off racing across the meadow up the valley and towards the woods beyond. Corbulo swore again. The boy had got away. Then despite the situation he chuckled. There was something comical about the naked youth's wild sprint towards the trees. He turned to the woman. She too was naked. As Corbulo turned she made a dash for the ladder but this time he managed to get there first. She backed away, trying to cover herself with her hands. She looked old enough to be the boy's mother. The woman was staring at Corbulo fearfully.

"Where will he go?" Corbulo gestured towards the damaged roof section.

The woman swallowed and tried to compose herself.

"He has family a few miles away," she muttered as she backed into a corner and stared fearfully at Corbulo's sword. "He only came here to fix my roof. Please, take what you want. I don't have much but don't harm us, I beg you."

"Where is your husband, where are your family?" Corbulo growled.

The woman swallowed nervously. "My husband is dead. He was killed last year during the fighting. I live here alone with my two little ones. Don't harm us. They are all that I have got left."

"I saw your children down there – they will be safe as long as you help me," Corbulo said, replacing his sword in its scabbard.

"Thank you, thank you," the woman murmured in relief.

Corbulo bit his lip in concern as he turned to look at the hole in the roof. He should not have allowed the boy to escape. They couldn't stay here now. He had maybe three or four hours before the boy could return with trouble. He would have to take what he needed and leave.

"I need food," he muttered.

"Take what you need," the woman replied.

"I also need horses."

The woman shook her head. "My husband took our only horse when he went to war. I don't have any here. I am sorry."

"What about weapons?" Corbulo grunted.

"There is a knife on the table and an old hunting spear beside the door," the woman said.

Corbulo gestured for her to start putting her clothes back on. He watched her thoughtfully as she quickly dressed herself.

"I am heading south," he said at last. "I was told that I will have to cross a wide river if I want to keep going south. Is that so?"

The woman shook her head. "No, there are only the mountains to the south of here. The water that you are talking about is to the west, a couple of miles in that direction," she said, raising her arm and pointing with her finger.

"That's good news," Corbulo smiled. "I didn't fancy crossing that river. I am a poor swimmer."

Chapter Fifty-Three – The Journey into the West

Marcus was crouching behind the boulders watching him when Corbulo returned carrying a pot of stew and a bag of supplies slung over his shoulder. It was early morning. Marcus looked exhausted and there was a sullenness about him as he accepted the hunting spear that Corbulo handed to him. Corbulo nodded in encouragement. "I got food and I know where we are," he said as he placed the pot on the ground. His son fell on it like a starving animal, scooping the hot food into his mouth with his fingers. Some of it trickled down into his beard. Corbulo reached out and placed a restraining hand on his shoulder.

"Easy, son, eat it slowly or else you will vomit it back up. Take your time. Let your stomach get used to the food."

Marcus shook off the restraining hand and continued to scoop the food into his mouth. When he'd eaten nearly everything he looked up. His mouth, chin and beard were smeared and dirty.

"What about you?" he said.

Corbulo shook his head. "I ate my fill down in the farm, don't worry about me. I am good. How is the leg?"

"It hurts," Marcus replied, wiping his mouth with his hand. There was a little more colour to the boy's face now that he'd eaten his fill.

Corbulo nodded and glanced at the farm. "The great river that we are looking for is just over those hills, a couple of miles at the most. But someone saw me at the farm. He ran away but he will come back. We must go now. We will rest once we're across the river. I told the woman at the farm that we were heading south. Hopefully if anyone comes after us they will think we headed off into the mountains to the south. Maybe it will buy us some time."

"They are already on our trail," Marcus said quietly. "But it's not the local villagers that you should be worried about."

Corbulo frowned. "What are you talking about?"

Marcus looked up at him with a sullen, angry expression.

"The girl who was imprisoned with me," he snapped, "I foolishly told her that I knew about the amber cave. I told her that I thought I knew where it was. I think the fucking chamber was right beneath my feet, under those cliffs that we climbed down."

Corbulo shrugged casually. "So what?"

Marcus shook his head. "You don't understand. The druid is her father. To know about the amber is a death sentence. That mad druid is killing everyone who knows about the amber. He is determined to keep the stones a secret. He will come after us. He cannot let us escape. I know too much."

Corbulo looked away.

"Well we had better be moving on then," he murmured.

Wearily the two men rose to their feet. Corbulo looked around at the barren hills but could see no one. He glanced back at Marcus who was limping along leaning on his newly acquired spear.

"Glad to see that the army has made a man out of you," he joked, trying to lighten the mood.

"Fuck you," Marcus replied sullenly. "You are still an arsehole."

They skirted the lonely farm and when Corbulo was satisfied that they could no longer be seen he turned due west in the direction that the woman had pointed out. There was no path and they stumbled on over the barren rocky and heather-covered hills. The sun rose steadily in the sky and Corbulo felt his eyes and legs growing heavy with exhaustion. They needed a rest but he didn't dare stop. If they stopped now they would fall asleep where they stood. Marcus fell further and further behind as he limped along, leaning heavily on his spear, and Corbulo would have to go back and half push him up the hills. His son was in a lot of pain but his stoicism was remarkable and not once did he complain.

"Come on," Corbulo said as he slipped his hand around Marcus's waist and guided him towards the summit of the hill. Then they were on the ridge and Corbulo cried out in joy.

Stretching out below him from horizon to horizon was a great valley, cut in half by a long lake that disappeared off into the distance. It was the largest and longest lake that he had ever seen. A dense dark-green fir tree forest covered the land beside the water and came crawling up the hillside towards them.

"A river that cuts the land in half. It's not a river," Corbulo cried out, "Agricola was wrong, it's a lake." He clenched his fist in triumph as if he had just won first place at the Olympic Games. "You know what Agricola told me," he said, gripping Marcus's shoulder. "He told me that no Roman has ever crossed that water. The land beyond it is unknown to us. But by immortal Jupiter, you and I are going to be first to do so. That is going to be a fine tavern story when we get back home."

Marcus nodded. "What now?" he said, staring at the vast expanse of water.

"We find a boat or something to help us across."

They stumbled down the hillside and were soon lost in the forest. A gentle breeze started up and the noise of the wind rushing through the treetops was calming and peaceful. At last they glimpsed the lake through the trees. The shoreline was marshy and flies were everywhere, dancing in swarms across the water. Marcus collapsed to the ground beside a tree, too exhausted to swipe away the midges that swarmed around him. Corbulo walked up to the water's edge and gingerly poked his foot into the lake. The water was dark, brackish and ice cold. He looked up and stared at the opposite shore; it seemed a long way off. He needed to find a boat but finding one was easier said than done. He raised his hand to his brow, shielding his eyes from the sun, and searched the opposite shore, but he could see no signs of people or human activity.

"Stay here," he said, turning to Marcus.

The marshy lakeside soon gave way to rocks and then a small shingle beach. He looked up at the sun. It was nearly noon. Up ahead along the shore a tangled mass of tall water reeds swayed in the breeze. He was just about to retrace his steps when he spotted a dark shape lurking amongst the reeds. Curiously he approached and using his sword he gently parted the reeds. He grunted in surprise. It was a log and it looked half rotten. He stared at the wood for a long moment knowing somehow that the log was useful but being unable to see how. It was the exhaustion. He could hardly think straight. Then at last it came to him. It wasn't just a log. It was an old log canoe. The tree trunk had been hollowed out to form a primitive boat. It must have lain here for months after being abandoned. He grunted in relief. It would have to do.

He looked up at the sky and then turned to gaze around at the hills and the distant mountains. But they would cross during the dark. He made up his mind. If that mad druid that Marcus had talked about was indeed searching for them he couldn't take any more risks. Anyone on those hills would be able to see them if they attempted to cross during the day.

The sun had gone and it was getting dark when Corbulo returned with Marcus. He waded into the water and pulled the primitive boat free from the reeds. The wood felt soft and the log wobbled dangerously as they eased themselves into it but to Corbulo's relief it floated. He began to paddle using a piece of wood he'd found in the forest. Marcus sat hunched in the front, his legs dangling into the water on both sides. He was using his hands as paddles. Neither of them spoke as they drifted further out into the lake and the darkness deepened. The water was placid and Corbulo peered over the side into the lake wondering how deep it was. Then he turned to look back at the shore they'd just left behind. Nothing stirred amongst the trees. Had they managed to shake off their pursuers?

The lake was completely silent and only the noise of their paddling disturbed the peace. They made slow progress. Soon the darkness prevented Corbulo from seeing the spot where they had set out from. They were alone in the midst of the dark and silent water. It was eerie.

"Marcus," he whispered, "can you see anything?"

His son shook his head. It was as if the very stillness of the lake had stolen the words from his mouth.

The log drifted on through the darkness. Then suddenly the shoreline loomed up out of the night and Corbulo felt the boat grind and bump onto shingle. They had reached the western shore. Corbulo rose stiffly and plunged into the lake. The water came up to his knees. He waded ashore, dragging the log higher up onto the beach as Marcus carried their bag of supplies onto dry land.

"We made it," Corbulo said fiercely as he plonked himself down on a rock.

Chapter Fifty-Four – Terra Incognita

Corbulo woke with a start as someone poured water over his face. He spluttered, coughed and leapt to his feet. Marcus was standing close by. It was dawn. His son looked stronger and wide awake. He scowled.

"I could have cut your throat whilst you were sleeping," Marcus snarled. "By gods you deserve to be punished for what you did."

Corbulo raised his hand. "I am sorry, Marcus," he muttered.

"I told you once that I never wanted to see you again. Do you know why? It wasn't just the beatings and your drunken foolish behaviour. I have endured worse in the army. No, it was because every time that I saw your face you reminded me of her."

Corbulo was silent as Marcus stepped up to him. For a moment they stood nose to nose with Marcus's angry eyes challenging him.

"Go on, hit me one more time. Then I will have an excuse to kill you," Marcus cried.

Corbulo didn't move nor did he say anything. He just looked at the ground.

"Do you know why she killed herself?"

Corbulo raised his head and looked his son straight in the eye.

"Go on, tell me," he said.

Marcus's eyes glinted dangerously. "It was because you were going to take her to Italy when you retired. I had already made up my mind that I was staying here where I was born. She was afraid she would never see me again. She couldn't bear the thought of having her family ripped apart. We meant the world to her. All she ever wanted was to grow old with us. She didn't want to go with you. She wanted to stay here. She knew I was not going to go with you. She tried to tell you. But you wouldn't listen. You never listened to her. You treated her as if she were a new recruit that you could just bully and order about."

Marcus fell silent. Out on the lake a thick mist obscured the far shore.

Corbulo's cheeks burned with shame. He swallowed and then touched the phallic amulet that hung around his neck.

"You kept this," Corbulo said. "Remember when I gave it to you? The three initials are our initials – yours, mine and hers. Why did you keep it?"

Marcus turned and looked away.

"I don't know, sentimental value perhaps."

Corbulo nodded. "There is not a day that goes by that I don't mourn for her," he said quietly. "That's why I came to find you. I need to try and make right the wrong from the past. I thought I could do that by rescuing you."

Marcus took a deep breath.

"You are a fucking hero," he said. "That's the worst part."

Corbulo scratched his chin and looked around.

"I have been thinking," he said. "When we get back home we should erect a headstone for her. A memorial. That is the proper way to honour the dead."

Marcus took another deep breath and nodded.

"She would like that," he replied.

"There is something else. I am going to stay here in Britannia," Corbulo said. "I served my whole career here so why not. Quintus is planning to retire to some hill just south of Londinium. I think I may join him when he goes. Londinium is not that far from where your unit is stationed. I could come and visit you regularly." Corbulo paused. "If that's alright with you?"

Marcus blew the air from his cheeks and stared at the mist-laden lake.

"That would be fine," he said at last.

Corbulo nodded and looked pleased. Then he stretched out his arm to Marcus and the younger man clasped it in the soldier's way.

"We should be going," Corbulo said, glancing at the mist.

The mist seemed to be growing thicker as the log canoe glided through the silent black water. Corbulo sat at the back of the craft peering into the fog but he could only see a few yards ahead. An eerie silence hung over the lake. He drove his piece of wood into the water with careful measured strokes, resting now and then to listen. Marcus sat at the front, his legs dangling in the water over both sides as he used his hands to help push the boat along. He too seemed to be listening. Then he pulled his leg up onto the half-submerged wood and twisted round to examine the long scab on his calf.

"How is the leg?" Corbulo whispered.

Marcus didn't reply as he examined the wound.

"I think the infection is spreading," he muttered. "I have seen wounds like this before. If I don't do something soon then the whole leg will have to come off."

"We will get it seen to by the army doctors as soon as we get back," Corbulo said, trying to sound reassuring. He tried to remember what the army doctors had told him about treating wounds but he couldn't remember much. Silently he cursed himself. If only he'd paid more attention.

Marcus shook his head. "No, I must do it now. A doctor explained it to me once. You boil a knife or sharp instrument in hot water. That makes it clean. Then you lance the wound and drain the infection. Once it's all gone you clean the wound with a disinfectant and bandage it. Then you pray to the gods."

Corbulo looked away, embarrassed.

"A good doctor is a soldier's best friend," Corbulo said. "If you have to bribe anyone in the army then bribe a doctor. He will keep you alive."

Marcus didn't seem to be listening.

"We have a knife, we can boil the water but I have no disinfectant or bandages," he said as he touched the wound.

Corbulo turned to look out into the mist. If the maps that Quintus had shown him at Inchtuthil were correct this lake would take them south-west. If they followed it they would be able to cut across the mountains to the south-east and make contact with one of the Roman forts at the valley entrances. He had no idea how long it would take them to cross the highlands but they still had some food. The druid, if he was indeed coming after them, would be watching all the obvious routes south. Maybe by going this far west they had thrown their pursuers off their trail? Maybe they would be able to slip away unnoticed.

There was no wind and the fog did not lift as the hours slowly passed. The mist hung over the lake, thick and impenetrable, hiding them as they drifted through it alone and undisturbed. Corbulo was glad for the cover it provided them. He kept the log canoe close to the western shore. Now and then he would glance towards the west, wondering what lay out there in those trackless wastes where no Roman had ever set foot. Whatever one's opinion about Caledonia, he thought, no one could argue that it was not a stunningly beautiful land.

It was dusk when they suddenly heard the voices ahead of them. At the front Marcus tensed and picked up his spear. Then Corbulo heard it again. Two men were having a conversation. Then up ahead a strange shape loomed up out of the mist and darkness. Corbulo gasped in surprise. The shape was a small circular island made of tree trunks that had been sunk into the lakebed and filled in with turf. On top of the man-made island stood a single small round house. Corbulo dug his paddle into the water and tried to force the craft to a standstill but the log ploughed on, propelled by its momentum. The men's voices were closer. They were coming from around the back of the house. Corbulo stared at the strange construction. Who would want to build a house out here in the lake?

"Let's go round," Marcus whispered.

Corbulo looked undecided. The mist and gathering darkness would surely cover them and allow them to slip by unnoticed but Marcus needed to have that wound tended to. Maybe the people who lived here could help? Maybe they wouldn't. Maybe they would be hostile. Corbulo was conscious that Marcus was waiting for an answer. The log was about to hit the island.

"Let's see if they can help us," Corbulo whispered.

Marcus said nothing as the canoe bumped gently into the island. Corbulo reached out and grabbed hold of a tree trunk. Then he called out.

"Friend, may we come ashore?"

The two of them sat tensely in their craft and waited. Corbulo had his hand on his sword pommel and his right foot rested against the island ready to push them off if they had to make a quick exit. The conversation they'd heard ceased abruptly. Then two men appeared around the side of the house and stared down at them. They were both short and stocky with dark hair but where one had a full black beard the other's face was pockmarked with red splotches. For a long, awkward moment no one spoke as the two men took in every detail of the canoe and its occupants.

"May we come ashore?" Corbulo repeated. "My son is hurt. He needs help. We will make it worth your time."

The two men on the island exchanged glances.

"Come round the back, you can get out there," the man with the beard said in a thick accent.

"Are you sure about this?" Marcus whispered as Corbulo manoeuvred the canoe around the island. "Did you see how they looked at us? They know we are Romans."

Corbulo sighed. "We don't have a choice, that leg of yours needs tending to. We won't stay long."

Corbulo felt stiff as he clambered onto the wooden platform. He stooped and hauled the log from the lake and laid it down on the island. Marcus stood to one side leaning on his spear, the sack with supplies slung over his shoulder. The man with the splotched face watched them from the doorway, his shrewd eyes taking in every detail and movement. A moment later the bearded man emerged from the hut closely followed by a young woman. The woman kept her eyes lowered as the bearded man muttered something to her.

"Do you have vinegar?" Marcus said, looking at the woman. "I think the cut in my leg has become infected. I need you to boil some water. Do you have any bandages?"

The woman kept her eyes turned to the ground.

"I have some apple vinegar. I will clean your wound with that but we have no bandages. Only the Roman settlements have such things."

The bearded man angrily slapped her over the head and the young woman abruptly fell silent.

"Follow her," the man growled. "She will tend to your wound."

It was dark inside except for a small wood fire in the middle of the space. Soft animal skins lay scattered across the floor and a boar's head hung from one of the walls. The woman crouched beside the fire and busied herself with the iron pot that was cooking over it. Marcus limped over to her and sat down beside the woman and showed her the festering cut on his calf. Marcus smiled encouragingly and the woman smiled shyly in return.

Corbulo turned to the two men who were watching from the doorway.

"Thank you," he nodded his appreciation. "We will not stay long. What can I do to repay your hospitality?"

"Where have you come from? Where are you heading?" the bearded man said, folding his arms across his chest as he ignored Corbulo's question.

"We have come from Cawdor, the Roman fort to the north, near the sea," Corbulo said guardedly.

"I know where it is," the bearded man interrupted.

Corbulo paused and glanced at Marcus. "My son and I came here to trade. We were on our way back south when this happened," he gestured to Marcus's wound. "He got injured."

"Looks like a knife wound to me," the disfigured man muttered.

The bearded man spat onto the ground. "What were you trading?" he asked.

"Silver for precious stones," Corbulo said hastily.

The bearded man shrugged. "I didn't see anything in your boat."

"We were robbed," Corbulo said slowly. "They took everything we owned."

"Is that how he got injured?" the disfigured man said, gesturing at Marcus.

"Yes, it happened a few days ago."

The house fell silent and Corbulo was aware of two sets of shrewd eyes studying him in the dark-red flickering firelight.

"Not very smart to lose your entire stock to a robbery," the pockmarked man muttered.

"No," Corbulo admitted with a resigned look.

"There are no Roman forts around here," the bearded man said, spitting once more onto the ground. "The closest Roman forts are to the east across the mountains. If you are heading south then the fastest route would be through the mountain passes. But he," the man pointed at Marcus, "won't get far with that leg. You are welcome to stay here until it mends. My name is Sceolan." He gestured to the man beside him and the woman examining Marcus's wound: "He is my younger brother and she is my woman. We will share what we have with you but if you touch her, I will kill you. Is that clear?"

Chapter Fifty-Five – The Warning

That night Corbulo could not sleep. Something was worrying him but he couldn't put his finger on it. For a while he listened to the gentle snoring and to Marcus muttering in his sleep. The five of them lay scattered about on the soft animal skins and the fire was burning low. The young woman had cleaned Marcus's wound with vinegar and had bound it with a strip of cloth from Marcus's tunic. She had told them that they should rest for at least two days to give the wound a chance to heal. Corbulo wasn't sure. Two days was a long time; a lot could happen in two days. He turned over on his side and stared at the dying fire. The woman lay curled up beyond it. Corbulo looked at her and froze. The woman had her eyes open. She was looking straight at him. Corbulo opened his mouth to speak but then closed it again. Silently she stared at him from across the dim fire. Then she closed her eyes and turned over onto her other side. Corbulo looked away and as he did so he remembered why he was worried. Sceolan had not bothered to take up his offer of redress. The man had been so quick to offer them his extended hospitality. Such generosity. It just didn't feel right.

Corbulo finally fell asleep and when he woke he found Marcus prodding him with his foot. Through the doorway he could see that it was light. The woman was pottering around in the corner and there was no sign of Sceolan or his brother.

"The younger one rode away at dawn," Marcus whispered in Latin. "I watched him go north. He looked like he was in a hurry. I don't like it. Something is going on."

"He rode away on horseback? They have horses?" Corbulo replied, looking up at his son.

"Yes, they keep them on the land," Marcus nodded.

Corbulo looked undecided. Then he glanced at the cloth tied around Marcus's leg.

"We will leave tomorrow at dawn," he muttered in Latin. "See if you can speak with the woman. There is something odd about her."

"I will try but Sceolan keeps an eye on her all the time. I don't think she is his woman at all. I think she is a slave."

Corbulo glanced at the woman but she seemed not to have understood a word of what they were talking about.

Then Sceolan was standing in the doorway.

"Come," he said, beckoning to them, "there is some good fishing to be had. You like fish, don't you? We will cook them tonight."

Corbulo nodded and rose to his feet. The mist had cleared and it was a fine day with a blue sky and a gentle south-westerly breeze. A fish net lay on the ground and Sceolan handed it to Corbulo. The lake was empty and silent and there was no sign of anyone on the water. The island itself had been built about twenty paces from the shore. Corbulo glanced round the side of the house. Their log canoe was still where they had left it.

That evening as they ate their fish Sceolan explained that his brother had gone off to visit relatives and that he would be back by around noon tomorrow. Marcus's leg was healing and he seemed to be growing stronger with every day. Corbulo had decided not to tell his host that they would be leaving at dawn. It would be best if they simply slipped away when the others were asleep.

It was dark when Corbulo was woken by a gentle shake. He opened his eyes and sat up. Close by he could hear Marcus still muttering in his sleep. He rubbed his eyes. A figure stood silhouetted in the doorway. Then the figure vanished. Corbulo rose as silently as he could and glanced in the direction where he'd last seen Sceolan lie down to sleep. In the darkness he could just about hear the man's gentle snoring. Carefully so as not to trip over anything he moved towards the doorway. Then he poked his head outside and looked around.

The moon hung high in the sky and in its light he caught sight of the woman standing beside their log canoe. She raised a finger to her mouth and beckoned him over.

"You must go," she whispered. "Eoin has not gone to visit relatives. He has gone to fetch help. They will be here by dawn, not noon." She shook her head. "They are planning to enslave you. That is what they do. You are in danger. Leave now while you can."

Corbulo nodded in agreement.

"Why are you helping us?" he whispered.

The woman fumbled for his hand and pressed something into his palm before closing his fingers around the cold hard object.

"I am a slave," she whispered. "My village is on the coast just north of Deva. These men came one day in their ships. They raided the coastal settlements and kidnapped me. I have been here two years. The ring I have given you, please, take it to my father in his village. He is a beekeeper. My village is known for its honey. You will find it. Tell my family that I am well; tell them that Efa and Dylis are fine and that we miss them."

"Come with us," Corbulo said at once.

But the young woman shook her head.

"No, I can't leave my child behind – Dylis is with Sceolan's family. I won't leave her behind. But you must go. Sceolan keeps his horses in the meadow over there. Take them." She paused and swallowed nervously. "There has been fighting to the south," she whispered. "Sceolan was lying when he said there are no Romans around here. A few days ago we heard that the Romans had landed two days' ride south of here and destroyed the Caledonian fort at Dun Deardail. The Romans are building their own fort on the coast."

"Fighting?" Corbulo muttered.

The woman nodded. "Sceolan said that the Romans came from the sea and attacked the fort and destroyed it. He says they are busy building their own forts. He says that Roman ships come and go all the time. If you make it you will be able to get home on one of those ships."

"What about the war bands, won't they be flocking south to attack the Romans?"

The woman shrugged. "I don't know about such things," she whispered, "but you can make it if you ride hard for two days. Follow the lake. After this lake you will come across another. Keep following the water and it will take you to Dun Deardail. Now go, please."

Corbulo and Marcus crept through the meadow towards the two horses that stood tethered to a tree. The beasts turned to look at them inquisitively. Clumsily Corbulo tried to mount one of them only to slither off. Marcus, however, was more successful and with practised ease swung himself onto the animal's back.

"Walk them," his son said firmly. "We don't want one of these horses to break their legs in the dark. When it gets lighter we will trot and make more distance. Trust me, I know how to handle a horse."

Chapter Fifty-Six – Ride Hard and Don't Look Back

Dawn found them riding south along the western shore of the lake. Marcus had led the way through the dark picking out the trail that ran alongside the water and Corbulo had become impressed at how easy and confident the boy handled himself in the saddle. As the morning had worn on Marcus had begun to mix up their speed, trotting for a while and then slowing to a walk before trotting on again. At noon Marcus ordered them to take a rest and for a while they led the horses by hand down the path. The two of them spoke little, each alone with his own thoughts, but it was clear that the rest on the man-made island had done Marcus a lot of good for his strength was returning. It was just as well, Corbulo thought. All that morning the sense of pursuit had been growing on him and every few minutes he had turned to look back but had seen nothing.

They rode on, feeling the wind start to blow against them.

"How long can you ride one of these animals before they collapse?" Corbulo called out to Marcus who was riding ahead.

"That depends on the horse," Marcus replied. "These scrawny horses are nothing compared to the horses that the army buys in Gaul. But if we had to trot without rest," he paused to do the calculation, "over this terrain and assuming the terrain stays like this I would say we could do forty or fifty miles before they are broken."

Corbulo looked impressed and patted his horse on its neck. Then he looked up at the mountains to the west. They were snow-capped. What more lay beyond those mountains? What lay beyond the great western ocean? There had always been a small part of him that had wanted to know how far from the edge of the world Britannia really lay. They were close. He could feel it. He could feel the great unfathomable, restless power of the ocean pressing into the land. Beyond the outer ocean that encircled the world lay the domain of the Hyperboreans, the beasts of the deep and the home of the gods. No one had ever been there and returned.

As a young man Corbulo had listened to story tellers speaking the tales from Livy and Polybius. But his favourite story, by far had been about a Greek explorer from Massalia, called Pytheas. He had travelled around Britannia and Caledonia and had written a book filled with detailed observations, called "On the Ocean." When Corbulo had heard the story, it had been written over four hundred years before!

It was late in the afternoon when they came to the end of the lake. Ahead of them at the southern tip of the lake the land turned marshy. Without hesitation Marcus led them on in a south-westerly direction and soon Corbulo caught sight of the second lake that the woman had talked about. The forests were growing more abundant the further south they went and the ground remained flat and they made good progress.

They had just reached the crest of a steep hill when something made Corbulo glance over his shoulder.

"Marcus," he cried out in alarm. From the ridge they had a fine view to the south and north. Emerging from the forest, beside the first lake, a couple of miles away behind them, were tiny figures on horseback.

"I see them," Marcus cried. "They've got hunting dogs and spare horses. Damn it, they are coming on fast."

"They don't look like slavers to me," Corbulo muttered uneasily. "This looks like something else. Come on, let's go. Ride hard and don't look back."

They wheeled their horses around and started off down the hill at a fast pace. Corbulo's cheeks burned with sudden despair. They would not be able to hide from those war dogs nor were they likely to outrun their pursuers. Their only hope lay in reaching the Romans at their beach head beside the sea but that was still at least a day's ride away. He glanced at Marcus ahead of him. His son was concentrating on finding the right path through the trees. Corbulo felt a cold savage resolve. If the worst became inevitable then he would not allow them to take his son. They would die together and meet each other in the afterlife.

They thundered through the trees. The track through the forest was fairly clear and Marcus was pushing the pace now. They burst out of the trees and into a colourful meadow.

"We ride without stopping, until the horses are broken," Marcus cried out. "We are going to make it. Maybe we will lose them in the dark."

Corbulo didn't reply. He glanced up at the sky. He had forgotten that dusk was approaching. He glanced back over his shoulder. Their pursuers would not rest during the night.

They rode on with the lake to their left. The bleak, barren mountains crowded around them like rows of spectators in the Circus Maximus. His horse snorted and nearly slid on a rock, sending a shower of stones down the slope. Again Corbulo glanced over his shoulder but the hills and the forest hid their pursuers. How many of them were there? He hadn't had time to count them all but there were enough to handle two fleeing fugitives. He was sure of that. He stared at the spear strapped to Marcus's back. That, the small knife he'd taken from the farm and his gladius were the only weapons they possessed. It was going to be a rather decidedly one-sided fight if it came to it.

Soon the ground levelled out and they began to move faster. Marcus had set a blistering pace and seemed to have no difficulty in picking a path. Corbulo blew the air from his cheeks. The boy was impressive on a horse. Damn impressive. The realisation brought about a sudden feeling of guilt. What did he really know about Marcus? He had hardly been there to see his son grow up. Now it was as if he was seeing the young man for the first time.

"How far to the sea?" Marcus cried.

"At least a day's ride, that's what she said. We just have to keep going," Corbulo shouted. "We ride through the night, we can't stop. Can you find a path in the dark?"

Marcus looked away and didn't answer as they galloped on. They entered another wood and Corbulo caught glimpses of the lake through the trees. They rode on without speaking and slowly the daylight slipped away like spectators leaving the circus. As it grew dark Marcus began to slow their pace. The horses were exhausted. White foam clung around their mouths and their flanks were heaving and covered in sweat and dirt. Just as the first stars appeared in the night sky Corbulo heard the faint baying and barking of dogs.

Marcus had heard it too. He snatched a glance over his shoulder. His face was concentrating hard.

"They are closer," he cried.

In the dark branches scraped and scratched at their arms and legs and one low-hanging branch nearly knocked Corbulo to the ground. The forest seemed to go on forever and to Corbulo it seemed like a disorientating mass of trees and undergrowth that stretched off in every direction but somehow Marcus seemed to keep them going in the right direction. Corbulo marvelled at his son's ability to keep to a path in the dark. Every muscle in Corbulo's body was tensed but he didn't feel tired; fear was making him feel more alive than ever.

"Marcus," he called out. "If it comes to it and we have to fight I want you to know that they are not going to take me alive. I have come a long way to find you. I am not going to let them take you."

"I know, I know," Marcus said. "But we are going to make it. This is not our time. You will see."

"Since when have you become such an optimist?" Corbulo growled.

"I always was," Marcus cried. "We're going to make it – now be quiet and save your breath and let me concentrate."

Corbulo blushed at the retort but he did as he was told. Behind them the baying of the dogs sounded closer. Corbulo glanced over his shoulder. Burning torches were moving through the darkness behind them. Their pursuers were riding hard.

All that night they rode without rest, guided solely by the moonlight and Marcus's unfailing instinct. They flitted past trees and huge boulders that had crashed down the mountainside long ago. But however fast their progress, their pursuers seemed to be gaining on them. During those long dark hours

Corbulo marvelled at his son's courage and strength. The boy had become a man. He was seeing a side of Marcus that he just had never known before and as the darkness dragged on his pride and respect began to grow.

At last the first lazy glimpses of dawn appeared in the sky. The two horsemen rode on along the shore of the lake. They didn't speak. As the light grew they pushed on into open meadows and fields. It was an hour later that Corbulo saw his first corpse. The man lay on his back in the grass. As he thundered past Corbulo caught sight of an ugly gash in the man's chest. He twisted his head to get a better view of the man but the grass concealed the body. What had the woman told him? There had been fighting to the south. He blinked and turned to look at the horizon ahead of them. If the woman was right they were riding straight into a war zone.

As the light grew Corbulo rubbed his weary eyes. To the south smoke was rising up into the sky. Was that from Dun Deardail, the Caledonian fort that the Romans had destroyed? There was no way of knowing. Marcus looked like he was glued to the back of his horse. He had been leading them now since they had set off from the island in the lake. Suddenly his son cried out a warning and pointed to their right. A troop of men were running parallel to them a few hundred paces away. They looked like a Caledonian war band and they were heading in the same direction. Corbulo stared at the men. The warriors had seen them.

"Keep going," Corbulo yelled. "We stop for nothing."

Marcus cried out to his horse, talking to her in words that Corbulo could not catch.

How much further? How much more could their horses endure? The brutal reality could not be ignored. They were not going to make it. The odds were against them.

A few minutes later Corbulo saw another group of men coming towards them from the opposite direction. The group was pulling a cart along upon which lay a number of wounded men. Corbulo and Marcus stormed past the men. The

Caledonians stared at them but made no effort to try and intercept them.

"We must be close," Marcus shouted. "Don't you dare give up on me now, old man."

Corbulo shook his head in weary disbelief. The arrogance of youth, he thought. The young thought the world belonged to them. He slapped his face to drive away the exhaustion that was gathering. The smoke on the horizon – what did it mean? How far did they still have to go? The land before them was open but on both sides of the lake the hills were just stepping stones to the mountains beyond. Grass and heather covered the barren slopes and across the lake he could make out the white stain of a waterfall cascading down a gully.

Behind them Corbulo heard the sound of barking dogs. The noise sounded horribly close by. He twisted his neck and blushed at the sight that met his eyes. Half a mile or so behind him his pursuers were coming on. There were twelve of them and they were riding their horses like mad men, their cloaks flying in the wind. A pack of war dogs was racing between them, baying in anticipation.

"Fuck," Corbulo whispered. The dogs by themselves could tear him and Marcus to pieces within seconds.

He turned to look at Marcus but his son had seen their pursuers too. Corbulo caught a glimpse of his son's leg. The piece of cloth tied around his wound was soaked red with blood. He looked up sharply. Marcus had not said a word. He had to be in a lot of pain.

"Are you alright, Marcus?" he cried.

The young man did not reply but Corbulo caught him giving a short nod.

The two of them tore on across the open meadows. They passed another corpse whose lifeless eyes were staring up at the sky. A few minutes later Corbulo spotted another war band. The men were crouching in the grass, gathered together in a circle. They rose as they caught sight of the two horsemen. One of the men raised his spear and shouted something at them. Corbulo and Marcus stormed past without answering.

"Come on, horse, a little further. Come on!" Marcus screamed, slapping the animal with his hands. Behind them the barking of the dogs was drawing closer. A surge of energy suddenly swept through Corbulo but it didn't lift his spirit. He knew it was a false hope for it would not last. It was just desperation.

They galloped on and Corbulo glanced up at the mountains on either side of them. There were no places to hide and even if they did find a spot those war dogs would find them and tear the flesh from their bones. Corbulo nudged his horse forwards so that he and Marcus rode side by side. Behind them they could hear their pursuers clearly now. There was no need to look over their shoulder. Corbulo's fingers found their way to the pommel of his sword. They were not going to be taken alive. He knew what the druid would do to them. He had seen what the druids had done to captured Roman soldiers when he and comrades had come across the druidic sacred graves on Mona Insulis, twenty-four years ago. There was nothing more terrifying for a Roman than to be captured by a druid. Every soldier understood that and every soldier accepted that the druids had to die as a consequence. There could be no negotiation between Rome and the druids.

Their pursuers were drawing closer. It wouldn't be long now. Corbulo could hear their voices now, crying out to their horses, their voices mingling with the slash of whips and the barking of the dogs. He snatched a sideways glance at Marcus. The young man looked grim but determined, his face full of concentration. Did Marcus know how proud of him he was? He felt a tear stir in his eyes. There would be no time to tell him. No time to tell him how proud he was to see his son. He'd had a whole lifetime to tell his son but now when he most wanted to tell him he didn't have the time.

Their pursuers were only a third of a mile behind them when Corbulo suddenly saw the watchtower. It stood on a hill half a mile away overlooking the valley. The smoke he'd spotted earlier was rising from another hill behind it.

"Marcus," he screamed, pointing at the watchtower.

His son, however, had already seen the fortification and was veering towards it. The horses, somehow sensing the war dogs behind them, seemed to find some extra speed. The two of them sped towards the watchtower. It looked Roman but Corbulo could see no one manning the observation platform. Then as they rode up the slope towards the tower Corbulo suddenly caught sight of water on the horizon. It was only a glimpse before his view was obstructed by trees. He turned and looked at Marcus riding beside him and for an insane moment they grinned at each other like two boys who had discovered something they shouldn't have.

"I told you we would make it," Marcus shouted.

Corbulo looked away. They weren't going to make it.

They stormed towards the watchtower. Their pursuers were only a few hundred paces behind them and closing fast. Corbulo stared at the watchtower. It was definitely Roman but it looked abandoned. Then he caught sight of two bodies lying half in and out of the V-shaped ditch that surrounded the small square tower. He stared at the gateway. The wooden gate was open. Then he saw another corpse propped up against the wooden parapet on top of the turf wall that surrounded the tower. It may be Roman but the men who had manned the place were all dead.

"Marcus," he cried, "this is it. We will make our stand here. Get inside and we will try and barricade the gate."

The watchtower drew closer. Then they were there. Corbulo leapt from his horse as Marcus did the same and the two of them charged through the gate into the small square enclosure. Corbulo tripped over a corpse and went tumbling to the ground. He was back on his feet in an instant.

"They are our men," Marcus gasped as he stared at one of the corpses.

Corbulo pulled his sword free and stumbled back towards the front gate and tried to close it but the gate was broken and the wood wouldn't budge. A spear suddenly hammered into the gate inches from his head and Corbulo looked up in shock. One of their pursuers had dismounted and was coming at him wielding a long sword. Another was close behind him.

"Marcus!" Corbulo screamed in alarm, but before he could say anything else Marcus had stepped into the gateway and flung his spear at their attackers. The spear struck the leading man in the abdomen, sending him crashing to the ground.

"The gate won't move," Corbulo shouted as he tried to move it. There was no time. The second man was nearly upon them. With an angry growl Corbulo gave up on the gate and stepped out to face the onrushing man. His assailant came at him with a cry, sweeping his axe down towards Corbulo's neck. At the last moment Corbulo twisted away and stabbed the man with his short sword. The man groaned, staggered, dropped his axe and collapsed to the ground.

A shout behind him made Corbulo whirl round. Marcus had somehow managed to get the gate moving. Corbulo rushed back and grabbed hold of the wood and heaved. From the corner of his eye he saw more figures rushing towards them. Then before he could react a big black dog sprang towards him, bowling him backwards onto the ground. The animal was snapping its jaws and barking. Something seemed to snap within Corbulo. He screamed like a madman and hit the dog with his fist. Then he grabbed the animal by the throat with both hands and sank his teeth into the dog's ear, ripping it off in a single movement. The animal yelped and fled. As he rose to his feet Corbulo heard Marcus cry out and with a mighty roar lift the gate and push it into place. It was not a moment too soon. Outside men's curses and shouts mingled with the barking of dogs.

"Get up on that parapet!" Corbulo screamed. He spat blood from his mouth and grabbed hold of a ladder and began to climb up the turf ramparts. Behind him Marcus snatched a sword from a corpse and rushed to another ladder on the other side of the small square enclosure. On the ramparts Corbulo crouched and then risked a quick glance over the side. The remaining ten men and the dogs milled around the watchtower surrounding it. He crouched behind the wooden parapet and stared at the corpse of a fallen auxiliary. The Roman had been killed recently. The body had not been robbed and had not started decaying. He caught his breath and snatched the dead man's spear. Across from him, six yards away on the opposite parapet, he could see Marcus too had taken shelter. His son had armed himself with a spear and a sword.

Corbulo took a deep breath and jumped up and raised his spear. Figures and shapes moved below him. He flung the weapon at a man but missed. Then he ducked below the parapet. The Caledonians had started to hack at the gate. The sound of axes and swords battering against the wood was demonic. A couple of yards away a hand suddenly appeared, grasping the edge of the parapet. A Caledonian was trying to climb over the wall. Corbulo slithered across and hacked at the fingers with his sword. The hand vanished with an agonising cry.

"It's the woman," he suddenly heard Marcus cry out. "It's the woman from the well."

Corbulo sat with his back against the wall. He was panting.

"I knew I shouldn't have hit her," he muttered to himself. The noise from the gate was getting more frantic. The wood creaked ominously. How long would it be before they broke in? How long before the men outside coordinated their attacks and rushed them? He looked up at the square watchtower. A Roman corpse lay sprawled in the doorway.

"Marcus," he shouted, "get inside."

Corbulo was last through the open doorway. The square tower was about three yards by three. A ladder led up to the second floor. They clambered up it and Corbulo hauled the ladder up. Just then he heard a crash and a splintering of wood. The Caledonians had broken into the compound. A dog stormed into the entrance hall below them and leapt up in the air. Corbulo stumbled backwards in fright but the distance between the ground and the second floor was too great for the animal. Growling and snapping its jaws it landed back on the ground.

Marcus was already climbing up the next ladder leading to the third floor and the observation platform outside. Corbulo looked around him wildly. The tower was a mess. There was nothing useful in this room. He saw a Caledonian looking up at him. The man's hard angry eyes gleamed. How long before their pursuers found a replacement ladder? Corbulo picked up a discarded earthenware pot and flung it at his pursuer. The man vanished from view as the pot smashed to pieces on the ground. Then he picked up another pot and flung it down through the hole and then another. Then there was nothing left to throw.

Marcus was shouting for him to come up to the third floor. There was an urgency in his voice that Corbulo could not ignore. He dashed up the ladder and pulled it up. He was at the top of the tower now. There was nowhere left to run to. Marcus was on the narrow walkway around the side of the tower. He was staring at something towards the south. Then Corbulo gasped. A few miles away was another narrow lake and yet this was not a lake, it was the sea. Riding upon the water were a dozen Roman galleys anchored just offshore.

"So close," Marcus cried in frustration. "We are so damned close."

The great barren mountains crowded around them, hemming them in on all sides. On one of the hills to his right he saw smoke rising up. It was the smoke he'd seen earlier. The Romans must have attacked the Caledonian fort and set it on fire. The strategic value of this place was instantly recognisable to Corbulo. He wrenched his gaze from the ships and looked down into the compound. The Caledonians and their dogs were all over the place. Then he caught sight of a woman. She had lowered the hood of her cloak. Her cheeks looked flushed and her long black hair fluttered in the breeze. She was holding a spear. She caught sight of him staring at her. With a cry she raised her arm and flung her spear at him. The projectile hammered into the wood inches away from him. Corbulo staggered backwards into the watchtower and tripped over a Roman corpse. He landed on his arse. Then he blinked. Beneath the corpse something glinted. He pushed the dead soldier onto his back and stared at the object that had lain concealed under the man's body. It was a long, straight and shiny tuba, a Roman trumpet.

His eyes widened as an idea came to him. He picked up the piece of signalling equipment and poked its long straight snout out onto the observation platform. Then he blew with all his might. The blast of noise echoed off the distant hills. Then he blew again and again until he was red in the face. Lowering the trumpet he gasped for breath and saw Marcus staring at him in stunned, awed silence.

"Blow the damn thing," Corbulo gasped. "I haven't got any breath left."

Below them in the compound he heard the Caledonians shouting to each other. Then the horrible, coarse trumpet noise erupted again as Marcus put his lungs to work. Corbulo poked his head out onto the observation platform and stared at the sea. Below him he suddenly heard a triumphant yell and a scrambling of feet and arms. The Caledonians had managed to get onto the floor below them. Again the trumpet cut through the air. Would the Romans hear it? Would they come? Marcus gasped, took another deep breath and blasted away.

Then Corbulo caught sight of a reflection in the sunlight. He slapped his face and tried to focus but his eyes were tired. He blinked. Then he saw it again. A mile or so away a troop of horsemen were riding towards the watchtower. The sunlight reflected on the riders' armour.

"Auxiliaries, they are coming!" Corbulo shouted with sudden fierce delight. "Keep blowing that pipe, Marcus, keep blowing that damn thing."

The riders were coming on at a steady but cautious pace. Below him Marcus suddenly heard a woman's warning cry. She must have seen the riders too. Then the woman was right below the hole in the floor glaring up at Corbulo.

"We will meet again, Roman," she cried. "That day will come. Do not think that you will be able to sleep peacefully in your bed. I will find you and when I do I shall kill you. I swear it before all the gods and when I do your spirit shall belong to me forever. Yes, mine forever."

"Oh, fuck off, bitch and leave us alone," Corbulo shouted back.

There was no reply from below. Then Corbulo heard cries and shouts. Cautiously he again poked his head out onto the observation platform. The woman and her companions were riding away, back the way they had come with the pack of war dogs running behind them.

"They are going," Corbulo yelled in triumph. "We made it, Marcus, we made it." Marcus lowered the trumpet and managed a broad grin. Then the two of them stumbled towards each other and clasped each other in a fierce embrace. When they parted Corbulo stumbled out onto the observation platform. The Roman auxiliary patrol was nearly at the fort. Corbulo raised his arm and shouted at the men. Then he slumped back onto his arse, leaning against the watchtower wall. He closed his eyes and took a deep breath. Marcus slumped down beside him. He was still holding the tuba.

"I always hated the noise this thing made," Marcus said, looking down at the instrument.

"I always despised the auxiliary cohorts," Corbulo grinned.

They chuckled at that together. Then Corbulo opened his eyes and ran his hand over his face. "If that woman who was after us had any sense she would simply move the amber to another location or just block up that narrow, twisting cave passage. Seems a better solution than trying to kill us," he muttered.

"Maybe she will," Marcus nodded. "But I don't like that promise she made. What does she mean, your spirit will belong to her forever? Sounds like trouble." Then he stopped and turned to look at Corbulo. "How do you know where the amber was kept?"

A guilty look suddenly appeared on Corbulo's face. Wearily he fumbled around for something on his belt. Then he produced a small leather pouch and undid the binding. Nestling inside was a beautiful piece of red amber.

"I found the cave," Corbulo said with a grin. "I found it when I came to rescue you. It was a bit of luck I suppose but I had to take away a little souvenir. This piece here should buy me a nice plot of land." Corbulo's grin widened. "Look, I even brought a stone for you."

Author's Notes

I first wrote *Caledonia* in 2009, inspired by a trip to Scotland. This book is a second edition of my original story.

In this novel I have tried to stick as closely as possible to the written historical accounts that we have about the first Roman invasion of Scotland. Tacitus, Agricola's son-in-law, who is the main contemporary source for this invasion, was very useful and therefore, to show my gratitude, I have included him as a minor character. The other excellent information source was David J Breeze's *Roman Scotland*.

The location of Mons Graupius is a hotly disputed topic but no one knows for certain where the battle took place or indeed in which year. In this novel I have opted for September 83 AD and the location as Bennachie in the Grampian Mountains, to the west of modern-day Aberdeen. The Celtic settlements of Tuesis and Bannatia are both mentioned in Ptolemy's *The Geography* but their exact locations are not given and we know very little about these places. Ptolemy mentions the Caledonian tribes of the Decantae and the Vacomagi but again, apart from that one mention, we know nothing more about these people.

The main amber-producing region during the classical age was of course the Baltic which is why the famous Amber Road from the Baltic, across Eastern Europe to the Danube, came into being. There is, however, a rich folklore and tradition that tells of amber being found in Scotland, although amber finds have actually been very rare.

One of the great enduring questions concerning Roman Scotland was why did the Romans abandon Caledonia after destroying the Caledonian confederation at Mons Graupius? No one knows for sure why and in his book *Roman Scotland* Breeze gives us a number of possible reasons. To my mind, having read a number of archaeological dig reports on abandoned Roman forts such as Inchtuthil, it seems that many of the Roman forts that encircled the Highlands were abandoned in a well-planned manner, suggesting that the

Roman withdrawal was systematic, organised and dignified. I do not believe that the Caledonian tribes drove the Romans out. It is more likely that changes in imperial defence requirements meant that the troops based in Scotland were simply needed elsewhere.

PARTICIPANTS OF CALEDONIA

Baldurix – A leader of the Decantae tribe

Bestia – Decurion in the Second Batavian Auxiliary Cohort

Calgacus – Leader of the anti-Roman Caledonian confederacy

Conall – Caledonian boy taken prisoner at Mons Graupius

Corbulo - Father of Marcus. Veteran legionary of the Twentieth Legion

Domitian - Roman Emperor AD 81 - 96

Dougal also known as Greer – A Vacomagi druid and Emogene's father

Efa and Dylis – Mother and daughter, slaves in Caledonia

Emogene - Daughter of Dougal

Gnaeus Julius Agricola – Roman governor of Britannia

Marcus - Son of Corbulo, auxiliary soldier in the Second Batavian Auxiliary Cohort

Quintus – Roman centurion in the Twentieth Legion and a friend of Corbulo

Vellocatus - A civilian slave dealer and merchant

Vespasian – Roman Emperor AD 69 – 79

GLOSSARY

Aesculapius - The Greek God of Healing

Aphrodite – Goddess of love

Atrebates - Celtic Tribe living in northern France

Balnageith – Possible Roman military fort in Caledonia

Bannatia – Emogene and Dougal's home village, in the territory of the Vacomagi. This area is now called Strathspey
.
Batavia - Now land between the rivers Lek and Waal in the Netherlands

Beltane - Celebration that marked the start of summer

Boudica – Queen of the Iceni Tribe

Brigantes - Celtic tribe living in northern England

Carnyx – Celtic war trumpet

Cawdor – Roman fort located about 15 miles east of Inverness, Scotland

Circus Maximus - Large stadium in the centre of Rome

Cohort - Roman military unit equivalent to a battalion of around 500 men. Ten cohorts made up a legion.

Camulodunum - Colchester, UK

Decantae - Celtic Tribe living in north east Scotland

Decurion - Roman cavalry officer

Deva Victrix - Chester, UK.

Dormouse - A Roman delicacy

Druids - The high-ranking professional class in ancient Celtic cultures

Dun Deardil – Iron age Caledonian fort

Eburacum - York

Equestrian order - The Order of Knights – minor Roman aristocracy

Falacrinae - Birth place of Corbulo. Close to the Roman colony of Narnia, some seventy-five miles north-east of Rome

Forum Julii – Frejus in southern France

Gallia Narbonensis - Roman province in what is now Lanquedoc and Provence in southern France

Galley - Long low ship with one deck moved by oars and sails

Garum - Fermented fish sauce

Hibernia - Ireland

Hispania - Spain

Hyperborea - Mythical land beyond the north wind

Hypercaust - Roman under floor heating system

Inchtuthil- Only legionary base in Scotland, just east of Dunkeld

Jupiter- Patron god of Rome

Legate - Roman officer in command of a Legion

Lictors - Bodyguards

Londinium- London

Massalia - Marseille, France

Middle Sea - Mediterranean Sea

Mona Insulis - Anglesey, Wales

Mons Graupius - Battlefield in Scotland where Agricola defeated the Caledonian confederation in AD 83. Location not yet confirmed.

Orodovices - Tribe living in north Wales

Palla - Army overcoat with hood.

Pennines - Hills running, north - south, through the centre of northern England

Praetorians - Emperor's personal guard units

Pytheas - Greek explorer, around 325 BC, who visited the northern Atlantic

Samhain - Festival marking the end of the harvest season and the start of winter

Saturnalia - Roman festival in honour of the god Saturn, held on 17 December

Spatha - Roman auxiliary cavalryman's sword.

Taexali - Tribe living along the north-eastern coast of Scotland

Tesserarius – Roman army watch/guard commander, third in line of command in a Roman army company.

Torc - Metal ring worn around the neck identifying the wearer as a person with status

Trinovantes - Celtic tribe who lives in Essex and Suffolk, north east of London

Tuba - Roman trumpet

Tuesis - Main settlement, in the territory of the Vacomagi. This area is now called Strathspey

Urban Cohorts - Soldiers tasked with keeping public order inside a city

Vacomagi - Tribe living in north east Scotland in an rea now known as Strathspey

Vexillatio(n) - Temporary Roman army detachment

Ynys Mon - Anglesey, Wales

Printed in Great Britain
by Amazon